St[illegible] Sturgis

by
Ryan Stattelman

PublishAmerica
Baltimore

To Carol Weiss –
Thanks and
happy reading!

First printing

ISBN: 1-4137-3143-0
PUBLISHED BY PUBLISHAMERICA, LLLP
www.publishamerica.com
Baltimore

Printed in the United States of America

For Adrienne, the cutest editor I've met.

Chapter One

To him, snow was like those Teletubbies his daughter liked so much—cute for awhile, but soon changing to just plain annoying.

Though the weather had slowly begun to take its turn for the better, the past few days had still been colder than normal, which received plenty of objection from Paul Morris. Thus far, the grass was not yet growing and the snow remained; the landscape would surely see no change for at least another month.

"If not two months, knowing this place," Paul said to himself quietly, so as not to wake the sleeping figure across the room. The previous winter had all but closed down every facet of the city on a couple of days, allowing for some much needed family time in a lot of households like the Morris's. They had huddled around the television, clad in sweaters and robes, just sipping their respective coffee or juice and watching school and business closings abound. Then came word from the weather man that, since no plows would be deployed until late the next morning, no one would be going anywhere that particular day.

Temperatures close to 40 degrees below had apparently been too much for the outdated boiler in their middle class apartment, as the thermostat on the wall never topped 50 degrees for the greater part of that cold spell. Still, with fingerless gloves for daddy and the popular two fingered mittens for the two lady Morrises, the three of them stayed in that living room most of the morning coloring in the family's new *Big Dog's Fun Day* book. The gift had been a surprise from mommy after one afternoon of seemingly endless fussing. Paul remembered thinking how only God himself could have acted with such magnitude as to stop the entire city in its tracks.

Mommy looked much more peaceful now than she had on that particular day, hair ruffled and mouth agape in the rising sunlight. Her day wouldn't begin for another hour or so, and Paul was always more than happy to let her sleep. Some mornings, like this one, he would just stand there after taking his daily look out the bedroom window to watch her sleep for a few moments.

Golden hair attached to a slender face reminded him of many girls he had known in his younger days, and he often had to stop and think before calling out her name, just in case of a slip-up. They had made love the night before. No special occasion this time, just two bottles of champagne (they each could handle one on a good night) he had picked up on his way home and a tube of Pillsbury chocolate chip cookie dough which was nearly the last food left in the refrigerator. After Shelby had been put to bed, her four-year-old eyes straining to stay open while Paul finished *One Fish, Two Fish*, he and his bride retired to their room to sit cross-legged in front of the television and a dirty movie, eating balls of dough with their spoons and sipping away at the twenty-dollar champagne.

In just her UND sweater and sensible white underwear, he thought her as seductive as any other he had seen. That same sweater was on her now, proving she must have gotten up sometime in the middle of the night. A room was never warm enough for Sam; even in a fancy restaurant after she had spent so much time getting to look beautiful, she wouldn't hesitate to throw on her old leather coat if it was a bit chilly.

He worried about her sometimes—he worried most of the time, actually. Just 110 pounds soaking wet Sam had always been small, but he knew she had fought with the disease of wanting to be smaller several times. They were both still in school the first time the sickness reared its ugly head, with Paul spending three solid days not leaving her side even for bathroom breaks. Only one class suffered, History of Film and Theatre, which Paul thought pointless anyhow.

Turning again toward the window, he caught his own reflection in the antique full-length mirror that had been a wedding gift from Samantha's parents. "Great notion, you dumb cunt," Paul remembered thinking when they had opened the huge package the day after their ceremony. "Give a bullemic woman a mirror; that'll send her cruising down the road to recovery *real* quick."

At 27, he no longer looked like he had at 18 but still had few complaints. What used to be a washboard stomach had faded some, and little Shelby had pointed out his few grey hairs once while he bathed her. All in all, though, he was doing pretty well for his age, far better than the tubs of lard he came in contact with every day. Paul had been heavy himself as a youngster—blame it on living with the best cook in Illinois—and was taunted until he finally did something about it in his early teenage years. He remembered those days when Samantha fought him to run to the toilet. Paul thought, though he knew deep down it was wrong, that someone with the strength of a man would never let that sort of thing happen to them.

From his window he could see the tower whose employees and patrons paid his meager salary twice each month. This little trick was nice to get Shelby off to daycare sometimes, as his wife would need to point out where daddy worked before the stubborn youngster would even get dressed.

"Or so they tell me," he spoke again, right index finger extended in the gun gesture, shooting the top off the building where he was stuck nine hours each day. It kept him away from the traditional family breakfasts he was used to, and he resented his job for that reason, among others.

As if people in general weren't unhappy enough in The City, Paul knew it would be an even more dire situation if he were unable to present a good portion of them with their morning cups of coffee. Unfortunately, in exchange for doing this invaluable public service he had to basically be up and at 'em before most everyone else. Though traffic was sometimes a hassle with the few go-getters left in the world who were out by 7 a.m., he couldn't complain one bit in that department. When Samantha had settled in and realized the finer things she liked would be no more if she didn't work, she ran out and in two days was assistant manager of a Barnes and Noble downtown. Things like that always came easily for her, as if someone up on high was just throwing good luck at her. It had taken Paul three weeks of pounding the pavement to put his degree to work in this land of opportunity, but in the end he took a job running a sandwich bar rather than pursuing a career in his chosen field of psychology. True, he still met with his share of crazy people each day, but at least there was little pressure to go with his work.

When all was said and done, the rest of the year was pretty much all for those splendid two weeks each fall when the three of them would load the Taurus with a few clothes and some snacks, and select a destination once they had left The City. Just last year, with a few hundred dollars in his pocket, Paul and his bride had awakened their sleeping child at 5 a.m., got her dressed and into the car by 6, and were well on their way to Disneyland by mid-morning.

Little Shelby breathed heavily now, her only nearby Adventure Land there in her dreams as she slept on that chilly morning in her ladybug-shaped bed. The combination of Paul's dark red hair and her mother's blonde had produced a sort of dirty brown color, which fell in tendrils over the child's green eyes. Paul leaned over to kiss her, stroking her soft cheek with the back of his hand.

In this day and age, although children not much older than she felt the need to massacre each other in the schools and parents relied on television and the Internet to raise them, Shelby could be anything she wanted to be. Though it was some time in the future, he would gladly stand behind her whatever she chose to be—president, congresswoman, astronaut, "just not selling sandwiches like daddy," he said to himself, though a little too loud.

Her eyes popping open one at a time, the little girl first wiped the sleep away with tiny hands, then smiled at what she saw.

"Mawneen!" she exclaimed, surprising herself by how loudly she had actually said it. "How come yow still heew?"

Whichever preschool he and Samantha chose, Paul knew for sure their speech program would be one of the most important factors. While the magazines Sam read told them the girl was right on track in development for her age, he felt sure she would need some help to speak correctly. The game he had ordered off television which boasted it would make four-year-olds read at a first-grade level had not done the trick. Shelby would just get bored and head for her favorite spot in the house—the bathtub. Then they had tried taking the board game into the bathroom to play, but after Sam dropped the instructions into the tub the $99.95 had officially gone to waste.

He looked around her tiny room, knowing it would soon be too small and he would have to start looking for a bigger apartment. As it was, though, things were stretched to the limit in the money department with car payments, two hefty college loans to pay off, and being way overcharged in rent, according to their friends. The only thing there was room for in Shelby's little room besides her single bed was one dresser and an old end table in the corner where she liked to play dolls.

Paul turned back to the bed to see the little one, only now she was gone. Sure enough, naked as the day he had first met her, Shelby sat cross-legged in the bathtub ready to get cleaned up. If she had her way, the entire world would simply revolve around that tub and except for going number two (though accidents had occurred), she would never have to leave it for any reason.

"Washey!" Shelby exclaimed, throwing her hands in the air.

"How about we wait until mommy can do that?" he asked her, as the child's smile began to fade. Clearly, a quick save was in order before a crying fit awoke mommy an hour early.

"You hungry?" he asked the little naked girl, who nodded her head in response. It wouldn't hurt for him to have an unorthodox midweek breakfast with his own daughter, would it? So what if a couple grumpy businessmen were a little more grumpy when their coffee wasn't ready and the doors of the tiny basement café weren't open by exactly 7:30 a.m.

"Aw you leeveen?" she asked, lip still quivering.

"Nope, got me a date with a pretty girl this morning."

Paul lifted the girl from the tub and got her dressed again, quickly finished dressing himself, and ignored the shaver this time. He gently closed the kitchen door behind them once they had entered and poured two bowls of Cheerios, slicing bananas for Shelby's.

He couldn't help but watch the clock as the time neared 7:15, Shelby already gulping down her cereal and milk. She kissed him on the cheek and bolted toward the living room, jumped onto the couch, and fired up the TV. Soon enough Sam would be up, and probably thankful Paul had done his fatherly duties for the day. Without another word, he snuck out the front door, grabbing his set of keys from the candy dish near his coat.

He would have to rush now to make it on time, though no one would ever know. He was the sole proprietor of the little coffee shop until 10 a.m. on the weekdays and the owners, two fat old women from Connecticut, rarely felt the need to visit. Each Friday he would lock up as normal, after placing orders for the next week, and not give one thought to the hot little dungeon portion of the building until three days later.

Traffic had already begun to build up early on that particular Tuesday morning, so Paul took a familiar shortcut he used often. Growing up in a town of 2,500 people, he had very little knowledge of how big city streets and interstates worked and he and Samantha had spent their first three weekends in The City just driving around, familiarizing themselves with their neighborhood and what was near them. This route would bring him to a two-way street, and as long as no trucks felt the need to block the way as they often did, he would have no trouble arriving by 7:35 or so.

The Taurus sailed along the empty street, as Paul met only a handful of cars in the first few blocks.

"Most *normal* people are probably still in the shower right about now," he told himself, yawning and remembering he had forgotten to pour himself a cup from the full pot of coffee on the counter back at home. All day long, if he wanted, Paul could sample one of the café's 45 varieties of coffee beans, but after working with them so long he would just as soon have the plain old Folgers he grew up with.

Besides the few minutes he would miss from his normal routine, he knew this day would be just like any other with most of the same faces whose names he never knew. Few of the state's tourists felt the need to travel down into the H. Francis Building's basement, or perhaps they just didn't know about the place at all, so the average daily customer was one of the hundreds of professionals who were there every day just like Paul.

"Yessir, same old shit, different day," the Taurus's lone passenger reminded himself once again, now just ten blocks from where he would spend the day.

Paul rubbed the sleep from his eyes to focus on a red object in the distance on the right side of the road.

A car.

A stalled car.

Back where he came from, before he moved on to the rudeness and self-sufficiency of big city life, he had helped more than his share of stranded motorists, whether in the middle of the night, in a blizzard, or the pouring rain. This sort of thing was understood in more sparsely populated places—you help some guy out and chances are, he'll get to return the favor when you break down some day. More than likely, it'd be someone you went to church with or who your father sold hardware to, so it'd be good business as well.

As Paul came closer, reading the digital 7:27 from his car's radio, he actually contemplated passing the car right by to make it to work on time. Sure, the java would be brewing right on schedule, but who knows who could have been in trouble in a strange city whom he had just left there for dead. It would bother him not to stop, even though Paul knew it could very well be a weirdo waiting to kidnap him and use him as his love slave. It would ruin his whole day and go against the small town values he possessed not to at least stop to see if everything was all right.

He resented where he lived, especially on days like this. It had been Samantha's choice and he even resented her for it sometimes. Leaving someone without helping them was exactly the sort of thing he had experienced when it came to most of the people he had met lately. Surely, he didn't want to be "just like they are," he finished aloud, pulling in behind what he now identified as a 1999 or so Grand Am.

The plates were from New York, but he'd try not to hold that against whomever was inside. The car's hood wasn't up, though, which Paul remembered as the universal "oh shit, my car died" signal. Still, it wouldn't hurt to ask.

As he shut off his car, pocketing the keys and locking the doors, he noticed only one person inside. A dark-skinned man with short black hair, the driver's head seemed to be nodding at some unseen thing, or maybe jamming along with the radio as Paul himself had just been doing to The Beetles' *Hey Jude* just two seconds before.

The figure appeared to be around Paul's age and build, and suddenly he felt like a police officer, assessing the driver and the situation in such a way. He was a small-town hick thrown into a big town and he knew it, but that notion would probably sink in only after he had been raped and left for dead in a dumpster. And all for helping his fellow man.

"You alright?" Paul tapped on the driver's side window as the figure lurched away from him, the handwritten letter he had been reading scattering across the dash and floor.

The man first looked him straight in the eye for a moment, eyes wide with surprise, before quickly gathering up the pages and stuffing them under the small black bag on the passenger's seat. Dressed in a polo shirt and khaki pants, Paul knew immediately the man was from out of town. His guess was reinforced by the Enterprise Rent-a-Car receipt on the dash.

"I said, are you alright?" he asked again as the man turned on the ignition, cranking over the motor several times before he gave up.

Though the same size as Paul, he looked small and frightened, even in that little car. He looked to be Indian or even a lighter shade of African American, but there were so many different kinds of people Paul saw every day that he knew it would be impossible to find out for sure. Deciding to give up before he got shot, Paul headed back toward his car, pulling its keys from his pocket.

Behind him he heard the Grand Am's door open and as he turned the man stood there before him, eyes still wide with surprise. The two strangers exchanged glances there for a second, unblinking, still sizing up one another. The figure's red- and yellow-striped polo shirt was tucked halfway into his khaki pants, all finished off by what looked to be Wal-Mart shoes. Finally, as Paul began to turn away a second time, the man spoke.

"There…there is no, uh, *gesaleen*," he said in a strong Brazilian accent Paul recognized from a foreign exchange student he had befriended back in high school.

It was clear now that the traveler was at least six inches shorter than Paul as the two approached one another. Paul stepped past him to the door of the little red car, reaching in to turn on the ignition. Sure enough, the gas needle remained at the bottom of the "E" mark.

"It's all right," he told the dark-skinned man. "I'll be right back."

Rummaging through his handy "oh shit kit" as Paul liked to call it, he produced a bottle of emergency fueling chemical he had picked up at K-Mart a few weeks ago. He could certainly be credited as the ultimate roadside helper, with two bottles of Fix-a-Flat, jumper cables, a battery powered lantern, and a complete 141 piece tool kit all packed amongst a spare car seat and Samantha's crafting supplies in the Ford's trunk.

All the way through the next couple of minutes, Paul pouring the chemical into the little car's tank and returning the empty container to his trunk, no cars passed them. The man just stood along the passenger side of the vehicle, again reading intently the handwritten pages he had stuffed under his travel bag. Occasionally, he would look over top of the pages at Paul, but glance immediately back down at his notes if the two made eye contact. Paul noticed that besides the travel bag, the man's lone suitcase in the back seat still had its price tag attached.

"First time in town?" he asked the man upon his return, who had sat back down in the driver's seat. He had calmed a bit now, but his eyes grew wide again when Paul approached the vehicle. "Where you headed?"

"Yes, uh, yes thank you," the man spoke, cranking the motor once again. It took a few seconds, but the chemical finally made its way to where it should and the car roared to life. Paul noticed the fuel gauge now read just above the "E." Putting the car in gear, the man sped away before Paul could tell him to get to the nearest gas station, saying nothing else.

"Welcome to town, psycho," Paul told himself.

-2-

"These dogs know all the tricks," repeated Andrew Falkness, reading aloud the cover of a matchbook he produced from the pocket of his favorite suit. On it, three women seemed to be mastering the art of holding themselves up on the bed doggy-style with one hand, while opening themselves for the cameraman with the other.

Fantasy Fred's, made famous on this particular matchbook, had been a frequent stop during Andrew's last vacation to Las Vegas, and he had long ago begun counting the days until the next one. With his clothes for the day laid out on his bed atop a yellowing sheet, Andrew headed for the shower. It had been two days since he'd last visited it, though he cared very little what those around him thought of his appearance. After all, nearly all of the business he conducted was via computer or phone, and since he was in charge at his little corner of the tower, no one dared make a remark about his looks within earshot of him. And as for what they said behind his back…

"Fuck 'em," he told himself confidently in the scratched mirror atop his sink.

As long as he had the bucks to dish out, it was he who called the shots. This rang true not just at the office, but at the massage parlor downtown he often stopped at after work en route to The City Gentleman's Club.

You'd find no bodybuilder here; quite the opposite, really. Though he'd ran a bit of track and boxed as a college man, it was mostly to get invited to the best parties at Dartmouth and little more. He took it about as seriously as he took his studies, which he breezed through each day much to the frustration of his roommates.

From day one, the potbellied software wholesaler had known his rung on the ladder of society, and Andrew fought tooth and nail to get there at any cost. He had gone even so far as to slash two of a fellow salesman's tires when he got his start in the late 1950s just so he could get to the 2,500 record album order first.

"Damn Jew didn't deserve it anyhow," he had told his boss that evening over whiskey sours of celebration. "Those people got some nerve, don't they?"

Seeing what he liked to call "those people" here in The City sickened Andrew, who would most likely spend his sixtieth birthday at the club alone next week. Even when a stripper of color took the stage, he'd be so polite as to laugh at the young lady and strut to the other side of the bar until a nice white girl came back out for him to ogle. After all, what could they do to their best customer, who often would tip with fifties later in the evening if he were allowed to take his time inserting them deep in the girl's g-string.

There would be no gym membership in the near future for Mr. Falkness. Nossiree. He felt it a waste of time to run around in circles or lift heavy things only to put them right back down again. And as for the caliber of females at those clubs, they were nothing more than bullemic little whores as far as he was concerned.

His ex-wife Coralie had joined up at a health club once, tiring of the monotonous housewife's existence she'd lived with already for 21 years. Sure, her husband enjoyed the reduction of her "old lady ass" as he lovingly called it, but she soon became frustrated with the effort she'd have to put forth and sunk back to where she'd been, where she was told she belonged.

Cranking his Wave Radio to near full throttle, Andrew stepped into the shower to be serenaded on this particular morning by the sound stylings of Mr. Elton John, who at present was remembering when rock was young.

"Goddam fag," he said matter of factly while lathering his thinning hair. "Helluva singer, though."

Checking the clock for the tenth time that morning, Falkness suited up for the day ahead in his favorite pinstriped J.C. Penney suit, horribly out of fashion by at least a dozen years. It was no matter, though. He had met a lovely young lady in the cereal aisle when he was wearing this particular suit not too many years ago, and he still felt it was good luck. Though their courtship spanned a mere three months, it was the only action he'd had since that fateful day in the early 80s when his Coralie left him. Her departure was preceded by little more than a notice of their pending divorce and a Polaroid of her and his lawyer on Andrew's bed.

Though he had found many uses around the house for his bride, perhaps the most valuable was that of the Windsor knot holding his tie together. Little charts on the wall and recurrent explanations of what he'd been doing wrong had never helped. Now, he resorted to having them tied properly when he bought them, giving the dry cleaner strict instructions they were to be tied when they were returned. And at the end of the day, he'd simply slide the loosened neckwear over his head carefully, leaving the knot intact for another day.

"Some dogs you just can't teach new tricks," he chuckled to the empty apartment, looking again at the girls on his matchbook cover. "I bet I could teach you guys some, though."

Though an okay husband, mediocre household handyman, and borderline pillar of the community, Andrew always thought he'd be best suited giving up his desk job and going after something a little more pleasurable—perhaps spinning the music at his favorite club.

"Alright, fellas let's hear it for the lovely Amber," he said, smiling to the girl on this month's Penthouse cover which lay across the back of his toilet. "Now let's all give a big hand to...Melanie! Waddaya think, guys? Isn't Melanie a little too chubby for her own good? Better lay off the doughnuts there, sweetheart."

For Andrew, the more routine life was, the better. Though he felt bored with it sometimes—most of the time, actually, there was just something about knowing where everything was supposed to be and having all of one's affairs in order which appealed to the man. As usual, his black leather briefcase lay atop the table by the door of his posh apartment, ranked one of the Ten Best Buildings by *The City Post* last year, thank you very much. Inside the case was the usual array of pens and note pads onto which he scribbled notes and suggestions he'd receive from friends during lunch. Other than that, the case remained mostly empty. Most of what Andrew did was not confined to a briefcase but on computers, a device he'd first heard about some twenty years ago and dismissed as simply a fad.

Surely, no one would want to make room in their homes and apartments for such a bulky, troublesome machine. But they had made room, and with those power-sucking appliances came other needs—for typing programs, new games from the latest Seattle long-haired weirdo, or maybe a recipe disk to help today's modernized women find their way back into the kitchen where they belonged. And Andrew was happy to help fill those needs, convincing himself almost daily he was more than just another middle man amongst millions of middle men. He was truly helping society to fill a need which would continue to grow by leaps and bounds as the years passed.

"And why not make a tidy profit while I'm at it?" he asked no one in particular as his tan trench coat fell from his grasp onto the floor. Beneath the table were boxes cluttered with Christmas decorations he hadn't put up since Coralie's voice had last filled the place. Though Christmastime had been good to him and his business each year, Andrew simply couldn't bring himself to deck the halls like he'd used to.

Also routine, just like Aaron the doorman who greeted the proprietor of Faltech Software on the way in and out each day, was the BMW in Andrew's parking space. For as long as he could remember, he'd traded up every two years for a new seven series, always black and never with a sunroof.

"Got my own one of those," he whispered, rubbing the skin on top of his head. In his college days the long, greasy hair that used to live there had gotten him far, including into the white cotton panties of a young Dartmouth professor. Now, he just let the area get worse and worse, not believing in Rogaine and too proud to try a comb over.

Along the way on his routine drive, always listening to the KPHR oldies station on the A.M. dial, he couldn't help but notice the two cars parked alongside this usually secluded route, hazard lights flashing in time with each other. From the looks of things, a skinny white man was helping some foreigner who probably was too stupid to realize the car needed gas in order to work. Neither one looked to be in need of any further assistance, and if they had been it certainly wouldn't come by way of Andrew. Janine Falkness hadn't raised any fools, you know.

He had grown up along a popular route for vagrants and the homeless, and watched his mother feed and clothe those people while his own family struggled for money. He'd return home sometimes to find his old toys or favorite clothes gone—given away to the less fortunate.

"Everybody wants *something*," he muttered. "Damn welfare cases and Indians living off my money. Maybe next time this gook'll remember to stop at the gas station."

Arlene greeted him as she always did, handing him a sheet of yellow legal paper full of messages, ranked in order of importance. Andrew detested those pink "while you were out" note pads with the sticky stuff on the back…too easy to lose and quite unprofessional looking. As for his secretary, she still looked somewhat professional after eight years with Faltech, though her widening bottom and greying hair kept Andrew looking at younger prey these days. He had chased her around the office on more than a few late night sessions, but that had been a long time ago.

For now, he'd stick to the strippers with their long blonde hair and fake breasts. They'd probably kill him eventually, but God, what a way to go!

At 10 a.m. Andrew's lawyers arrived, bringing with them an air of both condescension and distrust. Andrew hated lawyers, especially young punks like Estes and Sawyer, but when an old time business man tried to survive in today's modern world, they were, alas, a necessity.

This time it was bad news. Most of the time it was. Two of the *real* writers of a couple of popular software programs he'd pirated had filed suit, with a third threatening the same if her conditions were not immediately met and of course a healthy sum paid to her little company. As the two bloodsuckers continued to tell their tale, Andrew found his mind wandering to better places…to "greener pastures" as his father had said often.

All through his school days he'd been this way, daydreaming during lessons so often that his knuckles were numb from the beatings the nuns had given them. He'd been off in La La Land while they hit him, too. Hell, during most of his marriage he'd been there. Andrew was fond of his fantasy world, where only he and a tall blonde lived, riding his Road King down one of South Dakota's endless roads. There were no offices in this place, no ringing telephones, and no nights where he would wake up alone in the dark. When his mind departed the natural world, there would be no pain, no regret, "no lawyers," he finished to himself, making Estes and Sawyer pause. At present they had moved on to the remedy for the situation, which would most likely mean a sizable chunk out of Faltech's wallet, but on the bright side would keep the man out of court. Andrew hated court, too. He'd spent too much time there already losing money to Coralie and the man who used to be his lawyer. There was no court in La La Land, either.

When the discussion ended and the men left him alone, he decided lunch would be the next big decision of the day. Andrew could afford the best, but fast food places like Burger King and Hardee's (known to the rest of the world as Karl's Jr.) had gotten hold of him a few years back and hadn't let go since. Nothing helped him through the rest of his day better than a burger and fries. That, and a quick Manhattan at LeRoy's bar/restaurant for dessert.

Maybe two.

-3-

If Paul had been keeping count, he'd guess there were four dozen more people in the small sandwich nook than on a usual day. Soaked with sweat and the *au jous* spilled a few minutes earlier, he kept his mind turned off for the most part, which was what kept him sane. Every night on his way home from work, and later when he'd begin drifting off to his own La La Land, Paul would think about his much-deserved two weeks of immunity from the sandwich and coffee business. Just a few weeks away, he had everything planned down to the letter.

"For you see," Paul said to himself, taking advantage of a rare moment alone in the crowded kitchen, "every man must have a dream of some sort."

What good is a man who hasn't got a dream? 'Bout as good as a car with no gesaleen, he thought to himself, repeating the country song he'd heard earlier piped through the building's speakers. Paul smiled at this, wondering for a bit if his untalkative friend had found his way to where he was headed.

For the Morris family this year, at least for him and Samantha, it would be a trip like no other they'd taken. For one, the baby would stay behind at Sam's aunt's; she was glad to have her and Shelby was always glad to visit, and also their mode of transportation would change slightly. Fearing an early mid-life crisis, Paul had dipped into the retirement fund he'd contributed to faithfully each month since age 16 to buy the 2000 Harley Davidson Heritage Softail which now sat in a rented storage garage. Three thousand dollars more in chrome and he was feeling better already. There would be no mid-life crisis for Paul Morris this year, probably not until the need for a Camaro came along.

Yellow and white, the bike was nothing like he'd ridden as a kid on the farm. Those little machines were more trouble than they were worth, and most of the time was spent wrenching on them. Paul had heard the same regarding the new Harleys, but cared very little about that. He'd gladly spend all his Saturdays in that garage just to be able to hear the low rumble of a properly tuned V-twin.

Purchased in September, a surprise early snowstorm had not only frustrated Paul but nearly put him in tears when the garage door was locked and he knew his new toy wouldn't see the light of day for another six months. It shouldn't have gotten to him as much as it did. At his young age, everything was going his way. Sure, Sam would stay a little longer every week at those night classes she liked so much, and he couldn't escape the sinking feeling he got when he saw that Shelby looked nothing like him, but those were just little things and all in all, everything was going his way.

He worked hard like his father had preached he should his whole life, living only for the immunity weeks where nothing like that would matter. This year, he'd have immunity *and* a Harley.

Feeling a bit better about his whole situation now that some small ray of hope had been introduced into the day's events, Paul decided it was time to delegate his authority. Instructing the help to hold down the fort—the help consisting of two teenage dropouts whom he didn't trust and one older woman he did—it was now time for lunch. At this place, unlike that T.V. show and just like any other place Paul went, everybody *didn't* know his name, and that suited him just fine. The City wasn't the place for a small-town boy, anyhow.

About the only highlight of his day thus far had been the tall brunette who'd playfully asked him where he ate lunch when all this grease and sweat got too much for him. Sure, he'd never cheat on Sam, but it was fun to play around just a little with the customers. He'd told her his normal place, and almost hoped she'd be there waiting to meet him.

The open road winding on forever was where he belonged, the yellow lines passing by so fast they begin blending into one another. And at the end of those winding roads, after a few days in the scorching sun, was a little get-together Paul had always wanted to get to but never had the chance, where he wouldn't mind being unknown amongst thousands of people. For these people were like him, all working-class Paul Morrises brought together for the same reason—a little immunity from the day-to-day.

This thought made him smile as the Taurus pulled up in front of the dingy place on Fifth Street with mediocre French fries but amazing burgers. He barely noticed the old man in the terribly outdated suit entering for his Manhattan just in front of him. Paul barely noticed a lot of things these days, as immunity approached and his thoughts began turning to the road ahead.

Without a word to one another, not knowing the strangers would soon be strangers no more, Paul and Andrew stepped into LeRoy's at almost the identical moment, one for lunch and the other for a pick-me-up before returning to work. Not far behind them, tugging nervously at his red and yellow polo shirt, was a small dark-skinned man who eyed the pair carefully, the pages of the hand-written letter he carried blowing in the cold April breeze.

Chapter Two

"Well ho-lee shit," came Andrew's greeting from behind the bar. "Big time Andy Software, as I live and breathe!"

LeRoy "Lucky" Salvino was one of the few people Andrew came in contact with during day-to- day life who seemed to be even more crude and old fashioned than he himself. He loathed being called "Andy," had even hated it as a child, which is what made it such good ammunition for the bar's proprietor.

Though it was true some dogs knew all the tricks, this one hadn't learned any new ones in the past forty years, especially in the design department. The ratty red carpeting and peeling yellow wallpaper turned away most anyone who wasn't a long-time customer, and reminded people of a cheap Vegas downtown bar, where the strippers who'd still take dollar bills instead of fives went for breakfast in the mornings. Perhaps that's what Andy liked so much about it.

"Salvie, would ya quit telling your delivery guy to drop your Viagra off at my office? It's making me look bad."

A handful of people turned and looked at this, snickering to themselves. Insulting Salvino's manhood was the only way Andrew had found to really get under his skin. Andrew thought it must be some kind of a soft spot, since he'd worn a shot of sour back to the office with him the first time he tried it.

"Come on," the old Italian, who still oddly had most of his hair, replied, "You know I don't need that shit. I'm enough of a hard prick already."

Andrew didn't need to look at a drink list, or even to shout he'd have "the usual." After seventeen years of coming here off and on, he'd gotten pretty predictable—a tall Manhattan served in a beer mug. It didn't look like so much of a girlie drink that way. When his poison of choice arrived, Andrew looked suspiciously at the middle-aged black man who delivered it. It seemed like every place he went, he would meet someone who didn't belong there. It was bad enough he had to put up with hiring women as more than secretaries in his own company, but to deal with minorities as customers, where he had to kiss their asses to make an honest dollar, that really got to him.

About the only matter of business Andrew had dealt with this morning, aside from the crucifixion delivered by his attorneys, was a short trip to the bookstore downtown to pick up a rare programming manual for a customer who'd called him. Though they'd never met in person, Andrew was sure the soft-spoken man had been from some far-off nation, and was probably some sort of rich oil baron visiting town. When he was asked to do such medial things he'd generally decline, but his new customer had kept assuring him that his company would throw a lot of business toward Faltech if this first request could be granted. Foreigner or not, Andrew would gladly take his money. Its color was always green, no matter the source.

About halfway through his sandwich, he drummed his fingers atop the copy of *Small Business Applications for General Programming*, occasionally watching the door of the crowded bar for any unfamiliar faces. Andrew was in no hurry, though. Nothing awaited him back at the office but more lawyers, who likely wouldn't bring beer mugs filled with Manhattans. He'd be content to sit here all afternoon waiting for what could be his biggest customer this year, as long as the drinks kept coming.

He thumbed through the pages of the thin paperback, looking for nothing in particular.

-2-

"What kind of cheese is *that*?" Paul asked the fair-skinned redhead who sat his plate in front of him. As far as he knew, none of the letters in BLT stood for any sort of dairy product. He'd heard innumerable complaints about his own sandwiches, and had to admit he enjoyed the opportunity to dish them out once in awhile.

And away she went again, returning his plate to the kitchen to be fixed for the second time. As she walked off, after giving him a loathing look, he began hoping the cook wouldn't feel the need to add an S for Spit into the sandwich. A couple tables to his left, an older man in a tan coat kept spouting insults at the bartender overtop of Paul and another table full of businessmen. He recognized the group, one seeming to be a carbon copy of the next, from the Jemmings Land Trust office in his building.

"Why don't you put some liquor in this?" the man asked the old Italian behind the bar. "Unlike your kind, we Germans can hold our liquor just fine."

"Ah, just go back to that romance novel you got sitting there," was the reply. "That's the only action you'll be getting today, anyhow."

"You're as blind as you are stupid, Salvino." the old guy shot back, holding a book over his head. "This happens to be a very rare manual for a very important rich client of mine. He's meeting me here. Maybe then I can make some real money and afford to eat somewhere without so damn many cockroaches."

"Well la-de-da. Who you trying to impress with that crap, anyway? Probably thought you'd gone senile down at that bookstore; I suppose you were trying to impress some young cutie."

Smiling now, Andrew stood up and sauntered his way to the bar, beginning to realize he was disturbing about a dozen other customers with his shouts. He motioned for the Italian to come closer, and leaned on the bar with the book in his hand.

"Now that you mention it, she was a pretty hot little number. If you'd ever learn how to read, maybe you could swing by there sometime. It's that Barnes and Noble on Fifth."

Paul's ears perked up. Despite his position, he could still hear every word over the crowd.

"I tell you, I asked for this little gem here and she gave me the sweetest smile you'd ever seen, like she wanted to invite me behind the counter right then and there. This chick had the longest blonde hair and these big, blue eyes…"

Paul, looking down at the sandwich which still had mayonnaise on it, after he'd specifically said no mayo twice, leaned in closer.

"I bet she'd be the kind of woman who could send an old man like me to an early grave," Andrew continued, growing steadily louder and unaware that one more pair of ears was listening to his story. "I made sure I dropped my money behind the counter for her to pick up, too. And when she bent over to pick it up, I tell you, Salvie, I just couldn't help myself. I grabbed myself a big old handful of that sweet little ass. What'd she say her name was, now? Sabrina? Saltina?"

"Maybe Samantha?"

Andrew turned around, looking eye to eye with the skinny little twerp he'd bought coffee from five mornings a week. He recognized Paul at once, though without the hairnet he looked a little more proper. All he remembered about this man was that fake, friendly Hickville smile that made his stomach turn.

"Well, two points for you, pal. How'd you guess that one?"

"I suppose you could say we know each other," Paul replied through his teeth, sizing up the man in front of him. For his age, he seemed to be doing all right, though Paul would regret knocking out someone twice as old as himself.

"Lucky you!" was the reply as Paul received a healthy pat on the back and half a Manhattan spilled on his shirt. Supposing the man had skipped breakfast again (he never bought more than coffee), the three drinks he'd torn through so far had probably gotten the better of him. "Boy, I wish I could remember what it was like to be with a fine little thing like that. Me and Salvie here, though, we're too old for that stuff. I'd sure like to take that one home with me sometime, though. A handful of the old Italian's Viagra and I'm sure something would…"

Andrew Falkness, who once took great joy in boxing with men twice his size, and who once ignored the referee's whistle and kept on punching a man until he nearly died, never finished his sentence. The remainder of his drink flew with its glass behind the bar as the left half of his jaw met with Paul's fist.

Paul had never hit anyone before, and the closest he'd ever come to a fight was being kicked in the groin by a third-grade classmate once, in a skirmish over who was next up to bat. Maybe it was the fact he'd wanted to do anything in the entire world but go in to work on that particular day. Perhaps the same rude, tactless people like Andrew he'd dealt with all morning had gotten to him. It could have been the rude visitor to his city who hadn't even bothered to shake his hand, or his sandwich order.

Regret had already begun to set in before Paul had both his arms grabbed by the black man who'd served Andrew his many drinks. It didn't matter, though. He was into this and had no intention of stopping. Paul threw himself against the bar hard, sandwiching his captor, who let out a little yelp and bent backward over the bar. As the hospitable young bumpkin passed through the next few minutes, all he could think about was the day he'd met his pretty wife, and all the fights he should've gotten in when someone spoke badly about her. Usually, Paul thought as his view blurred from the sweat dripping into his eyes, he'd just let those jackasses say what they wanted to, knowing it was still he who would be taking her home that night.

Someone's elbow met with the side of his head and the world began to turn black. What had been a calm lunchtime crowd in a sleazy bar just moments ago was now an angry mob.

A younger lady with wide hips and a business suit had Andrew dumped in her lap after he was pushed off the bar. Even though Andrew was nearly unconscious, she still felt the need to crack her root beer mug over his head. Two men who looked like they had been skipping out on middle school that day each held one of the black man's arms while another punched him repeatedly in the chest. Their heads were all clean shaven, and Paul felt sure they wore white hoods when they weren't in such a culturally diverse place as The City.

A table fell over onto the feet of a dirty-looking old man wearing sandals. He'd have lifted it off, had it not been for Andrew's lifeless body being thrown on top of it, weighting it down. Soon, that was the least of his worries, as a metal chair struck his side. Then he was on the floor as well. Yelling in an unfamiliar language, the bar's proprietor felt that hosing down the crowd with seltzer water would do the trick.

It did not.

Getting up at the same time, Andrew and Paul staggered together through the stream of water, toward a face Paul recognized.

"I need to get out of here," the small, dark-skinned man from the rented Grand Am told Paul. "We both need to."

"Hey, it's you..." both Andrew and Paul said simultaneously, Andrew immediately recognizing the voice as the one he'd heard on the phone this morning.

They didn't have time to make any further connections.

All three men with the shaved heads rushed their little Brazilian friend, sending him to the floor kicking and screaming. While one sat atop his chest, the others kicked wildly at his sides.

In the confusion, no one had heard the sirens.

Before either could come forward to help, Andrew and Paul found themselves being held from behind and dragged backward out the door. Paul raised his hand to strike his captor, saw the shine of a badge, then thought again. Andrew wouldn't be going so quietly.

"...the *fuck* off me!" he yelled. Since the officer had hold of the back of his coat only, both Andrew's hands were free, but trying to hit something behind his back was difficult. Eventually, the back of his hand met with the side of Officer Friendly's head, and Andrew was dropped onto his stomach.

The last thing Paul saw as he was dragged out were the handcuffs being placed on the old man. Sweat and blood trickled down the side of his weathered face, and Paul suddenly felt that shameful feeling returning. He came in contact with innumerable dirty old men every day. Why did he have to pick a fight with this one, who now looked so small and brittle?

Now the action could be watched from the luxurious back seat of a Crown Victoria Police Special. The seat felt far more comfortable on Paul's back than having that wooden chair broken across it, but the car's lack of operable door handles on the inside left something to be desired.

Despite the pain he was in, aside from the ribs which he felt sure were broken and notwithstanding the few teeth which he spat out onto the floorboards, the little fish in the big pond was smiling to himself. In his memories, as he watched Andrew Falkness being forcefully helped into another squad car by three uniformed escorts, Paul was atop his very first Harley Davidson, and reminiscing about his first ride in a police car.

-3-

Whatever AMF stood for, he didn't care. Paul had been 11, and knew nothing about the financial troubles which had been plaguing his favorite motorcycle maker for years. What did matter, however, was that the dirt bike, dark red with a yellow, white, and red stripe weaving through the tank, was marked Harley Davidson on the side, too.

It seemed to be calling him in his dreams from beside his father's Christmas tree. His dad would save up a few government checks secretly in his little stash in the basement, then as a surprise to his youngest son who had been begging for it for months, he'd make sure to deliver on his promise and have the shiny SX 250 home for the holidays.

It was only fair. He'd bought that Pinto for Howard, the oldest, the year before. Harley had discontinued the SX a couple years before, something about too much foreign competition. That didn't matter, though. Paul had seen one just once en route to Chicago for the family's annual school clothes shopping trip, and that was all it took.

In the *Tribune*'s classified ads each week there were always two or three for sale; only a couple hundred bucks, usually. Surely Paul could have been doing enough chores and staying out of trouble sufficiently to deserve his first Harley.

Of course there would be no motorcycle for him under the Christmas tree that year. His old man, who was minus his left arm and the top portion of his left ear thanks to his second tour in Dong Ha twenty years earlier, cared very little about motorcycles and other useless expenditures of his pension. If it was a car, that at least it served a purpose…namely driving him places when he was too far on the better side of a 12-pack to do so himself.

Paul did have a bicycle, though. Bought by his parents? Nope. It took a month of shoveling out corn bins for a nearby farmer and some negotiating with the retired guy down the block who fixed them just to get that. And now, now he was almost in high school for Christ's sake! Bikes were for little kids. He was in the double digits now.

It was a Sunday morning at the Morris home, with smells of dinner beginning to waft up through the heat vents. This was always torture, especially on Sundays when his mother really went all out, because it would be two hours before he could finally sink his teeth into that ham. And no breakfast was allowed, so appetites would be at their maximum.

Fortunately, an argument between his father and the pastor at First United Methodist a few months before kept the family from having to attend church. It seemed like he was always arguing with someone about politics or an equally stupid topic, and would usually feel the need to start a fight with no cause. At the present moment, Paul saw the man alone in the spare bedroom as he descended the stairs. The room, which had become his dad's own personal den, was filled with old black and white photos, an old rotary knob black and white T.V., and a strange smell Paul's brothers kept telling him was marijuana. Of course it was a crime in their household for anyone but the patriarch to enter it, and even yelling in to the man was forbidden when he was reading one of those thick old war books or was deep into a television show. Most of his free time was spent in there, while the rest of the family did homework or fiddled with one of the old project cars behind the garage.

His mother, skinny as a rail like her boys were, huddled over the stove watching four boiling pots at once. Below her the oven light was on, and through her tiny legs Paul could see buns rising, signifying the meal was nearly ready. Her long dark hair was pulled back with a rubber band, showing the pale white skin of her neck and shoulders. No matter how often she was outside in the garden, taking her turn with the lawn mower or whatever the chore, the woman never seemed to tan.

Almost instinctively, his father sensed the meal was ready and the door of his room was shut behind him. Once he was seated at the end of the old chrome-edged table, the others began to filter in, taking their respective places while examining the old man to see how much conversation he would allow.

Annie Morris had a place at the opposite end of the table, but it was rarely used. Most of her time was spent refilling glasses or fetching ketchup and mayonnaise for her four men, and she usually ate her meal, then cold, once the others had finished and returned to what they had been doing before. Dishes and cleanup were also women's work in this house, and she knew better than to ask for help.

"There's one in Elgin for four hundred and fifty bucks," Paul said to the entire table, feeling out his father's mood. The man simply frowned, having heard the same story every week for nearly a year, especially on Sundays when the classified section was larger.

There was no need to say what the item was. Everyone knew.

"And do you have that much?" the head of the table asked, concentrating hard on his sliced carrots. This was what he always responded with, and after the usual reply of "no," that was the end of the discussion for that week. This time would be different, though.

Every now and then, if he felt up to it, Paul's father would go into the narrative about how the company was in ruin and their product was junk, and how his friend had owned a 1948 FL which did nothing but break down.

"Look, I know what your problem is with all this," Paul shot back suddenly annoyed, as his brothers stared and his mother slid toward the sink, "but I'll learn how to fix the damn thing myself. You can just sit in your room all day and not have to worry about it."

The man dug through his potatoes, still looking down. The familiar red color was beginning on his forehead. He took a moment, calming himself, then spoke to his plate, "Can't afford it, 'nuf said."

"I've got a hundred and thirty-two dollars. I'll pay you back the rest, with interest if you want, just please…"

"Did I stutter, boy?" He looked up now, big brown eyes fixed right on Paul's. "Said, can't afford it. 'Nuf said."

"Fuck this!" Paul slid back in his chair, hitting the refrigerator hard enough to nearly tip over the cookie jar on top of it. He exited the back door, ran around the garage, and slumped into the seat of a '46 Ford with no fenders.

What was so hard to understand about this whole proposition? Their house was at the edge of a huge wildlife area, owned by the city's mayor whom Paul had already gotten written permission from to ride on his land. From there, a countless number of minimum maintenance and gravel roads wound all over the state. No one ever traveled most of them, and if someone was coming he'd simply dip down into the ditch where riding was nice and legal. And the farmers he'd been working for would gladly allow him to ride on their land, as long as he didn't squash any crops. What was three hundred and eighteen dollars in the grand scheme of things, anyway? There was even more than that in the cookie jar, and he would have been able to count it all had he used a bit more force on his exit from the Sunday dinner table. He was working almost every free moment for someone or another, being as miserly as possible about spending money on movies or cassettes, but it just wasn't adding up fast enough. It was tough not to just dip into that jar, help himself and go buy his Harley.

Of course, he was smarter than that. His father would just return the cycle, then keep all the money for the jar as a punishment.

"He'd like to chat with you," Mrs. Morris, always trying to fix the situation, said as she sat down beside him. Paul wondered how it felt to be a grown woman, yet still unable to leave the house without permission, and, like her children, spending from an allowance doled out by Al Morris, the lone bread winner.

"I've been trying to soften him up a little, Paulie, so who knows, maybe today's the day."

She looked so tired all the time, though he wasn't sure if it was from her chores or putting up with them all. Sometimes Paul wanted to cry for upsetting her like he did, but he just couldn't let go of the idea that he'd get what he wanted, one way or another.

"Yeah, right," he said sarcastically. "I'm sure he'll wanna run right out and get it for me right this minute."

"You never know."

As he entered the house, he could hear *Mutual of Omaha's Wild Kingdom* blaring from the forbidden room. He thought, under the circumstances and since he'd been requested to enter, a step or two into the room would be allowed. In his old green chair, spotted with duct tape to repair holes, his father just stared blankly at the screen. Paul stood there, watching the lions wrestling with one another thousands of miles away. He tried to make conversation in a manner Al Morris would be sure to enjoy.

"Wonder if they chase down all the niggers…"

"Shut the door, Paul."

He did as he was told, and as he crossed back into the room his father rose, pulling down the shade on the room's solitary window. As it closed, he caught a glimpse of his brothers and mom pulling away in the family's old Caprice.

Sweaty hair hung just above the man's eyes as he stared over the boy's shoulder to one of the many framed photos on the shelves. Paul turned and looked too at the two men holding up their socks for the camera, smiling with matching cigarettes protruding from their mouths. He recognized them as Ab and Jimmy, who usually attended the reunions held at the Morris home every other summer. Paul had only asked once to hear stories about war days, when he was nine.

"It'd make your fuckin' head spin," Ab had said, grinning in an evil way and planting a firm hand onto the boy's shoulder. He'd ran away in tears and never asked again.

"I think at one time I would have traded everything I owned for a pair of dry socks," his father spoke, gesturing toward the photograph. He drew closer, picking up the faded print. His voice seemed to have a sadness in it Paul couldn't understand. Why couldn't he just forget about stuff he did that long ago? Paul decided it would be best not to ask.

"So where was this one taken at?" he asked casually, figuring this small probe for information couldn't hurt. After all, he was under the impression they'd sit down man to man and discuss the motorcycle proposition before reaching a mutual agreement in which Paul would finally get his way.

But on this particular day, no such thing would be happening.

In the blink of an eye, the man's face hardened as his thick, calloused hand clamped around Paul's throat. Eyes open wide in surprise, Paul stared at his father and the sweat now rolling down his cheeks. As his grip tightened, both of the boy's hands trying to pry himself free, he felt himself being lifted off the ground, then slammed into the bookcase behind him.

"I was just wondering," the man spoke, unusually calm for such a situation, "why you thought you needed to embarrass me in front of my family."

Paul choked, tears streaming down his face and the world beginning to turn black.

"Do you think it's easy keeping this house running on the measly chump change Uncle Sam gives us? Do you think whining like a little bitch is gonna change my mind? DO YOU?"

With his father's last words, Paul was spun around and thrown into the desk like a rag doll, his head cracking the mirror behind it. Oblivious to what he'd just done, the old man just stood there, calmly glancing at the other photos on the shelf. Paul wanted to pick himself up and run, but his legs wouldn't move. He felt things on the desk jabbing into his back from underneath but was frozen in terror.

How could his father just stand there like that?

-4-

With the house empty and his father still comatose, staring at his wall of shame, Paul watched the stairs fly by through teary eyes as he ran to his room. He knew that in order for his plan to work, the last resort idea he'd hoped would never be an option, he would have to move quickly. There would be little time to spare before the rest of the family returned.

In the small red case that held the best cards of his collection, Paul began packing. Left behind would be the great Hank Aaron; Willie "Say Hey" Mays from 1960, the oldest of the group; and the 1979 rookie card for Nolan Ryan, his favorite of them all. In their spot, he placed a fresh roll of electrical tape he'd been hiding (a valuable commodity in a house full of car nuts), the new pliers he'd splurged on at Ehlert's Hardware last week, and one of each kind of screwdriver out of his desk drawer.

The television was blaring once again in the little room as he snuck by, and on the way out the back screen door he stopped briefly to look at the cookie jar. It would be so easy to do things that way, and he could probably get away with blaming his brothers for the missing loot, but the wheels had already been set into motion on Plan B.

One hundred and thirty-two dollars would have to be enough for now.

A stop in the empty garage and Paul's tool kit was complete—two pieces of paper from the notepad kept by the phone, a pencil, two soda bottles filled with gasoline and tightly sealed, and two feet of 12-gauge wire. Onto the latter he used a crimper to fashion an alligator clip, then added the crimping tool to his box.

Up the road he could hear tires approaching, so he slipped through the garage window and was at least 100 yards into the wildlife refuge by the time his mom and brothers returned.

"Nothing but a bunch of cowards, all of them," he spoke to himself as he walked, the broken tree branch he carried acting as Luke Skywalker's light saber. He'd seen the movies at least six times each, and it was still all the kids at school could talk about.

"Fucking weenies, they are," he managed in his best Yoda voice and laughed, not sure if he sounded more like the little green man or Fozzie Bear from The Muppet Show. "Know how to defend themselves, they do not."

More humor came when he'd made his way through the woods and into Harper, the nearest town. On its western edge, the second house across the railroad tracks was where Chewbaca lived.

Zachary Moss was 13, but still wasn't too cool to hang out with Paul. While trying to grow his first bad teenage moustache, Chewy had gotten the idea he'd just stop shaving altogether. Besides the fur coat, fluffed-up mullet haircut, and the fact he'd already topped six feet, Zach could do that whining Chewbaca groan just perfectly. They'd usually sit together in church, but his father's disagreement with Zach's dad, who was coincidentally the pastor, had kept them apart for the past few weeks.

"Hey, furball!" Paul called out as his friend waved from his front porch, throwing aside the *MAD Magazine* he was studying. More hair had grown on his chin and neck, but his cheeks were still bare, reddened from the sun. "I need The Bandit for a suicide mission."

The Black Bandit, named after Zach's favorite movie, *Smokey and the Bandit*, began as a junked Schwinn they'd found at the dump. After some paint, new tires, and Paul's best effort at drawing a screaming eagle on the front fender, it had been a job well done. Since Zach's family couldn't afford to get him his own bike (they couldn't afford much by the looks of the house) Paul let him keep it at his house, as long as it was kept hidden from Chewy's three little brothers at all times.

"Wadda you mean, suicide mission?" he asked, one furry eyebrow raised.

"I'm afraid it won't be coming back," Paul answered, then dropped his case, slanting each eye with an index finger. "It is kamikaze mission, Chewy-san."

"Bullshit! It's half mine, you know."

"And do you ever get to ride it?"

"No."

"And why is that?"

"You know why, jackass."

"C'mon Chewy, why not?"

"Cuz mom said if I can't share it with Alan, Joey, and Mike then I can't ride it either."

"So what's the big deal, then?"

Just to be fair, since each boy had sunk $8 into the project, Paul gave his friend a ten-dollar bill before strapping his case to the rack and heading north on the usually deserted County Road 51. One hundred and twenty-two dollars now, but it would still have to be enough.

If he'd read his directions right, and usually he was pretty good with those things, Paul's destination would be the farmplace just up ahead, one mile west of Elgin. Two of the largest corn silos he'd ever seen were the first things to come into view, big and blue with American flags toward the top of each that had to have been twenty feet tall by themselves. Below the flags were huge letters advertising the site as the property of The McCormacks, and on the second, three names were listed—Arnold, Peggy, and David.

An only child, Paul thought to himself. Already this had begun to seem easier than it was back in the planning stages.

The sun had departed from view about an hour earlier, bringing out the mosquitos and lightning bugs, but more importantly—darkness. He worried little about the late hour he'd return, since his family would be thinking he was upset and had headed off to his hiding spot deep in the Hasslund's grove he often visited. Adding to the ease of the operation was the house's proximity to the other buildings on the farm. For some unknown reason, the McCormacks had been smart enough to build their house on the south side of their grove, offering protection from winter snowdrifts, but all the farm's buildings were on the grove's opposite side. Even a city kid like Paul knew a tree claim was essential in the winter months, otherwise kids would be sledding off the top of their houses and freezing to death in the 40 below nights.

Paul dismounted the Black Bandit and pushed it silently across the gravel yard, staying as far as possible from the house. He hadn't taken into account the possibility of a dog, which he kicked himself for once he realized, but fortunately not a growl or bark was heard.

First came a two-car garage, freshly painted with new doors and windows, identified by the manufacturer's stickers still in their corners. Why would anyone care about how their garage was painted on a farm, especially when it was way out here in the trees where no one could see it? No luck here, just a Buick with chipped paint and a Ford pickup with chrome rollbars. Next came a small red shed, which Paul knew would immediately be the place as soon as he read David's Clubhouse on the door. Sure enough, opening the hasp that was being secured by nothing more than a screwdriver, his prize sat waiting.

He went to work quickly, loosening the necessary covers with his screwdriver to reveal the Harley's battery and primitive electrical system. Paul dreamed of someday being an electronics expert; he dreamed of many future jobs, but this was one of the bigger possibilities. One cut red wire, with half held to the frame and the other fastened to his alligator clip, then a quick touch to the positive side of the battery, two kicks, and the engine cranked over.

Now that he was sure he could start the bike, Paul removed the paper and pencil from his case, then strapped the remainder of his toolkit to the motorcycle's rack.. On the paper, which he stuck with electrical tape to the wall along with $122, he wrote:

Dear David,

When you first read this note, I know you're going to be mad. Please know your Harley is in good hands and I'll treat it as good as I'm sure you did. I've wanted a bike like this my whole life, but I didn't quite have enough money to actually buy it from you. Here is my life savings, which is $122, as well as a really cool bicycle my best friend and I fixed up. I know it's not as much as you were asking, but it looks like you've got it pretty good here so I'm sure your dad will give you the rest.

Remember, I'll treat your Harley like it's the coolest thing in the world (because it is), and if I ever get the rest of your money, I'll give it to you.

Thank you so much.

P

It wasn't a lie, either. Paul actually had every intention of sending his victim the remaining $328 as he earned it.

"Like Robin Hood," he told himself as the McCormack's farm got smaller and smaller behind him, "Take from the rich kids and give to the poor ones."

Paul felt something deep in his brain, though he wouldn't fully understand it until years later. He'd been getting all kinds of funny feelings lately—about girls, his parents, school—but this one was different. He formed a mental picture of young David standing in the doorway of his clubhouse that next morning, bawling his eyes out while he examined the spot where his prize possession used to be, and for some strange reason it didn't seem to bother him that much. Maybe it was because the boy was the only child and was therefore spoiled rotten anyway; maybe it was because David had, for some strange reason, wanted to sell that magnificent piece of machinery (most likely a newer, bigger one was on the way to replace it).

He knew better, though. Somehow, even in the years to come when he'd do this same thing over and over again, he knew better.

-5-

That magnificent rumble, not really like the big ones but close enough for Paul's taste, was something he became familiar with in the coming days. The routine would consist of Paul getting frustrated at his family, which was totally normal considering his situation, then wandering off into the woods like he often did. In his own clubhouse, which was homemade from a plastic tarp and nowhere near as professional as David's had been, he'd carefully park his new motorcycle each time he was through with it.

Normally, Paul would stay deep in the woods during the daytime when people might see him, but after dark those gravel roads belonged to him. He'd never known how interesting abandoned farm places could be until he had begun to explore every one within a 50 mile radius of his clubhouse. It was interesting what could be hiding in those old buildings that most people just assumed were empty. In one, Paul found an old Chevy he figured to be about a '65, still in pretty good shape except for the window someone had broken out and the condom wrappers littering its mint green carpeting. In another old farmhouse, where the center of the living room floor was mostly gone and allowed him to view several dozen bats hanging in the basement below, Paul was poking around in a closet when he came across an interesting, and valuable, surprise. In an old shoebox taped over the top of the door frame was a small plastic bag keeping the moisture out of 200 or more old baseball cards—names he recognized from his own collection like Hank Aaron, Jerry Koosman, and the high-dollar Mickey Mantle cards from 1955 and 1956.

For someone his age, he was meticulously careful about his range, in regard to the gas that would be consumed. Going too far would mean running out on the way home, which would cause him to have to push his hog and increase the possibility of getting caught. With a full tank of gas, though, which Paul hauled in a milk jug from the family's fuel tank each day when no one was looking, he would just head out across a random field if he saw a car coming.

He did feel a little bit bad about damaging the crops of people he knew, but in an emergency it was worth the sacrifice to avoid getting caught.

When nightfall came, and his bike's headlight was turned off for the night, Paul would lie in bed, sometimes wondering why he didn't feel guilty for what he'd done. In the past three weeks, he'd earned a record $86 for his miscellaneous labor, but had no intention of sending it away to some spoiled brat in Elgin when he could keep saving for the bigger Harley he'd need soon. As sleep approached, he would picture the young boy lying in his bed back at their poorly-arranged farmplace, cursing Paul's name.

And did he cry when he pictured this? Paul laughed, giggled about the little brat all the while he was touring the back roads of Illinois, feeling guilty only about the fact he'd left so much money for the spoiled little fucker, and wishing he had it back.

Saturday night came, which meant his brothers would pile into whichever car they had running at the time and head uptown to get into trouble and look for girls. And for his parents, it was their tradition to hit Pal's Bar until closing time, one of the only times his father agreed to leave the house, mostly because he and his fellow Vietnam buddies could sit around and feel sorry for themselves in a group all night long. Paul's only instructions were to always keep the door locked and, of course, stay out of dad's room.

Although he was expected to just eat junk food and lay around on the couch watching music videos all night long, Paul of course headed out to the woods for his nightly ride.

He'd had his eye on a junkyard outside of Henning, about a 30-mile trip one way, but hadn't had enough time to go there and back until now. It was rumored from a semi-reliable source, the great Chewbaca, that there were hundreds of junked Harleys there too, just waiting to be bought for cheap and fixed up by someone like Paul with little money, but a lot of time to fix them up before he was old enough for a street bike.

Chewy had been the only one Paul trusted with his little secret, but since the hairy teenager had a girlfriend to hang all over now, it seemed like he didn't care much.

This time Paul filled two milk jugs, pouring the first into the bone-dry tank and strapping the other to the back. There was no way he'd run out of gas now. He thought the myth about "junkyard dogs" was just an old wives' tale, and wasn't worried about getting bit after he climbed the fence.

There was more traffic on the usually deserted roads now, with everyone either heading into or out of town for the night. Even though he had to duck into the corn seven times, he made the trip in just under an hour. Berning's Auto looked from the outside to be nothing more than a long wooden fence, but after a little climbing it revealed more old cars than Paul had ever seen at one time. It was sad to see the 40s and 50s era vehicles, which were his favorites, sitting down in the mud with no tires, broken windshields, and weeds growing up through the hoods.

There were, however, no motorcycles in the entire place.

Paul was a little disappointed, but spending a couple hours with his flashlight taking a trip through automotive history cleared that up pretty quick. When he was old enough for all three of them, he told everyone he'd have a '57 Chevy, turquoise and white, and a matching Panhead with a dual seat for his gorgeous blonde girlfriend.

The mostly full moon guided him home, and after twenty miles the motorcycle began to sputter. David's father had put some sort of filler plug into the tank, probably to make sure the little moron wouldn't get too far from home and be left stranded. A flip of the reserve switch yielded him three more miles, but that was the end of milk jug one.

Refueling was an especially vulnerable time, so he coasted into the nearest cornfield, steadied the cycle on its kickstand, and reached around for jug number two.

All he felt was an empty rack, and a broken strap dangling down near the back tire.

Paul was no little weakling, but pushing a dead motorcycle up a steep ditch took some serious grunting. And, during those last few miles, all the while pushing harder to beat the clock and his parents' return from town, he failed to notice the figure riding bicycle ahead of him. Finally he saw the reflection of a yard light on one of the stickers he could have sworn he'd stuck on the Black Bandit, a silver Harley eagle that spread across the back of the bike's sissy bars.

"Chewy?" he called out into the darkness. A figure came into view just far enough away that he couldn't make it out, riding a bicycle into the cornfield, not answering him back. Whoever it was, they had been riding ahead of him and watching his whole escapade this evening. But why would Chewy do that?

Suddenly another figure, this one much larger, came into view.

In the dimming beam of his flashlight stood Al Morris, Jack Daniels in one hand and his belt in the other.

"Chewy called to have a talk with me tonight about you and that motorcycle. Now I gotta have a talk with you."

Chapter Three

"So then what happened?" Andrew asked, spitting what Paul figured to be the sixth tooth out onto the floor of his adjoining cell. The old man, who looked much older now, looked through the bars at Paul with one blackened eye, the other swollen completely shut.

"My punishment, along with the buckle end of ol' Al's belt, was that as long as I lived under his roof, there would be no motorcycles of any kind. And believe me, that hurt far worse than the half hour ass whipping."

"So the little hairy guy dropped a dime on you?" Andrew asked. His interest in the little punk whom he'd only met to hand his coffee money to every morning had been piqued somewhat during the two hours they'd spent together at the Morrison County Courthouse's jail facility. It was rare for Andrew Falkness to like anyone new, especially one of the younger people he thought were nothing but drug addicts who could get the good caliber of women without charge. This one, however, seemed to have respect for older folks, even those whose noses he'd just tried to relocate.

"I guess he was jealous because I had a new toy that no one knew about and I was getting away with the whole thing," Paul said. "We were literally out in the middle of nowhere, and even with that loud little dirt bike no one ever paid any attention to me riding through the woods at all hours of the day and night. I guess the most embarrassing part of it all was that next morning when we loaded my bike in my dad's truck and hauled it back to the rightful owner. That spoiled little bastard kept my money and got his cycle back, and my dad told Chewy he could keep our bicycle all to himself, but if he ever saw me riding it he'd come take it away from him."

"And who cut that strap and got you stranded? Was it your buddy or your dad, cuz it sounded like they were both following you."

"To this day I still don't know. Maybe the thing just broke from all the bouncing around. It just goes to show how you can get it in the ass sometimes and never really know where it's coming from."

Paul suddenly longed even more for the contents of his storage garage, to hear nothing more than the steady growl of a V-twin beneath him. Having worked so hard these past few weeks, he'd forgotten about the summer plans of immunity which would be coming up soon. Andrew asked if that was Paul's last grand theft auto experience, which made Paul smile from ear to ear.

"Not by a long shot, old man. Just a few weeks after that…"

Paul's words trailed off as both men turned to watch the action coming down the hallway toward their cells. Mr. Polo Shirt, who was neat as a pin when Paul had stopped to help him just a few hours ago, was now about the sorriest looking mess he'd ever laid eyes on. The doctors had wrapped one bandage diagonally across the man's left eye and around his head, and a similar one encompassed his entire midsection. There was no more polo shirt, and in its place was the man's brown chest, stained everywhere with dark red patches. He limped noticeably as he passed both caged animals, one hand held over the bruise on his hip which was about the size of a coffee cup.

"Was it worth it for a fucking *book*?" Andrew asked the man, suddenly turning from someone who almost cared about his newfound friend's childhood back to his normal bigoted self. "Little sand nigger. Got no business wasting my time, or even being here, ya know. Leave the computer business to us big boys, all right? Can you hear me through your busted head, you little fuck?"

The man sat down gently on the wooden bench opposite his toilet, saying nothing. Andrew continued the interrogation.

"So what'd I do, huh? Did I not give enough money to your sister at the titty bar last week so you set up a bunch of assholes in my bar to pound the crap out of me? Or maybe you're one of those little Starbucks coffee-drinking fags who think I can't borrow their precious computer programs. Which one is it, Mohammad? You just tell me so when I sue your brown ass for every penny you've got, I'll at least know what it's for."

"Leave the guy alone," Paul broke in. "It wasn't his fault; he got his ass kicked worse than either of us did."

"Sure, maybe you were in on all this, too." Andrew's rage switched directions. "Didn't I put enough money in your tip jar this morning, coffee boy?" As the two bickered back and forth, they failed to notice their bloodied friend's smile growing wider, his gaze turning to them both. Later, right about the time Andrew was going into his dissertation about what young people were doing to ruin society, Polo stood up and moved toward them, silently sliding his hands through the bars of Andrew's cell. In an instant, Paul watched Andrew's eyes go from an angry glare to nearly popping out of his head as two hands grasped around his throat, setting Andrew's arms and legs thrashing out of control. He watched as the man bent over the old racist, sexist idiot, now looking much tougher than he had underneath the kicking legs of a group of skinheads. Polo whispered in Andrew's ear as he continued to struggle against his grasp, and though it may not have been meant for others to hear, Paul made out every word.

"If you're quite finished," Polo said in a thick accent, "we have some business to take care of." He turned his stare from the back of Andrew's reddening neck to Paul and added, louder, "You too, my friend."

As the small man loosened his grip on Andrew's neck, he fell to the cement, grasping his throat and silently deciding whether or not to continue throwing insults at someone he'd just learned was far from defenseless. All the while, Andrew crawling away from him and Paul standing silently watching the whole thing, the dark-skinned gentleman's smile kept getting wider and wider.

Mr. Yellow and Red Polo Shirt had a plan, even though it hadn't included those broken ribs. The two men he'd been asked to find were now in place, and how they got together wouldn't be important later on. There was work to be done regardless of how the pieces of the puzzle were brought together.

So far, though, everything was still right on schedule.

-2-

"Ev-a-woo-shun," repeated the red-faced little blonde girl, her frustration already beginning to show at this, her fourth attempt to pronounce the word. Twenty years later, she would still have trouble with that word. Inside the dirty two-car garage, she watched intently as the much larger figure pulled the oil plug from the same gigantic, chrome-plated monstrosity that had sent her into the house crying on several occasions because it was so loud.

"There ya go, right on the money, honey." Wyatt Scott stood up from his bike, wiping his oily hands on an old rag but saving just a smidgen to smear on his daughter's nose. Patting one of the V-twin's massive cylinders, he added, "Evolution, that's what they call this thing here."

Quickly losing interest, as most three-year-olds likely would, the youngest of the Scott family glanced intently at the posters on the garage wall. Perhaps her favorite of the bunch was the cartoon elephant with the zookeeper standing behind him, covered in doo-doo. From the man's mouth, the words "I said SIT" were written. She wasn't sure what that meant, but she did know the elephant was smiling, and that was the funniest part.

Covering the walls were scores of women in miscellaneous poses, usually wearing skimpy clothes, and always shown with a motorcycle. At the bench now, removing an oil filter from its box, was the man who'd given her her first ride just six months before.

He was skinny; her mother always yelled at him for that. Bryn's favorite feature, though, was the man's sandy brown hair. At night when he'd read her stories, she would run her fingers through it as he lay next to her, making his eyes immediately start to droop. Many times he could be found still laying in that same spot the next morning.

"And what do we call a bike that's not made in America?" he asked, catching her attention once more.

"Wice gwinder!" she exclaimed, the man laughing so hard now he had to grasp his sides. He tickled her sides with his still-black hands, but somehow she didn't mind getting dirty when she was in the garage with her father, especially not when he was laughing and happy.

After replacing the filter, Wyatt told his young shop hand it was time for her to get to work, and she knew exactly what that meant. He held the funnel steady while she poured the oil into the Harley's crankcase, being careful not to spill a drop. Even when she slopped a little onto the floor, he'd only smile at his daughter and ask in that Bryn-can-do-no-wrong voice for her to pour a little slower, patting the girl on her tiny head.

"Is this a big motorcycle?" she asked, still holding the oil container steady. He smiled again now, knowing that indeed, yes, it was a big motorcycle, and telling her about it always made him happy.

"See if you can remember all this. A nineteen eighty-five Harley Davidson Tour Glide Classic FLTC, with a one thousand, three hundred and forty cubic centimeter evolution engine, S and S carburetors, a modified exhaust, and custom paint."

"Ev-a-woo-shun!" she yelled again, this time coating his boot lightly with spilled oil. "Mofadied eghost!"

Wyatt filled the remainder of the engine on his own, while his helper traced her fingers along the gas tank's airbrushed Yogi Bear holding an eight ball. She had watched her uncle Jerry for nearly two hours while he made his mark on the motorcycle last week, following a drawing of the cartoon character in meticulous detail. About the only things she knew about her father and his brother were that they both worked together five days a week at an electronics store Wyatt had purchased with his rather sizeable inheritance from an elderly uncle. He worked in a dusty little corner in the back while Jerry got to run around up front, talking to everyone who came in and usually ending up selling them a television.

Bryn and her mother would mark the days off on the calendar each morning, and she would wait patiently for that fifth day to pass, so she could spend hours over the weekend playing with her Matchbox cars and, of course, daddy. Couch cushions and a blanket here and there made one hell of a make-believe town, in her opinion. And if the Barbie giant came along and smashed some cars here and there, it was just one of the hazards of living there.

Love it or leave it, as her dad liked to say.

With the oil transfusion completed, the two shared tuna sandwiches out on the porch swing. This particular Saturday found Sandra Scott and Bryn's brothers off to buy new pants for the remainder of the school year, meaning it was daddy/daughter day. That suited her just fine, though. She hated shopping for pants.

"Ready for a spin, squirt?" the man with tuna breath asked. "Since you helped out today, I think I'll even let you drive."

Not ten minutes later, they were puttering down their home street of Atlantic Avenue, the small figure in front of the larger one, running the handlebars. Even though she was forced to wear an itchy old helmet, which was so big the wind sometimes pulled it down onto the back of her head, she still hopped on the cycle whenever the opportunity came up. She had conquered her fear of the big rumbling thing, which had lasted all of two days. Twice around the block and she was ready to turn the steering duties over to the other rider.

They stopped into the parking lot of Samson's Bar, where she climbed out from in front and mounted the foot pegs to get on the back. There, with arm rests and a soft cushion behind her, Bryn would often fall asleep if a journey became too long.

"Sparky Scott, you big stud!" Bryn heard a man call from in front of the bar. Turning her head and adjusting the helmet so she could see, there were two men leaning on an old pickup truck, waving to her father.

"How's it goin', Spark!" the other exclaimed, winking at Bryn. "You taking your old man out for a ride today, sweetie?" Bryn nodded her head in agreement, her helmet slipping down over half her face as she did.

"You know what, honey?" the first man asked, leaning in close enough to Bryn that she could smell the beer on his breath. "Your daddy here saved me a whole shitload…I mean, a crapload…of money last week. If it wasn't for him and his magic soldering iron, your uncle would have screwed me out of four hundred bucks for a new TV."

Both men then insisted, a little too much in Bryn's opinion, that she and her father join them for a round of drinks. Her father had always subscribed to the belief that the customer was always right, and wouldn't dare turn the men down.

As the group bellied up to the bar, the minor enjoying her Shirley Temple, she watched the two men buy round after round. Bryn didn't mind the men too much. One would even ask her about how her day was going, when she would start preschool, and all the other traditional adult questions. They shot two games of pool, with her father holding her up to the table each time it was her shot. She made two balls, which was two more than usual.

After their game, the men insisted everyone have a round of something called a stumplifter, and bought two large pitchers of the reddish concoction, enough to go around the entire bar. The one who bought the drinks, the bearded man who had wondered about her day, said something about junk bonds and how he was making a killing selling them. Bryn wondered why they were so valuable if they were junk. She had a whole box full of broken toys that her mother called junk, and wondered if they were worth anything.

"Here's to good times, good company, and pretty ladies," the bearded one said, winking at Bryn after the last part. Though her father seemed reluctant, he drained his glass like the others. After another game of pool (only one ball this time, but still better than average), she caught her father looking at the pay phone in the corner, then the door, then back again.

Oh, how she wished she would have figured out what he was thinking then; twenty years later and she still wished she would have caught on!

Out to the motorcycle they went, with the itchy helmet strapped on her head once again. He never put one on because he said no one else had to, and that was one of the freedoms he had fought for. But kids, they had no choice.

"Should we stop for some ice cream at Benny's before we get home?" he asked her. The man's words sounded a little strange, like he had to think hard about what he was saying. Bryn nodded vigorously, the helmet again sliding over her eyes. He cranked over the motor and they were off.

"Daddy, wasn't that light lellow?" she asked him after he passed through the second stoplight. He just stared straight ahead, concentrating hard. Soon after, she saw the dog running, saw it stop to relieve itself on a light post, then run toward the intersection.

"Puppy!" she exclaimed, pointing at the black lab and tapping her father on the shoulder.

"Bryn, do not— " he looked down to scold her, but collided with the dog. Bryn shut her eyes and screamed, a sound that echoed through her head so much it made her scream more. She felt an impact, then wrapped her arms around her father as she felt the two tumbling over and over, her helmet repeatedly colliding with the pavement.

All that she could hear, besides her screams, were crunching noises that reminded her of Cap'n Crunch cereal. She would later find out it was her father's neck and back, and her own arm.

Bryn's eyes opened only once when she quit rolling, long enough to see the bloodied dog staggering its way across the rest of the street. From there, she covered her ears and screamed, the tears stinging her eyes until a stranger finally picked her up.

She wore the dark blue dress to the funeral, which was the last time she ever had it on. In the last three months, she had grown nearly an inch and the seams on the tattered dress were nearly ready to burst. As the group filed in, she couldn't help thinking about what had happened to the dog, and silently cursed herself for thinking something so terrible when she should be remembering her daddy.

He looked a little bit funny wearing makeup, which was something she thought only girls wore. Her mother said it was one of the two things he would need to get into heaven, the other being a goodbye kiss from his little girl. Teardrops dribbled onto his forehead as she leaned over the casket, and though she knew the vision would haunt her for years, she had to kiss the man's forehead to get him into where Jesus lived. Nothing less would do for such a great man.

-3-

Not long ago, but nearly two decades after her final kiss to Wyatt Scott, she could still taste the makeup on her lips when she first saw her birthday present. Malcolm had bought the 883 Sportster at the dealership in Harkin, then immediately paid to have it stripped down to nothing and have every piece of it that wasn't chromed painted bright neon purple—Bryn's favorite color.

On each side of the tank, hanging from the symbol and looking like he was almost ready to be sucked off by the wind, was Taz, her favorite cartoon character. As a final touch, painted in red letters across the bottom of the windshield was her nickname—Brinnie.

She stood in front of the garage with both hands cupped over her mouth, unsure of whether to scream, cry, or both. How could something so considerate and perfect for her make her feel like running the other way at the same time?

"It's all you talk about, whether you realize it or not," Malcolm said, pulling his cell phone from his breast pocket to check the time. "I even hear you mumble about these damn things in your sleep."

Malcolm knew about Bryn's father; had comforted her on many nights when she recalled the story or had nightmares about that day. She knew that this was his way of being considerate, a character trait he rarely had exhibited during their two-year relationship.

"That's not all, either," he said, turning her away from the neon Harley. He led her into the back yard to reveal a maze of orange cones, extending all the way to the back of the 12-acre property. "This is your training course, since I know it'll probably take awhile for you to get the hang of it. We don't want you out on the road running over little kids until you know what you're doing."

Believe it or not, Bryn thought, *he* is *actually trying to be nice.*

She looked at him, tears of some unknown emotion wetting her cheeks, and did the only thing she felt she could right then—hugged him tight to her. Bryn smelled his familiar Aspen cologne and felt comforted; it was not often he would let her be this touchy-feely.

Malcolm Devane was a real estate genius, or so he liked to think. Straight out of school and after passing all the licensing requirements, his first deal with the tiny firm back in his hometown had been a three-quarters-of-a-million beachhouse that was not only the largest and most expensive, but had proven to be the most difficult sell on the lake. As the story went—and he told it often—he figured out early that he had a knack for this line of work, and branched off on his own.

To date, Devane and Associates Realty was pulling in a dozen new listings every month, and hanging "Sold" signs on more than a hundred homes every year. Their motto, "Bringing your family home," could be heard on six radio stations throughout any given day, and his long, thin face even graced the television here and there with an exclusive listing or two. Their current abode, which he had paid for with his first three commissions (another story told often), was a three-story colonial with a huge backyard and enough work for a full-time housekeeper.

"Well, anyhow, happy birthday Brinnie. Hope my guys painted it good enough. Don't hurt yourself with that thing."

With that he was off, headed for a full day of two-hour lunch breaks and glasses of Dewar's on the rocks at his desk. God only knew what he did in the evenings—something about continuing education of some sort. Usually, he would find the time to poke his head into his most recent investment property, a customizing shop for cycles on Sherman Street in The City. It was the only one of its kind within two hours' drive, Malcolm would tell her, making the shop a goldmine for whomever had the balls to own such a volatile investment.

He would usually straggle in each evening after Bryn had already gone to bed, when she ended another boring day. Not that being able to stay home or go shopping half the day was necessarily a bad thing.

"Just a poor little rich girl," she told herself as she strolled back over to the motorcycle, eyeing the machine up and down like the devil himself had placed it in her garage stall. Bryn had never ridden one in her life, had never even *gotten on* one since her little accident. Truth be known, it scared her to death. And fascinated her, too.

She ran her perfectly manicured fingernail along the shining tank, over the soft vinyl of the custom-made seat, and traced the letters in her nickname along the windshield. Malcolm's boys down at the shop had done quite a number on this bike, and the fact that her husband would keep his staff from making him money to put their time into a birthday present for her made her feel good about the man once more.

Maybe she was more than just a token for showing off on Saturday nights, with her long hair and Malcolm-purchased artificial enhancements. The fact that he would lose money on her made her think he truly did care for her. Malcolm never lost money, and if he did, there was one hell of a reason for it.

Certainly it wouldn't hurt to try out the course once or twice. She would wheel the Harley to the back yard, get it pointed in the right direction, then decide whether or not she wanted to ride it.

To look the part, or perhaps just to kill time until she had to make a decision, Bryn spent the next two hours on a drive (in her properly enclosed Cadillac) into town. When she returned, after a long lunch of course, the motorcycle was where she had left it, pointing its nose toward the twisting lines of cones. At Macy's, she had picked up a leather jacket, leather gloves, and boots to match, and of course had stopped for a properly-sized helmet at a Suzuki dealership.

"No more procrastination," she said, pointing to the sky. "Keep me on the wheels this time, Dad."

On the first try the engine sprang to life. In the distance, or maybe in her own head, she heard a dog howling.

-4-

It had begun three weeks before, with what most would have brushed off as a little harmless flirting—a miscellaneous comment here and there on her assignments, or a passing glance in the hallway after class.

But now, after two dates and a couple dozen little notes passed back and forth, Samantha Morris was beginning to feel like she was back in high school again.

Not that she was too far off, though. In her mid-twenties, she had religiously paid her dues to the local Bally's U.S. Swim and Fitness, and had successfully gotten back to her target weight (a sum she'd disclose to no one) just five weeks after having her child. Very little had changed about her since her school days, aside from the marriage and child, that is. Given the occasion, she could still drink most men under the table on the rare nights she found time to go out with the girls.

Only one thing had been lacking since her entry into the real world—attention. In a military family, herself, the Colonel, her mother, and her twin little brothers had moved around a lot, meaning many cities and all the boyfriends to go along with them. And when she would return home from a date, her parents had felt the need to coddle her as much as possible, to keep her away from drugs and on the straight and narrow path. Though she never would admit it—girls weren't supposed to do such things—Samantha loved every minute of the attention she had gotten. But after her college years, and after marriage and a couple seasons in everyday life, that attention had begun to dwindle.

"It would be just as much their fault as it would mine," she told her coffee mug (Not another crisis, my schedule's full!) over a hastily prepared lunch of dry toast and strawberry yogurt.

No longer would her father sit up late and talk to her about all aspects of life, no longer did her brothers come running to her about every little scuffle they found themselves in, and no longer did her husband even take the time to ask her how her day had been.

"I'm just not getting what I need, that's all."

When Paul would return home in the evenings, provided he didn't spend three hours in that horrid little storage locker talking to his fucking motorcycle, he would play Barbies with Shelby, take a hot bath for a good hour, then would usually be asleep on the couch by eight. He was no help with dishes, and quite often no help after the lights had gone out for the day, either.

So when Wednesday nights came around, and she longed for Wednesday nights, Samantha had begun to feel less and less guilty about leaving the dirty dishes and heading out to Athen for her night school class. After all, there was no reason she couldn't better herself, was there?

She hadn't had the opportunity to finish college because of a forgotten lapse in her quarterly Depro-Provera shot that brought about the young Shelby, so why in the world shouldn't she be given the chance to finish what she had dreamed of finishing since the second grade?

"But what about the other activities?" she asked the empty kitchen, Shelby having already boarded the daycare bus for the day. "What about denying all those things you agreed to do, like stand by your man and all that?"

Samantha reasoned with herself for the full fifteen minutes it took to throw a few curls in her hair and smear on a bit of lipstick. Any notions of turning back had apparently vanished, as her last attempt at stopping was launched and she fought to start her car. The Carmen Ghia had been a Christmas present from Paul, who remembered all the times she had admired them back in college. It was getting old and didn't get the attention someone had once given it; maybe that's why she loved the little car so much—they had so many things in common.

While the engine warmed up she made herself read the note one last time. *One last chance to turn back*, she thought. And it *would* be a last chance, because after this there would be no turning back. All the movies she had watched, silently cursing the unfaithful women but even more silently admiring their courage, would soon apply to her. Either she wouldn't want to stop, or he wouldn't allow it; that was usually how these things worked out.

Sam-

All kidding aside, I must say that your grasp of the material we have been covering has impressed me very much since you began coming to my class. I hope you know I am only teasing (perhaps flirting a bit, too) when I single you out in class sometimes. I just want everyone there to know how wonderful I think you are, and I want to do anything I can for you to show them that. When the day comes when you're running your own business, I have no doubt you will prove yourself as among the best of the best.

Of course, a recommendation from myself, something everyone knows I only give one student each year, would also be a great help. I can't help but think that your chances would improve greatly if you were to join me for lunch on the tenth. Shall we say one p.m.?

Looking forward to seeing you!

The Prof (But you can call me Stinky)

The note had been placed in her handbag as the group exited the classroom last week, just like all the others. Most of the time she would know he was behind her, but she always ignored his comments just to make him want it that much more. It was a cruel game that many women sometimes took to a much higher level, but she enjoyed toying with his emotions when given the chance.

Things had been so innocent up until now; one night after class he helped her prepare a paper for the next week, and most recently they had sat and discussed their families over coffee. The subject of childhood nicknames and how cruel children could be came up when Samantha spoke about her daughter's problems with the other kids. That was when The Prof., who had been known back in Riverview, Connecticut as Stinky, had first begun to capture her interest.

Maybe it was the way he joked about life, and never took anything too seriously. He had a stroll when he walked that suggested he didn't have a care in the world—no bills, no worries. More probably, it was the attention she had not been getting anywhere else, which he was more than happy to direct her way.

She had just eleven hours of vacation time left in her account at the Barnes and Noble, having taken two days off the month before to herd around Shelby and several of her toddler friends on a daycare class trip. The afternoon would burn up four of those hours, as she puttered along Highway 23 after dealing this morning with a smelly old pervert grabbing her ass, to the nearby city of Pendleton, the city where the postcard had come from.

Good 'ol Stinky had written only two lines on the card, which showed a photo of happy visitors to Pendleton's Native American Days on one side. It had named the Country Vista Inn, Room 41 on the first line, and "One p.m., remember?" on the second.

Glasses rattled as she knocked on the door. She heard wine or champagne being quickly poured. Soon he greeted her, with long, greasy black hair and those nerdy professor glasses that made her giggle, though still looked sexy. No one could tell Samantha Morris that she should think this through.

In fact, thinking it through was all she had been doing for the past few weeks, while her husband slept and her daughter cried. Yes sir, she had thought it through plenty.

It was not Wednesday, but it appeared that school was still going to be in session. Only now, both teacher and student would be learning things from one another.

The door closed gently behind her, creating just enough breeze to slightly move the sign asking no one to disturb them on its knob.

Chapter Four

It wasn't too long after she had knocked over countless numbers of orange cones that Bryn graduated to the mean streets, looking every bit the part of a biker chick. Since her first leather-filled shopping excursion, she had also taken to wearing a neon purple scarf when she rode, even if only in the backyard. The look of the fabric flowing in the wind reminded her of the women from those old cycle movies back in the 1950s when Marlon Brando was still young and skinny. Only then, the girl rode in back of her man. Being a modern woman of the world, she was bound to help break that stereotype.

It had been three months since she took her first ride through that course. Heads turned as she rumbled past minivans filled with soccer moms and screaming ten-year-olds. Oh, how she felt sorry for them! Working forty-hour weeks only to spend forty more being a mommy, hoping they could save enough to finally retire by the time they were too old to enjoy life anymore. Wiping noses and asses, sometimes both at the same time, and never getting a thank you for any of it.

Bryn had taken up the habit of strapping her gym bag (purple, of course) to the rack on back of the Sportster, then heading to the gym each day for a two-hour workout. Of course Malcolm hadn't noticed the change, males seldom do, but she was feeling better about herself than she had in years.

Two weeks before, with her health kick in full swing, Bryn had woke up starving at two a.m. and headed downstairs for a rice cake and a glass of water.

"Fucking things taste like styrofoam," she told herself when she heard the ring—Malcolm's distinct cell phone tone of *The Entertainer*—coming from the pocket of his suit jacket. At first she thought of heading back upstairs, munching on the pickle she had opted for instead. Something, though, made her reach into the inside pocket of his coat, hung like it always was across his chair at the dining room table, and tap the button flashing "answer."

"Christ, good…is that you, Malcolm?" a female voice asked, slurring her words like she had spent the evening at one of the bars uptown.

"Yuh," Bryn grunted into the receiver, sounding genuinely tired and as masculine as possible, though not knowing why. Perhaps it was because the likelihood of a real estate customer calling at this hour was very tiny.

"Look, I know you said not to call you at home, but I gotta ask you a favor. This *asshole* here at The Lion's Den wants to cut me off, so I told him my rich boyfriend was gonna come down here and kick his fucking ass for him." The caller accentuated the word "asshole" so that Bryn could tell she was yelling it at whomever had been serving her the drinks that night.

"Will you just come down here this one time, sweetie? I know it's late, but I'll make it worth your while—you know I can do that."

"Yuh," Bryn repeated, though the false testosterone had left her voice. She was simply too shocked to care.

The woman said something else, but Bryn pressed the "end" button before she heard any more and slipped the phone back into its place.

Starting her escape plan at that point would have made sense. Having started it unknowingly two weeks after she met the cheating bastard now was more logical than ever.

As degrading as it was, Bryn was given a weekly allowance to spend on whatever she wanted, and needed only to ask nicely if she wanted more money. It was hard work staying in shape and well-dressed enough to be a token on a rich man's arm, and Malcolm knew that all too well. When Bryn first opened the account with a four hundred dollar deposit, twenty percent of her weekly budget, she had intended to save for her very own car. Somehow in her mind, if she were to save the money and buy it herself, then it would be almost as good as if she had earned the money on her own.

As the weeks passed and her savings grew, she thought a few times about telling Malcolm her intentions, but always stopped herself. He was the typical rich man, and would simply make fun of her for trying to do something on her own. In his mind, a woman's place was in the home—well fed, clothed, and pampered, but always in the home.

At present, she had just under $140,000 in her own name that no one else in the world had any claim to. All her debts had been wiped clean with a wave of the hand when she had first met her beau—the college loan that was a waste of both time and money, the Nissan that had blown an engine after two payments, and of course what she still owed Binion's Horseshoe back in Vegas.

Until that phone rang, she thought a hundred grand and some change was plenty of money to use as a cushion just in case the bottom fell out. But now, after she had put all that time and effort into trying to change the ways of a man, she deserved more. Not only had his late hours begun to get later, he had finally let her in on some of his financial data, and now that spring was here and houses were selling like hotcakes, Malcolm had even entrusted her with management of Midwest Custom Cycles. Much to Bryn's liking, she only worked as many hours as she wanted, but enjoyed putting her accounting skills to work now and again when there were no good sales going on.

Plus, half the men working there were in their twenties and built like Greek gods. Eye candy is always a good job benefit.

"All that time…all that work," she muttered to herself as she climbed back up the stairs. She never did call Malcolm on the mystery lady, but snickered to herself at the thought of some bimbo waiting in a sleazy bar for her knight in shining armor who would never show up. He must have known she had answered the phone that night, or else just dismissed it as a drunk woman's hallucinations. Bryn also took comfort in the thought that the little whore had probably bitch slapped him the next time she laid eyes on the bastard.

The next morning, Bryn made a stop at Starbucks for a cheese Danish to treat herself. She had, after all, shed six pounds and was once again a size six like she had been her entire life. Surely, a little celebration wouldn't hurt, and a little comfort food in her situation was always a good idea.

Arriving promptly at ten, she seemed almost surprised that the crew at Midwest Custom Cycles had been working so diligently that they were already dirty. Her idea of a full workday consisted of a mid-morning arrival, a two-hour lunch with Malcolm or at the gym, then out of there and home no later than three to catch Oprah. She sometimes thought it *passe* that she dropped everything like a traditional housewife to catch afternoon television, but at least she didn't look like those other fat cows did.

Steve Desharo was eighteen, fresh from high school and still wet behind the ears. If she were to sink to Malcolm's level and climb on the nearest good-looking hunk, it would probably have been him. Steve had wrestled in school, but was dumb as a post and had no future educational plans—all the things she figured a woman would look for in a lover.

Bryn's office had a large window overlooking the shop, where at any one time as many as ten men would be grinding, welding, or pounding on something. As per her strict orders shortly after she began managing the business, the room was soundproofed so she could concentrate on keeping the books, paying the bills, or reading the latest from John Grisham. Anyone disturbing her concentration for anything short of a broken bone or blood squirting out from a severed limb could face immediate termination. Though she had only made good on that promise once, when the door was closed not one of the men would dare interrupt her.

"My rich boyfriend will come down and kick some ass," she mumbled to herself, imitating the drunk mystery woman from the night before. "Maybe his rich *wife* should have come down there and kicked *her* ass for her."

A knock on the door stirred her from her daydream of clawing some tall, skinny blonde's eyes out. Bryn yelled into the speaker for whoever it was to turn and run the other way if they valued their job, but the knocking continued. On the other side of the door was Steve Desharo, grease smeared across his pecs underneath a thin white T-shirt. At Steve's side was a balding little man in his forties, clutching a black leather attache case and gawking at her through thick glasses.

"Um, sorry Miss Scott, but this guy said he had an appointment to see you," Steve said, sounding every bit like the backwater hick he was.

"You're not the fucking IRS, are you?" she asked the gentleman, who was taken aback by such harsh language from a young lady. Finally, a smile began to cross his face as he shook his head. "Good, then if you're not a salesman either, you got five minutes."

Bryn crossed back behind her desk and sunk into the big leather chair, in dire need of a Midol or a margarita; maybe one of each.

"Avery Czimanski, Miss Scott," the man held out a card in front of her nose. "I'm Malcolm's insurance agent. We spoke last Thursday? Remember?"

No, in fact she did not remember his call, but last Thursday had been an eternity ago, and on some mornings she would forget where she had left her car keys. She blamed stress for her little lapses of memory; this made Malcolm laugh.

Czimanski explained that it was time to compile her husband's annual inventory, an event which he billed the company for each April. The multi-talented man was also Malcolm's accountant, which made Bryn warm up to him a little bit.

Love your husband, but love his accountant even more, she replayed in her head from an old movie she had seen once. She thought it had been Marilyn Monroe who had said it.

Czimanski had been going through the shop, the smaller of Malcolm's two businesses, for the past two days, and after reviewing sales figures and deductions for the last year, it was time to pay into the government before the mid-month deadline. Malcolm had already sent over all the financial records from the business, something which was supposed to be Bryn's job. Now all that remained was to get a check from her and to decide on their level of insurance coverage for the next quarter.

He placed copies of financial records in front of her, which had been sent from the shop. The problem was, she had never seen them before.

"With an ever-changing inventory of motorcycles and equipment, not to mention numbers of employees, we've found that it's cheaper this way," he said, as though she were a secretary and not the person in charge of the place.

"Yes, I'm quite aware of that," she shot back, though she was not aware in the least.

"At present, Malcolm is sitting on one hundred and seventy-four cycles at the two dealership locations, valued between eighteen thousand and twenty-five thousand apiece. We recommend he maintain coverage of four-point-five million for the inventory and equipment, and stick with the group health insurance plan he is currently enrolled in."

As the little troll droned on about deductibles and occurrences of doctor visits, Bryn watched Steve hammering on a gas tank he had fabricated that morning, the sweat dripping from his chiseled forehead. It occurred to her that Steve would be to her what she was to Malcolm—a good-looking airhead who couldn't handle any responsibility whatsoever. Not only did that son-of-a-bitch think he could run around on her behind her back, but Malcolm had the nerve to keep on making all the decisions at his other business, the one he had entrusted to her, without telling her about it.

After Czimanski left, she contemplated just heading off for lunch and letting the whole thing drop. *She* knew she could handle the responsibility of running her own business, and maybe that was enough. All Bryn would have to do was slide underneath one of the hot men at the gym to balance out Malcolm's little escapades, they were forever hitting on her anyhow, and everything would be right in the world again. She would talk to him about the business responsibility, but would be professional about it.

That idea lasted about twelve seconds. Forgiving and forgetting just weren't what Bryn Scott was about. She believed in the old "eye for an eye" rule. Sure, she had it very good and didn't have to do any more in life than what was absolutely necessary. But it was the lack of money and distrusting parents who wouldn't believe her when she promised to pull up her grades that had nearly kept her out of college. The fat assholes at Binion's hadn't trusted her with another marker to make up for her losses; the old woman in charge of the dancers hadn't trusted her when she called in sick four days in a row. To make a long story short, Bryn had very little patience for those who lacked trust in her.

Before leaving at noon, not for lunch but for the remainder of the day, Bryn checked the caller identification box at the shop. Between a call from a wholesaler and a sales call from the phone company that morning was the name of the Lion's Den Bar.

The call time was 2:04 a.m., just before the call from the same place to Malcolm's cell phone.

"She's been meeting him here!" she yelled to herself, though the door wasn't closed all the way and others would hear. "He's probably fucked her right here on top of this desk!"

Delinquent account summaries, pens, and the small lamp were swept to the floor. Two workers turned to look at her, then quickly thought better of it and turned away.

"And the worst part is," Bryn said to the empty room, much quieter and sobbing, "I love the stupid bastard. Why can't I have just one thing in my life that works out? Why won't he trust me? Why doesn't *anyone* trust me?"

This was nothing like her. Sitting around, crying and feeling sorry for herself would never have been tolerated in the house she'd grown up in, and those values had stuck with her. When someone close to you, especially someone you loved, hurt you, the best thing to do was to get back at them in the way that it would hurt them the most. Just taking on another guy, even two or three, or even sending Malcolm pictures of the whole thing, would not be enough.

Deep down, she had known this day would come. Everything he had told her up to this point had been lies manipulating her into staying with him just so he could look good to his snooty friends.

Bryn dried her eyes with her purple scarf, smiling smugly for the few workers who dared look at her as she exited. By the time she slammed the door behind her, the little wheels in her head had already begun to turn.

-2-

It's amazing what a couple hours spent doing squats and burning up the miles on the Stairmaster can do to calm a woman down. By the time Bryn climbed back on her bike, she had cleared her head of any thoughts about a quick retaliation. Getting to Malcolm Devane would take time and planning, because he knew all the dirty tricks people liked to play, and more likely because he was, though she hated to admit it, smarter than she.

Bryn stopped off at the Safeway for fifty dollars worth of groceries, purchased with her own money and not on the credit card like he had given her permission to do. This would be just one bit of ammunition tonight. Strapped to the back rack in a large cardboard box were the ingredients for Malcolm's favorites—swordfish, steamed vegetables, and cherry pie for dessert. Along the way she passed by the Southside Technical Institute, and took the time while waiting at a stoplight to watch the students through the large picture windows. On one side of the building, eager young people her age were listening intently in rows of desks, while on the other side she could see four or five future beauticians styling the hair of their willing volunteers.

Maybe when all this was over, she might like to return to school. Surely, with plenty of tuition money so she didn't have to hold down a job at the same time, Bryn would have the opportunity to study as much as was needed. The willpower to hit the books instead of party? That one was still a toss-up.

Bryn dug through the cupboards to find the dusty cookbook that had been her birthday present from Malcolm's mother. Apparently, he had been unsatisfied with the quality of the food at home, too.

"I should just poison the shit," she said, dropping the slab of fish onto the counter from its package. "He isn't dumb enough to put me in his will, though."

Malcolm's mother must have thought her to be as much of an airhead as her son did, because this particular cookbook was focused on dishes with six ingredients or less. It didn't take much effort to cook a meal like this one, just a lot of patience for the delicate swordfish to keep it from shriveling up and turning black. The veggies? Just pour from the bag and heat. And pie? Canned filling and store-bought crust. This was the way he liked it, and she didn't complain.

Bryn instructed the housekeeper to take the afternoon off, and whatever chores were left could be finished in the morning. She said it was a special occasion and she wanted to surprise her beau with his favorite meal, prepared all by herself. The servant was asked to return later in the evening, however, for a short conference with Bryn.

Since it was Wednesday night, Malcolm would return from the office at precisely six, with just enough time for a quick shower before he headed off for the evening. She no longer believed his rambling about some sort of class he was in; Bryn now knew where he was really going.

"My God, what's burning in here? It smells horrible!"

Just as planned, he burst through the side door and into the kitchen, right on time. Over the back of his chair went his jacket, and he was halfway through the door going upstairs before he realized it was Bryn behind the apron.

"That's just the broiler, babe," she assured him. "It smells sometimes on these old stoves."

"Broiler? As in…?"

"Your favorite. Cherry pie, too. Seemed appropriate for a special occasion like this, doesn't it?"

The look on Malcolm's face was priceless. Not only was he still recovering from the shock of seeing one of the nation's worst cooks in an apron, but he was trying hard to remain calm while he racked his brain to figure out what occasion this could possibly be. This Saturday was his annual celebration for his customers from the past year, a big dinner for a couple hundred people, and if he wanted his wife there to show off he knew he had better think fast.

"Sounds wonderful, Brinnie. I'll just take a quick shower and be right back."

She giggled while stirring the boiling vegetables, picturing him standing dumfounded in the shower upstairs still working on why this date was so important. He must have thought a quick exit would bring him some more thinking time, but it wouldn't do any good.

Of course there was no occasion at all; she loved to make him squirm, though.

He returned in a different suit, smelling fresh as a daisy. As Malcolm combed his hair with one hand, he kissed her on the cheek and ran his fingers through her hair with the other.

"I must say, my new housekeeper looks a lot more sexy than the old one."

He ate, and she poured the wine. He drank, and she dimmed the lights. Bryn held up her wine glass, toasting.

"Here's to the most wonderful man in the world." This was blowing his mind, and she was loving every minute of it. When she leaned in to peck him on the cheek, she could see the tiny beads of sweat forming on his forehead. Bryn could almost hear his thoughts: *Anniversary? No. Birthday? Nope. First date anniversary?*

"Sweetheart, can I ask you something about the bike shop?"

"Absolutely," Malcolm replied, very much relieved to change the subject.

"Your accountant was in today and we talked about some stuff."

"What kind of stuff?"

"Oh, you know. Sales figures, profit margins, all that boring stuff. We went over a couple of ways to help move some more inventory this spring, and talked about health insurance for the guys."

Bryn explained, while sitting on Malcolm's lap, that the two had put their heads together and come up with some great ways to boost his sales for the next fiscal year. It was all about exposure, and they had figured out just the ticket to get the business' name out there.

"Sturgis?" he asked. "As in South Dakota? Do you have any idea what that would cost to move everything up there, not to mention what I'd pay for display space?"

He was reluctant at first, she could hear it in his voice. Who wouldn't be? But what Bryn could also hear were the numbers clicking around in his head. Midwest Custom Cycles, which had posted a profit of a little over $100,000 in each of the first six years Malcolm had owned it, had slowly seen those numbers shrinking. Blame it on the slowing economy, or the safety concerns from all the half-bald lawyers who usually bought custom bikes, but the figures didn't lie. Last year, for the first time since the business opened its doors in 1964, the "chop shop" as the local gearheads liked to call it, had lost money.

Malcolm hated losing money.

"You know you couldn't be alone for this; not saying that I would approve such a thing. But if I did, you'd need to take someone with you."

Bryn told him that yes, she was well aware that such a trip and such an undertaking as cleaning out two stores worth of bikes couldn't be done alone. Fortunately, the housekeeper was also a trusted member of the family. That was just a saying, of course; the Devanes were white as white could be, and had been damn proud of it for all of their two hundred years in America. Common help, especially dark-skinned common help, would never carry the name Devane.

He cleaned his plate, wiped up the last bit with a slice of bread, then enjoyed two pieces of pie before loosening his belt a notch and scurrying out the front door. Almost instinctively, as soon as the headlights of Malcolm's Mercedes had pointed down the driveway, his trusted advisor returned as ordered.

She laughed to herself at the sight of the little dark-skinned man. There was just something about a man who cleaned houses for a living that she found funny.

And that polo shirt; sometimes in different colors but always that stupid polo shirt.

-3-

"Okay, wait just a second…" Andrew gasped for breath for the third time that day. The first had been after he got a policeman's nightstick to the belly before he was hauled off to the pokey, and the second when the little diaper head had launched his sneak attack on him. This time, the tears rolled down his cheeks as he laughed hysterically, and tried hard not to wet himself. "Wait…wait just a second…you're a fucking *maid*?"

Polo glared at the old man, anxious for the second he'd walk too close to the bars so he could strangle him some more. Because of this tub of lard and his quiet little friend, who seemed all too amused to be watching Andrew laugh, Jorge Zapate had been beaten half to death, slapped around in a chair by a member of the police force which he thought was supposed to protect and serve, and now he had nowhere to go and nothing to do but to listen to them laugh at him.

"You're-gay," the skinny one taunted, "what kind of a name is that?"

They had listened intently while he told them about how he'd gotten wrapped up with the Devane family, but now they were beginning to get on his nerves. He probably should have expected the teasing as a bit of retaliation for his part in instigating this whole thing, but to hear someone poke fun at such a sad story made his heart heavy.

While stationed outside of Sao Paulo for a brief time in the late 1950s, Joseph Devane, Malcolm's father, had befriended a streetwalker and contributed most of what Uncle Sam was paying him to his new friend—one hour at a time. Over time, a trust was built up between the two, and despite

Joseph's story about having the mumps as a child and being sterile, the woman was soon pregnant with a child that was never supposed to exist. His lies had led to the birth of her only son, Jorge, named after the Spanish version of George, Joseph's father's name.

Twenty years had passed until one morning in early April, a dark-skinned young man simply walked up to the front door of the Devane estate and rang the bell. He was homeless, jobless, and was sent across the border strapped underneath a truckload of bananas to find his dear 'ol dad. All Jorge carried with him was a worn photograph of his siblings, five girls, and the two hundred American dollars that was the last of the money his family had. Joseph Devane had taken him in, and secretly found him a job at the docks and a tiny apartment in exchange for his silence. No one could ever know that such a pillar of the community had an off-colored son. It was agreed that Joseph would send for Jorge's family as soon as he could find a way to import them—maybe a month or two, Joseph had told him.

That month had turned into six, then a year. By the time disco had officially died and given way to the cocaine-snorting decade of the 1980s, Jorge had stopped asking. Either the opportunity to smuggle six people into the country wasn't going to happen, or Joseph simply didn't want to put forth the effort.

On the day George Bush Sr. was inaugurated, Jorge received the telegram saying that his family was no more. A new kind of fever had wiped out all three hundred people in his village. His mother, even though she had carried a rich white man's child, had died in a tiny shack trying to tend to her sick family. Lacking money, as they had since the sole bread winner left to find his father, their bodies were simply burned.

They could not afford anything better.

And so, from the docks Jorge graduated to a jack-of-all-trades who cleaned the mansion, prepared the meals, and even served cocktails at the farewell party for his white grandmother after her death in 1993. How degrading it was to be a servant at his own family member's funeral! But where else could he go?

Only Malcolm knew the secret about Jorge, and kept his brother employed and fed as his father had done in exchange for his silence. Jorge had only called him "brother" one time, during an argument over wages, which resulted in a beating with a golf club. He was also forced to watch while Malcolm burned that old photograph right in front of his eyes—the only evidence that Jorge's family had ever existed.

"He made you watch?" Paul asked, now sorry he had laughed at the little man. "I would have left right there, money or no money. No one is worth that kind of treatment."

"Yes, but it has all been forgotten. Mister Devane seemed as though he was truly sorry to hear about what our father had done to me. He paid for me to attend college, and to get my degree as an accountant."

Paul turned to Andrew, laughing again. "You got your ass kicked by an accountant!"

"Sit and spin, coffee boy," Andrew replied with a one-fingered salute.

A gradual trust had begun to seep into the relationship between Malcolm and Jorge. Upon completion of his degree, the housekeeper was allowed limited access to Malcolm's financial affairs, and was quickly finding ways to save his employer money in taxes. Malcolm had liked the results, and soon he was asking for Jorge's opinion before making any major decision that dealt with money.

"So this guy's wife wants to take all his money?" Andrew asked. "Why doesn't she just get the dumb bastard to divorce her, then she can take as much as she wants? Worked for my wife."

"Malcolm is smarter than that. I've known him most of my life, and he has one of those agreements where she gets nothing if she leaves him. Malcolm wants to hold onto every penny of his money."

Jorge, or Polo as he had already been dubbed by these two, had explained the whole story. Bryn had sat him down at the kitchen table, fed him some leftover swordfish which tasted disgusting, then detailed exactly how she would take more than two million dollars from Malcolm Devane.

That was two days ago. He had been given strict instructions to head into The City and find these two, then arrange a meeting. The little bar brawl had been unexpected, but worked nonetheless. Polo used his single phone call to notify Bryn, or rather Bryn's cell phone messaging service, about their little difficulties and how she could bail them out.

"But why does this involve us?" Andrew asked, suddenly curious.

"She can tell you that herself."

"Why does it involve *you*?" Paul asked suspiciously.

"My family died because I left them behind, and I left them behind because of my father's sloth. The satisfaction that I can avenge their deaths will make things right between myself and the Devane family. The fifty thousand dollars I have been promised will help as well."

All three turned toward the sound of the woman's voice down the hall.

"Promises won't mean anything unless all four of us can work together." Bryn Scott stood leaning against the entrance door of the cell block that contained her three potential accomplices. Her new boots, which she had bought on the way with part of her weekly allowance, made her stand four inches taller than normal. The leather pants helped to shield the early spring cold as she rode on her Harley, and the jacket would pad her in case of a fall. Of course, her entire ensemble was purple.

Neither Andrew nor Paul had ever laid eyes on the woman before, but she paid their bail, which made Bryn their new best friend.

"How about we chat over dinner?" the slender, dark-haired woman asked them. "From what I understand, you guys didn't have a chance at a decent lunch today."

-4-

While Andrew picked away at his hash browns, Paul happily devoured his cheeseburger. It had been his only food since twelve hours earlier. Polo, meanwhile, kept to himself while he sipped from his soup spoon. It was clear that whenever Bryn was around, he knew to keep his mouth shut.

"You do know that I just sell *coffee* for a living, right?" Paul asked between bites, both amused and bewildered at the same time by this little meeting.

"And I sell video games and tax programs, *not* motorcycles," Andrew chimed in. "Are you sure you got the right people?"

Bryn only smiled, knowing full well who they were and what they were both capable of. The old, fat one had ties overseas—ties that he had been using for quite some time to sell more than just software. And the young one, who couldn't seem to keep his eyes off her breasts, he had a little-known criminal background that fit her needs quite well.

"Look, gentlemen," Bryn spoke slowly, trying hard not to show her impatience. The convincing would not be difficult, but she knew she had to take her time. "I've already taken the liberty of having Jorge here look into your pasts. I know exactly what you're capable of."

While Paul kept right on eating, with that poker face he'd used to clean the dollar bills off of unsuspecting freshmen back in college, Andrew had begun to sweat it a little bit. Faltech Software, after all, would not still be open for business if Andrew only peddled twenty-dollar computer games. It was all about the connections; his little black book of important names and numbers overseas and extensive knowledge of U.S. trade laws meant all sorts of things made it into his repertoire.

Another reason the old man was nervous was that the formula here just wasn't right. Pretty girl, little dark-skinned lackey helping her out—two strangers trying to pry information from someone they didn't know. Put the pieces together and it spelled "cop" to him.

"All right, let's just say I get a wild hair up my old, wrinkly butt and decide to climb on my Harley, which I no longer have, I might add, and help you out. The minute I let you know about my connections you slap the cuffs on me and haul me back to that stupid jail again."

"I'm not a cop, if that's what you're asking."

Yes, as a matter of fact it *was* what he was asking—what he was sure of, actually. Andrew knew all too well that he had screwed over one too many distributors and program writers, and now the heat was on. A young, pretty girl like this didn't need to do anything illegal to get the money she wanted. She could simply latch onto another rich man and bleed him dry.

"If you aren't one of the boys in blue, you have to convince me so."

Bryn tried to conceal her smile, knowing he was following along exactly as Jorge said he would. Over a period of two months, her little housekeeper had hidden in bushes, tapped phone lines and tailed these two— all skills he had learned from Malcolm's family over the course of many years. In the case of Andrew and his big, greasy BMW, Jorge had even contacted some of the Devane family's buddies in Taiwan who were into the latest in technology and purchased a tiny receiver and microphone. One day while Andrew was leaving the drive-thru at Burger King he figured out they had shorted him on his order, and he ran inside to raise hell with the teenage servers. Jorge had been following him that day since early morning, and had the little transmitter and wireless mic in his pocket. While Andrew's car sat in the parking lot unlocked, Jorge had wired it up in a matter of two minutes, and by the time the old man returned with all his fries, Jorge was long gone.

"I know about Hans Weickhoff, and could've had you arrested a month ago."

Andrew, who had finally begun eating his meal, stopped dead with his fork in mid-bite. Weickhoff, after all, had made half a million of Andrew's dirty money squeaky clean again all the way from Germany via creative wire transfers that were not anywhere close to being legal. Only three people in

The City knew about this little laundry service. It was a quiet operation, and Andrew liked it that way.

"But how…?"

"Check your defroster vent in that shiny car of yours, big boy. I could have sent you to prison for a very long time, and had our buddies in Berlin arrest your little washmaid overseas. That is, of course, if I was a cop. I'm not, though. I'm just a girl with a lot of really interesting audio tapes with your voice on them."

Now it was clear. Though he struggled to keep his composure, Andrew was getting the sinking feeling that he would have no choice but to do what this young lady was asking.

"Blackmail. So that's your angle."

"If need be, yes. But I'd rather just have you help me out and reward you accordingly."

Paul was enjoying himself, even though he figured his turn was coming soon. The old man had been beat up so far today by a skinny coffee peddler, a little foreign guy, and a 100-pound woman.

Justice had been served.

Bryn's reward for the old man would begin with a gesture of her trust—a 2003 Heritage Soft Tail 100th Anniversary Edition with a clear title in Andrew's name. Her plan would call for the two to arrive on bikes, and she intended to have things her way.

"What about me?" Paul could wait no longer. While Andrew sized up the young lady who could bring him to jail with one phone call, Paul needed to know how he fit into this. "Yeah, so I took a bike or two in my younger days, but so what?"

"One hundred and twelve, I think you mean. Paul James Morris, held fourteen times for questioning on fourteen different occasions, but only convicted of property theft one time. You're good at what you do, Paul Morris. One conviction out of a hundred and twelve thefts is pretty good in my book."

"It's a hundred and fourteen," he shot back immediately. "Not that I was counting."

From what she had known about Andrew, Paul thought nothing she would say to him could come as a surprise.

"And you're still a lifer with the Gearheads, if I remember correctly." Her investigation of Paul had been much easier—one of Bryn's old clubbing girlfriends worked in the records department at the police station, and two hundred dollars had bought her all the info she needed. The Gorham Gearheads were small town Illinois' answer to the Hell's Angels—a group of four hundred that had started with one tenth of that amount back when Paul was riding his first stolen bike through the tooley bushes. It had been three years since he'd heard from any of them; they weren't exactly the kind to call just to say hello, after all. Even with the wife and new child, though, he still held a pretty high position with his old crowd.

"You can't blackmail me with that," he said, keeping his poker face intact. "I've already been questioned about my time with those boys and sent on my way. I've got other priorities now."

Andrew suddenly felt connected to the little punk once more. He had been teetering back and forth all day about the young man, but now that he knew more about Paul's illegal endeavors… He was like the son he'd never had. Or wanted.

"I think what he's saying, sweetheart, is that you can find a couple other idiots for your little bike raid." Andrew's confidence was back now, knowing it was two against one. "Maybe we'll just take a walk to the police station ourselves and let them know about your little plan."

All three locked their eyes as the two men left the booth. They pocketed the cards Bryn gave each of them with a cell phone number on it, just in case they changed their minds. He doubted that would be happening, though. Jorge, as usual, stared at the table. Andrew kept right on smiling as he pulled a twenty from his wallet and laid it on the table.

"This meal's on me and my laundered buddy Mr. Jackson. I don't take charity dinners from women." Andrew flung his arm around Paul's shoulder, who was smiling right along with him. With one final dirty look they turned and headed for the door. He knew the next day would bring more lawyers and more trouble, but he was still the king of his castle and the head of his business. In all his years, no one had made good on their threats to Andrew Falkness. They didn't dare. He would eat her alive if she crossed him again.

He offered Paul a drink, but he declined. The baby would be wondering where he was and his wife itching to head off to her now twice-a-week class. Andrew could see Bryn watching as he unlocked his car, so he dug out the tiny microphone from his vent and looked briefly at the bean-sized device.

"Listen to this, bitch." He smiled through the window at the girl before swallowing it whole. *He* made the deals in this world, especially when it came to women. Andrew thought he might just have some old friends of his track her down and cut up that pretty face of hers, just to show her who was the boss.

"Two days." Bryn chewed her Reuben confidently, watching them leave—the rich man's BMW and the poor man's Taurus.

"*Que*?"

"I give them two days, Jorge. If there's one thing I know, it's men, and in two days they'll be back, with their bags packed and ready for Sturgis."

Chapter Five

The burger hadn't been nearly enough, so before he tucked Shelby in for the night Paul poured half a box of Cheerios into a large bowl and doused them with half-stale milk. The house was all his, since Samantha didn't return from her class until quite late. She said it was on the other side of town and blamed traffic, but he wasn't so sure.

Paul set the empty bowl on the night stand and tried hard to stay awake long enough for Letterman's Top Ten list, but soon found himself fast asleep, dreaming of days before his father kicked him off to college and his family began.

The Gorham Gearheads, so named by his old buddy Zachary "Chewbaca" Moss, started as a dozen high school kids who sat around and watched old biker movies from the fifties on Saturday afternoons. They had dreams of terrorizing the small nearby town of Gorham, with its rival football team and the home of numerous fights between high school boys. They named their "gang" after the town in the hopes they would one day ride in on their bikes and raise hell.

In reality, though, the gang was ill-equipped for hell raising. Only three of the boys, who were all a couple of years older than Paul, had motorcycles of their own, and the bikes they did have were a far cry from the rumbling Harleys on the silver screen. They were high school graduates still hanging around the little town taking turns riding each other's Hondas. The other kids at school had several nicknames for the boys— "Rice Rocketeers," the "Jap Bike Jokers," but Paul's favorite was the "Honda Heckraisers."

It had been three years since Paul's little excursion to hotwire his first bike, but Chewy still remembered it well. He caught Paul sitting in the town square one Saturday night getting drunk by himself and asked if Paul would like to join their gang. Maybe it was the alcohol, or the fact he had been trying to fit in with the older kids his whole life, but whatever the reason he reluctantly said yes. Chewy swore up and down he hadn't ratted out his best buddy that time, and being young and stupid as he was, Paul believed him.

His initiation was to steal another bike, then show the rest of them how it was done.

The following Saturday, seven guys packed into Chewy's Mercury Zephyr and headed for Chicago. In Paul's back pocket was the same screwdriver he'd used the first time, and other assorted tools he would be needing. At a gun show he'd attended with his older brother, Paul picked up a small leather pouch full of funny-shaped picks and a tensioner which the seller boasted could pick any lock in the world. He studied the little book that came with it religiously, and practiced daily on the old cars in his yard. His best time was down to twelve seconds.

Outside of a shitty little bar called Pumper's, the pseudo-gang sat in their car for nearly an hour listening to the sirens all around them before one finally got up the courage to speak. Burly, hairy bikers, most of whom outweighed them all by a hundred pounds, came and went from the bar, urinated on the side of the building, and swore at one another like sailors.

"You guys still think this is a good idea?" asked Matt St. Vincent, one of the three Honda owners in the bunch. He would just as soon have returned home. He could take the teasing from his friends about his cycle; it was nothing compared to getting killed trying to steal a better bike.

"Don't be a pussy," Paul shot back, proud to be the bravest of the older boys. He was the youngest in a family of big, angry men, and had little fear of a beating at this point in his life. He wasn't yet old enough to be sent to adult jail, and figured the worst that could happen was a stint in juvenile hall before he turned 18 and was set free.

Paul climbed out of the back seat, patting the inside pocket of his old leather coat to make sure he'd remembered the picks. The rest followed silently behind him into the alley, their lights turned off. The next three minutes were some of the finest in his young life. Paul not only gained the respect of the wanna-be biker gang, but was instantly promoted to one of its leaders.

Without even looking at the tools, he removed the pouch and felt for the curved pick with the tiny nub at the end that worked in most motorcycle ignitions. He glanced both ways up and down the alley to make sure no one was there, then slid the two-by-four into the handles of the bar's back doors.

Two dozen bikes lined the narrow alley, wedged in wherever they would fit near dumpsters and cardboard boxes filled to the top with beer cans. It was clear that the men with the best bikes were higher in the pecking order and got the privilege of parking away from the others. Paul recognized most of the models—a 1979 FXEF with forward pegs, a decked-out brown FLT Tour Glide, and a couple of 1980 FXWG's with blue flames painted on the side. One was blue and the other pink, making him think the man let his old lady ride her own bike.

By the time anyone inside had a chance of hearing the engines, they would quickly find the door blocked, and if things went according to plan they would have to fight their way through the crowd to the front door, then run all the way through the crowd in front of the building to get to the alley. Even if those guys were the biggest gorilla sons of bitches in town and could throw anyone out of their way, Paul figured it would take them at least three or four minutes to get to the alley.

Plenty of time.

Overconfident now, he turned to the carload of waiting hoodlums and asked, "So, which ones you guys want?"

Paul worked quickly with his little wire device, only running into trouble on the pink FXWG. He figured no one would want a girlie bike, so he kept that one as his own. Paint jobs were easy, after all, especially with the array of tools in the Morris boys' shop. Even today he could still feel that cold shiver when a big hand grabbed for his shoulder, but he had sped away just in time. That's a lot of what his life had amounted to so far—getting away just in the nick of time.

-2-

To say their little plan went off without a hitch would be an understatement.

It was as if they were professionals, not just acne-ridden teenagers with bad moustaches. Paul always felt as though he had someone watching over him, even when he was doing something bad. The proverbial "rabbit's foot up the ass" as Henry O'Neill, one of the Gearheads, liked to say. Sure, the last of the crew heard angry voices and cycles being kick started as they rode away into the crowded streets, but the important thing was that they never looked back.

That was the key to stealing, Paul had found. If you looked back, you just might catch a glimpse of the little boy crying in his clubhouse at that fucked-up farmplace, or the six foot six, 230 pound monster just half a step behind you. It was then that you either choked or gave up the fight.

A bigger-than-average urge to piss woke Paul up, head down on his folded arms next to his empty cereal bowl. Once again, the sandwich dungeon had taken its toll on the young man—or perhaps it was the unexpected trip to the big house. There had been many nights when Paul had awakened the next morning to find himself in the most interesting places—the uncomfortable chair he'd had since high school, still soaking in the bath tub, or today's choice, the kitchen table.

Paul soon knew what had roused him when he heard the water running into the tub. Shelby had taken the liberty of drawing the water herself, although she was strictly forbidden to do so. He caught the toddler just as she was straddling the edge of the tub, toes dangling above the rising water.

"Hey, hold on a second there, sweetie." He checked the temperature and, sure enough, it could have boiled rice if the need arose. Paul set the child, naked and smiling with no clue she had been seconds from scalding herself, onto the toilet while he cooled the bath.

"You know you shouldn't take a bath without mommy or me," he said, trying hard to scold but too soft-hearted to really get into it. How could anyone be angry at a child whose only ambition in life was to spend every waking moment naked and in the bathtub? She could grow up to be a world champion swimmer, build a better bath tub, or be a hippie nudist, he supposed.

While Shelby busied herself with a more moderate temperature of bath water, Paul wandered back out into the kitchen to the spot where he'd slept last night. Should he tell Sam about his little run-in with the law? Surely she had seen the cut on his lip or the gash on his forehead when she came in last night, so how could he avoid it?

Why hadn't she woken him up?

"Aiwpane!" Paul heard from behind him, Shelby standing there with her favorite pink towel wrapped around her neck, dripping onto the carpet. He told her to get dressed first, before Captain Daddy would let the plane leave the hanger. This seemed to work, as she returned two minutes later in a Hello Kitty sweatshirt, green tennis shoes, and one of those pink ballet dresses, whatever they were called. Shelby's inexperienced parents made the mistake of allowing her to dress herself however she chose.

"Pretty stylish there, goofball. Ready for that airplane ride?" Shelby held out her arms as high as they could reach, which, of course, wasn't very high, and Paul twirled her around the room over and over again, both of them giggling wildly. He didn't give any thought to waking up Sam until the ride was over and he sat at the table with his daughter on his lap, trying to brush her tangle of hair.

"We waited a wong time, Daddy."

"We did?"

"Uh huh!" she said, nodding despite the brush tearing out her hair.

"You went to sweep on the table, and I tucket mysewf into bed."

"When did mommy get here?"

"I donno, but I could see the sun outside the window. She took a showuw and went to bed, but it was light outside."

Paul fumbled through the magazines for the remote and turned on the electronic babysitter, which seemed to be permanently set to Nick, Jr. While Shelby watched the dancing squares he snuck into the bedroom to find Samantha fast asleep, hair still wet.

In all the years he'd known her, Sam had never taken a shower before bed. She always said it was pointless when you were going to do it in the morning after working out, anyhow. She still had another 20 minutes before the alarm according to the clock radio, so he started investigating, even though he knew he shouldn't. Samantha was a loyal mother and wife, who liked raw cookie dough and cheesy old blues records while they made love. She told him every day that there was no one else in the world she'd rather be with; no one who could understand her like he did. She had likely gone out to the bar with some friends after class. There was no harm in a bit of mid-week drinking, after all. Hell, they were still young people, and most people their age were still going to college parties trying to scam on unsuspecting freshmen.

So why did he find himself going through her pockets, then? It certainly wasn't because he had extra time on his hands, because today was inventory day at the sandwich shop and he was already running late. Still, he had always been very careful and suspicious of people, even those close to him. Maybe it was because he always though his mother would come through for him but she never stood up for herself. Maybe it was his brothers or his friends who stole from him, and led him to want to steal from others. Whatever the reason, he felt silly digging through the hamper and even more so when he smelled her underpants from the previous day.

What would she say if she woke up and caught him? What he felt, and smelled, confirmed his fears.

So did the note in her back pocket from some asshole named Stinky.

He wanted to shake her awake, pull back his hand across his chest and slap her as hard as he could, over and over, until she swore to God she would never do anything like that again. Samantha's slim face would be nothing but a puffy, black-and-blue mess when he was finished. He wanted to find out where the man lived and hunt him down, as he was sure most men in his situation would have been feeling. Those first thoughts are always the worst—where do I get a gun? What about a kitchen knife? Should I catch them in the act and kill them both?

But in the end, he would take a few deep breaths and leave her sleeping there, taking care to be long gone by the time her alarm was set to go off. Paul's mind raced with what if's: Shelby, their apartment together—fuck, their *life* together.

He kissed his daughter on top of her head, and when he did he saw a tear splash into her still-tangled hair. She shouldn't see him like this, so he turned quickly and headed for the door. Maybe he would just keep right on going, right past the shitty little sandwich shop and back where he grew up, where women respected their husbands and life was peachy-keen, jelly bean. Where a good woman cooked your meals and kept your house clean, raised your children and, Jesus Christ, the most important "and" of all, they were faithful to you one hundred percent.

No exceptions.

"And never look back," he told himself. Paul turned the note over and over in his hands, then slipped it back where he found it. Truth be known, there was a member of the opposite sex he hadn't been able to get off his mind, either. Maybe he was nearly as guilty as his wife.

Last night when he picked up his daughter, who would depend on him for several more years to chase away monsters and, later, horny teenage boys who were after her virtue, he had no intention of giving any further consideration to Bryn's plan. But, as his father liked to say, "Times change and shit happens."

He may have beaten up on his children a few too many times, but the old man had some real insight. Paul had spent most of last night, while he waited for his wife to return, convincing himself he was still debating the Sturgis issue. But he had actually made up his mind as soon as he laid eyes on Bryn Scott.

The air outside was warming up some. Finally. Maybe he would drag the Harley out of the shed and take the long way to work. He deserved a bit of recreation, after all.

Paul suddenly longed for the old days like he had dreamed about the night before, without a care in the world or a woman to slow him down. That sealed the deal. He pulled Bryn's card from his pocket and dialed the number.

"What the hell," he told himself, smiling like he had on the night all those burly bikers tried chasing him down. "I was going to go there anyway."

-3-

Andrew awoke once again soaked with sweat. He'd had that same dream again, the one where he is alone on some godforsaken piece of pasture land just south of Sheepville, North Dakota. He sits alone by the campfire, the chuck wagon blocking the prairie wind, when all at once a great commotion stirs the ground. His coffee begins making waves in his cup. The pots and pans rattle on the side of the wagon. Then someone yells "Stampede!" and he begins to run.

Andrew is naked, of course; people in dreams are often naked for some reason. From behind him he can hear them coming. Two thousand? Maybe three thousand head at least. The cries of all those voices blend together behind him into a low roar, which grows louder the faster he tries to run away, his middle-aged beer belly flopping from side to side.

He can't look back. He *mustn't* look back because that is when the real terror really sets in—when he can see all those faces so close behind him, ready to trample him down like they have done to so many before him. But, careless like he often is, he ventures a glance over his shoulder and sees them all. Good lord, there must be five thousand this time, chasing him over endless grass-covered hills with no tree or rock to climb on in sight.

Then those objects are flying at him, being thrown from behind and wizzing past his ears, some catching him in the back and cutting up his neck. Blood flows from those cuts now, not deep but deadly just the same. Finally, one of the missiles falls into his hands and he can't help but look down at it, just the way he couldn't help but look back to see all of them chasing him.

It is horrible! And he screams at them, and at what lies in his trembling hands as he runs.

It is his bill. One of many bills in their proper white envelopes, disguised as mail someone might actually want to open. And behind him, numbering ten thousand now and growing the faster he tries to get away, is a herd of lawyers—all of them clad in the same boring black suit, carrying the same boring black attache, and shaking the ground with their $300 Gucci loafers.

Like all the other times, he gives up eventually—just lays down on his belly and covers his head, praying they won't trample him. But, like always, the vultures just gather around him and keep on throwing those plain white envelopes, cutting away at his ears, his back, his bare buttocks.

And their cries! Oh, how he hates to hear their cries!

"Pay us!" the fat little Jewish one says.

"Pay us!" echoes the pretty woman in heels.

"Litigation!" cries a tall bald one as he slices at Andrew's ear with an envelope.

"Alimony!" they all chant in unison, as Andrew feels his blood draining and his body becoming weak. He will die soon, broke and naked in the middle of God knows where.

But he woke up. That was the best part—he always woke up.

The shower's warmth usually helped take away the memories of his nightmares, though sometimes he would still see blood trickling down onto the floor as he washed, like all those deadly paper cuts were still there. Today, though, it was nothing but clear water, dribbling down past his aging belly into the drain.

Andrew dressed as he did every morning in one of his tired old suits, one of the last remnants left on the street of the cocaine decade known as the 1980s. He still snickered at the idea of some little bitch, even younger than the coffee boy, trying to get the best of him and take advantage of his connections. So what if she knew a few details about his past—who didn't?

He had made the papers more than his share of times with indictments that never produced results. Each time, ironic as it may have been, he turned to those he hated the most to set him free—the lawyers. They were blood-thirsty, money-sucking leaches, but they always got him out of a tight spot if need be. And was that such a surprise? Immunity was, in fact, what he shelled out half a million last year alone for.

Andrew viewed himself as a twenty-first century O.J. Simpson who was a little more careful with where he left his bloody gloves. At times he slept better knowing that there were very few messes he could get himself into that his ol' faithful boys in black couldn't clear up for him.

Wealth means different things to different people. Andrew often laughed at some of the rubes on television who responded to that newsman's questions—he thought McFain was the guy's name—about how much cash it would take for them to consider themselves "rich." Most said a million would suffice; others said half of that.

As of tax time in February, Andrew was known to the government of the United States of America as being worth a tidy five hundred thousand on paper. Of course, in reality that figure was more likely to be multiplied by four (five before the Enron ordeal). Offshore accounts, creative use of wire transfers via his old college buddies in the right places, and Andrew Falkness's money was kept on the move so much that only a handful of people knew it even existed.

And on the back of her little card she had the nerve to quote him a price for his time. His help, all his years of hard work and finding little holes to tuck money into, or skinny little windows through which goods could be shipped overseas; all that was supposedly for sale in her little bimbo mind. He was like any other whore who would come running from wherever she was hiding when she heard the sound of a little cash whipping in the wind.

"I don't think so, sweetheart," he told the empty bathroom, ripping the card into four pieces and stuffing it in his back pocket. Andrew was nothing if not careful, and he would never throw away anything at his own house that would tie him to anything even remotely illegal. He knew about the hundred-dollar-an-hour scavengers who would sift through people's trash; he had even caught one a couple of years back and hired a friend of his to re-arrange the little weasel's thinking. No, Andrew was smarter than that by a mile. Any credit card statements, wire transfer authorizations, or little cards with the name of a gal who was fixing to get herself in a lot of trouble would be run safely through the shredder at his office by the only woman he trusted in the world—his secretary Arlene. A lot of good people had done a lot of time in bad jail cells from dealing with him, but nothing could ever be tied to Andrew, and he intended to keep it that way.

And into the BMW he went, accompanied by the sweet voice of Mr. Pavorati on this particular day. At precisely 7:19, he entered the drive-thru at Burger King, and the same girl (single mother, likely a college dropout but at least not a welfare case) asked if he would like the usual. Of course he would, thank you very much sweetheart, he told her just like always. The potato cake went in his belly first, the wrapper thrown out the side window before he even left the parking lot. Then the bagel sandwich, alternating between sips of coffee and orange juice. He laughed again when he passed the spot where the little foreign man had started this whole ordeal the day before.

Perhaps one of Andrew's friends (maybe the same one who dealt with the garbage thief) would like to meet Mr. Polo Shirt, Mohammad, You're-Gay, or whatever the hell his name was.

Yes. Yes, Andrew liked that idea just fine. Let someone strangle *his* skinny little neck for awhile and see how *he* liked it.

"The nerve of some people these days," he said to himself, pulling into his reserved spot in the parking ramp, the same one he'd parked his seven series in for decades. "Some folks just don't know who they're fucking with."

Andrew handed two stacks of papers to Arlene on the way past her desk. One, with which he gave explicit instructions, was that day's listing of wire transfers and account numbers. Of course, Arlene's name was always required on each one, so she could never up and quit then turn stool pigeon on him. Her ass would be just as red as his once the paddling was done, and she knew it. No matter, though, she was paid well and was good at keeping her mouth shut.

The second stack included the previous day's account balances, printed off and left in a plain brown envelope slid under Andrew's door each evening. He didn't know who brought it and didn't care, either. All that mattered was that one of the guys he paid for kept him in the know about how much he had and where it was located. Into that envelope he slid the pieces of Bryn Scott's card.

He thought about calling his little friend about a little intimidation for Bryn, too, in case she tried to use any of the information she had gathered. But she was, alas, a woman, and Andrew had always had a soft spot for women. Especially pretty ones like her who looked all too familiar.

Arlene nodded her head behind what was likely her fifth cigarette of the day so far. Damn the building's little rules. Andrew came from a different time where men smoked while they made their deals, and anyone who didn't could never be trusted.

Yes, Mr. Falkness, she understood the instructions just fine. They were the same orders as she had received every morning for the past sixteen years, so why wouldn't she understand? Of course Arlene just thought this to herself, silently wondering what would be on Letterman that night. She wanted some mornings just to shred the whole works, to send the old man into a fit about where his ill-gotten money was. Arlene was a churchgoing gal, after all, and always thought of what Andrew did as stealing. But her paycheck came from that stealing, and it kept her and Ruffles the cat well fed. And so she tried not to think about the moral dilemma too much.

Three people had called while Andrew was doing time in the big house that previous afternoon. And what a surprise! All three were his wife's lawyer.

"Goddam leaches," he said, pouring a Dewar's. "Getting my old lady's snatch isn't enough, now he wants all my money, too."

Another part of the usual routine, Andrew dreamed of his next vacation. He took many, but the destinations had always stopped short of being, well, exotic. He feared venturing into other countries—too much diarrhea and disease, and being outnumbered by colored people. So that left the good 'ol U.S. of A. Vegas had been visited seventeen times, by far the most popular. New York trailed not far behind at twelve, and bringing up the rear were Miami, Houston, Reno, Lake Tahoe, and last year's choice—Hollywood.

With all the towel-heads blowing up their airplanes, Andrew thought it was time for the good old- fashioned road trip, like the ones he had taken as a boy. Dad loads up the car, mom packs about three times as much food as they could ever possibly eat, then they all head off in the DeSoto for the Grand Canyon or somewhere equally as wholesome. They would return better friends, even he and his sister Wilma, and would count the weeks until they could do it again.

Maybe Sturgis wasn't such a bad idea. But not to do what *she* wanted, though. To be where old men with beer guts can be themselves—ride their Harleys when they want to, party all night, and watch the ladies bare it all. And the best part was, he wouldn't have to pay to see their goodies. Hell, they paraded around every night showing it off for free, from what he had been hearing.

Yes, Sturgis was the place to go when that August heat wave hit, which wouldn't be long according to the weather man. Andrew dozed in his leather chair, imagining himself on a shiny turquoise and white Heritage Softail with those leather stringy things on the handlebars, his sleeping bag and tent rolled up on the back and some beautiful twenty-year-old hitchhiker clinging to his shirtless body. And as she slid her hands up and down his chest, she leaned in closer so he could feel her breasts against his back. Then she whispered her name.

"Missy Fuckness."

An odd name, sure, but as long as she was pretty.

"*Mistah* Falkness!" Andrew nearly jumped out of his chair as the skinny British geek better known as his wife's lawyer/lover glared at him.

"*Mistah* Falkness! Please do wake up, *Mistah* Falkness. This is very important."

Only twice had Reginald Sloane set foot in Faltech Software's offices. The first time was shortly after Andrew's wife hit the road, and ol' Reggie was right there with the divorce papers. Andrew had slammed the door in his face. The second time came a few months later, and even though he had signed the stupid papers, giving up half of what (as far as the feds knew) he owned, Andrew still had that little friend of his follow Mr. Sloane home. It was reported back to him that Reggie-boy went home to his new girlfriend with two broken ribs that day.

"Jesus Christ, Sloane! You've already bled me dry. What the hell else do you want?"

"It has come to our attention, *Mistah* Falkness…"

"And for goodness sakes, don't call me *Mistah Falkness* like I'm some chump you *didn't* go to high school with. Grow some balls, admit to me you're fucking my wife, and for God's sake call me Andrew!"

"Your *ex*-wife, Andrew."

"Whatever. You interrupted a perfectly good dream where I was having someone kick your ass for you again. Wanna hear about it?"

Sloane explained he was far too pressed for time to shoot the bull with his old football buddy. Coralie was unhappy, as Andrew had expected, with her settlement. She wanted more, and knew without a doubt that Andrew had more.

A lot more.

"Two hundred grand and a Mercedes, all for me working to put a roof over her worthless head for all those years, and she has the nerve to ask for more money?"

"She's entitled to half."

Half of what, that's what Andrew wanted to know. He had already divided up his net worth and property with the old bat. As far as she knew, he was left with his car (leased, by the way), a couple hundred thousand for his retirement in the bank, and his condo.

"We've become privy to information recently which indicates you may be a much more wealthy man than you've let on," Sloane said, with that knowing grin Andrew would have liked to have punched right off his face.

And just who, Andrew wanted to know, had made him privy to this information?

"It was a most interesting call, that's for sure," the little weasel continued. "Last night, a young woman called into my office to let me know that she had account numbers and balances showing you had squirreled away a good two million and some change in a different name. The signatures, though, were a spot on match to your own. She wouldn't tell me her name or any more details, just gave me a message for you."

She was young enough to be his daughter, and seemed about as dumb as a post, but Bryn Scott was poised and ready to take The City's third largest software mogul to the cleaners. Instead of being angry, Andrew simply smiled to himself. He admired the guts some people had, and Bryn reminded him of himself a few short years ago. With a much nicer ass, of course.

"This is a serious matter, *Mistah* Falkness. I wouldn't be giggling to myself if I were you."

"Sloane, my boy, if you only knew what this chick has been putting me through lately, you'd be laughing, too."

With that, the sleazy lawyer (as if there were any other kinds) knew he was beat. It appeared that Andrew had the situation under control and Sloane didn't anticipate another call from the young lady. He would have to settle for his fees from the first two hundred thousand, and slink back home to his aging girlfriend who used to be Falkness's wife.

"Well," he said over his shoulder on his way out, Andrew still giggling to himself, "don't you want to know her message?"

"Sure, shoot."

"She said, 'Don't lose the card.'"

"I figured she would."

Andrew reclined in his now-empty office, imagining just how this little girl planned to defraud her husband, who just happened to be one of the most wealthy men in the state. It seemed silly to him that she could make such a plan work, since rich men were often the ones most likely to cover their asses the best. You can't just make a hundred and fifty motorcycles vanish without someone getting suspicious. He would get caught, then spend the rest of his days behind bars with the goody-goody coffee boy and the foreign guy.

They could all become the best of friends—eat together at chow time; play grabass in the shower. This made him laugh even harder. He dozed off again, this time being transported to a lush golf course in Arizona or somewhere equally as warm and dry. This would be his retirement, funded by his more-than-modest holdings which would keep him golfing every day and out on the town each evening. Once he paid off all those who were helping him to keep the money moving, sold the business, and headed for the hills, Andrew would come away clean with a half million. Hardly enough to be considered among the elite in Phoenix, or Palm Springs, or wherever he was headed, but a tidy sum nonetheless. He would purchase a modest condo, lease another seven series, then live off the rest as best he could by cutting corners where possible.

Still, he wondered as he dreamed, *wouldn't a whole million be better*? And what would be involved, anyhow? Using his contacts one last time to sell a few hot motorcycles to the Chinese? That part would be easy. As soon as the little girl mentioned the idea, he already had the names of who could help figured out. Andrew had sent a lot of money to these certain people over the years, and there were still a few favors they owed him. Could he really retire a millionaire just by taking a little motorcycle ride and giving Bryn the right names? It could land him in jail, but men like Andrew Falkness with money on the outside were generally respected in such a place. On the other hand, doing nothing could wipe his accounts out completely, leaving a lot of angry people he owed money to and one rich ex-wife who hadn't earned a penny of it.

Deeper into his dreams now, Andrew watched each tee shot go straight as an arrow, or bend miraculously around doglegs, much to the dismay of the rest of his foursome. At the final hole, and over cocktails at the clubhouse that evening, he would collect on the many wagers he had won for the day. Lowest score, of course. Longest tee shot? Hell yes, he could outdo any of those old codgers even on his worst day. During all of this money exchanging hands, though, all he could hear was the tremendous noise coming from the imaginary kitchen in the imaginary clubhouse.

Andrew rose from his seat, hundreds hanging out of every pocket, and walked in that dreamy walk that people do to the kitchen window. There, near pots of boiling water and sinkfuls of dirty dishes, was none other than Bryn Scott, shredding lettuce.

Only it wasn't lettuce, was it? She fed brown envelope after brown envelope into the food processor, cutting the papers inside to unrecognizable bits. Then she smiled at him, and said, "Don't lose—"

"—the card!" he finished out loud, jumping from his dream and his chair. Andrew ran to the office door, screaming at Arlene to stop, for Christ's sake, stop!

If she hadn't already, Arlene now thought the old man had completely lost his marbles. Here he was, yelling like prohibition was back, running toward her with his gut flopping from side to side. It was hardly her vision of a tanned hunk running along the sand toward her. Arlene flicked her ashes into the shredding basket as today's little brown envelope started running through the machine. It was halfway through when the old fool toppled her from her stool and sent the shredding machine crashing to the carpet.

Andrew pulled what was left of the envelope from the jaws of the shredder, tearing it open to reveal the half-eaten contents. He fumbled through the papers inside, sending them flying everywhere, groping for the pieces of that damned card. One, then two, but where were the rest? He dropped to his knees, searching through the paper-littered floor while Arlene picked herself up and others stared. There, appearing under Arlene's ass as she stood, were the other pieces.

As quickly as he had come, Andrew ran back into his office, leaving the mess behind for the women to clean up. He taped the pieces together so that he could make out the girl's cell phone number, then re-read the other side.

"Five hundred thousand dollars for a few hours' work."

Andrew calmed himself now. He would call her, but the first rule of business was that when you wanted something, the best way to get it was to make people think you didn't want it. He would play her game, not because he was scared of what she could do to him, but because it was a chance to retire properly and live out the rest of his life among the millionaire crowd. His last act in the software business would be an illegal one, but would pad his wallet more than any ten deals he had made this year.

"What the hell," he told himself, echoing his new buddy Paul at precisely the same moment, but not knowing it. It wouldn't be admitting defeat, but would be a final business venture where he stood to make a lot of money. The fact that someone one third his age could ruin him if he refused meant nothing, at least that's what he told himself. People didn't get the better of Andrew Falkness, it was Andrew Falkness who got the better of them. Why not retire a millionaire for a few hours' work?

"Besides," he said, reassuring himself one last time as he dialed the phone, "I was going to go there anyway."

Chapter Six

Watching them come crawling back into the same diner parking lot gave Bryn Scott more joy than she had felt in quite some time. The old one, who told her how it was going to be before sticking her with the check at their last meeting, had now turned into a slinking dog like most men eventually did. The young one, who looked like Howdy Doody not quite grown up, followed close behind.

While Andrew backpedaled through her cell phone line, the buzzing indicated Paul was on call waiting and ready to do the same. Her estimated crumbling time was only off by an hour and a half, which Bryn felt the need to brag about to Jorge as often as possible.

"I ought to just punch in that pretty face of yours and send you off to jail like you did to me." Andrew's greeting was about as pleasant as she had expected. A few phone calls to Malcolm's buddies down at the Bureau of Justice, whom Bryn had flirted with in their swimming pool that last fall, and they were crawling all over her to give her whatever information she required. It was not tough to track down Mr. Falkness's hidden riches, since they had been keeping an eye on him for years now.

Then, another quick call to his ex-wife's lawyer and the game was underway.

Bryn didn't blame the woman for leaving such a creep, and she would get more than she had before no matter what Andrew said. If Andrew agreed to help her out, Bryn promised the former Mrs. Falkness a check for two hundred thousand dollars for her silence. If Andrew declined, he would have a lot of explaining to do to the courts, the IRS, and his ex-wife about his unclaimed money. Just to keep things running smoothly, Bryn had copies of Andrew's last three wire transfers, complete with his signature as "Andrew

McLain" in her handbag. It was amazing what one little brush of the leg, wearing her tiniest bikini of course, could do to the ethics of a federal agent.

She was surprised at how many uses there were for a size 6 young woman among older, richer men.

"You can run and tattle to whomever you would like," she said to the old man, flashing her most smug smile. "But don't forget who my husband is and who we know. Personally, I wouldn't waste my time if I were you. You'll figure out soon enough that it's just easier to go along with what I say."

Andrew knew already he would go; he was scared to death of this little bitch to tell the truth, but he had no intention of rolling over quietly.

"I think you forget, sweetie, that what you're trying to do is probably more illegal than anything I'm doing."

"All right, smart guy. And just how are we planning to prove what I asked you guys to do for me, eh? I'm sure you thought to bring your trusty tape recorder with you to catch me in the act. You did think that far ahead, didn't you?"

Whether it was the lawyers, his ex, or his AA sponsor back when he was still on the wagon, Andrew knew when to give up and cut his losses. He sat down without another word across from Bryn and the little diaper head who had put him in jail, knowing full well they both could seriously mess up his life with only a phone call or two.

"Et tu, Brute?" Bryn turned her attention to Paul now, who had once again been silently enjoying the exchange between the hogtied old man and the pretty young woman. He'd nearly forgotten that she had some dirt on him, too. Also through her fun in the swimming pool, she had found out there were several police departments in several cities with incomplete records on one Paul James Morris. Separately, they were not worthy of further investigation in a time of meth labs and terrorists, but add them together and Howdy Doody would likely be doing ten to fifteen in Folsom Prison.

There were a lot of former motorcycle owners with a lot of unanswered questions about where those motorcycles went who were strewn all over Illinois. Most of them would love to learn that their assailant had moved away, and Bryn was sure all those burly biker men would love to have his address and telephone number too, not to mention the names of his wife and daughter.

The ammunition in her handbag against Mr. Morris would not be needed. For some reason, he seemed almost like he was looking forward to jumping back into his old ways. Bryn understood this, she guessed, since she sometimes enjoyed rubbing on Malcolm's powerful friends in the swimming pool a little too much. She liked doing strip teases for him more than the average housewife, too.

"Once a whore, always a whore," is what Malcolm had said a few nights ago, probably after seeing his little mistress. At least Bryn was being faithful to *her* vows. Who, then, she asked him before he backhanded his wife for the very first time, was the *real* whore?

Over burgers and fries, she detailed what had been spinning around in her mind for so very long. Today could be a grease day. What the hell, right? It wasn't as though Bryn's husband would notice a couple extra pounds, anyhow. Malcolm would first have to stay home long enough.

Waving a french fry for emphasis, in a dark corner of a nearly-deserted diner, she began teaching the lesson to her three pupils, now very much interested in what she had to say.

-2-

Over the course of the next several weeks, leading up to the rally in August, Bryn explained that both of their asses belonged to her. If, at any point, she felt they could not perform as expected, all deals were off and her handbag full of goodies would be delivered to the nearest police precinct. It was, after all, her money being paid out to these two, and she reserved the right to kick both of them to the curb any time her little heart desired.

"Capice?"

"I suppose so," said Andrew.

"Yeah, whatever," said the other one.

Jorge remained silent. He had learned when to answer and when not to.

In her aunt's garage, an aunt who had recently been moved to the old folks' home and left Bryn in charge of watching her meager house, they would rehearse until it was perfect. Nothing less would do. She offered to purchase any and all supplies that would be needed, but insisted on knowing what each was for.

Oh, and no guns, either. They made her nervous.

Bryn would supply the pair with a complete listing of every cycle that was being hauled to Sturgis. Every title would be signed and ready to be transferred by the receiving party. This was her portion of the job, and was easily accomplished with a little finesse and the longstanding flirting contest she had going with the old, fat guy at the DMV. Bryn transferred a lot of titles while running the bike shop, and was usually in to see the guy at least once a week. She had no doubt that her womanly charm, and fifty grand, would convince the lonely old fool to bend a couple of rules for her.

Every week, while Malcolm was off doing God knew what, the four of them would meet in the same garage and practice the same operation until it was engraved in their brains. Every one of them would know exactly what their part was, and also what the other three members were supposed to do. If one was caught or ran into trouble, the remaining legs of the animal would have to keep it moving.

On such short notice, Bryn explained that Midwest Custom Cycles had only been able to get a small display space about the size of the diner they were sitting in. Of the one hundred and fifty bikes that would be hauled to the rally, twenty-five in each of six custom semi trucks, only fifty would actually be seeing the light of day. Anyone purchasing one of those bikes would be told the company's computers were down and their cycle would be held until the Tuesday morning after the celebration, at which time they would be able to come and pick them up. She said that most people would not be suspicious of this, since the average customer of the cycle shop who could afford to put down thirty thousand on a bike was a doctor or lawyer who most likely dealt with moody computers all year long.

Bryn would arrive with Jorge and the fleet of truck drivers earlier in the week, set everything up, and take as many sale orders as she could. Whether it was one or one hundred, it didn't matter. She was just hoping some morons would actually be naive enough to pay in cash up front. That would mean more to split amongst her accomplices later. The first part would be the easiest, and things would get progressively more difficult from there.

Bryn had selected four of the six truck drivers, who were also mechanics for Midwest Custom Cycles, to participate in their little plan. The four trucks which would be packed with approximately 100 of the bikes would never be unloaded, and the drivers would simply pick up and leave the night of the job. For all they knew, Bryn had just made a huge sale of several bikes for export and they would just be following orders by delivering the trailers to Minnesota where they would be shipped out through the Great Lakes chain and overseas. None would be suspicious enough to give Malcolm a call, and they would be especially happy at the $5,000 bonus Bryn planned to give each one for the unexpected extra trip.

"And why would they think anything is wrong?" Bryn asked the table full of men. "These guys have made that same trip for me probably three or four times apiece, just not with such a sizeable load. Every now and then I get a call from a dealer in New York who sends me a cashier's check for twenty or twenty-five bikes and we ship them up there the same way."

By the time Paul gave the first turn of his screwdriver, which would be his first attempt to hotwire a motorcycle in six years, two thirds of the work would already be over.

"So why don't you just load up the whole bunch and have a great big convoy to Minnesota?" Paul asked, cleaning up the drippings from his Reuben sandwich with his fingers. "Save us all a lot of hassle."

"It's like the old saying—don't put all your eggs in one basket," Bryn said. "It's a one in a million chance that one of these boats will be searched before leaving U.S. waters, but on the off chance that happens, we'll have another one right behind it. They'll never get to them both; there's too many and not enough money to police all the ships leaving the country. Plus, it would look awfully suspicious if we just packed up all these bikes from the main street of Sturgis in the middle of the night."

Paul was once again confused. He had run several questions through his head since their last meeting, but probably the most important one was why do you need a thief when you already own what you're stealing? Bryn saw the puzzled look in his eyes and beat him to the punch.

"He's not stupid, you know. Rich guys might be inexperienced in the street smarts department, but they're not stupid. Malcolm never has, and never will, allow me to hand over even one set of keys to a buyer until the check has cleared the bank. It's lost him more business than it's gained, but I have to admit it's a smart policy. I married the son-of-a-bitch, but he still won't hand me the keys to even one fucking Harley until I can prove that the customer's check didn't bounce."

"Imagine that," Andrew said. "He doesn't trust the woman who's trying to rob him blind."

Bryn ignored his comment and continued with her story. Paul and Andrew would arrive on Friday, August 8, near the end of the rally. From there, Paul would have until 8 p.m. the following evening to have keys made for all 100 bikes packed in the trailers.

"No way," Paul said. "It can't be done, so just forget it. No one's ever made a hundred keys in one day, even if they had all the privacy and tools in the world. I'd need more time, like two days more."

"Well, you can't have it." Bryn was already frustrated by both their attitudes, and was tottering back and forth over whether or not to just call the cops on them and make a clean getaway with her savings. It wouldn't be enough to last for long, especially with her ever-increasing love of shopping, but she could always go back to the gentlemen's clubs in Vegas when she was broke. "Look, Paul. Malcolm already has enough doubts about me taking nearly everything he owns on a week-long vacation. I told him we would leave that Wednesday and I can't go back on it now. Shit, if it wasn't for Jorge's tagging along, he wouldn't have even given me as much time with his precious motorcycles as he did. The trucks get there Friday afternoon, we set up for the weekend crowd, and he's expecting us home Tuesday morning. I can't change it now."

Paul flashed back to his late teens, spending precious minutes in alleys behind biker bars with his battery-powered soldering iron, lighter, and 10-gauge wire. It was primitive, but as far as he knew there was no other way to make your own keys. With the newer bikes came more complex wiring, and the old "wire and alligator clip" trick didn't work as well anymore. He figured most of what would be in those trailers would be the custom-made choppers, with all new parts and the security features to match.

Bryn told him a handful of their bikes were considered "classics," unrestored originals dating as far back as the 1900s, but confirmed that most were new customs.

"Even if I kept at it all night long, that's only like fifteen minutes for each. You need to trip each tumbler in the lock mechanism, make the necessary adjustments to your wire key, and go back and forth like that until you get it exactly right. Then you have to cut the key blanks using the wire pattern, and if you mess that up even a little bit you have to start all over again. Plus, add on the fact that I haven't done any of this in a few years…"

"All right! I'm sick of your shit," Bryn stood up and began heading for the door. This time she would stick them with the check. "You either tell me you can find a way to pull this off right now, or you can practice your whining next to your cellmate Bubba!"

She stormed outside, strapped her bag to the back of her Sportster, and cranked the engine. Bryn was crying now, and turned her head away from the diner's windows so no one would see. She guessed her two-timing husband would get the best of her after all. Hell, she knew that deep down in her mind from the start. At least Bryn would take down those two whining assholes before she cleaned out her savings account and blew town. They could share a cell all over again and get to be best buddies for all she cared.

"I need the whole works—just like your friendly neighborhood locksmith."

Bryn turned, wiping her eyes with her purple scarf. All three of them stood there in the doorway, staring out at her and the deserted parking lot. Her three knights in shining armor—the little foreign guy, a fat old man, and Howdy Doody's slightly taller twin brother. This made her laugh, and Bryn tilted back her head to cackle like a witch, still crying but finding the situation hilarious at the same time. Surely a damsel in distress, especially one as pretty as she, could have sought out some more charming Prince Charmings. They all smiled back, even Andrew, who wiped mustard from his chin, and that made Bryn laugh even harder.

She would have her revenge. She would have the money her mother always told her she deserved. And, Bryn just might have a little fun in the process. Bryn ran to Paul and hugged him, silently kicking herself for showing such typical feminine weakness in front of her new business associates.

"Whatever you need, Paul. Whatever it costs, I'll get it for you." And then, the words she regretted most of all, which truly showed how desperate she was to make their little plan work— "Thanks. You guys are saving my life."

As the gang trooped back inside, the waitress gave each an equally cursory glance. She likely thought they were skipping out on the check.

"All right, boss," Andrew said. "Let's continue before we change our minds."

Bryn took careful notes of Paul's required items—wax key blanks in several thicknesses, a key blank cutter with a grinder attachment, as many picks and tension pins as she could find, and some other brand name items Paul wrote down himself. A couple hours playing around on the Internet would yield most of these tools, and what she couldn't find there she would send Jorge to sniff out. He was good at that sort of thing.

"Okay, so now it's Saturday evening and Paul has just finished his little job. The trucks are rolling down the road."

"So what am I doing this whole time?" Andrew asked.

"You'll be in the trailers assisting Paul. If he needs a flashlight shined over here, then you do it. If he needs you to run out for something he forgot, you do that too."

Great, Andrew thought. *Just what I wanted to be, a gopher for some coffee-brewing kid.*

He didn't make his feelings known, though. Andrew Falkness may have been one tough cookie in the business world, but he hated like hell to see a woman cry. It was his one weakness (aside from Manhattans and porn magazines), and he couldn't bear to see this pretty young thing get upset again, even if she did have some nasty papers that could send him up the river.

"After the four trucks are all on the road, you guys get a little vacation time. Go out, blend in with the crowd, just don't get in any trouble. I'll need you both sober and rested by Sunday night."

Through her knowledge of the business's insurance, and of their agent's total lack of attention to detail, the four would have a window of exactly one hour in which to complete the next phase. Bryn explained that she would be planting two or three of her friends near Midwest Custom Cycles' tent on Sunday night, who would be more than happy to tell the police what had happened later on. The girls were already going to Sturgis, and welcomed the chance to make an extra couple thousand dollars just for telling the cops they had seen something that, in fact, they hadn't. They had all grown up in the same trailer park together near Death Valley, and Bryn knew she could trust her friends. After all, they had lied to the police lots of times before and had never even gotten paid for it.

"What do you mean 'insurance'? What's that got to do with anything, sweetheart?" Andrew thought she had calmed down enough to meet with at least a little of his wonderful way of talking to women.

"Malcolm might not trust me with any of the keys to his bikes, but he does let me maintain the insurance for the whole inventory, the building, and the shop. I signed up to change companies, which is a pretty routine deal for us. The old policy ends at midnight central time, since the business is located in the central time zone."

Andrew suddenly grinned from ear to ear. Not only did he fully understand what she was doing, but he was remembering the time he had done something similar to a former business associate. She might have the means to bankrupt him and put him behind bars, but he had to admit he was starting to like the sneaky little bitch.

"So let me guess, you told your insurance guy the new policy would be starting while you were in Sturgis, which is an hour behind us."

Bryn smiled back. "That's pretty much right. The old policy lapses at midnight central, and I set the new one to begin at midnight mountain time, which is the zone we'll be in when we're in Sturgis. I checked on all the fine print on Midwest Custom's new policy, and it said something to the effect of 'the understood time of all claims will be recorded according to the zone in which the business resides, regardless of the location of inventory.' Since both times are recorded as midnight, some agent's computer won't catch the discrepancy."

"You're saying that for exactly one hour, Malcolm won't be covered for all those bikes?" Paul, who found the situation a bit more difficult to understand than a professional businessman like Grandpa Falkness, was starting to come around. "Won't he know it was you, though? I mean, it'll look a little suspicions when you never come back home."

"And so what if he does? I am technically an employee, and regardless of how much I steal, his lawyers and the police will just tell him that he should have had insurance for employee theft. Without insurance, he's up shit creek without a paddle. I'll have the law looking for me, but I don't plan on sticking around long enough for them to catch up with me anyhow."

"Where are you going?" Jorge spoke his first words of the day. This part had come as a surprise to him. Spoiled brat or not, he had grown quite fond of Mrs. Malcolm Devane.

"That's just for me to know. Maybe some exotic island in the South Pacific where I can drink margaritas all day and stare at cute cabana boys."

Now came the tough part. Bryn said she could only trust four of the six drivers to keep from calling Malcolm or the police if anything seemed suspicious. She didn't want to take the chance of trying to involve people she didn't know as well as she knew the other four.

"This is another little job for you, Paul. That little gang you used to hang out with—we need a few of them to help us out. On Sunday night, I'll close up the display tent at 10 p.m. just like the sign says. You guys will have from then until 8 a.m. Tuesday to have the remaining fifty cycles going. Some go to Two Harbors, Minnesota, complete with keys and ready to load on the second boat. I figured a lot of your old pals ended up like you did—working in a dead-end job and dreaming at night about how they'd love to get back to their old reckless ways again. Call up the ones you can trust, forty-eight and a couple spares if you want, and tell them you're having a nice little reunion at Sturgis this year. Since Sunday the tenth is the last day of the rally, no one will ever question a group of fifty Harleys rumbling across the Midwest. Now, it'll take a good thirteen hours to wind your way through the countryside, and probably a little longer without using the interstates. I don't want to take any chances, so stick to the back roads."

"Hold on a second." Paul was offended, even though she had hit the nail right on the head. "What makes you think that I, or any of my old buddies, are all in dead-end jobs?" He couldn't help himself, and burst out laughing. Tears were rolling down his cheeks by the time he caught himself. Just picturing all of the old crowd, loading hardware trucks or working in factories all over Illinois, then getting together once a month to see who had developed the biggest beer gut, nearly split his sides. Bryn was pretty perceptive for such a cute little thing.

"Anyhow, I've got five thousand dollars for each of them. It'll be waiting when they leave, and just so they don't get any wise ideas of splitting away from the group and heading for home, I've got a back-up plan. I'll have the VIN numbers of all fifty of those bikes ready to give to the nearest sheriff's department if you all don't show up."

"Of course we'll show up," Paul said, still laughing nearly too hard to talk. "If we didn't that would be like stealing or something. Just what kind of men do you think we are?"

They all laughed together this time, even Jorge. It was a bit disturbing for him to see the men making light of such a serious matter, but he figured that a bit of humor never hurt. Bryn continued.

"Tell them all they can take their cash, hop on the nearest plane, buy themselves an old pickup truck, or go blow it all at one of the Indian casinos up there. Frankly, I don't care what they do. And as for the three of you guys, when I get my money for the delivery, we'll all go out and have a little celebration while we divide it up for ourselves."

"How in the world did you ever convince Malcolm to let you go through with this?" Andrew asked. "Why didn't he start hauling bikes out there a long time ago?"

"I think it was because of Malcolm's dad. He went out to Sturgis a few years back on a Honda, all by himself; Malcolm only mentioned it once. Some guys caught him in an alley and beat him within an inch of his life. Whether it was because of his Jap bike or just because the old guy was an asshole, I'll never know. But he apparently told Malcolm never to go near that place. And Malcolm is a guy who always listens to daddy, since daddy gave him everything he owns."

Paul said he still wished she could just find a way to get hold of all the key sets, but that would not be happening.

"This practice dates back to when Malcolm's dad was selling Chryslers. Whether the car was brand new or twenty years old, whether it cost thousands or just a couple of dollars, no one got their keys until after the check cleared. They could test drive the car, and today I can let guys test ride these bikes as often as they want, but at the end of the night we lock those keys back in this big old safe. Malcolm unlocks it for me every morning, and he's always right there at six to lock it up again every night, no matter what he's in the middle of. I think it's the same safe his old man had, and it's built like Fort Knox. Even if I did have someone break in, he would know it within a few hours. I can't make copies, either. I tried copying the keys to my own cycle at a hardware store across town, and within five minutes Malcolm was calling me on my cell phone thinking I was stealing from him."

Oh well, Paul thought. *Can't blame a guy for trying.*

Once again, the waitress was sending dirty looks toward the residents of table four, probably because they all had been sitting there for two hours and had only eaten a combined ten dollars worth of food. Bryn excused herself and agreed to meet everyone at 417 West 42nd Street on Wednesday evening, when she would have all the tools on Paul's shopping list ready to go.

"There's still the small matter of my wheels," Andrew reminded her. "You promised me a new Harley and I'm planning on taking you up on it. I'd look a little funny riding through the streets in my Beemer, now wouldn't I?"

All three men watched the woman with the amazing plan walk off into the night. It sounded so perfect that even seasoned crooks like Paul and Andrew had given their approval.

"Don't worry about the bike," Bryn called back over her shoulder. "Or anything else for that matter. I think you'll be pleasantly surprised."

From what they had heard so far, they already were.

-3-

The first evening the four spent together was nothing short of frustrating. Andrew complained that he couldn't work things out for distribution overseas in time, which was, of course, a lie. If this little lady was going to make him crawl on his belly, he was going to make it as tough on her as humanly possible. Paul, in the meantime, followed suit and expressed his dissatisfaction with the key making equipment Bryn had found, though it was far superior to any tools he had ever used.

Jorge "Polo" Zapate kept silent and learned. He listened intently as Paul explained how the wax key blanks were heated, then how important it was to take one's time to grind every peak and valley of every key exactly. The two practiced on the Harley Davidson key blanks Bryn had bought through the dealership so as not to arouse suspicion. There were four hundred, plenty to account for errors and practice while still keeping enough to make one for each bike.

Andrew spent much of his time on the phone while stuck in Bryn's aunt's little garage. Any calls he made would be on her phone bill, in a place no authorities would think to look. That was, of course, if they ever looked at all. He awoke old friends at odd hours, rattling off models and years from a master list which Bryn made sure to take home with her after each meeting.

Perhaps the bikes receiving the most interest were among the oldest of the bunch—twelve identical 1908 Model 4 Harleys, each with a book value upward of $100,000. Andrew already had seven of the bunch committed to before the crew's first meeting was over—a businessman in Taiwan apparently had some old photographs of his grandfather and then-infant mother on one similar to it, and felt the need to buy one for himself and each of his six brothers.

Two hours into it, and already half a million in cash committed. Andrew knew the family, and remembered that they cared little about where their possessions came from. In their world, having the most toys was next to Godliness. He guaranteed delivery by August 15, and was informed the cash would be sent via courier to the docks when the four would arrive. Once the courier confirmed the authenticity of the purchase, the cash was theirs. The Chinese men would be happy, because such a rare item would easily sell for $150,000 in their home country, though its sentimental value was worth more, they said.

Things dried up for awhile, but then by mid-June, Andrew had commitments for a 1931 DLD Sport Solo, a pair of 1911 7D Twins, and twelve newer custom Soft Tails, which added three hundred thousand to the pot. If he played his cards right, the complete list would bring far more than the anticipated $1.5 million.

He often watched Paul and Polo playing with their little wax keys, and couldn't help but wonder why it was the old man who was being forced to do all the work.

A retired Naval officer living in Hong Kong scraped up enough money to purchase a 1939 EL with the 61 cubic inch motor, the twin brother of his very first bike. A small order, but ten grand was ten grand, after all. Whenever possible, Andrew mentioned that the merchandise might not necessarily be legal. Over the years, he had developed good relationships with many of the folks he was calling, and could deal honestly with most of them. Few cared where their ill-gotten goods came from, anyhow. Who would look for a stolen motorcycle a couple thousand miles away?

Two weeks later, that same officer spread the word to his brother in Taiwan, who committed fifty thousand toward a 1919 F Twin for himself and half a dozen classic choppers for his kids. The thought of all those five foot tall Chinese men riding around on big, shiny, rumbling Harleys kept Andrew laughing much of the time. He knew those guys were infatuated with anything American, but to pay such a premium price for stolen merchandise just to have a toy that your neighbors didn't? He was growing to like this little Bryn girl more and more with each dollar he earned.

It was the last week in July, coincidentally the last of their meetings before the big day, when Andrew Falkness worked his magic on the one hundred and fiftieth, and last, cycle. Throughout all of his calls to all those places, just one bike, the most valuable of the bunch, refused to be sold. The group often joked that because it was so old, a key wouldn't even be necessary. Paul said a five-year-old could hotwire this one.

Bryn had taken a photograph of the plaque, which was the first sight to greet visitors to Midwest Custom Cycles. Behind triple-thick bulletproof glass and more alarms than Fort Knox was one of the three existing 1903 Harley Davidsons. Little more than a bicycle with a gas tank, the motor was a 25 cubic inch, single cylinder. Only three were made, and all three still existed. This one cost Mr. Yoshiro Chin of South Korea, a wealthy software mogul Andrew had read much about, a cool million cash.

Seated around the old kitchen table where the four had pounded the same plan into their heads for weeks, Andrew revealed the results of his little fishing excursion. After paying off Paul's buddies, Bryn's couriers who would be making arrangements to pick up some of the cash, the truck drivers, and all others involved, each of the three would earn $420,000 for their efforts. All American cash, laundered to sparkling perfection.

Andrew saw an even bigger condo.

Paul dreamed of owning the biggest farm in Illinois, and having enough cash to take Shelby with him, leaving his cheating wife penniless.

Bryn visualized Maui, cabana boys, and lavish parties.

Polo would return home, finally. He sought to buy every member of his family something special. They sat up until the early hours of that Thursday morning, Paul caring little if he made it in to work the next morning, along with the other three. The first thing he would do is call up the old women who ran that little sweat shop and tell them where they could stick their silly rules and "always smile for the customer" attitudes.

When Paul went home that night, and after reluctantly making love to the wife he had been ignoring for weeks, he found his thoughts changing. Ever since he began to suspect her affair, he would lie in bed every night, watching her sleep until he finally joined her. Often he would cry a little to himself, remembering how he had fought for her, how he had stood by Samantha's side through all the years of problems with her family, her health. And now, to think that she could do such a thing to the man she vowed to remain faithful to, in her mother's wedding gown in front of three hundred visitors at a wedding that had cost Paul more than $10,000.

The tears would trickle down his cheek as he stared at her, picturing another man on top of his pretty wife, both of them sweating together while they enjoyed what they were doing to each other, what they were doing to him. Sometimes he would wake up and look over at her, then picture some nameless figure there, pumping away, oblivious to the family he was hurting.

And the worst part of his vision—his wife would turn to him, then smile.

But tonight, it was right to sleep, and to a world where Paul did nothing but rehearse his part of the job over and over again. Every last move was accounted for. He thought about his old friends and seeing them again, and how happy they had been to hear that the Gorham Gearheads would once again be a pack of hoodlums. Just as he had suspected, the former hard asses he'd been calling over the past few weeks had fallen on hard times, either spending time in jail or just having been released, working in their factories and garages for peanuts.

Polo dreamed of being back home, that same dream he'd been having for years. He would run into his family's arms, returning victorious from the white man's world with a small fortune of the white man's money. Few of those who left his small village returned, and even fewer returned with more money than they had left with. Jorge Zapate would be a hero, a martyr.

They would build a new school and name it after him. Pretty girls would fall and kiss his feet as he walked along the dirt streets. He would finally take a wife, and planned on sampling every woman he could find before making his decision.

Maybe he would sample some twice.

As for Andrew, who would have slept in his garage on this particular night if he was able, he remembered just how much of a rut he had settled into. It was amazing how one young lady, a few phone calls, and the chromed machine he rode around the block over and over at two in the morning could bring new hope to an old man.

Shortly before she turned out the lights in the garage, the makeshift hideout where they had come to know one another, Bryn pulled the sheet from the object that had stood in the corner for nearly a month. She made Andrew swear he wouldn't look until the last deal was complete, and for once he'd made good on his promise.

It was exactly like he'd pictured it—a brand new Heritage Soft Tail, turquoise and white, leather saddle bags and those little leather stringy things dangling from the handlebars. Andrew tried it on for size, and remembered he hadn't ridden a cycle since 1995, on one of his more recent trips to Vegas where he'd rented one for a week. And the best part about it was he had signed his name to a clear title on the machine. If at any point in their excursion he felt trouble looming, all he would have to do was ride off into the sunset on his Harley, clean out his accounts with a couple phone calls, and ride around the south in the warm weather until he got too crippled up to straddle the bike anymore. He believed in what they were doing, but having a Plan B was never a bad idea.

Both he and Paul would store their bikes in Sturgis until they returned to claim them. Storage garages had been rented in false names, and Bryn gave each a key. She didn't care how they got back or if they got back at all. She would be well on her way to the tropics as soon as she had the cash in her hand.

Andrew waited until the other two left before he took Bryn aside and thanked her for all she had done. In the past few weeks he had escaped his routine of fast food every morning and drinking all day. Instead, he took walks when he felt up to it, and spent his days rehashing his part of the plan. He went out to restaurants he'd never visited before, and called up old friends to watch football with him on Sundays. Not since before Coralie left him had he felt so alive, like there was a purpose for an old man in this young man's world after all.

"You've made my old routine into a new one, and I've loved every minute of it," he told Bryn, the two of them alone under the porch light. "Even if we don't pull this thing off, I can say I'm a better man for having known you."

She hugged Andrew, said he was very welcome to the 'cycle, and thanked him for his help so far.

"Think we can pull this off, old man?"

"I think a woman like you could do damn near anything she set her mind to. You've surprised me, that's for sure. I just can't shake this feeling that I've seen you somewhere before. Any ideas?"

"Nope," Bryn said. "I think I would have remembered you."

Bryn watched him ride away, a little wobbly on his new toy. As he crossed the intersection, she could have swore she heard him yell, "Yahoo!"

When the night was through and Bryn herself was drifting off to sleep, her husband still running around into the wee hours of the morning, she cried to herself. Not because of Malcolm, but because of Jorge, and her two new friends. She didn't want to call them that, but that's what they were. She had been trying hard not to like any of these three since she would never see them again after a few more days. The old sexist bigot had actually grown on her a little, Jorge would always have a special part of her life, and Paul, the Howdy Doody wanna-be, just made her laugh by being around. He tried so hard to be like the other big city people, to act like a two-bit thug who used to be in a motorcycle gang, but Bryn thought he was failing miserably. Paul was a kind and gentle man, and she was starting to think Andrew was coming around, too. He reminded her a bit of her own father at certain times—how he would be such an asshole when the other men were around, but would soften right up if it was just the two of them.

It was almost a shame to think about what she was planning to do to them.

Almost.

Chapter Seven

It warmed his heart to hear his native Portuguese once again, even if it was from the operator. Years had passed since Jorge Zapate had telephoned back to Brazil, though a day never went by without him feeling as though he had shamed his family by not removing them from such a terrible place.

"*Metropole, por favor?*"

Since his boyhood home of Guinea Donca was no more, and his family had been taken with it, Jorge chose to try contacting his next closest family. His cousins and one uncle had moved to the nearby city of Maninho de Sao Paulo (Sao Paulo's little brother) shortly before Jorge left home. He had grown up with them all around, participated in neighborhood gatherings with them, and now he felt as though he owed his extended family a phone call to tell of his upcoming wealth.

He would no longer be considered a failure in his family's eyes, and would avenge the deaths of his mother and sisters by making life better for what little family he had left.

"Jorge?" his aunt Mariana asked. Then, in a flourish of Portuguese Jorge could barely understand, she asked where he had gone, why he had not written or called, whether or not he was married. And did he have children? She told him the future of his family lied in his having children.

Lots of them. And fast, too. American aunts and Portuguese ones were much the same in this respect.

His cousins, or *los primos* as she called them, had both stopped attending school and were headed down a dark path. She explained that Hector, the oldest, had been influenced by a neighborhood gang after having a crush on one member's girlfriend. He had come home a few months ago nearly beaten to death, but smiling from ear to ear and talking about how he was now a member of some sort of movement to free his people. All this mattered little to his mother, but Marianna said what did bother her was that he smelled of liquor all the time and stayed out all night. What got to her even more was that her other son, Jesus, who was just shy of his fourteenth birthday, was following close behind.

Marianna cried when she told Jorge about the nights she spent at home alone, hearing the shooting of guns and praying all the while that her boys weren't on the receiving end of those shots. She could not control them. Her drunken husband had left them to her nearly a decade ago, and between her hours at the factory and keeping up a house, there was just no energy left to scold them when they came stumbling in at dawn. The police had visited her home four times now. They cared little for her concerns about keeping her sons out of those gangs, but always came running when they thought one of her boys was involved in something illegal. A few weeks before, she said her boys had returned drunk on a Saturday morning, laughing about their trip to Sao Paulo and how they had helped steal the Minister of Justice's car. It was only a matter of time before one, if not both of them, were hauled off to jail for good.

"This is nothing compared to what your sister has been doing," Marianna said in her at-my-wits-end slur of Portuguese. "My boys may be using the drugs, but her, she is selling them, selling her body too."

Jorge sat down hard on his lone kitchen chair, just one of the three pieces of furniture he owned, and dropped his peanut butter sandwich onto the table.

His sister? But the telegram had told him no one survived from his village. He lapsed back into his native language without thinking, grilling his aunt with questions about his sister.

Which sister?

How old was she now?

Did she say selling her *body*?

Marianna waited for Jorge to calm down a bit, then told him the entire story of how Jorge was actually one of two Zapate children still walking the earth. Rosa, his youngest sister, had been playing at the home of one of her friends when the friend's father had taken ill. Without thinking, she began running the six kilometers to the nearest doctor's office. Just halfway there, she was picked up by a harvest truck full of field hands, who took her to their house in the hills and raped and beat her for three solid days.

By the time they let her go, the fever had taken control of everyone else in the village.

"All that she had to return to," Marianna said, "with her eyes blackened and her innocence taken away, was the sight of men from the health organization with torches setting fire to her home and the bodies of her mother and sisters."

The sight, and the whole experience, had taken its toll on Rosa. Such a sight, Marianna said, would likely be too much for a grown man, let alone a 12-year-old girl. Rosa, nearly naked, beaten, and with all of her possessions burned, was sent to live with her aunt and cousins. She rarely spoke to anyone after that day. She was teased at school, and soon stopped going altogether.

Marianna had found small plastic packages and far more cash than a woman should safely be carrying in the now-older Rosa's pockets, and overheard the men talking to one another in the marketplace about how they enjoyed being inside her.

This made Jorge furious. He had never met either Hector or Jesus, the youngest of Marianna's boys, since they had been born after he left. Therefore, he cared little for their safety. A man was responsible for a man's decisions, as his grandfather often told him, but the entire village was responsible for the ill-mannered behavior of its women. This was especially true of the women in your own family. While the Americans he knew cared only about their wealth, sloth, and getting fat, back home it was all about pride. What hurt him the most was not the fact that his cousins were causing trouble to others, but that a woman carrying his family name was prostituting herself.

Jorge didn't understand how people in this country could walk down the street when their own flesh and blood had done such terrible things. This was especially true with the Devane family, which, like it or not, he was a part of. So many cousins, brothers, uncles, and even wives and daughters had disgraced their family name with drugs, drinking, and unclean living. Some had even made newspaper headlines for their exploits!

He spoke to his aunt for quite some time about this—how he had tried his hardest to save enough money to send for his family, and how the Devanes had continually postponed his efforts until it was too late. They even joked about the situation in his presence, saying things at the dinner table like "You cannot do this to my people," trying to copy his accent. Then they would all laugh.

He wanted for so many years to pack his things and leave, but they kept him basically as a slave, paying him only enough to feed himself and never enough that he could save even a little money.

Jorge remembered only a little of Rosa—playing on the swings with her in his arms when she was a toddler, putting the medicine on her skinned knee because he was the only one she was not scared of. What stuck in his mind the most, though, was her smile. Few people he had known before coming to America had pretty smiles. Health and dental care in his part of the world was unheard of. But Rosa, pretty little Rosa, had the straightest, most white and beautiful teeth he had ever seen.

He imagined the other children were very jealous of such a gift; Jorge certainly had been. Had those terrible men, who violated not only Rosa but the name of his entire family, knocked out those pretty teeth? Jorge thought it best not to ask; the pain of knowing would be greater than the pain of not knowing.

Once he had done his final work for the Devanes, just another illegal act in a long line of illegal acts, he would return home. He would first hug his sister close to him like he had before, tell her she no longer had to sell anything for as long as she lived, especially not her body. Then, he would find the men who did this to her, because no one else would. The Zapate name would be resurrected.

"You must not fail," Marianna said. "I fear for Rosa. I fear for my boys. I fear for all of us."

"I must not fail," Jorge repeated to his family thousands of miles away, though mostly to himself. "I will not leave my family behind again."

-2-

Bryn enjoyed her last ride on the little purple Sportster, which she figured had been more of a gift to keep her from making noise about Malcolm's little girlfriend than anything else. Her first stop of the day, after a breakfast of Special K and sliced bananas, was at the Prairie Commerce Bank downtown. There, she signed the forms and authorized the transfer of her little nest egg to a little place in Aruba called the Trans-Global Holding Trust. Malcolm had used this same business to hide money, and, according to the papers in her handbag, so had Andrew Falkness. With a couple of shrewd characters like them hiding their riches there, Bryn figured her $218,112 would be safe.

Her contingency plan was a simple one—any calls on her cell phone about any sort of searches, or even one of the drivers getting stopped for as much as a hundred dollar speeding ticket, and she would bail out. She had grown fond of Andrew and Paul, each with their own little quirks. They made her laugh, and she enjoyed bringing a little bit of joy and hope to a couple of otherwise joyless men. And Jorge, he had been a faithful person for a very long time, one of the few faithful men she had ever known. He would likely be beaten within an inch of his life if things went badly and Malcolm found out that Jorge was in on the plan. Then they would leave him in the street, penniless. Bryn would feel the most sorry for Jorge. The four drivers, her old friends she was paying to lie, and Paul's old gang buddies were all just pawns in the game, and would bounce back.

With some creative accounting and a little discipline, Bryn could live out her days just fine on a couple hundred grand. She would find a rich man, or rather lots of them, and get whatever little extras she wanted by simply turning on her womanly charm. If worse came to worse, there was always Vegas. Pretty girls were a dime a dozen there, but could get paid well if they chose the right career.

After her stop at the bank, she rode across town to an unfamiliar ATM location and withdrew the maximum cash advance from the credit card she and Malcolm shared. By the time he got the statement, if things went well, he would already be broke. The $5,000 Visa bill was the proverbial salt poured on the wound.

She only wished the limit were higher.

At Brach's Department Store, she charged the maximum to Malcolm's account like she often did. Later that day, their truck would deliver the $200 sleeping bag, tent, cook stove, power inverter (she wasn't even sure what that was), foldable chairs and tables, an inflatable couch, portable television/ DVD player, stereo and ten complete new outfits for Sturgis. Bryn left strict instructions, as she often did, to stow everything in the shed out in back of the house. Whatever Malcolm didn't see her buying, he couldn't complain about.

Hey, if a girl was forced to camp out on the ground like an animal, she was at least going to be a very comfortable animal.

It gave her great pleasure as she handed over their Brach's credit card imagining Malcolm having to borrow money from his daddy just to pay the bill. Nothing embarrassed her husband more than begging for money, and he had vowed long ago that he would never have to do it again.

Since she would be leaving the following morning, Bryn Scott's last act of bankrupting her hubby was to put a big fat charge on the only other account he allowed her to use. She arrived at Destorando's, one of the most expensive places in town, at 11:15 a.m. Bryn treated herself to lobster thermidor, and instructed the staff to prepare five other similar meals to go. It was an unorthodox request, but all she had to do was flash her smile at the maitre d' and he always bent over backwards to keep her happy. And why not? The Devanes were among his best customers.

Before leaving, she signed off on a $50 tip for each of the wait staff and instructed them to put the meals of the next five guests on Malcolm's account. Bryn told the staff she had had a fight with her husband and wanted to hit him where it hurts.

They just laughed. Apparently this sort of thing happened a lot.

To work off her meal, she took a walk behind the restaurant and kept making her way up the alley until five fortunate homeless people were all eating $200 lobsters, courtesy of the generous Mr. Malcolm Devane. Such a humanitarian, that guy was. Maybe some sort of award was in his future, hopefully with a cash prize so he could recoup his losses.

It was 1 p.m. before she finally arrived at Midwest Custom Cycles, amidst the hustle and bustle of shirtless men loading motorcycles into semi trailers in the August heat. This was certainly fun to watch and it entertained Bryn for a few minutes, but she still had work to do before the next morning. A few clicks on the Internet, and she confirmed the gap in the insurance policy still existed. It certainly wouldn't be the end of the world if Malcolm's agent caught the error and fixed things, but it would be nice to know that she was leaving the cheating bastard with nothing. That thought would help the tropical drinks go down that much easier.

As the men finished up their loading duties, Bryn was surprised to see Malcolm stroll through the front door. Usually, he didn't come in until after she had left for the day, to lock up the keys and check the books. She was even more surprised to see the man walking at his side.

Roger "Junior" Devane, the youngest of the Devane boys, was the textbook example of a poor little rich boy. If one were to look up "spoiled brat" in the dictionary, that's where he'd be. He looked like a shorter, fatter version of Malcolm, and had spent the greater part of his 22 years smoking marijuana and trying to start his own band. Daddy's money had gotten him gigs here and there, but when you suck, you suck, no matter how much money you had. Most of Junior's high school days were spent at home playing sick while he polluted his brain with video games and cocaine. By the time daddy gave an endowment large enough to get him into Penn State, Junior had more piercings than any ten women Bryn knew and had been to rehab three times.

Malcolm barely ever spoke about the black sheep of the Devane family, just updates here and there about which treatment center the boy was in or what the newspapers had printed about his latest escapades.

But what bothered Bryn the most was the fact that he had absolutely no interest in her. She was the type of girl who could walk into a room, wiggle her behind, and get just about anything she desired. It had been this way her whole life, and few men had ever dared resist her. Junior was one of them. Bryn even made it a game at the few family functions she was allowed to attend. She pulled out all the stops trying to catch the boy's attention, but nothing worked. Bryn couldn't even dub the kid gay, since he always had some white trash skank on his arm.

"Brynnie," Malcolm called from her office door. It had been two days since she'd seen him last, between work and his little bitch on the side. "Fire of my loins, pain in my wallet. How's my lovely bride doing today?"

"Ready to drive all these trucks over the nearest cliff and bankrupt you," she shot back. "And yourself?"

Malcolm smiled. Junior judged his mood and dared to smile too.

"Hello, *Roger*," Bryn said to the shorter one, knowing very well he hated being called by his real name. "How's the family's biggest embarrassment today? Out of treatment so soon?"

"Put the claws away, darling," Malcolm said before Junior could answer. "You and Junior here are going to be real good friends a week from now. You'd better be nice to him now."

"Friends?"

"He's been pestering me for a job, so I found him one," Malcolm said, enjoying the visions of all the suffering this would bring his little gold digging wife. "Junior will be accompanying you to Sturgis. Show him around, introduce him to the other guys, whatever you have to do. He's your right hand man."

Bryn was hit with the force of a truck, but couldn't dare show it. She could tell that Malcolm had been nervous about letting so much of his wealth out of his sight, and the slightest twitch could cause him to cancel the whole thing. Aruba would be nice, but Aruba with her asshole husband's millions would be even better.

"And what job's he going to do—whiskey sampler? Drug tester?"

Malcolm didn't flinch. He was quite used to his wife's sarcasm. No, Junior would be driving out with the prize plum of Malcolm's collection. Truth be told, he said, Bryn couldn't be trusted with something worth that much money anyhow. Nope, the 1903 would remain locked in its little plastic cube, loaded in the back of semi numero uno, and never let out of the sight of his brother.

"You could buy a lot of new clothes with the amount of money that baby's worth," Junior said, knowing he was making her squirm. "We wouldn't want you to get any ideas, would we?"

Everything was crashing down before her eyes, but she had to keep it together if there was going to be even a slim chance her plan would work.

"So that's that," Malcolm said. "He'll be seeing you at seven tomorrow morning. Jorge, too. Just one big, happy family. I'll be out tonight, but I'll see you when you get back."

Like hell you will, Bryn thought.

"Peachy" is what she actually said, through clenched teeth.

As quickly as they had come, the two men, one nothing more than a smaller, more pierced version of the other, turned and exited Midwest Custom Cycles. Malcolm thought that last minute addition would make her blood boil, but he had no idea of the real problems it posed. He didn't need anyone to escort that bike; he trusted the drivers to do the job, but it was true that Junior needed a job, and his father was pressuring him to help out. Plus, since his wife could neither cook nor clean, this was one of the few benefits he got from Bryn—watching her squirm.

Through her picture window, the men out in the shop were all watching Bryn's reaction to the news. Apparently they all knew what was going on, and were well aware of her dislike for Malcolm's brother. Bryn calmed herself, closed down her computer, and walked calmly out of the building, much to the disappointment of the four mechanics watching.

They would rather she threw a fit, kicking and screaming and tipping over the desk. Just watching that pretty little thing was entertainment enough, but watching her have a temper tantrum was the greatest. She left through the side door, sent one halfhearted smile toward the shop as if to say, "I'm just fine, get back to work."

Bryn even made it as far as two miles out of town before the flood gates opened and panic set in. As she sobbed uncontrollably, she pulled over beside a large oak tree and sat down beneath it, burying her head in her hands. All her life, men had gotten the best of her. Her father had squashed any hopes and dreams she had as a child, to the point where she kept all her thoughts to herself. Boyfriends, an endless string of them dating back to just before her twelfth birthday, had not been much better. Like all men, they were only after one thing. Just because they were young men meant nothing. Bryn thought all males were born with that gene—to say what the girl wants to hear just long enough to get in her pants.

It was surprising that after all their planning and rehearsing the same thing over and over again, she had never grown tired of Paul or Andrew. In fact, as she sat there wiping her eyes with her purple scarf, Bryn could think of no one else in the world right now she trusted as much as them. How pathetic was that? To have a life so riddled with mistrust that you spill your guts to a couple of morons you'd just met a few months before.

As she sobbed, Bryn flipped through the listings in her cell phone's memory. Lawyers, judges, cops, and other friends of Malcolm's she kept on file just in case, but not one could make her laugh and feel secure like Paul Morris had. When a concern came up during all those long nights in that cold garage, he would be so kind to her that it actually scared her a bit. Sure, he was getting paid well for his efforts, but Paul was going above and beyond.

"Paul, is that you?" She was pleased not to hear his wife or daughter answer the phone. Bryn had no idea how she would explain the situation.

"Hey, Bryn. Just packing up. You still heading out in the morning?"

Then, for the second time since she had met him, she let her guard down and rattled off everything that was going wrong. Junior's presence would only be a small part of it. Bryn told him about Jorge and how she was nervous that he wouldn't hold up his part of the bargain, and how she had been kept up at night by the thought that Andrew would just ride off into the sunset on his new Harley and not show up at all. Why wouldn't he? Who would want to risk their neck for someone they barely knew, to possibly rot away their remaining years in a jail cell?

It took a good ten minutes, during most of which Bryn was nearly hysterical. She had convinced herself that it didn't matter if their plan worked or not, but deep down inside her head it really did matter. For once in her life, she wanted to have the upper hand over a powerful man. Dear God, with the past she'd lived through, no one would argue that she wasn't entitled.

"The worst part is Junior," she told Paul. "Not only can I not work my charm on the little bastard, but he won't take a bribe to help us out, either. All that matters to him, besides drugs and booze, is pleasing his father. Shit, he's just like Malcolm. All the Devanes are the same—keep daddy happy and treat your women like crap."

While Bryn broke into another crying fit, Paul considered the options. After all, he was the one who had the most to lose if things didn't go well.

Bryn had her little savings account and would find another rich daddy's boy to latch onto. Andrew probably had a good nest egg put away, too. Polo didn't have any family left to return to, and seemed to have lost all ambition in life. But Paul, hiding out in a big city with a cheating wife and six hundred dollars in his own savings account, he needed this to work out. He needed to get back home where he grew up, with enough cash to make good on all the bad deeds he'd ever done. Maybe then he could sleep a little better at night, and never have to sell another sandwich.

"So this guy likes the liquor, eh?" he asked. "Little Junior would probably be more easily persuaded with a few drinks in him, then. We'll just have to take him out on the town."

There it was again. Bryn knew for sure the world was crashing down around her, but with a few calm words from Hick Boy Morris, she was ready to follow him anywhere. She didn't know how, but for some reason things looked a bit better than they had an hour ago.

"Don't worry, we'll take care of him, sweetheart," Paul said, holding the phone with his neck while using both hands to roll up his sleeping bag. "See you in a couple days."

"Thank you, Paul. Really. I mean it."

Bryn hung up the phone, watched the combine in the adjacent field make one more round, then headed for home to finish packing.

All the way there, she cried even harder than before.

-3-

It was 7:30 a.m. on a Thursday morning, but Paul Morris was a little more excited about his day than usual. Today there would be no coffee-stained aprons. No hair nets. No hot little dungeon full of ungrateful business people. No, today marked the beginning of something new and different for Paul. He would leave The City for the wide open spaces of the countryside, much like where he grew up. Today began the much-anticipated vacation, only without the two women in his life.

Samantha, who was now working evening hours at the bookstore (or so she said), really didn't take the news so badly. This was part of the reason Paul had grown increasingly suspicious of his lovely bride. Even before the car pulled up in front of their apartment at the completion of one vacation, she was already whining about the next. Coming to The City in the first place had been her idea, but in their first few months there Sam was always ready to leave it behind. But when Paul had sat her down at the kitchen table a few weeks before, while Shelby snored in the next room, she didn't seem to care one way or the other that Paul was leaving without her. Sam tried to hide it, but Paul was sure he heard a little bit of relief in her voice. This was how he knew the heist had to succeed. Something told him that when he returned to that apartment, *if* he returned, things would be a lot different. Samantha Morris, who often helped her husband eat cookie dough right from the tube before licking moderately-priced champagne off him, was no longer the same woman he had married.

When Paul tried to ask her what was wrong, she would run away either to the bathroom or straight to bed, citing migraine headaches most of the time. It had been more than six months since they had taken Shelby to the spring opening of the Meadowland Zoo. A stranger had taken their photo while all three Morrises wore their new hats—Paul a rhinoceros, Sam as a monkey, and Shelby still giggling about how silly she looked with a stuffed buffalo on her head.

Even Shelby had noticed the change. The pictures she drew on the big easel with the oversized tablet wired to it were becoming less and less about a happy threesome. The last two hadn't even included Sam, and when Paul asked where Mommy was, Shelby just said she was "wooking again" or "taking another showah."

All that money would buy his only child one hell of a speech therapist.

Today, he wouldn't be taking the Taurus, with its cushy interior out of the wind and ample cup holders, so Paul gulped down his second cup of coffee while he watched Shelby pick her way through a bowl of Cocoa Pebbles. Sugared cereal was generally a "no-no," but under the circumstances he thought it best to spoil her a little bit. Paul planned on spoiling her a lot once he came back home, with or without the aid of her mother.

"I've gotta get rolling, Sam," he called into the bedroom. "You taking Shel to daycare by eight?" She managed a mumbling version of "yes" from beneath the hum of the hair dryer. Much of their communication of late had been from beneath the hum of the hair dryer.

Paul slung his leather duffel bag over his shoulder, rinsed out Shelby's empty cereal bowl, and started to turn for the door. As it hit him, he buried his head in his hands but fought with everything he had not to cry. No, not only could he never show weakness in front of his little girl, but Paul mustn't give his wife the satisfaction of knowing how much she was really hurting him.

"She's four years old," he said through his hands, sitting down alone at the table. From the living room, Barney sang to his daughter via the electronic babysitter. From the bedroom, the hair dryer continued to blow. "For Christ's sake, Sam. Think of the baby when you're doing what you're doing. She's four *fucking* years old."

No. He was so close now, dammit. Paul would take a little trip, clear his mind, make a few bucks, then come back to get Shelby. If her mother was still being a whore, he would use his money to make sure she never got near Shelby again. There were plenty of high-priced lawyers who would help make that happen. It was all planned out, and he refused to change it now by showing any weakness. He couldn't risk doing anything to show his girls what was going on inside him—the rage he felt, how he wanted to slap Samantha across the room every time he thought of her screwing up all that he had helped to build.

How dare she do anything to take his family away! Paul Morris, with a few T-shirts and two thousand dollars in traveling money in a duffel bag, took one final look at his humble apartment, the one he alone had paid for most of the time. There were no goodbye kisses for either of his ladies. Samantha would surely get over that little detail, but it would scar Shelby for life if he got caught and never saw her again. Still, a lifetime of her hating her daddy for not saying goodbye was better than her seeing him in a moment of weakness. Al Morris may have been one hard-nosed son-of-a-bitch, but after all he had been through Paul never saw him cry. Vietnam. Danang. All those surgeries. He planned to be just as strong, no matter what.

The door closed behind him, and he was halfway down the hall before he heard his daughter's words that broke the dam. Tears rolled from Paul's eyes as he ran down the stairs, praying he wouldn't meet anyone before he could calm himself.

"Daddy? Aw you leeveen?"

Yes, Paul thought as he ran. *Yes, if this all works out, we both are.*

Chapter Eight

If it's too goddam loud," Andrew told the empty apartment, dousing his cupped hand with cologne and slapping it across his cheeks and neck, "then you're too goddam old."

And speaking of being too goddam old, Andrew had wandered through his friendly neighborhood Wal-Mart at least three times before he found camping items more suitable for a gentleman like himself enjoying the golden years of his life. The young man in sporting goods, he thought Daniel was his name, was getting a bit testy by the time 11 o'clock rolled around the previous night and Andrew's shopping list was finally complete. He was in such good spirits that before throwing his purchases in the BMW's trunk, he even tipped his little helper. Sure, it was against store policy, but with the place nearly deserted and, Andrew guessed, most of the cameras turned off for the day, no one could turn down a fin.

Andrew even visited a different bar before returning home last night. It was out of routine and cheating on Lucky Salvino and his cast of regulars, but at present Andrew was all about breaking tradition. He'd had a tall draft beer rather than a Manhattan. He'd eaten pizza instead of greasy french fries and loved every minute of it. And when he'd returned home, he tried dialing a familiar name at an unfamiliar number, only to make it to six digits and quit.

He was proud of the progress, though. The farthest Andrew had made it prior to then was four. But why shouldn't he call Coralie? He'd spoken to her each and every day for decades, then all of a sudden cut off all ties just like that. Surely they would have some catching up to do.

Maybe it was because he didn't really like coming home to an empty place every night, or the fact that he hadn't been with a woman for a very long time. Not likely, though. Andrew knew that he nearly made it all the way through dialing that number, which also belonged to his former best friend, because a certain young lady had reminded him of how pleasing it was to have a woman around. Bryn Scott was like a young, female version of Andrew—scheming, manipulative, and ready to use any trick she could to end up with what she wanted. All that crying, the temper tantrums and the sobbing—Andrew saw right through all that. It was just what women did to get their way.

And it had worked like a charm.

He wanted to tell Coralie he was working with someone now who told him stories about how terrible her husband was to her. He wanted to tell her that all those stories reminded him of what he'd done to his own wife, and finally made him realize how much he'd hurt her. The fact was, Andrew was no spring chicken and when he skipped town with the better part of a million in cash, he wanted someone to share it with him. Maybe Coralie would come along because he now had more money than that lawyer asshole, or maybe it would be because she still loved him.

Andrew really didn't care which one it was. He missed her company.

"Good Christ, Falkness, you're going soft," he said to the telephone that never rang; never rang because Andrew couldn't think of any friends or relatives who'd want to call. "Just call her up and see what happens. The worst she can say is buzz off, then you get on your bike and go without her."

"Twenty-one sixty-five," he told the phone. "Just those last four and you're through."

Two.

One.

Six.

Maybe at the best possible time and maybe not, Paul rapped on Andrew's door at precisely 8 a.m., clad in the leather jacket he hadn't worn in five years, old jeans and a T-shirt (Shovelhead, Genuine Harley History).

"Wonderful," Andrew said into the phone line to no one at all. "Coffee boy's a punctual one."

Paul laughed when he saw Andrew, and figured everyone else would too. Leather vest, cowboy boots, and blue jeans, all of which were brand new. In fact, the vest still had the tag on it. Paul decided not to say anything about that. If the old man's hair were any longer, he could have been Jerry Garcia. The sad thing was, he would fit right in where they were going. A lot of the old Harley riders now had grey hair and dressed the same way. Andrew looked like any other doctor or lawyer, the only ones who could afford the new bikes, who grew out their beards and tried to look tough for one week a year.

"What's so funny, Fonzie?" Andrew said, eyeing his riding partner's old jacket. "I bet you're enjoying this whole revert back to teenage hoodlum days thing."

"Sure am." Paul smiled from ear to ear. He *was* enjoying himself, thanks for asking.

With the sun already beating down hard, both men could tell the day's ride was going to be a long one. Andrew had checked the weather report on the news last night. One hundred degrees was the anticipated high in downtown Sturgis. At noon, Paul had been assured over the phone that no less than 50 members of the Gorham Gearheads would meet them in the parking lot of the Watertown, South Dakota Mall. Everywhere they went, the guys liked to show off their bikes, and Paul figured they would probably set up in rows so the kiddies could get a look at all the chrome. It might be a problem getting them to leave, though. Teenage girls like Harleys, especially bad teenage girls. And the Gearheads liked bad teenage girls. Paul could remember two members off the top of his head who had been sent up for statutory rape charges.

"Well, Kimo Sabe, ready to hit the trail?"

"Who's Kimo Sabe?" Paul asked, making Andrew feel even older than he did already.

He might get the senior citizen discount at Burger King, but Andrew Falkness was feeling better now than he had in twenty years. As long as he could still hoist his leg over that bike, he planned on riding it.

"There's just shy of three hundred miles between us and Watertown," Paul said. "We don't want to keep my boys waiting."

-2-

Paul marveled at how long it had actually been since he'd felt so alive—a stretch of winding road ahead of him and the machine rumbling underneath. This one far surpassed his old SX250, with the ignition switch you needed a screwdriver to operate and the wire wheels so rusty and out of round you felt like you were riding through a plowed field all the time. The new Heritage performed beautifully; it was just a couple years older than Andrew's, but on the newer ones it was hard to tell anyhow.

He remembered his younger days with the Gearheads, and how people that young had to have a certain level of immortality. There was no other explanation, because Paul would easily be dead several times over if he tried some of those stupid stunts now.

Directly below him (he'd achieved such high status due to his pioneering efforts at stealing bikes for the whole crew) was Eugene "Charger" Monroe, probably the last surviving wearer of the 80s mullet cut style. Charger had grown up in much the same environment as Paul had, with an abusive father and a mother who always ran around trying to smooth things over. He'd never left the cocaine decade, and still wore his nearly shredded Metallica T-shirts and bandannas over his long, greasy hair. Paul figured Charger's daughter would be around 14 by now, and he laughed to himself thinking of the old headbanger having to bring her and a carload of her screaming friends to see one of those new boy bands like N'Sync or the Backstreet Boys.

When Paul left town with a new bride and a baby on the way, Charger, the oldest of the group, had taken the reins of the gang. At that point, most of them were in their 20s and realizing they had to find real jobs and move out on their own to survive, and that there was no future in stealing motorcycles. Their little garage-based operation had done pretty well, though. Paul got the great idea that the sum of a cycle's parts was worth more than the complete bike. Through a nice little network of their Gearhead buddies around the region, Paul and his friends had packed and shipped out thousands of parts for rare cycles, and collected their envelopes full of cash every two weeks. But, with an ever-increasing number of aftermarket parts makers, the risk soon outweighed the profitability and Paul checked out of the business.

The last time he'd heard any news, Charger worked in a factory painting implements for a living. Charger still got together with the Gearheads on the weekends for a little hell-raising, but when you've started raising a family and many of the others had, too, there's not a whole lot of hell left to be raised.

Marty "Smith" Smithwick, who likely spent the Gearhead reunion weekends fantasizing about Charger's young daughter, was the one Paul had spoken with several times on the phone in the past few weeks. He wanted to make sure nothing went wrong, and felt the need to call Smith every few days to remind him of the exact place and time they were to meet. The guy may have been a convicted pedophile, but he was by far the most reliable of the bunch.

Smith kept the books for the gang when they were still doing their parts shipping business, and everyone trusted him to keep things fair for all involved. He paid the bills, kept track of which dealers would accept which stolen parts and which ones they would not, and told the boys which deadbeats they should pay personal visits to in order to collect what they were owed.

Of course Smith would never accompany the group on their little collection visits; the intimidation factor was non-existent. Just 140 pounds soaking wet, he was one of the only people Paul had ever heard of who both entered and exited a four-year commitment to the Marines looking exactly the same. He came out with no more muscle and not a pound heavier, though he had lugged his backpack and trudged all those miles just like the rest. What he had gained from Uncle Sam, though, was a vast connection of military buyers, who knew how to manipulate the paperwork correctly. At one point, thirty percent of the Gearheads' stolen parts were being shipped off to various military bases, where some smart G.I.'s would use the cheaper parts and pocket the difference. Who would ever suspect the defenders of freedom of doing such a thing? No one; that's why they kept it up for more than a decade, and helped fund the often-robbed college fund Paul had set up.

Paul and Andrew finally arrived at their lunch destination—a little truck stop called Stone's on the outskirts of Watertown. The smell of frying beef and diesel fumes mixed together in an interesting combination that reminded Paul of being back home on the farm, mom watching out the kitchen window while she made supper and the older boys making ungodly noises in the shop with the welder or grinding on a fender.

Burly truckers waddled in and out of the attached convenience store, and one washed the morning's dust off his Kenworth and attached reefer trailer with a power washer. The wind out here was something Paul couldn't believe—the open prairie let the gusts build up enough to push his bike all over the road, and the shoddy construction of the concrete highway they were traveling on, with its ruts and potholes, didn't help a great deal either.

The usual Thursday afternoon crowd—or what Paul thought would be the usual crowd—filed into the café one after the other, businessmen in short-sleeved shirts and only a few with ties. Others wore uniforms from various implement dealerships or fix-it shops, with their names neatly embroidered on the pocket. These were Paul's kind of people, the small-town folks who took life with a grain of salt and were never in too much of a rush to chase down the almighty dollar. Business out here was done with a handshake and a man's word, and people still had a little shame. Nothing was worse in a small town than taking from others without earning it, whether it be the government, relatives, or otherwise. People took care of their own and worked hard to support their families, with no help from anyone else, thank you very much.

The two amigos ate an early meal while they waited for noon to arrive. The mall was supposedly a couple miles farther up the highway, and Paul knew very well that the Gearheads would be fashionably late. Good coffee, excellent steak and eggs meals for them both, and the waitress's name was even Flo. It was like he was ten again, going into town for lunch on a Saturday.

Paul felt even more homesick now.

"I bet this takes you back," Andrew said, feeling out Paul's mood. "All you need is the *Green Acres* theme playing in the background and I bet you'd be so happy you'd wet yourself."

"Yeah, you grew up with things a little nicer than I did," Paul shot back. "Big deal. When you get right down to it, though, you just had a more expensive version of everything I had. I bet you didn't have even one thing we didn't."

"Sure. Indoor plumbing."

"Fuck you."

Paul would have to live with the old man for the next few days, but after that he didn't think their paths would ever cross again. He was thankful for that fact.

"So," Andrew said, changing the subject, "you think these inbred weirdos can get the job done?"

"They'll do what they're told, as long as there's enough money involved."

"My kind of guys."

The waitress, who Andrew watched through the window as the pair saddled up, was amazed to find the ten dollar tip on her table. Andrew was wealthy enough to tip everyone he met on the street, but he gave special consideration to strippers and waitresses. A certain ex-wife of his had once been a waitress. Maybe lightning would strike twice and the next one would be found pouring his coffee too.

Past a Wal-Mart, a few car dealerships, and a pawn shop was the mall, a much smaller version of the ones the men were used to, but a mall nonetheless. Five minutes after twelve and no large group of leather-clad hoodlums to be seen. This didn't surprise Paul much.

While Andrew waited near the main entrance for any sign of the Gearheads, Paul went inside to find a gift for Shelby. She was currently in her dinosaur phase, and had at least a dozen plastic ones that accompanied her into the bathtub, slept with her at night, and stabbed the undersides of Paul's feet late at night when left in the middle of the floor. They had names like Grrrawr! and Tyrasanorus, and since they were small, they inevitably got left at some unknown restaurant or were thrown out with the trash. Paul's last promise to his daughter was that he would make up for the lost toy with a big picture book on the little girl's favorite animals.

Inside the B. Dalton, packed into a corner behind the ice cream shop, he pawed through coffee table books on Harleys, classic muscle cars of the 1960s, and the pictorial history of Marilyn Monroe before he came across *Land Monsters; An Illustrated Dinosaur Hunt For Children*. Paul paid the young woman in glasses behind the counter with the friendly smile (Kim was her name), returned with a grin of his own, and strolled back outside. Friendly people in little stores, who probably knew you by name if you came in more than twice. This was where he would like to take Shelby when his job was done. She could grow up across the street from a big park, one that was always full of kids playing something, and Paul would never have to worry about anyone taking or hurting her. Of course he still would worry, but that was his job as daddy. He just wished mommy had been doing her job, and not doing her professor.

Andrew sat where he had been before, happily watching people go here and there and no doubt finding something wrong with every one of them. Paul joined his partner in crime and kept checking his watch every two minutes until one o'clock had come and gone.

"You think they forgot— "

"They'll be here, just shut up and be patient."

While Paul thought of pushing his daughter on the swing set in some nameless Watertown park, the screams and laughter of children filling his ears, Andrew envisioned himself and Bryn on a tropical beach, her bikini-clad breasts brushing against his hairy back as she rubbed him down with suntan lotion. Neither one noticed the big purple thing until it pulled up in front of them and the horn sounded.

Da-na-na-na-na-nam! Da-na-na-na-na-nam!

The first two bars of *Bad to the Bone*.

How appropriate, Paul thought.

The bus looked like something a rock star would have been proud to tour the country in. Fifty years ago, that is. But in 2002 the monstrosity was bright purple, belching black smoke from one chrome stack that shot straight up into the air from the driver's side of the hood. Paul noted the rust patch over the rear wheel where someone had apparently stuffed a blanket into the hole to keep out the cold and fumes. In red letters on the side, the old Harley-rider motto, "Live to Ride, Ride to Live" was painted. And the finishing touch, hanging from the rear on a large noose, was a tiny old Honda cycle.

Paul glanced over at Andrew, whose eyes had doubled in size. He just shook his head slowly and stared at the sidewalk.

Charger met Paul on the bus's stairs, one of which had a hole rusted through it. He looked much the same as the last time Paul had seen him, which wasn't surprising at all. These guys didn't exactly embrace progress. After a brief handshake and the usual exchange of pleasantries, Paul went right to work and counted heads.

Exactly fifty-two. Perfect. A couple could get arrested or thrown into detox and they still would have enough to get the job done.

He noticed Charger and Smith, who waved a skinny arm at him from near the back of the bus, but no one else. According to the club's rules, if you moved away or did any number of no-nos, you were automatically out of the Gorham Gearheads and couldn't ride with them or share in the profits from their operations. Paul, of course, was the only exception to this rule since he had achieved such a high rank and basically left town only to appease his wife and escape some bad people.

Most of the men looked about the same—dirty leather jackets and T-shirts, long greasy hair. Paul guessed most had no idea what they were getting themselves into, they had just followed along to collect their money and get away from home for a long weekend. The married ones were escaping their wives and kids, and the unmarried ones, most of whom still lived at home, were probably there to get away from mom and dad.

"You coming home after all this?" Charger asked. "We miss ya like crazy, Paulie."

"I just might."

They would all get to know one another tonight, when they stopped to make camp somewhere along the trail. Bryn wouldn't have things set up and ready for them until the next day, so there was no sense in hurrying. Paul figured the guys were ready to get out and party in Sturgis, but they had also been driving through the night and wouldn't mind a few hours' sleep away from the noisy purple death trap.

He told the driver, Jerry Garcia's long lost twin brother, to follow Andrew and him until they got sick of riding. Then they would find a decent place to pitch their tents. The man nodded, and winked one of his marijuana-reddened eyes at Paul.

Paul turned to leave the bus, then remembered the most important thing.

"Hey, Charger, one little detail I need you guys to take care of."

"You name it, boss."

"There's gonna be a guy hanging around where Andrew and I will be working. I don't know much about him, but he's supposed to be sticking real close to Bryn, the gal running the show. She told me he's not real sociable, but loves his booze. I need a couple of you guys to take him out on the town, get him so wasted he won't wake up until we're gone, and hopefully get his ass thrown in jail for awhile. Just remember, he's the only one who could stand between you and your money."

"What's he look like?"

Paul had always pictured Malcolm Devane during his conversations with Bryn, and felt he would look like the average rich boy—skinny, perfect hair, dressed like a banker even on Sundays. Since his little brother was the target, he described Junior to Charger the same way.

"He likes to look like he's rich, and probably dresses that way too."

Charger nodded, clapping Paul on the shoulder. "Consider it done, *mi amigo*."

Even over the rumbling of their own engines, Paul and Andrew could clearly hear the squealing belts from the bus behind them. Brakes squeaked and the rock and roll music blared as the caravan pulled up to the stop light. Since the group had shown up, Andrew hadn't said a word.

"So what do you think our chances are?" Paul asked him, waiting for the light to change.

Behind them, fifty-two men chanted along with the music, "Gonna see my smiling face, on the cover of the Rolling Stoooooone!"

"I dunno," Andrew said, burying his head in his hands and snickering. "But from now on, whenever I hear that song *Get a Haircut and Get a Real Job*, I'll always remember this day. The ones who don't end up killing themselves will probably get us caught."

Paul just stared ahead, remembering all the people who had felt exactly the same about these guys, then ended up minus their hard-earned cash. He knew very well that the stupid drunken biker thing was all an act, and that the Gearheads were still in existence because they knew how to make people underestimate what they could really do. In reality, they had made very good money for a very long time doing something illegal and not getting caught. Everyone just thought they were incapable of most of the things they did whenever it came time for the law to start pointing fingers.

Yes, it was all an act, and his boys would soon be proving what they were made of.

God, he *hoped* they were just acting.

-3-

For the first hour, rolling along Highway 212 west, Andrew couldn't believe how many people passed them by. The three-vehicle group was traveling well above 70, but they were being consistently passed like they were standing still. It wasn't long, though, before he figured out why. Over every hill, with the sun beating straight down on the top of his head, was nothing more than another hill, and another one after that. Cows, endless stretches of fenced pasture, and hills.

Christ, he needed a Manhattan.

Several things weighed on Andrew Falkness's mind as he rode, stretching every few miles to help work out the kinks in his back and soothe his aching behind. For one, he thought about Coralie, and what she might be doing right now. That woman always had a love of helping out the less fortunate, which went completely against what Andrew thought about the lazy bastards. She was probably handing out bread and soup at a shelter or sweating away in some industrial-looking kitchen, cooking up stew for the vagrants.

While they were still married, Coralie made the tour twice a year with the Bloodmobile, riding shotgun in the big white truck all over the region. Her smiling face had likely greeted thousands of donors before she asked each one a few questions about their sex partners and other invasive things. She did the same job over and over again, day in and day out, just in different towns. It was satisfying work—to her, at least, but it continually bothered her husband. Not only would Andrew have to find his own meals and wash his own laundry during those month-long stretches, but the worst part was that when Coralie returned, she wouldn't have a dime more than when she had left. All that work and putting up with all those people, for no money.

All Andrew's life, he had found that anything worth putting effort into was worth getting paid for. The bigger the lawn he mowed, the more money he asked for. To hell with just seeing the smile on the face of an old woman. They had more money than anyone else, so why should he be a chump and let them ride free?

He weighed his options around the time the caravan got smart and pushed their speed up to 80. On the one hand he could stick with the group, take his chances with a busload of idiots, and risk going to jail or to the poor house. Something would definitely go wrong with this bunch; there was no doubting that. And when the time came for the proverbial shit hit to the fan, he would be in it just as deep as any of them.

Or he could sneak off in the night and take his chances with Bryn's little bag of mystery. She had some dirt on him, but was it enough to put him away? Would John Law really waste that much effort on tracking down an old man who had made a few shady deals in his life?

What it came down to was getting paid. If he stuck around and actually pulled this deal off, the final deal of his illustrious career, he would be set for the rest of his life. Andrew was tired—tired of cheating and stealing to keep a roof over his head, and tired of worrying about what his lawyers would lay on him next.

Most of all, Andrew Falkness was tired of being alone.

Although the thought of Bryn running off to Mexico with him was extremely appealing, it wasn't likely to come true. What he wanted most of all was to return home victorious just long enough to gather up his things, call Coralie, and take her with him to wherever she wanted to go. Ireland, China, Australia—he didn't care, he just wanted his wife back. It would take some changes to the way he'd been thinking and acting his whole life, but the end result would be worth it.

Maybe one of those retirement communities down south in Arizona or Florida would be the key. Andrew could waste away his final years playing cards and legally taking away the retirement funds of other old men. Coralie would fix sandwiches and lemonade, and they would go out dancing like they'd used to with the whole geriatric crowd. He was a little fish in a big pond now, with bigger and bigger companies laying down tough rules and regulations to keep him out of the software game. But down *there*—ah, yes, down with the old buzzards like himself—he would be king once again, complete with his queen.

For the teenage boy working alone waiting tables at Buzzy's Roadhouse, the group's stop for supper, Andrew thought the young man now knew what hell really was. At seven o'clock on a Thursday night, just as the kid was sweeping up from the supper rush and getting ready to lock the doors, fifty-four people packed into the little shack. The Gearheads, who notified Andrew that they had been drinking and playing cards the whole trip, stumbled over tables and fell into booths, yelling out orders in unison. He stood outside near the bus, watching the whole ordeal and doing a closer inspection of their chosen transportation.

"So, whatta you think of the old girl?" the driver asked, stumbling down the stairs. His foot caught the rust hole, and he tumbled out onto the gravel. Andrew smelled bourbon on the bearded man's breath, and figured the one driving was probably the most drunk out of the bunch.

He stood up, brushed himself off, and kicked the bus's side.

"Stupid bitch! That's the fourth time this month."

"Uh, she's a real dreamboat," Andrew said, starting for the restaurant door.

"Thanks, man. We all got together a coupla years ago and pooled our money for her. Us guys drive around to all the bars and drink like we're nuts, and pick one poor fucker to drive us and stay sober. Keeps the cops happy."

"It must've been your turn today, huh?" Andrew asked, stifling a laugh. The man looked to both sides, pulled a flask from his jacket and took a sip, then began urinating on the front tire. The old couple leaving the place, after watching the hoodlums stumble off their hoodlum mobile, walked past and gave him a dirty look. Mister Indecent Exposure just grinned at them.

"Don't be jealous, old timer," he yelled to the man, who was quickly ushering his disgusted wife into their Buick. "They can't all be this big, ya know."

Andrew left the man to his business and made his way in the door of the restaurant. It reminded him of the old Marlon Brando movie where the bikers take over the diner and the town. Every booth was filled, as was the counter and most of the floor. From the kitchen, he caught a glimpse of the young man running rampant trying to flip hamburgers and lower the baskets of fries, while running back and forth with sodas. Not only had the boy been the only one waiting tables tonight, but he was also the cook.

It took a good two hours for them to get their food and finish, during which the Gearheads broke the pinball machine, instigated a ketchup squeeze-bottle fight and covered at least half of the floor surface in the restaurant with spilled soda. Paul watched two individuals vomit on the floor beneath the booth they were sitting in, cover the mess with about a hundred napkins, then simply move to another table.

The sun was getting low when they finally left the diner. Each man left a few dollars near their plate, not caring how much their bills were but rather leaving what they thought was fair. Who would argue with them, anyway?

Certainly not the waiter/cook. He was too busy cleaning up to notice. The group filed out much like they had entered, pushing one another and laughing, some cracking open the bottles of Budweiser they had in their pockets. Paul looked around, shook his head in disbelief, and followed them. By the time Andrew came out of the restroom, only the kid and the man who had relieved himself on the bus were left in the building.

"Helluva mess, eh boy?" Andrew overheard the man telling the youngster, who was now sobbing. He figured the boy to be no more than sixteen.

"Yuh…yes, sir."

"Well, everybody pretty much paid their tab, and this should cover the damage, plus a bit for yourself." The man reached behind him, pulled out the wallet chained to his belt loop, and produced ten crisp hundred dollar bills. "Sorry my boys made such pigs of themselves. You should put that toward a 'cycle for yourself, son, but make sure it's the right brand, or I'll come back here and bash your teeth in for ya. Understand?"

The kid nodded, and the bearded man headed for the door, noticing Andrew watching him. They walked together toward the bus, both giggling to one another.

"Robert Breslin," the man said, extending his hand. Andrew ignored the grease and took it.

"Andrew Falkness, wanna-be but too old software guru. Nice gesture there, Robert."

"Well, eleven months out of the year I'm a tax attorney. Being a drunken ignoramus is just a hobby. Don't tell anyone I did that, though, or I'll slit your throat ear to ear. *Capice*?"

Andrew said he understood, and headed for his Harley.

Another hour of driving and it was becoming clear that a stop for the night was in order. Greasy food and a bumpy road didn't mix, so they pulled into a rest stop just past a little town named Arden, noting the sign that said 100 miles stood between them and Sturgis. Camping out was best, since neither Paul nor Andrew wanted to leave any sort of paper trail from their trip. If caught, they would both need to dream up some sort of alibi, and a credit card receipt from a motel near Sturgis wouldn't do anything to help them.

The Gearheads quickly set up their tents in neat little rows by the headlights of the bus, as the mosquitoes and darkness were already descending on their little campsite. Paul had been looking forward to sleeping out under the stars like he had as a boy, but his older, more arthritic counterpart was not. Andrew felt every bit as old as he was, and often woke up with aches and pains even after a night on his thousand dollar adjustable mattress. Surely a sleeping bag, whether new or not, wouldn't help matters much.

Paul's days of escaping his family to camp out in the woods were all coming back to him now as he readied his tent and sleeping bag inside of two minutes. His supper weighed hard on his belly and his lower back was sore from riding all day, something he was definitely not used to. Before turning in, he sat outside in the cool South Dakota night air, listening to the Gearheads laughing and swearing. Paul debated taking a walk over to their part of the camp to meet and greet the ninety percent of them he didn't know, but soon found his eyelids growing heavy.

In and out of his dreams, Paul thought about riding along the endless highways of this part of the country, first packed in amongst his former gang buddies and later with his daughter clinging to his back. She shouted "Fastuw, Daddy!" over and over again and he would oblige, winding through the turns as she squealed with delight.

It just wasn't fair—not that life ever had been for him. All those years back home, while he dreamed of getting away, he had actually had it made. Good friends, a good job that kept him in shape and money in his pocket. Then, after a parts delivery run to Chicago he just had to stop for the night instead of pushing his limits. Out there on the lonely midnight roads there weren't many hotels to choose from, and those that Paul could find were packed due to the impending snow storm. When he finally couldn't see more than a few feet ahead of the van, he pulled into a bed and breakfast, one of those cutesy, old people kind of places, near Grolier. The innkeeper had gone into town for the night, but her replacement was vastly superior to the original. Two years later, Samantha St. Claire would be his wife.

He followed her to college, something he had always sworn he would never do. College was for smart kids from rich families, of which Paul was neither. While she did the full-time school thing, he took a few classes just to keep her happy while working at the auto parts store and, unbeknownst to her, maintaining his ties with the Gearheads and their money-making operation. By the time she had earned her bachelor's degree, they were already married and she was four months pregnant with Shelby. And, since Paul had made a few enemies in the wrong places back home, he thought it best to stick with his bride and move on to The City. Those big dreams he had of expanding the Gearheads' parts stealing/sales to the big town faded quickly, and it wasn't long before they were out of money and he started running the sandwich shop.

"And the rest," he told the blanket of stars staring down at him, as Andrew snored away inside his adjacent tent, "is history."

He just couldn't understand it; there was something about that woman that made him cave in to any request she had. Samantha could just look at him the right way and no matter how angry he had been, she'd get what she wanted. The night she'd scraped the side of the parking garage with the Taurus, which was nearly new at the time, she sent him down to assess the damage and was waiting for him in just her bra and panties when he came back upstairs. It was this skill that most women had—to make you forget what you were angry about.

But running off with someone else, that was a different story. His long ride today had eased the pain a little, pushing back the bad thoughts with anticipation and fear of the job ahead of him. That was one thing he was proud of—no matter who or what was on his mind, Paul could sweep it all under the rug when it came time to earn his money. Regardless of which girlfriend had been doing what before he met Sam, when Paul was in an alley or warehouse with a bunch of sweet bikes, it was just the machines and him. This little excursion would be the most profitable ever, in more ways than just money. He would keep the police off his back, pay back some of his debts back home so he could safely walk the streets once again, and have plenty left over to give his daughter all the things he'd never had when he was young.

So, with everything fitting so neatly into place, why in the world would he want to complicate it all by including his little whore of a wife? He didn't buy the Casanova theory, that women were powerless when confronted by a kind, knowledgeable professor or some other professional type. Women made their own choices in every aspect of life, no matter how much they whined about how men still ran the world. They had brains just like anyone else.

He was convinced that anyone who could make him feel those extremes the way Samantha did—all the fear, hate, and loathing, then right back to needing her so badly again—was evil. She could run off into the sunset with whomever she wanted, but not everyone would be willing to put up with her. She hated work, but still complained constantly about their financial situation. Samantha was a spoiled little rich girl who had never had to make it in the real world.

It was simple. Paul Morris didn't need her, and she clearly didn't need him. It was just too bad it had taken all this time to realize that, and that they had brought another human being into the picture who hadn't created the problem but was being forced to share in the pain. The only world Shelby knew contained Teletubbies, Barney, and about six thousand little plastic dinosaurs that liked to wander underneath daddy's bare feet. She knew nothing of the desire to be with another person when you already had a great man at home. She only felt love for her parents who tucked her in at night, and fear when one of them was gone. One day she would also be a woman, probably much like her mother, but in the meantime Paul planned on enjoying his daughter without the aid of the cheating bitch he'd foolishly given his heart to.

No, his daughter could live without her mommy if it meant she had a chance of growing up to be a normal, responsible woman. And Paul could definitely live without her too.

Why, then, was he sitting there dialing her number?

Chapter Nine

Paul was not the only member of the Morris family taking the day off. In fact, they all were.

Samantha hurriedly shoved about a dozen of Shelby's plastic dinosaurs into her Hello Kitty backpack, along with two juice boxes (Mrs. Finzell never had the right kind, Shelby said), a few half-completed coloring books and the mega jumbo crayon assortment which, after just five days in the house, was already missing half of its contents. The runaways were likely under the refrigerator, had gotten melted in the bathtub, or were test divers on little Miss Morris's freshwater flushing expedition into the toilet.

"But mom, Missus Fiznull smells like ooold people!"

That wasn't very nice, Sam told her daughter, even though it was a known fact that Ione Finzell, with her three cats and self-knitted mint green sweaters dating back to the Hoover administration, *did* smell like old people. When Shelby developed the sniffles or an all out barfing frenzy, she was banned from daycare and ended up at the Morris's neighbor's apartment two doors down. The concept was a good one too, since the more Shelby grew to dislike the old woman, the less she seemed to get sick. Further proof that illness was all in one's mind.

With her rations and entertainment, more than enough for a couple of hours, Shelby slung the bag over her tiny shoulder and marched down the hall under Samantha's watchful eye. If she had to go to the stinky old lady's apartment, at least she could make the twenty-foot trip on her own like a big girl. Her tiny hand rapped on the door and Mrs. Finzell answered immediately, waving to Sam as she ushered Shelby inside and closed the door behind them.

It was now just after 10 a.m. on a Thursday, right about the time Samantha would normally be taking a break from the book store for a Diet Coke and some chocolate. But not today. Today, as far as her superiors knew, Samantha Morris was suffering from "female troubles," as she'd told them over the phone earlier in the morning. Such an excuse to use up a sick day, which she had an abundance of built up anyhow, meant the old man in charge of her would ask no further questions. He was right on the verge of retirement and very old fashioned, and certainly didn't want any details on exactly what those female troubles might be.

Samantha stepped out of her robe with the bathroom door hanging open and the apartment all to herself, made sure the door was unlocked, then crushed a handful of bath beads into the warm water. Having the tub to herself, especially when it was Shelby's second home, was a rare occasion by itself. But getting both her and Paul out of the apartment for a while was absolute heaven. Growing up, Samantha was the second youngest of five sisters, so time in the house's solitary bathroom was a premium. Then she went off to college, and an industrial type facility with a dozen floormates always dirtying up the showers and leaving hair in the drains.

"But now, I am queen of my castle," she said, easing down into the bubbly water. Then, in her best Eric Cartman voice, "Respect my author-tah!"

Such an unorthodox event as a quiet bath in the middle of the day was simply unheard of in her world, and Samantha intended to enjoy every minute. While Carole King serenaded her, she munched on the handful of chocolate chips she'd gotten from the cupboard. Not exactly a fitting meal for Ezmerelda, Queen of the Bubble Bath, but there were few other choices in the place. As long as it was some sort of food.

She would need her strength for today.

For the past six months, Samantha had jumped back and forth to different classes at Northfield Community College—book keeping, insurance, pre-law—but her final choice had been the perfect one. Not only was the professor handsome beyond belief, she had actually learned a few things too. Her family was always big on college, and even though they hadn't had all the luxuries that other children did growing up, there was always a free ride waiting for each daughter to the university of their choosing. An education, her father said so often it had made her crazy, was far more important than fancy toys or lavish vacations.

Just two months ago, the constant barrage of cute little notes and comments atop her papers had finally hit their mark, and Samantha started thinking seriously for the first time in her life about cheating. Her mother had done it, and dealing with her infidelity had actually saved her parents' marriage. While all her friends were living in single parent homes, Samantha ended up with a mom and a dad, all thanks to a used car dealer named Franklin and his wayward penis.

With a husband working long hours and interested in nothing more than staring at his stupid motorcycle, she and Stinky met at a cheap motel. After having made love to the same person ever since her first time, Samantha finally had something to compare it to. He took his time, kissed her everywhere like Paul had done in the beginning but was starting to forget to do, and made her feel like her body was the one thing in the universe he desired most. From there, every week after class was spent in that same room, where she would tell him exactly what she was wanting at home but not getting and he would oblige.

Samantha lathered her hair and fought with the tangles, argued silently to herself over whether or not to chop it all off and end the frustration, then took the washcloth to her privates.

"It's a shame to clean my pussy up just so I can get it dirty again," she said. Talk like that would never have been tolerated at home or by her goody-goody husband. Paul shied away when she even tried talking a little dirty. Now, it felt good to be with someone who let her do what she wanted to do and say what she wanted to say.

Two knocks on the apartment door and he entered, six feet three inches tall with a body sculpted by three nights a week at the gym. He stood just behind the closed door and stared at Samantha for a few seconds, then removed his clothes as he walked across the apartment toward her. Without a word, he knelt down in front of her and took the washcloth from Samantha's hand, gently scrubbing her back and neck.

"So, my husband seems to be out of town for awhile," she said, enjoying the attention. "What do you suppose we could do about that?"

"Dunno. Pretty good coincidence, though. My wife seems to be gone, too."

He slid around to the front of the tub, then kissed her gently, running his hands through her wet hair. She kissed back as though it were their first time doing so, and ran her fingers over the bulges of his muscles. Samantha's fingers traced the outline of the tattoo on his bicep, mocking the name of his little bitch of a wife who couldn't satisfy her man.

"M-a-r-j-o-r-i-e. What kind of stupid name is that, anyway? Sounds like an old fat lady's name."

"It was more of a joke than anything else," he said. "She really didn't want me to get it tattooed on me; it really pisses her off."

"And what about me?" Samantha asked, kissing his nose and forehead. "I bet I piss her off, too."

"You, my dear, are a secret. The best secret I've got."

Samantha was picked out of the tub and carried into the bedroom, where they took their time and made as much noise as they wanted in the empty apartment. She came an unprecedented four times today, the final two while she felt him finish deep inside her. After the first couple meetings, she was surprised when any lingering feelings of guilt had just gone away, and there was nothing left but pure, slightly evil enjoyment.

When they'd finished, with her head resting on his chest, she outlined the day ahead of them, one they'd both been waiting for. The Sarlette County Historical Society had had the good fortune of obtaining a rare traveling dinosaur bone exhibit, which was on display downtown for the next few weeks. After Paul mentioned it to Shelby last Saturday, it was all she talked about. He, of course, didn't have time to take her since people at the sandwich shop were always getting sick and Paul was forced to go in on Saturdays. What a joke! Bossing around a bunch of old ladies who didn't really listen to him anyway. Then he came home and tried to boss her around, too.

It wouldn't make much sense to Shelby at first, but in the end she would figure it out, and Samantha promised to tell her the whole story once she was a little older. For now, it would just be something like, "Mommy and her friend want to spend some time with you, and he thinks you're the sweetest girl he's ever met."

He gathered his trail of clothes while she slipped on her red and black dress. Today was a good day, and her favorite outfit was in order.

"Are you sure you're ready for this?" she asked, feeling his hand. No sweat. No trembling or heavy breathing. She was nearly wetting herself from worry and Stinky stayed cool as a cucumber. Yet another thing she admired about him.

"I've been ready for a long time," he said, kissing her cheek. "We both still want to do this, right? There's no going back now."

"I know."

Samantha Morris, after thanking Mrs. Finzell for babysitting, walked proudly down the hall in broad daylight, happily showing the world what she was doing. Her husband was off on his little vacation, which he had insisted at the last minute he had to take by himself. Now was the time for her to finally enjoy life, and to do what she wanted to do, what felt right in her heart.

Holding on tight with her tiny hand and shooting confused glances at her mother was little Shelby Morris, bound for the "disonaurs" and a day with her mommy. She was happy the day had finally come when she could see a real dinosaur with his bones sticking out, but wondered why Paul couldn't be there to share in the excitement. Daddy liked dinosaurs too, except when he stepped on the plastic ones and said naughty words that made Shelby laugh.

On Samantha's left was her baby, who had kept her from finishing her education and making a proper life for herself. She was loved—at least Samantha thought she loved Shelby—but was unwanted both then and now. Unfortunately, Shelby was needed as the ticket to a better life. Behind her was Paul, whom she would have little trouble getting over when that time came. And on her right, smiling across at what would soon be his new family—Paul's replacement.

-2-

Around the time Paul was leaving the standard "I'm okay, we're almost there and, oh, by the way, love you both" message, Shelby was tossing and turning on a stranger's couch after a full day of dinosaurs and pizza. Everything felt odd to her, but the nice man had bought her a giant stuffed stegosaurus at the museum's gift shop, and mommy seemed very happy to have him around, so Shelby guessed she was too. Besides, she was far too tired to give it any serious consideration just then. She thought the noises and giggles coming from the next room were all in her dreams, but couldn't be exactly sure.

Paul awoke on Friday morning to the smell of frying bacon, which reminded him of being back home again. In his dreams that night, Shelby was turning into a young woman and now that the time was right, Paul had taken her around to all the dealers he could find so she could pick out her very first Harley. They looked a little different a dozen years in the future, with rockets in place of their tires and computer gadgets galore, but the style remained the same. Shelby had jumped up and down, clapping her hands when she saw the bright red machine, much like she did whenever Paul brought home a new plastic dinosaur for her. As he stood there watching her ride away, waving, his body began to age rapidly, his hair fell out and his pot belly grew. Soon, he was rocking on the porch of an old shack when an ancient station wagon pulled up in front, a middle-aged Shelby got out with four toddlers in tow, and coughed violently. Her hair was thinning too, and she walked with a terrible limp.

"Mommy wouldn't have let this happen to me," she had said. "Why did you make my mommy go away?"

This image, along with the bacon, was enough to jerk Paul awake. He dressed, ran a comb quickly through his hair, then poked his head into Andrew's tent. The old man was in exactly the same place as he'd been the night before, snoring up a storm. A long day of fresh air and the persistent sun on your face was enough to tire out even a youngster like Paul, so he guessed it would be best to let a man more than twice his age get his beauty sleep.

"You need it more than me, anyhow," he told the snoring lump inside the sleeping bag.

Even though they had likely stayed up drinking and telling lies most of the night, the Gearheads were, for the most part, bright-eyed and bushy-tailed by 7 a.m. Paul had given strict orders that the wheels would be turning, with or without them, by eight. While nearly a dozen bathed, yelled, and swore in the stream beneath the bridge at their roadside campsite, others rolled up tents, shaved, or watched Charger frying bacon and eggs over their fire. The temperature was already climbing into the 80s at least, but all were clad in black leather and most wore chaps. Five bearded Gearheads with big bellies stood in the bacon and eggs line, probably awaiting seconds or thirds.

"Morning, sunshine!" Charger called from beside the fire. He thought it was illegal to just start a fire at a rest stop, but what cop in his right mind would question fifty big, dirty bikers? "Grab a plate and get some chow in ya 'fore we saddle up for the day."

"No thanks. Let's go over all this again so you're sure these guys can get it right." Through about a dozen conversations over the phone, Paul had gone over and over their plan again, much like Bryn had done with her three men all those nights in the garage.

Charger said he and the boys would have the night off tonight and Saturday, but would be needed to saddle up late Sunday evening. Two friends of this Bryn girl were going to tell the police they saw all 150 bikes, including the 100 in the trucks that would already be long gone, being stolen by masked men at just after 11 p.m. and no later than midnight according to Sturgis's time zone. "This fucks the rich guy with insurance and helps us with our alibis too," he said. "You and the old guy do your fancy locksmith shit for the ones in the trailers, which are the ones headed overseas. When they're gone, you do a little more fancy locksmith shit on the other 50 in the tent, the ones we're supposed to ride off into the sunset with. We all head off to Two Harbors, Minnesota, as soon as all fifty are running and ready, then that Bryn girl gives us all a separate destination once we arrive. Some get on a boat and some get ridden clear across the freakin' country. You sure you can trust a woman, Paulie?"

"Yes, now keep going."

"We each get an envelope with some cash and a destination at Two Harbors, and if we haven't made our deliveries by the right time or wind up wanting to keep the bike for ourselves, this broad calls the cops with the VIN number. Damn, she thought of everything, didn't she?"

Yes, Bryn must have been thinking this one through for quite some time. Paul asked what the Gearheads planned to do with Junior.

"We find the rich guy's brother, who'll also be dressed like a rich guy and hanging around the sale tent, then we get all buddy buddy with him Friday night. Come Saturday, after we've kept him out of your hair long enough to get the semis on the road, we turn up the volume a little, get him a hooker or two, add some booze and pills, and have us a little photo session. If we can't get his ass arrested, then we can use those pictures to keep his mouth shut."

That was beautiful. Perfectly tuned and totally accurate. Paul's faith in the drunken bunch, or at least in their leader, was restored.

"Andrew and I will ride into town first, and go right to the trailers," Paul said. "We'll hang around and play looky-loo with the tourists until we make sure Junior is gone, then we'll start. Get him out of there however you can, just do it as soon as possible."

Gearheads, some still naked from bathing in the stream and caring little about what passing motorists thought, had begun packing their gear into the rusty rack on top of their bus. When the first phase was complete and Paul had a little time on his hands, he looked forward to getting to know some of the guys. Likewise, many of them, who still told and retold stories about the great Paul Morris and his pioneering efforts with the club, wanted to get to know him. One hundred and fourteen thefts and only one conviction, which he later appealed and ended up only serving two months due to a lack of evidence. Paul knew how to get the job done, cover his ass in the process, and keep one step ahead of whoever was after him. He never ratted out his friends, never took more than his share, and always gave one hundred percent to the gang.

To the fifty-two men drying off their hairy bodies, staggering toward the smell of breakfast, or kneeling in the nearby ditch trying to puke away a monster hangover, Paul Morris was a hero. Forget John Wayne or President What's-his-name; Paul Morris could steal the moustache right out from under your nose, and that was an admirable quality. He was revered back home, as more than a kid piling pastrami on rye and pouring coffee, as more than a big fish in a little pond, with his cheating slut of a wife and four-door family car.

Paul felt this admiration. Hell, he'd missed it every day of his life since leaving home. As he turned from the group, he felt fifty-two pairs of eyes watching him.

"Hey Paulie?" Charger asked as Paul walked back to his tent. "We've come a long way from the old screwdriver and wire trick, ain't we?"

"Sure have, Charger," he shot back without looking. "It's the big leagues now, boys."

Another hour of boring hills, down endless stretches of endless tar, and the traffic began to pick up a little. It was as though they knew Paul and Andrew were coming into town and had rolled out the welcome mat. For the last twenty miles, the pair found themselves minus a busload of allies but gaining a thousand more. Motorcycles of all sizes, ages, and colors with black people, white people, fat women and skinny ones too, began to crowd in around them, all headed for the same place.

It was a feeling Paul couldn't get enough of. That same feeling made Andrew a bit nervous, but he was definitely loving it too.

Though they were traveling at 75 miles per hour, a Kawasaki carrying two teenagers too young to know what a real motorcycle was buzzed by. Then came a green and black Suzuki, packed with enough gear to last any one person at least a month. Other Harleys passed carrying the standard middle-aged, beard-wearing lawyers, with their brand new tents and sleeping bags strapped onto their brand-new bikes. Perhaps the most despicable of them all were the ones with button-up shirts, driving their pickup trucks or, far worse, their SUVs, and hauling their bikes behind them. To Paul, nothing was more pathetic than spending all that money and time on a machine that you didn't have the balls to ride into town on. Harley Davdisons were made for the open road, not just cruising up and down main street all night. Other groups reminded him more of the Gearheads, with their older, sometimes pre-Evolution bikes that were scratched, dented, and worn but were at least being ridden. This bunch was Paul's favorite.

Andrew spent his last few miles rapidly jolting his neck to each side, watching the cycles and the pretty young girls on them as they sped past. It seemed that for every 20-year-old, skinny, long-haired blonde clinging to her boyfriend on the back of a Hog there were at least ten fat, ugly ones. The worst part was that the unattractive ones wore just as skimpy clothes as the cute ones.

Plus, Andrew knew that in today's liberated world there were women riding cycles, but he had never actually seen it happen until now. One middle-aged woman, in her bikini top and shorts, passed by on a Heritage Soft Tail much like Andrew's. Another, who he met and had little time to look at, reminded him of Coralie. Imagine, that old woman in a skimpy top riding her own Harley!

Over the last hill and there it was—spread out a lot more than either of them had imagined. On their right, three parachutes with big fans attached to a giant tricycle beneath flew over a large pasture, near a billboard offering powered parachute lessons. Every other sign seemed to be offering camping or lodging in one form or another. They passed an RV park, and Andrew watched as a quarter-million dollar rig was being leveled. Next to the house on wheels were about a hundred just like it.

"Probably lawyers," Andrew said to himself, regretting having opened his mouth as soon as he swallowed a bug. "Sons of bitches got all the money. Not for long, though."

The detour Paul had looked up on the Internet led them away from town and directly to the Buffalo Chip Campground, a massive pasture offering hundreds of acres of camping and exactly three shade trees. He and Andrew idled up to the little shack, parked near the window, and stretched their legs. Two hours worth of riding wasn't too bad, and both men were surprised at how they weren't even sore from sleeping on the ground the night before.

As was Paul's luck lately, one of his favorite bands, Blues Traveler, would be performing in the camp that night at 10 p.m. But by that time, he would be up to his neck in wax key blanks and grinder shavings. Each man paid his fee, then followed one another down the dusty road into the campground. Even this far away from town, a steady stream of bikes went one way or the other. Paul couldn't wait to see what the action was like in the heart of Sturgis if it was this wild even at the campground.

Andrew dusted off his tent and began the process of setting it up again. The chrome on his bike gleamed in the midday sun. He hated to leave his new toy sitting in some farmer's makeshift storage garage, but that was the plan. They would stow the bikes this afternoon, then hoof it the mile-and-a-half walk into town. That was one thing about Bryn, she didn't treat Andrew like an old man. She never thought twice about some of the crazy things she was asking someone more than twice her age to accomplish.

After setting up camp and leaving their gear inside the tents at the mercy of any passerby, Paul unwrapped the sandwich he'd purchased at their last fuel stop and munched away inside his tent, glad to be out of the sun if only for a few moments. Andrew traded lunch for a short nap, an activity he was growing increasingly fond of these days. This time his snoring was no match for the constant rumble of Harley pipes.

An hour passed, with Paul hanging half out of his tent watching the constant stream of people. It was insane to think that motorcycle lovers from all corners of the globe had made their way to someplace as hot, dry, and desolate as this, then slowly turned it into the most kickass week-long party in the world.

Finally he could wait no longer, and shook Andrew awake. The desire to get back to his old ways was intense. Who said you could never go home again?

With just his black duffel bag that held the wax key blanks, key cutter, and grinding wheel along with some other miscellaneous tools to make the next few hours go a lot smoother, the partners took their final ride on their Harleys, two bikes they wouldn't see again for several months. Paul wanted to wait until fall before he chanced returning here to claim his ride, and Andrew agreed. Maybe they'd "do lunch come next spring," as Andrew had said.

The two rode side by side back the way they had come, smiling like two kids despite the temperatures now in the high 90s and absolutely no wind. Sweat trickled down Paul's forehead onto his shirtless chest, but he was in heaven just the same. Andrew, great lover of the Whopper, chose to keep his shirt on for fear of disgusting others, but he shared Paul's feelings on the whole heaven thing.

"My ass hurts, my back hurts, and I have a splitting headache," Paul said, "but I wouldn't trade this day for any other."

"Consider yourself lucky," Andrew said. "Poor Bryn had to ride all this way in a semi with Junior Devane and some smelly truck driver. She must be pulling her hair out by the roots by now."

"Yeah," Paul said. "I wonder how she's making out."

-3-

It seemed as though the worst qualities of all the men—all the stupid, chauvinist, crass, women-should-be-barefoot-and-pregnant men—who Bryn Scott had ever known, had been combined to form the two wastes of human skin she was presently sandwiched between. Not only did they have to leave at the crack of dawn, but she was forced to spend all those hours as the meat in a Junior Devane and Abe Morrovich hoagie.

While Junior either crinkled his newspaper, burped up the remains of his breakfast, or told dirty jokes to the driver, Abe preferred to stay quiet. This was wonderful for Bryn, except for the fact that Abe was kept silent by the three-inch diameter cigar he had been puffing on all morning. It was one of those expensive ones, which seemed inappropriate for a man who made just over minimum wage, but the thing just kept on burning and burning, never getting any smaller.

"So this guy walks in a biker bar," Junior would say, taking a break from studying the Wall Street Journal. "He's a rich lawyer, right, so he just bought his first Harley and wants to be a big man. Of course, all the big bikers in there are laughing at him, right. So he says to the bartender, 'I bet I can prove I'm the meanest son-of-a-bitch in this place.' What happens? People keep right on laughing, right? So the bartender says, 'You think you're so tough, let's find out.' He pours five shots of tequila, then he says there's this bulldog in the back room, right?"

"Yeah," Abe shot back, probably listening as little as Bryn was.

"So the bartender tells this guy, the bulldog's got a bad tooth, right? And in the basement, there's this hooker with a terrible case of herpes and nobody'll touch her. So he says, 'You finish these shots, go fuck that hooker, and take a pliers and go pull that dog's tooth. I guarantee you nobody in here will ever laugh at you again.'"

Bryn turned her head the other way, trading a stupid male joke for cigar smoke. She had been trying to sleep for the past three hours, but with no success.

"So this lawyer starts pounding down these shots, right? And he damn near falls off his bar stool. The guy staggers into the back room with that bulldog, and all of a sudden you hear this terrible growling noise, and this guy's screaming his head off. About ten minutes later, the lawyer staggers out of the back room, all cut to shit and bleeding all over the place. He turns to the bartender and he says—this is the *best* part Abe—'All right, I fucked the bulldog, now where's the hooker with the bad tooth?'"

Abe chuckled, staring straight ahead at the endless stretch of tar. Behind them were five more trucks, most with only one driver and no one in their passenger seats, but Junior had still insisted on riding with Bryn. She figured he thought of her as a threat to the Devane fortune, even though she had signed Malcolm's little paper before they tied the knot, and was doing all this just to get on her nerves. The only other passenger in their convoy was Jorge, who seemed to get along all right with the foreign guy in truck three.

Abe was one of the two men Bryn didn't trust to take part in their plan. He and Bradley Swenson, a portly old man with a wife and four kids, would be sent off to the nearest big town for parts while everything went down. If things worked right, by the time the two returned that next morning it would all be over.

The other four drivers—Benny Ardy, Jamal Williks, Mark Osage, and Jorge's friend Carlos Vosalgo—had been given strict instructions not to breathe a word to anyone about what was happening. They were all long-time employees of the Devanes in some form or another, and had gotten screwed over in their wages and benefits for a combined total of 64 years. Three of the four were on the verge of quitting anyhow, and felt their $5,000 would be a nice severance package, even if they weren't quite sure their little trip would be legal. Bryn just told each one that she would hand them a destination Saturday night, and an envelope full of cash upon delivery. All they had to do was go into town and enjoy themselves until then, and ignore the guy making grinding noises all night in their trailers.

"Truck driver from Alabama likes to entertain hisself while he's driving by hitting niggers with his truck," Abe said, breathing smoke into Bryn's face. She turned the other way. "One day, he picks up this preacher stranded by the side of the road and is givin' the guy a ride to the next town. Sure enough, a couple miles up there's this nigger walking along the roadside. So this guy's debating, should he hit him with a preacher in the truck or not? So he swerves over a little, swerves back, swerves over again. Finally, just before he gets to this old boy, he shuts his eyes and cranks the wheel, and he hears this thud."

"So, what happened?" Junior asked.

"The trucker turns to this preacher, and he's just feeling awful, ya know. They go a few more miles and finally he can't take it anymore. He asks this preacher, 'I gotta know, did I hit that guy or not?' And the preacher says—"

"Nope, but I got him with the door," Bryn finished, surprising both men. "There, you've insulted every race and creed on the planet. Now do you suppose I can get some fucking sleep?"

Junior just laughed; it was that high, squeaky laugh of his that drove her insane. Abe smiled but was obviously embarrassed. Bryn finally had some quiet and drifted off to sleep, thinking about Paul and Andrew camping out under the stars, eating beans out of a fire-roasted can, or whatever else it was that men did when they felt like roughing it. She never was much for nature; the bugs and snakes never bothered her much, but it was the wide open space that Bryn hated. Just standing somewhere and being able to see for hundreds of miles in any direction was unnatural in her mind. She had grown up in a place like that, where there was just sand as far as the eye could see. Honestly, Bryn never got a decent night's sleep until she moved to the big city and was lulled to dreamland by horns and gunshots. She wouldn't mind staring at the ocean all day when all this was through, though. There was nothing unnatural about that.

Most of the ride, when she wasn't trying to tune out the bad jokes and burp smells, Bryn worried about all the details of the next few days. This amazed her, because she had never been the kind of person who would put enough effort into anything to need to worry about it.

Would her girlfriends show up, and would they tell the right story?

Would Paul and Andrew change their minds and skip town?

What if one of the drivers changed his mind and calls Malcolm?

She decided that no matter what happened, her savings would cover the money she'd promised her friends, the truck drivers, and the rest, while still leaving her enough to get a place of her own. Just not in Aruba. More like some shitty little town in Utah where the cops would never think of looking for her. But she would still be making it on her own. Bryn would probably have to go back to dancing for dollars on "sniffer's row"; it was the only thing she was truly good at.

And if she did get caught and sent to prison, for what would likely be a very long time, Bryn was confident she could talk her way out of most of the fights her big mouth would get her into.

Over a few more hills and there it was, the site of Malcolm Devane's soon to be devastating financial loss. Bryn had never seen so many people in one place, and they were all riding motorcycles in every direction imaginable. This kind of place, and not the desolate country they had driven through all day, was more her speed.

Abe navigated the Kenworth through one of the main roads at about 10 miles per hour. Everywhere, motorcycles darted out in front of one another and clogged up traffic. It took nearly an hour to get to their spot, which was just past a large grocery store advertising cheap bottled water and air conditioning inside. Bryn figured the place would be quite busy, and hopefully the traffic would come by their tent too. Then those poor suckers needed to put nice down payments in cash on their new Harleys. A little more money for herself was never a bad thing.

A bank thermometer read 99 degrees as the trucks lined up in the marked-off space along the road. They would be parked in an alley behind the tent, which blocked the view from the busy sidewalk. Bryn stretched her legs and decided to try out the grocery store's bottled water special, while the drivers congregated and smoked. Jorge, who flashed her a smile as she walked away, held up his crossed fingers.

When Bryn returned with refreshments for the crew, the blue and white tent was already laid out on the grass. Benny and Mark fumbled with the poles while Jorge read the instructions. Bryn wiped her forehead and thought of Paul and the old man, who would be stuck inside those metal trailers all night, then in the hot sun the entire next day. She hoped neither would get sick, because there was no time to be sick.

By four p.m., the tent was set up and anchored properly, even though there wasn't so much as a breath of wind to try knocking it down. Bryn had told Paul and Andrew to stop in around mid-afternoon, and searched the crowd frantically for either one. She kept her mind off them by giving orders to the drivers on where to put the bikes, and by yelling at Jorge to polish this one or that one a little better. She and Mark hung the Midwest Custom Cycles banner on the side facing the sidewalk while the remainder of the first two trailers were emptied. By the time all the bikes were placed neatly into rows, Bryn hung the last price tag on a 1947 FL and people had already begun walking through, it was six o'clock.

"All right boys, listen to me for two minutes then you can go drink beer and look at boobies all you want," she yelled, waving her hands for attention. Bryn Scott may have let men walk all over her most of the time, but when it came to the grunts from the cycle shop, she was the bitch who ran the show. It was almost a shame to give that up—barking orders five days a week at 13 guys who were all twice her size.

Bryn reached into her handbag, which contained everything needed for their covert operation, and produced a list of parts. It had been made up two weeks ago, but no one needed to know that.

"First things first. Abe and Bradley, I need you guys to unhitch the Peterbilt and run to Sioux Falls for me."

"Like hell," Bradley shouted. "I've been looking forward to getting here for months. You're not making me leave already."

"Yeah," Abe added. "That's a five-hour run one way. We wouldn't be back 'til tomorrow morning."

"Actually, you probably won't be back until Sunday morning," she said, smiling. Bryn knew they had to listen, or she would just tell them to find their own way back to The City. "Mark called me just as we were pulling into town and said his engine was knocking again. He told me what he needed and I called around. The only place that's got the right parts is in Sioux Falls, and they won't have them until closing time on Saturday night."

"Bullshit," Abe said. "Go yourself. I can stand here like a lump and sell a few motorcycles for you."

Bryn took a deep breath, strolled casually over to Abe, and took the cap off his head. She placed it backward on her head and forced herself to move in so that her nose was nearly touching his.

"I was just wondering, sweetheart," she whispered, "who's the boss here? I think it's me, isn't it? You think it is?"

Abe stared at her, but quickly backed down. He made more than the other drivers and had child support payments to make.

"Fine. Gimme the damn list."

She looked at Bradley, who followed suit.

"Whatever, *boss*."

What the two didn't know was that once parked outside the parts store, which coincidentally wasn't even open on Saturdays, they would get a call from Bryn telling them the shipment would actually be delayed until Monday morning. She'd say that they were selling so many bikes that they would just lock up the empty trailer and leave it for the pair to pick up on Monday. By the time they got back to Sturgis, ready to fix the broken truck that wasn't broken, she'd be at the Hubert H. Humphrey Terminal in Minneapolis with a handbag full of cash and a flight to catch.

The two men unhitched from the trailer, took the list, and headed back the way they had come. As Bryn watched Junior walking toward her, she wished there had been some way to send him away with Bradley and Abe.

"So does my brother know about this little change in plans?" he asked. "Seems to me like you're trying to get rid of those guys."

"And why would I do that?"

"I don't know…yet."

"Why are you here anyway? You've got all the money in the world, so why can't you just go skiing in the Alps or whatever it is that spoiled little rich boys do?"

As always, Junior just smiled back at her. Little did she know that the respect of the Devane family, a family that was threatening to cut off his allowance if he didn't straighten up and fly right, was worth more to him right now than anything. That little whore in college and her baby who was supposedly his had cost the Devanes $500,000 just to keep quiet. Most recently, Sergeant Marshall at the state Department of Justice had drained the family's bank account by another quarter of a million to keep little Junior's drug escapades out of the papers. Truth be told, he *had* to come here, not only to appease his father but to insure that his life of ease would continue. No way would he ever work for a living.

At least Junior and Bryn agreed on that much.

"Just remember," he said, "I'm keeping my eye on you. I'm not going to let you out of my sight this whole time. Something's going on, I just haven't figured it out yet. You've never had any ambition to do anything, then all of a sudden you're gung-ho to load up all these bikes and truck them halfway around the country? And for what? To impress Malcolm? I don't think so."

"Why am I here then, smart guy?"

Junior stopped short, knowing very well he had no idea what, if anything, was going on. Silently admitting defeat, he walked over to one of the lawn chairs set up under the tent and plopped down in it. Jorge glanced over his shoulder at him, then at Bryn's worried face, and went right back to polishing the handlebars on a burgundy 1971 FLH. Out of the corner of his eye, Jorge saw a wonderful sight, and immediately went about what he had been told to do.

"Would, eh, would you care for some dinner?" he asked Junior. "Perhaps a beer too?"

Believe it or not, that was the best offer Junior had heard all day. It had been nearly a full day since his last drink, and he was beginning to get the shakes. At this point, he would have gone for beers with Dr. Martin Luther King, Jr. himself if he'd been there to offer.

"Sounds like a plan, Jurgy."

"Jorge."

"Yeah, Jorge. Whatever. You thirsty or what?"

Junior walked off with Jorge to a seemingly random bar where the Gearheads were later scheduled to take him out on the town. A few drinks and a few snapshots here and there with the right women, namely women of any race other than white, and a few threats of sending those pictures to mommy and daddy (or a few newspapers dying for dirt on the Devanes), and Junior would be putty in their hands. He wouldn't want to risk losing his meal ticket, now would he?

Bryn watched them walk away, then noticed what Jorge had just seen. She smiled and waved, trying not to be too obvious.

Exactly three hours behind schedule, Paul and Andrew climbed the stairs into the first semi trailer, armed with a lantern and a whole bag full of tools. Jorge had been told to stick with Junior as long as was necessary to make things work out, so Bryn was left with the job of sitting alone, watching the customers and banging on the trailer if trouble arose. Her guys had made the journey, and looked ready for anything.

Bryn realized as she sat there, while bearded bikers checked out the merchandise, that everyone involved with their theft, aside from her girlfriends, were all men—the drivers, Paul and Andrew, Jorge, the Gearheads and the DMV man. All her life she had depended on them, for their tips or the minimum-wage factory jobs that were all short-lived, and now here she was depending on them again. What had become of her dreams of being an independent, respected woman?

"What kinda deposit you need on this Hog, sweetheart?" a grey-haired man in a brown leather coat asked. "Or do I need to ask your husband about the business stuff, pretty lady?"

Bryn smiled. She would end up independent the best way she knew how, by using her mind to outsmart old-fashioned idiots like this guy.

"No, you can ask me."

"Well then. I'll put down half now just so you'll hold it for me; I'll pick it up on Monday. How's that sound, babe? Maybe I'll take you for a ride on it later, too."

She put on her best flirting act, and played stupid until the man asked how she needed the money.

"Cash only."

With an extra eight thousand dollars in her handbag, Bryn handed him a receipt and settled in for the evening. Along the street, motorcycles of every shape and color rolled by, ridden by people of every shape and color, too. Was that what men really thought of her, that she was a stupid, pretty girl who couldn't fend for herself? Was that what Mr. Grey Hair thought? And Malcolm?

Their minds would change quickly, though, when Monday morning came.

Chapter Ten

It's just not fair, you know," Andrew said, panting. With the 99 degree heat, which the steel trailer had been absorbing all day, he figured the temperature inside their makeshift workshop to be somewhere in the neighborhood of the flames of hell. Andrew had stripped down to his T-shirt, and was consistently mopping his forehead with the discarded one.

"What isn't fair?" Paul asked, struggling to see the ignition on the Panhead from the cheap lantern's light. He too had stripped down to his T-shirt and was beginning to grow weary of his work. Unfortunately, there were still 81 cycles left.

"What isn't fair, young man, is that a rich prick like Junior Devane gets to go out on the town all night long, probably in a place with air conditioning and the works, so he can drink beer and stare at all the women while we're in here sweating and dying. I'm too old for this crap, Paul. When's Jorge coming back so I can get the hell out of here?"

"Sorry, old timer, but it's Jorges job right now to make sure Junior gets as drunk as humanly possible and back to that motor home he rented as late as possible. I don't care how, but between now and whatever time we get the rest of these bikes on the road, it's his job and the Gearheads' job to do whatever it takes to keep Junior out of our hair."

Paul removed a wax key blank from the ignition, then placed it inside the tiny ice chest which held their water supply. Three minutes later the wax was hard, then he removed the blank and placed it in the tracing side of the grinding machine. He flipped through the manual, found the right key blank number for the model, then screwed it into the other side of the grinder. While Paul began fiddling with the next ignition, it was Andrew's job to carefully guide the machine along the peaks and valleys of the wax model, being sure not to press too hard. Once completed, Andrew used a wire brush to eliminate any burs, then tested the new key in the ignition.

Nineteen Harleys down, and he had already messed up more than 40 times. Fortunately, they had enough blank keys in the little black box for a thousand cycles.

"So how do you think they're gonna steer him away from us?" Andrew asked, happy that for this bike, his first attempt at making the key had been successful.

"Dunno," Paul said, pausing for a quick drink. They had gone through more than a dozen bottles of water since they had entered the trailer four hours earlier, but neither one had gotten the urge to urinate. That had been a problem area identified earlier, since they couldn't be seen just walking in and out of the trailers all night long. Paul figured it was all sweating out as fast as he could put it in.

"Do these guys really know what they're doing?"

"For the last time, *yes*," Paul said, a little irritated, but still unsure himself. "Just because they look like hoods doesn't mean they're stupid. They'll buy him a few drinks tonight, get to be his buddy, then make sure he stays out all night long. Tomorrow, right about the time he's waking up with a splitting headache, the Gearheads'll be right there again with some hair of the dog to get him going again. Deep down, I think Junior wants to be bad ass like those guys, so he'll probably take to them easily. They go out on Saturday, get a few hookers, take some pictures, and one of the guys with a laptop threatens to email them to every newspaper in the country. Oh, and to Junior's parents too. After that, he's ours."

Andrew sat down next to Paul on the floor of the trailer. It was a good thing neither man was claustrophobic, because the space they were working in could hardly be considered abundant. Each of the 25 bikes in the trailer was wrapped in styrofoam material and strapped to a series of posts. Inside the trailer were two levels, with 12 on the top level and 13 below. The ceiling height on each level was no higher than about four feet. To even the weight, every bike on the top level was strapped to the driver's side of the trailer, and those on the bottom were strapped to the passenger's side. For each one, Paul would have to pull off all the material, wrestle it into the tiny alley behind the row, then crawl back and forth between the ignition and the machine, usually while dripping hot wax onto his hand. When he felt the blank was ready to be cut, he would hand it to Andrew and proceed to wrestle out the next one while Andrew made the key and put back the finished bike.

It was a pretty good system when you thought about it, but most people who did such a job had at least room enough to stand up. Soon they would be finished with the first trailer, and would call Bryn on Paul's cell phone to see if the coast was clear for them to move on to the next.

"So what's your deal, old man?" Paul asked, wedging one of Andrew's freshly made keys into the ignition of a 1952 Panhead. "You got any kids running around anyplace, or grandkids for that matter?"

"Nope. My Coralie and I always tried, which they say is the most fun part about children, but it seemed like one of us just didn't have the right ammunition. Later on we thought about adopting, which was getting to be a big craze right about then, but it all started going south and we figured we wouldn't want to bring a child into a world where mommy and daddy were just yelling all the time."

Andrew wiped his brow for perhaps the millionth time that night. It was well into the wee hours of Saturday morning by now, but the metal trailer just held on to the heat and refused to let go. If he believed in those ridiculous cellular phones everyone had to have these days, he would probably have excused himself a while ago to try his wife once again. It wouldn't be like you saw in the movies, though. Usually, the man gets left and cleans up his act—quits the drinking and smoking, stops looking at girls too young for him to get without paying. In Andrew's case, however, that behavior had just gotten worse in the past few years. He went through a 1.75 liter bottle of Lord Calvert twice a week, and that was just what he drank when he finally made it home for the night.

"I think I'd better just face the facts, young fella. There's never going to be any grandkids for this has-been. I'll just be happy to die in bed with some beautiful young thing, staring up at some firm tits. How about you? You don't have it so great either, I bet." As always, he felt the need to be vulgar and offended whenever someone asked about how he felt.

Paul thought of Shelby, and how she must be dreaming of sitting in a magic bathtub in some faraway land right about now, watching fluffy marshmallow clouds roll through a perfect blue sky, while mommy's little friend stayed over for the evening. All that would be waiting for him when he got back, though, and right now he needed to keep his mind on his work.

Paul got Bryn out of bed with a call to her cell phone and asked her to come check if the coast was clear outside of the first trailer. She didn't seem too overjoyed about being woke up at 3 a.m., but was glad to see everything was going right on schedule. They shared coffee and a sandwich outside the trailer as Paul tasted the cool night air. All around him the town was still going strong, and the rumble of motorcycles seemed as steady now as it had been at noon the previous day.

Even in her pajama bottoms and tank top, Bryn was still very much a spectacular looking young woman, a fact which both motorcycle thieves realized at the same time. Her hair was tied back into a pony tail, but even that was sexy. Maybe it was because Andrew hadn't been to the gentleman's club in so long due to preparing for the job, and maybe Paul had been feeling sick to his stomach every time he reached out to touch his cheating wife. Andrew decided then and there that as soon as Tuesday was through, he was headed straight to the Twin Cities for a night at the jiggly room, en route to warmer, drier weather for the rest of his days. Paul just thought of how he might just ask Bryn to ride off into the sunset with him when he saw her again that Tuesday.

"Seems like everything is going all right behind the scenes," she said, looking both ways for people and finding none. "I called my girlfriends, and they just rode in tonight. They seem to know just what to say and when to say it, so I'm not worried."

"And the money?" Andrew asked, still not fully trusting this kid.

"The courier called me a couple hours ago from Bombay. He's been a trusted friend of my family for many years, and there's no way he would ever double cross me, so don't get any ideas, all right?"

Andrew, who considered himself one of the great scam artists of all time, had been spending a lot of his free time in the hotbox thinking about how this little lady could end up screwing him over. Now he felt the need to share some of that knowledge.

"Sure, but what's saying you two don't just run off together to your tropical island and leave Paul and me standing there by a big lake with a lot of stolen wheels?"

"You've just got to trust me, I guess," Bryn said, smiling. "If not, keep in mind that I do still have some tapes of you and a certain money launderer talking on the phone, and some papers the department of the treasury would love to get their hands on."

"Seems to me I'll be going to jail either way, sweetie, so why am I in there sweating my ass off?" Andrew began to raise his voice now; since he had carefully practiced what he was going to say for the past several hours he was confident he could get the upper hand.

"I won't be out of your sight, you dumb old fuck, so how could I get away from you? I'll be riding with Jorge right along with you guys, calling and making arrangements for these last 50 bikes the whole way. If I magically vanish into thin air, then you can worry, but until then, just do your job and let me do mine. I'll be right there at the docks Tuesday morning with you to collect my share of the money."

Andrew liked this part of the plan, and no, he didn't plan on letting this young lady out of his sight. If so, he would just dump his stolen goods, buy a new Cadillac somewhere along the line, and take his chances on the open roads of America.

"Look, Andrew. Everything will be all finalized by the time we all get to Two Harbors Tuesday morning, but not until then. After that, all of you get what's coming to you and you deliver your 'cycles to where I say. Some get on another boat, and some might get rode a thousand miles back the way you came. It's all still being worked out."

"Why don't you let a man make the business deals and you can get in that trailer and sweat for a few hours?" he asked. Andrew's fears were slowly going away, but he never gave up on an argument that easily.

"Apparently the man can't make business deals too well," she said, calmer now, "because he let some little bitch catch him in all his dirty dealings, didn't he?"

Andrew threw up his hands and stormed over to the second trailer. At this point, he was enjoying the fresh air but wanted to be as far away from Bryn Scott as possible. It wasn't because he couldn't stand her—quite the opposite, actually—it was because she was just like any other woman in the world who knew just how to get under your skin.

Plus, she was right about what she could do to him and he knew it well.

"You trust me, don't you, Paulie?"

"Don't have much choice, do I?" Paul said.

Bryn liked the sound of that. There was nothing better than a man who knew his place.

"So you're right there with us out on the road the whole time? And we all get paid when we get to Two Harbors?"

"Would I lie to you, Paulie?"

"I guess we'll find out." He polished off his drink, took his last deep breath of fresh air for the next few hours, then turned away from her. Over his shoulder, he said, "Just don't fuck me, Bryn. I mean it."

The second trailer would be the most difficult, even though the pair had nearly mastered the technique of key making by now. Most of the bikes in this trailer were custom jobs, some so new they'd never been ridden, by big name chopper makers from California. With newer Harleys came not only more reliability and a smoother ride, but one thing that would prove to be difficult for an old thief like Paul Morris. Ignition systems had come a long way in the past few years, and these would not be easy. Many were double tumbler setups, which Paul had always had trouble with. The key blanks broke easier when trying to push in tumblers on either side, which meant fishing the broken piece out with a dentist pick and using up valuable time.

By the time Paul and Andrew stopped for lunch and a number two break at noon on Saturday, the sound of the crowd was deafening, even inside the trailer. This didn't help in a process where hearing each piece of the lock click together was essential, and 23 cycles had yet to be attended to. Bryn told Paul that everything seemed to be working as planned in the Junior department, since she hadn't seen him since he'd left with Jorge the night before. Paul snickered to himself when he thought about his old buddies and what they could do to humiliate such a high standing member of society as Junior Devane. Between the drugs, the booze, and the wild women who seemed to follow the Gearheads around, Junior wouldn't know what hit him.

"Well," Bryn told them as they sat down in the deck chairs behind the tent, "one of the Gearheads passed through about an hour ago, and even though he was still pretty drunk from last night, he managed to mumble something to the effect that they found the rich guy we were talking about, and showed him one hell of a time."

Bryn was happy, not just about being free from Junior, but about the way this whole thing was going. No one could ever say that she wasn't capable of something big after she had organized such a perfect plan. Someday, she might even tell her grandchildren about how granny had outsmarted just about every man she could find.

"This guy said they slipped some kind of drug into Junior's drink, and just like that he was dancing on the table, naked as the day he was born. They took him in back with two hookers, one Mexican and the other black, and made a porn video that I'm sure Junior's old man would just love to see. I asked them to make copies for the Devane's country club buddies and Channel 8 News too."

Paul leaned back and laughed. Even though he didn't know the black sheep of the Devane family, he came in contact with people just like that every day of his life. Preppy morons who had everything handed to them their entire lives loved poking fun at the man behind the lunch counter, and Paul saw this as a blow for blue collar workers the world over.

"I wonder what happened to Jorge, though," Andrew said. "He was supposed to check in by now, wasn't he?"

"He's probably holding Junior's head out of the toilet right about now," Bryn said. "I'm sure he had a few drinks himself, and enjoyed watching the show Junior was putting on. He'll be along soon enough, right after he makes sure Junior won't be able to leave his motor home until you guys are through with those trailers."

"Twenty-three to go," Paul reported happily. It was amazing what a thousand dollars worth of locksmith tools could do. "I don't foresee a problem with us getting done at least an hour earlier than expected."

Bryn walked to the large cooler, checking inside the tent for potential buyers, then returned with three bottles of beer and a small portable television. Biggest motorcycle rally in the world or not, she simply would not miss Judge Judy. The three partners in crime sipped Bud Light in the shade, taking a much-deserved rest. Although the job was nowhere near done, things were going smoothly, which hardly ever happened for any of them.

"Turn the news channel on," Andrew said. "Maybe our buddy will be on."

More than four hundred thousand visitors, the anchorman estimated, had visited the tiny city of Sturgis, South Dakota, over the past few days, and as the rally wound down for another year, some folks just weren't taking the hint to head home.

"*A fistfight involving more than two dozen rally-goers broke out last night at the Full Throttle, resulting in five bikers being taken to the hospital*," the anchor said. "*Police used tear gas in one area of the bar, and this exclusive amateur video shows just the kind of destruction that one rally goer was capable of.*"

A shaky video panned across the crowd, picking up the yelling of one table full of bikers Paul immediately recognized. There was Charger, breaking a pool cue across a stranger's back, and another Gearhead kicked away at a fat man's sides as he lay on the floor. Paul smiled, remembering just how rowdy his friends could get, but he soon stopped smiling.

Simultaneously, Andrew, Bryn, and Paul all dropped their beers as they watched the tiny television. Dancing atop the table was none other than Jorge Zapate, who appeared more filled with drugs than anyone they had ever seen. As one officer approached, Jorge picked up a chair and broke it over the woman's head. The video showed him kicking two more police in the face before he was dragged off the table by his ankles and handcuffed. They watched in silence as the anchor continued.

"Police arrested four men in connection with the incident, including the man shown here, thirty-one-year-old Jorge Cabande Zapate. Zapate, who is being held in the Sturgis detention facility, has been charged with possession of cocaine, first degree assault, resisting arrest, soliciting prostitution, and instigating a riot. And, upon this morning's search of Zapate's tent, Channel Four has learned that an additional charge of possession of child pornography has been added. Officers allegedly pulled a three-ring binder from the man's tent earlier today containing images of children in compromising sexual positions, some believed to be as young as four. A video was also allegedly found in Zapate's possession portraying prostitutes involved in sexual acts."

Andrew could say nothing. He just stared at the television. So did Bryn.

"Oh my dear God," Paul finally managed. "They drugged the wrong guy."

When the channel played the video the second time, Paul noticed that Jorge had been wearing a Midwest Custom Cycles jacket, and as he was pulled by his ankles closer to the camera, he read "JUNIOR" on the front.

"But how…" was all Andrew could say.

Bryn added, "Then where's…"

Paul felt a hand on his shoulder and froze, knowing exactly who it was.

-2-

"Stinky! Stinky! Everybody calls him Mistuw Stinkeeee!"

Samantha laughed, but only because she thought she must. Beside her, the ticket to a new life piloted their rental car south on I-94, and she could tell the driver was becoming more and more annoyed with her daughter's singing with each passing mile.

"Does she *really* have to keep calling me that?" he asked, leaning in toward Samantha. "It's driving me fucking nuts, you know."

Samantha turned over her shoulder and gave that stern mom look to Shelby, who was now happily enjoying her third package of fruit snacks that morning. The child just smiled, gobbling down a blue stegosaurus and following it up with a red pterodactyl. She knew very little about their unexpected vacation, only that she had spent last night sleeping on a stranger's couch, her stuffed animals were all back home because mommy wouldn't let her bring anything more than a change of clothes, and the man her mother was with, who insisted she call him Uncle Stinky, was now getting angry at her for doing just that. She had gotten yelled at already for asking too many questions, which had gone something like this: "Mommeee! Where's daddy?"

"He had to go away for awhile, so the two of us and Uncle Stinky are going on our vacation this year."

"When is he coming back?"

"Soon, sweetie."

"But where did he go?"

"Away, I said. Eat your fruit snacks."

"Can I have Larry the tyrasonosaurus?"

"No. He had to stay and guard the apartment. I told you that."

"But where are we goeen?"

For the tenth time, Samantha had explained that the three of them, under daddy's strict orders, of course, had to take the family vacation without him this year, all the way to sunny Miami, Florida. They would walk on the beach, visit Mickey Mouse, of course, and play in the ocean until daddy came home and they would join him. Samantha hadn't yet figured out a way to tell the girl that there would be no more daddy, just a couple of women off on their own who would likely be changing names as soon as they got to where they were going. Sure, the questions about her father would linger for some time. That would be the toughest part of it all, but in the end she was young enough that Shelby would forget all about Paul Morris. They would have everything they'd ever dreamed of—Samantha could go back to college and finally make something of herself, Shelby would attend the finest schools in the finest neighborhoods, and all three of them would mingle with the rich and powerful.

Oh, how Samantha hated being poor. She came from a middle-class family who couldn't give her a dime for anything and had married into a partnership with a sandwich salesman. He drove a Taurus, didn't work out like he used to, and was often too tired from work to even make love to her anymore. That was all changing now, though. Samantha Morris was truly happy for the first time in years, with just one little girl standing in her way.

"Us girls need a potty break, honey," she told Stinky. Then she leaned in closer, putting her head on his shoulder. "I'm sorry about the name thing, babe, but we don't want her learning too much about you until we get everything changed over, right? If the police ever tracked us down, this way she won't know anything about who we used to be. In a few years, she won't remember any of this anymore."

The Buick pulled into a Stop-N-Fill station just outside of the Tennessee state line, where the driver gassed up and Samantha unbuckled Shelby from her seatbelt. Her blood was absolutely boiling now, but she knew she mustn't show that in front of their new daddy. She just calmly helped her daughter out of the car, held her little hand until they were out of sight, then pushed her into the women's bathroom.

"Go in the stall, honey. I'll wait right here."

It sometimes worked, but not today. Whenever Shelby spilled her milk on Samantha's night school homework, broke a lamp, or threw a fit in the toy store, Samantha would step back, take a few deep breaths, and calm herself before she even moved. She herself had come from a household where children who spoke when not spoken to or, Heaven forbid, acted up in a public place, would get an open hand slap right across the face. Her mother hadn't cared if there was one person or a hundred standing there—she would show her authority whenever and wherever it was questioned. Over time, through years of bruises and the makeup that covered them, Samantha had gone from hating her mother to actually respecting her for working to raise her so well. And now she found herself on the opposite end of this situation, with a daughter who was jabbering and singing away and fucking up the good life Samantha was trying to build for them.

As Shelby tinkled, Samantha stepped over to the smeared mirror and splashed cold water on her face. There she was, pushing 30 years old, and she had not yet made a name for herself. By the time her Aunt Jean, Samantha's hero, was 21, she was already married to the second richest computer distributor in California. Jean had sent photos of the famous people she met and the decorations at the lavish parties she threw in her 4,500 square foot mansion. Samantha had saved them all, and while she battled with her mother, battled with bullemia, and even when she settled down in that shitty apartment, she pulled out that little box at least once a week and dreamed of how life should be.

And now, imagine her luck at meeting a powerful man who not only respected her beauty, but wanted to take her away from all of that and give her what Aunt Jean had always told her she deserved. But at night when she couldn't sleep and was thinking of her escape, she couldn't help but wonder what "Uncle Stinky" was really interested in. He and his wife were unable to have children, and it seemed like he had only begun hitting on Samantha so much after she ran out of time to take Shelby to the babysitter one night and was forced to bring Shelby to night school with her.

In the mirror, she saw her mascara streaking and her eyes getting puffy. Tears could not have come at a worse time, but she couldn't help it. Once again in her life, the man chasing her was only after one thing. Only this time, it wasn't her pussy—it was her daughter. Stinky had fallen in love with Shelby the first time he'd seen her, and had even brought gifts to class in the hopes that Samantha would once again forget the babysitter. He had money. He had power and recognition in society, and that meant he could get any woman he wanted.

"But what really matters is the child, Samantha," her reflection, with her red eyes and evil smirk, told her.

It was inside her head, *really* inside there, and that little voice had been yelling all her life. Putting her down. Calling her a fat cow no one would ever love. Calling her a stupid blonde whose opinions no man would ever care about. Shelby yelled that she was done and ready for mommy's assistance in cleaning up, but Samantha didn't hear her. All she heard was that voice, that awful, awful voice that kept pounding at her temples day and night.

She looked at her reflection again, only this time it wasn't Samantha Morris she saw. It was her mother, who had months ago taken the mighty dirt nap but was still tormenting her from beyond the grave.

"Look at you, Samantha," she said with her cold, dead eyes that had always been cold—even when she was still alive. "Look at you, dear. What are you doing in this place, anyhow? Little girls like you—little whores who go off and get themselves in trouble before the wedding day—you don't deserve any of this. That man out there loves you for your daughter, Samantha, and that's all. He can find a little whore like you anywhere, so why would he go after you?"

"Shut up, for Jesus' sake, shut up!" Samantha yelled, clutching the sides of her head and striking the mirror with her fist. "Just die, you old bitch! Why don't you just *die* already?"

"Just stand there and look at yourself, Samantha. What makes you think you deserve someone like him, with his money and his charms? You deserve exactly what you have, that good-for-nothing restaurant man who keeps you living in poverty and makes you work all the time."

Samantha covered her head, and shielded her eyes from that terrible reflection. When she looked again, the old woman was gone, replaced with a thirty-something mother with smeared makeup and red eyes. She got closer to the mirror, thankful the old woman was finally gone, and began to fix herself up. Then, without any warning, her mother was back again.

"I almost forgot, Samantha. You're getting a bit lumpy again, aren't you? What was it that the children used to call you? Sam, Sam, the Big Fat Ham. Yes, that's what it was, wasn't it?"

Samantha pounded the mirror now with her fists, and could hear Shelby crying in the stall. All that she cared about now was making that horrible old woman go away.

"Sam, Sam, the Big Fat Ham! Eat some Spam!"

"Shut up, for the love of God, all of you shut the fuck up!"

"Strawberry jam, eat a rack of lamb…"

"Please, Mom. Please just die and leave me alone. I'm trying as hard as I can."

"It's not hard enough, Samantha. Sam, Sam, the Big Fat *HAAAAAAM*!"

Two things happened after that. First, Samantha's hand shattered the mirror, sending her mother's taunting voice back to the pine box where it belonged. Then, for the first time in six years, Samantha Morris broke her promise to everyone. Back in the days when she was fighting to be skinny, turning down all those college beers and food service goodies, eating 10 calories worth of pickles and feeling so guilty she had to throw them right back up, Samantha had made a promise. She promised Paul, promised her parents who called the infirmary when she was checked in, and she promised herself that there would be no more of this eating disorder nonsense. Her mother said it was nothing more than a weakness, and women could not afford to show their weaknesses in a man's world if they ever expected any recognition. But on this day, Samantha Morris's weakness was showing brighter than ever.

She rushed into the stall beside Shelby's, lifted the seat, stuck that familiar pointer finger down her throat, and vomited the contents of her stomach into the toilet. It felt terrible to be right back where she had been before, but there was also a feeling of control there. Like if she kept on doing this for long enough, she would finally earn her mother's acceptance and be as skinny and beautiful as the other girls. As she watched the brownish puke swirl its way down the drain, Samantha was feeling good about herself again. She was in control of her life now, including what she ate, who she went with, and why she was getting such a break. It wasn't her daughter, it was the talented, pretty, skinny girl who now looked back at her in the mirror.

"Mommee! I'm done now. Are you arwight?"

Yes, little one. Samantha was doing just fine. She opened the stall door, finished the remainder of the job that Shelby hadn't yet learned to do for herself, then helped her daughter wash her hands in front of the broken mirror.

"What happened?" Shelby asked, trying to touch the broken glass.

Samantha pulled her hand away. "Nothing, baby. Mommy just had a little accident, like when you broke the lamp the other day, remember?"

Yes, Shelby nodded that she did remember. She pulled Samantha over to the next mirror, this one just dirty and not yet broken.

"Look," she said, pointing at Samantha's reflection. "We're both pretty girls, aren't we, Mommy?"

Though she didn't want to look, Samantha did. In her daughter she saw her eyes, her hair, and Paul's nose. But New Daddy could spring for a nose job someday if need be. How could anyone not love this little girl, with her freckles and a blue smear from the fruit snacks drooping down from the corner of her mouth. Shelby was a beautiful child, the kind who old women she didn't even know would give quarters to on the street. They lived in a world that rewarded beauty above all else. It was still a man's world, even today, and in a man's world, beauty was one of the few useful tools women possessed. Samantha stood there with her arm around Shelby's shoulder, but couldn't help wondering if her daughter was more beautiful than she had been at that age.

"Of course she is." The old woman's face appeared again, standing behind them and looking at Shelby. In the mirror, the old woman ran her fingers through Shelby's hair, the way Samantha always wished her mother would have done to her. "Be honest with yourself, Samantha, this little girl is prettier than you'll ever be. That's why the man in that car out there wouldn't care if you *ever* came back, as long as he got to take pretty little Shelby with him. That's all he wants, anyhow."

Samantha began to cry, and covered her face with her hands again.

"Mommy? What's—"

Shelby didn't have the opportunity to finish, since she was now being picked up by her hair. Samantha's head was swimming with her mother's years of insults, teasing, and abuse, and now she was choosing Shelby over her own daughter! All those words thrashed around inside her skull as she slapped her daughter as hard as she could, causing a surprised scream to escape the child. Shelby didn't cry, she was too afraid.

"You are not prettier than your mother, young lady, so just get that idea out of your little fucking head!" Samantha yelled in Shelby's ear, reaching over to turn on the hot water. Steam rose from the sink, coating the mirror but not enough so Samantha couldn't see the old woman staring at her again. She thrust Shelby's hand under the faucet and it immediately scaled the child, causing her to scream in pain and fear.

"We'll just see how pretty you are when we burn that cute little face of yours, won't we?"

"Momeeee! No, Momeee! I'm sowwee!"

As the child kicked and struggled, Samantha drew her face closer to the boiling hot water until the steam was burning Shelby's eyes. She looked up at her mother through the steam and her own tears, wondering what she had done so wrong this time. Normally it was just a swat on the behind, but now Shelby thought she must have really made a mess of things.

Outside, the horn on the Buick sounded. Samantha stopped just as the water was nearing Shelby's nose, took a deep breath, and turned off the faucet.

"I want my daddeee!"

She threw Shelby hard against the door of one stall, then kneeled down in front of her and shook her shoulders hard.

"Listen to me, Shelby."

The little girl howled, fighting furiously to figure out what she had done wrong.

"Shelby! Quit your crying and listen to me. That man out there is a hundred times the man your father is. He's going to be your new daddy now and there's nothing you can do about it, do you hear me?"

This reminded Samantha of how her mother had shaken her twenty years ago, desperately trying to pound into her head that good, skinny, pretty girls are the only ones who belonged in her family.

"Shelby, this is not a choice for you here. You will be good and keep your mouth shut for the rest of this trip or I'm going to leave you by the side of the road somewhere. I swear to God I will."

The little girl had finished screaming now, and the tears had slowed to a trickle. If it was possible, and Shelby hadn't thought it was until now, she was too terrified to cry.

Samantha cleaned her face up, wiped off Shelby's, then the two Morris women strolled back out to the car. At first Shelby fought her mother's grasp when she picked her up, but then decided she was in enough trouble already. She was too embarrassed and scared to say anything, but she had wet herself too.

As soon as they were back on the road, Samantha insisted that the group stop for the night at the first available motel. She paid the $34 at the desk, wrapped Shelby up in a blanket on the couch in the second room of the suite, and gave her a little shake while she reminded the child of their agreement. Yes, it was only 6 p.m., but when mommy said it was bedtime, she damn well meant it. After all, Samantha Morris, and not Shelby Morris, was running the game here.

As soon as she could get through the door, she threw "Uncle Stinky" on the bed, then turned to lock their room just in case.

"I'll show you what big girls are good for," she said, too softly for him to hear.

The first time she cheated on her husband, it was awkward to say the least. They just kissed for the longest time, since Samantha hadn't gotten nearly enough kissing lately. Then, it was as gentle as her first time had been. She slowly stripped for him and he did the same, their eyes locked on each other's. That was months ago, and things had been nice and slow since then.

But tonight, with Paul Morris as far from her mind as possible, Samantha was going to show her new husband why he should keep her around. Even though she could hear Shelby sobbing through the paper thin walls, she unbuckled his pants and nearly ripped them off before he could say anything, and soon he was in her mouth. This was something he had been bothering her to do since the start, but she'd never had the guts to try it with any man.

She worked her way through it just like she'd seen in the videos Paul liked to rent, and apparently Samantha was doing something right because Stinky looked like he'd never had such a fun time in his life. After a few minutes of this, when she knew he could take no more, she threw him down and climbed on top of him, sliding him inside just in time for him to explode. Whether he was done or not, she rode him hard, and for the first time ever she didn't mind yelling out while doing it.

"You hear that, Shelby?" she yelled at the door, pumping him and feeling herself ready to come. "This is why mommy needs to stick around!"

After her body shook and she collapsed on top of him, she curled up in his arms and listened for the voices again. Nothing. No mother. No husband. The only voice in the room was the one too low for her to hear, because the speaker was almost too scared to breathe. It was the sound of Shelby Morris praying.

Shelby listened to the sounds of the stranger with her mother, unsure if he was hurting her or not but too terrified to ask. She had found that under her blanket, without any stuffed animals to keep her safe, the tears wouldn't come out anymore. There had just been too many of them today and no more could be found.

"Please, God," she whispered. "Make mommy not be mad at me anymow. I'm sowwy for what I did. I want mommy and daddy and me to be togethuw again. I don't like Uncle Stinky anymow."

And her last request before going to sleep was one that made her father's heart hurt nearly two thousand miles away.

"And please, God, let my daddy find me. I want to go with him now."

Chapter Eleven

Little did Shelby Morris know, her father was having his own difficulties right about then.

With a handful of 'cycles still left in the trailers, not to mention those in the tent, the surprise visit from Junior Devane couldn't have come at a worse time. So many things flashed through Paul's mind as he sat there staring ahead, feeling the evil smile from the man behind him—for starters, he thought about how it had felt the first time he was caught by his father on that gravel road in the middle of the night. That sinking feeling in the pit of his stomach, the sting of his father's belt, and later on the regret that he had let such a thing happen to him. From that day forward, he had promised himself he'd never get caught, and managed to keep that promise pretty well until now.

"I presume these are yours, then," Junior said, working his way around to face Paul. He dropped a handful of wax key blanks onto his lap. "Wow, pal. Grand theft auto times, oh, I'd say about a hundred. Any way you look at it, I think you're fucked."

Paul just stared at his feet. Andrew tried to speak, but for once in his life could not. Finally, the shock began to wear off for Bryn, who was also studying her feet closely, and the tears began to flow. After all that planning, all that preparation and risk, it was all about to be taken away by the one man she never expected would have the brains to figure it out.

"How?" Andrew asked finally. "Before you do whatever it is you're planning on doing to us, I just want to know how."

Ah, how the sun was shining bright on the black sheep of the Devane family this afternoon! Junior planned on using all the drama he could come up with to tell how he singlehandedly had outwitted his sister-in-law at last.

"For the longest time, I knew damn well she was up to something," Junior said, pacing back and forth in between the group like the prosecutor about to close his case. "This chick had absolutely no ambition to do anything for as long as I've known her, and then, boom! She just one day gets a wild hair to take all of her husband's 'cycles on a thousand mile road trip just for the hell of it? I don't think so, Brinnie."

Bryn lifted her head finally and glared at the little weasel. He almost could have passed for anyone else at the rally now, with his Sturgis 2003 T-shirt, blue jeans, leather boots, and his greasy hair pulled back into a ponytail. Of all the scams and all the money she had conned out of men in her life, never would she have expected someone who was such an alcoholic, pathetic loser to finally take her down.

Bye bye, tropical island.

"So anyhow," Junior continued, "my brother started getting a little suspicious too, so he sent me along to keep an eye on things. At the start, we figured Jorge would be enough of a watchdog, but my family never puts too much trust in a darkie."

"Just get on with it," Bryn said, wiping her eyes.

"Right. We got out here and I kept my eye on things, but nothing happened. Then, when I went to get a bite to eat with Jorge, something just connected in my head."

"First time for everything," Bryn said. "Maybe it was women's intuition."

"That's cute, sweetie. Remember that one when you're getting your cooter licked by some dike in the big house."

Bryn just stared, anxious to get this over with. She was going down, but not easily.

"So Jorge and I are heading out for some supper when he seems like he's acting all funny. He keeps on looking over his shoulder like somebody's following us or something. I figured you guys were up to something, so I made sure we stopped back at my motor home so I could change clothes. It was…I don't know, just a feeling I had, like somebody was after me. Since he didn't know how to pack for this trip, the dumb ass didn't even bring a coat, so I insisted he wear mine. So we're sitting in this bar, and I noticed there were about a dozen bikers who were staring at us a little too much for their own good, right? And when the waitress came over with our beers, they really started staring."

Paul shook his head slowly. All this time, everyone who had doubted the Gearheads had been right about how well they would handle the job.

"I sent Jorge over to the bar to get me an ashtray, and got a good look at his beer. There was some kind of purplish tint to it, not enough to really notice, but I was already suspicious that something was going on so I slipped a little of my own medicine into it. All of a sudden, these guys started looking at me like I was their best buddy, and they just glared at the little foreign guy with 'Junior' on his jacket. We drank up, had one more, and before I knew it ol' Jorge was taking a walk on the wild side. He ended up getting drugged twice."

Andrew thought about the situation, and he too would never have expected such a young punk to be so perceptive.

"So, for all the Gearheads know, they've got the right guy," Andrew said.

Junior continued pacing as he tossed his cellular phone from hand to hand, using it as a pointer for emphasis. He had taken the liberty of looking up the Sturgis Police Department's number before heading over here, and it was right there on speed dial, ready as soon as he needed it. There was nothing they could do to him here; there were at least a thousand people mingling around no more than twenty feet away, and he could run like mad if need be.

"Grand theft auto." He pointed the phone at Paul. "Some more grand theft auto," he said, pointing at Andrew. "And, the kicker, conspiracy to commit a felony and defrauding an individual of lots and lots of money." He stared across the phone at Bryn.

Paul wanted to get up, run as fast as he could to that storage locker, and try to blend in with the rest of the bikers until he was as far away from here as he could get. He grasped the arms of his chair and prepared for a moment when Junior's attention was elsewhere. Unfortunately, he wouldn't get that chance.

"Paul James Morris, born 1976, with lots of questioning about lots of stolen motorcycles, and a great bunch of folks still wanting to track him down." Junior turned back to Paul, pointing again. "Tell me, my friend, am I pretty close here?"

Paul sat back down, suddenly exhausted.

Andrew leaned back his head and stared at the clouds. All those years of work, and he would likely live out the remainder of his days in the state pen. Either the government or his ex-wife would get what little money he had saved, and if he ever did make parole while he was still vertical, there wouldn't be anything for him to look forward to on the outside.

"And as for you, Andrew Fitzgerald Falkness, sole proprietor of one Faltech Software, which has been subject to seven…no, eight federal investigations in the past decade. I hear you like to launder dirty money with your buddies overseas and steal computer programs from honest, hard-working geeks the world over. Currently facing indictment for—"

"How did…"

Junior was now in the final act of his show, and it was time for the grand finale. He reached inside his jacket and produced Bryn's handbag. While she had gone to fetch sandwiches for her crew, he had just picked it up from behind the cash register and found all sorts of interesting papers inside.

"You *fuck*," was all Bryn could manage. She was suddenly very tired too.

"The way I see it, lady and gentlemen, we have ourselves a bit of a situation here. I could call the police; I've even got them on speed dial ready to go, but I think there's something else I'd rather do."

Just get on with it, all three future prison inmates thought in unison.

"I think jail would be too good for someone trying to steal from the Devane family. I'd rather just call my brother up, give him some information from this little bag here, and let the chips fall where they may. I'll be a hero either way, so why not? Malcolm knows some awfully talented people who could tie you down and keep you just alive enough to experience the worst pain in the world for a good week or more. Then they could give you over to the cops, I guess."

Junior began dialing his phone as all three gang members thought furiously of a way to stop him. Just whacking him on the head with a two-by-four was out of the question, since there were too many people around. Plus, they were already in enough trouble with the law.

"It's ringing," Junior said, enjoying the suspense terribly. He was in control now, the way it was always meant to be.

Bryn jumped from her seat, snatched the phone from his hand, and pressed "end call."

"You have three seconds to give me that phone before I walk to the nearest cop. One— "

"Please, Junior. I'll do anything you want me to, just don't tell Malcolm that— "

"Two, Bryn. That's two."

"You don't know what it's like in that house." The tears now fell like rain as she sobbed, though she hated showing her weak side to this greaseball even more than she would hate jail.

"Whining don't work, Bryn. And that's three."

Junior walked past the tent and up the sidewalk, leaving all three of them just standing there, feeling like their feet were planted firmly in cement. Then, much to her surprise, the answer came to her.

"Do you like Jorge, Junior?" she called to him. "Do you like that little foreigner?"

He smiled, turned, and walked back to them.

"Why are you wasting my time with this, sweetheart? You know I can't stand that little bastard."

Bryn smiled, too. Finally, she had thought of a way to get the upper hand.

"It's funny you should call him that. But the fact is that he *does* have a daddy, and I'm sure you know the guy too."

"So?"

"So, why do you think ol' Jorge has been around the house for so long, and why do you think your parents always trusted a foreigner when they were probably part of the founding fathers of the goddam KKK?"

"How should I know? And what has this got to do with you and your little criminal buddies?"

"Wow, you really are as stupid as they say you are. For Christ's sake, Junior. Jorge has been around your house all these years and he's such a trusted friend of the family because he's your *brother*. Your daddy's wayward dick got him in some trouble awhile back, and— "

Junior turned again, not believing her. Never would someone with the stature and history of the Devanes have anything to do with a woman of another color. Their family history was white, gleaming, perfect white, and it always had been. It had taken only one warning from his father that if any son of his ever brought home the wrong colored wife, they would be immediately disowned.

"You lie…" he said, faltering and getting frustrated at himself for doing so. "You lie just to buy yourself some time. Well, it won't work, Bryn."

"Oh, I'm not lying. My husband may not have trusted me with a lot, but one night when we got drunk on wine and started telling secrets, he told me the whole story. Your dad felt guilty and brought Jorge up here to live a better life, but ended up treating him like shit and keeping him poor. They threatened to have his family back home killed if he ever said anything, and when they died off anyhow, the patriarch of the Devane family got really nervous. He started putting Jorge in a position where he could be respected and live a decent life, but vowed that he'd be tortured and killed if he ever told anyone about who his father really was. Just think about it, Junior. Think about all those business contacts your family has with all those old world, racist assholes just like you are. Just think of what a few phone calls and a blood test could do to your family. And that would all be because of you, wouldn't it? All because of the black sheep in the Devane family screwing things up once again. And what about the social circle? The family would be ruined, wouldn't they? And who would they blame, Junior?"

He felt like a championship boxer had just gone ten rounds with him. Junior clutched his chest and struggled to breathe. Could this be true? Why else would his family give their kindness to such an outsider? Once again, he had gone from being on top of the heap to tumbling toward the bottom.

"And what about you, Bryn?" he said, down but not out. "Malcolm would divorce you in a heartbeat, and his friends would find you too."

"Oh, I assure you, Junior, I have plans for after this job so that no one will ever find me. And what then? Go after my family? I don't have anyone left but myself, asshole. And as for Malcolm and his divorce, I couldn't care less. I signed his precious papers before we were married and I know I wouldn't get a cent of his money. But I've been keeping a little savings account that's waiting for me to claim it. You'd be surprised how fast I can fuck up your life, then vanish like a fart in the wind."

Paul and Andrew had strolled over now, becoming more confident of their team leader with each word out of her mouth. From the beginning, she had known just how to tackle every obstacle, and this unexpected turn of events was nothing for her. Paul thought of Bryn as an amazing woman, the kind he wished he had met long before his wife came along. This was even more true now, since at that moment his wife had another man's cock in her mouth and was well on her way to a new life in Florida.

"Better listen to her, Sparky," Andrew said, smiling again.

"Yup, we've got this all planned out and we can take you down with us," added Paul.

Junior Devane weighed his options. He could take his chances and call his brother, but it was clear that Bryn had all the bases covered here. Sure, they would all be hunted down eventually, but the shockwave that such a bit of news would have on his parents' lives would last long after they were all dead. So what should he do now?

When in doubt, punt.

"So what are you going to give me here?" Junior asked. "Money? I don't need any of your money, folks; I've got plenty of my own."

"Not if you're cut off," Bryn said, pouring a tablespoon full of salt on the wound.

"So what's keeping me from reaching out and touching someone about all of this?"

It was Paul's turn to help. "When all this is over, Junior, the truth is that your family won't have a whole lot less money than they did to begin with. All we're doing here is bankrupting Malcolm, then making him look like a loser in his father's eyes for screwing up the old man's dream business. Admit it, pal. You've always been jealous of Malcolm, haven't you? Wouldn't it be nice to have *him* be the black sheep for awhile?"

"Yeah, but all this is going to happen under my watch," Junior said. "Somebody's going to have to take the blame for this mess, and it sure isn't going to be me."

Now it was Andrew's turn. "That's why I've got a fabulous idea where you can look like a hero, your brother gets the shaft, and so does your other brother."

"Don't call him my brother, you old son-of-a-bitch!" Junior yelled. "Don't you dare call that dark bastard my brother again!"

"All right," Andrew said, holding out his palms. "Sorry. We can work this out so you're the hero, Malcolm is broke, and Jorge gets the blame. We get our money, you're the prize of the family, and everybody's happy."

But what if, Junior thought, *Jorge opens his mouth about his family history.*

Andrew read his mind. "Jorges'll be in jail for so long, you can pay some guy a couple packs of cigarettes a week to make his life a living hell if he says a word about whose kid he is. I'm sure there would be guys inside that jail just lining up for such a fun job—beating on a foreigner and getting paid for it. All the skinheads could butt rape him as a group activity."

This made Junior smile. Such a punishment was perfect for anyone who tried to defame his family.

Bryn couldn't say anything. She was glad her men had jumped in when they did, because her plan was non-existent after blowing the whistle on Jorge's family tree, and that wouldn't have been enough. But Jorge Zapate had been like a member of her family since day one, and she didn't want him to take the fall for all of this. Unfortunately, there weren't any other options.

Paul had grown to like the little man too, but he knew all too well that you had to let someone else take the fall from time to time if you wanted to live to steal another day. He imagined that if he were to get sent to prison, he would likely meet up with one or two of those fall guys from the old days. And they probably wouldn't give him too warm a reception either.

"So Jorge gets the blame and I'm the good guy, and all I have to do is look the other way?"

"Yup," Bryn said. "And as for your little secret, you'll just have to take our word that we'll never tell. Hell, we'll all be so far away from here in a week, you won't have to worry anyhow."

Junior weighed his options, but found he had none.

"How do the cops catch Jorge?"

"I've got some friends here who are planning on telling the police a nice story right after we're gone," Bryn said. "I just tell them to say that same guy who was on the news was the one they saw hot wiring bikes in the alley, and they recognized him riding in one of our trucks stealing all those Harleys too. The police already think he's a criminal, and a pedophile besides. They won't think twice about throwing the book at him. And don't feel bad either. It's not like he has any family to go home to, right?"

As unbelievable as it was, the members of the Bryn Scott Gang, along with their newest partner, began to laugh. It was the laugh of the evil genius in those old movies, where he knew he had the good guy by the balls. But when you thought about it, all four of them were all evil in their own way. Maybe it was the tension between them, or the fact that they had all found a way to reach their goals, but they just stood there and snickered for a full minute before anyone spoke.

"So what do we do now?" Junior asked.

"I've got a job to finish, and we have to get the drivers on the road before eight," Paul said, looking at his watch. He couldn't believe how much time their little confrontation had wasted. "I need Andrew to stay and help me out, and Bryn has to watch the sale tent."

"Yeah, and Junior can help us out by bailing his little buddy out of jail," Bryn said. "He sure can't steal all these motorcycles while he's in there, now can he?"

And that was that. All four looked at one another again before going their separate ways. Paul and Andrew were going back in the hotbox, Bryn was going to try making a little extra cash off the rally goers, and Junior was on his way to the ATM for some bail money. If things went bad, they could each do some major damage to one another, which actually helped make up a good criminal gang.

They all had something to lose, and, more importantly, a lot to gain. Jorge, the poor Brazilian boy who had never asked to be sired by a rich man, would pay the price for all their sins, and not one of them seemed to mind at this point.

In fact, they were all still laughing.

-2-

By 7:30 p.m., Paul and Andrew were still fumbling around with the final ignition system, a 2002 V-Rod with more tumblers than Paul could ever have imagined. He thought technology was supposed to make things easier, but apparently that was not so for thieves. They had gone through at least a dozen blanks on this bike alone, and the truck drivers were knocking on the doors complaining about how they'd just as soon get on the road a little early.

But despite it all, neither man was nervous. The only real threat to their plan, besides themselves, had been neutralized.

"All right, I think this one will be it," Paul said, trying not to breathe while he slid the hot wax mold from the ignition. Andrew chipped away the chunks of wax from the tumblers with his tiny brush as Paul blew gently on the blank and slid it into the machine.

"This one's the one, kid," Andrew said, sweating up a storm. "I can feel it. Just one more and you and I get some time off. I'm about ready for a shower and one helluva nap."

Paul guided the metal arm of the machine across the peaks and valleys of the delicate wax model, so frustrated he was ready to scream but fighting to keep calm at the same time. The only thing that kept him in that trailer for most of this time, whenever he felt like just running away and admitting defeat, was the thought of himself and his daughter cruising down a country road in a new convertible. With the top down and her tiny bare feet on the dash, they would sing the songs he had learned as a child and enjoy the simple life away from the traffic, away from the shooting and the drugs; they would go to a place like the one where Paul had grown up.

"How's it going, Paul?" Andrew asked, also fighting to stay calm. Both men knew very well that the process of making another model if this one were to fail would push them well past the deadline, and complicate things further than they already were.

Paul removed the key from the machine, ground off the burs as delicately as possible under the circumstances, then quickly asked God for a bit of help. Fortunately, God was known for being able to hear more than one voice at a time, since he was presently listening to the plight of a terrified preschool-aged girl in a strange motel room in Tennessee. And just as his wife, who he had pledged to love through thick and thin, a pledge he was now beginning to reconsider, was informing his child of Shelby's insignificance in her plan for a better tomorrow, Paul felt a pain in his heart so intense he nearly snapped the metal key right in half. He didn't know at that moment what he was feeling, and simply dismissed it as fear and anticipation, since he had no idea his child and wife were not safely at home. Paul stopped, took his final deep breath of the stale, humid air inside the cramped trailer, and tried one last time to guide the new key into the V-Rod's ignition.

Lucky number thirteen was a perfect fit.

Paul cranked the motor on Harley's newest model, which he thought a bit too futuristic looking for its own good, surprising Andrew, and cracked the throttle repeatedly in excitement. The roar was deafening inside the tin box, and soon the exhaust fumes were too much for them. But Paul didn't care one bit. He was well on his way to a fortune and a simple life for himself and his daughter. With one more twist, taking the rpm gauge to the redline and nearly bursting his eardrums, he screamed with absolute joy and couldn't remember the last time he had done so. There were no marriage troubles now. No longer would he have to worry about money, or a college education for Shelby. Soon enough, there would be more than adequate cash for all of that.

Bryn opened the door and was flooded with smoke immediately, though she smiled triumphantly along with her partners.

"About damn time," one of the drivers mumbled, but Paul didn't care. They were a full 18 minutes ahead of schedule, which was more than enough in his book. Three-fourths of the job was now complete.

"Way to go, boys," Bryn said, clapping them each on the shoulder. "Let's get these bikes out of here and get you guys to bed for awhile. You look like you haven't slept in a couple days."

"That's because we haven't, smart ass," Andrew said.

"All right, have a nap. You've earned it. But I want you guys back here right after lunch tomorrow. I've got a little insurance plan for our buddy Junior I've been working on."

Paul asked if Junior had succeeded in getting Jorge out of jail yet.

"He called a few minutes ago. There's a bail of twenty-five thousand, which is a loss we're all going to have to share. I told him not to post it until as late as possible, probably tomorrow afternoon. That way, we'll get him out just in time to get him right back in."

"And just how are we going to work that out?" Andrew asked. "The guy's no dummy, that's for sure. If he sees Junior waiting outside the courthouse for him, he might get a little suspicious."

Bryn assured the men that all those details were being worked out extensively, since she was having an extremely boring evening watching fat, hairy bikers eye her breasts and the bikes in the sale tent. No one was buying, or hardly even asking any questions about the 'cycles. Most just wanted to gawk at all the chrome they couldn't afford. This dry spell had given her a chance to formulate a plan for the remainder of their trip. Though she hadn't quite ironed out all the details, Bryn assured Paul and Andrew that everything would be figured out when they came back the next day.

Though he needed a Manhattan more than just about anything, Andrew Falkness needed a hot shower and a good night's rest even more. He could no longer stay up until all hours of the night and run for weeks on end with little sleep. These days, he was usually snoozing by the time the 10 o'clock news team made it to the weather forecast, and he enjoyed sleeping until noon on the weekends.

Paul felt much the same way. The constant sweating and hours of breathing that stale air had taken its toll even on one of the youngest partners in the gang. As the trucks warmed up for their long journey, loaded down with a few dozen motorcycles and their brand new keys, the drivers stretched and each climbed into the passenger seat of a separate semi. Even though Paul would have loved taking his Harley out of the storage locker and riding up to Mount Rushmore or into Deadwood, he could barely keep his eyes open. Plus, there were strict orders from Bryn not to draw any attention to themselves by riding around. Yes, she was a woman and yes, she was half his size, but she had thus far proven herself worthy of his respect by the way she had handled things.

Paul and Andrew waved to the trucks after they were dropped off at their campground, watching until their hot, tin homes for the past two days disappeared over the hill. The sun was setting now, but there was no sign of anything slowing down in the campground. On their way out to their tents, the pair stopped and watched the constant parade of Sturgis rally goers, who rode back and forth along the gravel road. One man, rather than riding a cycle, had converted his bike into a large arm chair, complete with an end table and a seat way up high in the back for his girl, who was of course flashing her tits at whoever would look. They passed a group of young men holding up a homemade cardboard sign reading "PLEASE STOP FOR PHOTO" and they gladly posed with their arm around every topless woman who would oblige them. The local law enforcement kept a pretty tight leash on partiers in town, and handed out hundreds of tickets to both women and men who exposed themselves, but in the campgrounds, just about anything went. Even a handful of wrinkly, fat old men rode by naked, proud as hell to just be a part of it all.

There could have been ten million people in that little town, but it wouldn't have made either man any less exhausted. Andrew stripped down to his undershirt and boxers, gave serious consideration to a shower since he smelled terrible, then reconsidered. He would likely fall asleep under the warm water, crack his head, and force someone to call an ambulance. That wouldn't exactly be staying low key, now would it?

Instead, Andrew zipped up the door to his tent and produced his wallet from his pants pocket. Inside it was a photograph that had been nearly worn down to nothing, and if staring could deteriorate a picture, this one would have been confetti long ago. In it, he and Coralie stood in front of a 1972 Chevrolet, turquoise with matching interior. The car had been a gift from Andrew to his wife for Christmas that year, though it had given her nothing but problems from that point on. Come to think of it, so had Andrew.

Coralie was a nut for painting, and she had made her husband spend an incredibly boring Saturday afternoon sitting behind the wheel of that thing while she immortalized him on canvas. She had left the painting when she left him, and he soon after fed it to the fireplace. A few drinks later, he had burned every photograph in the house that included every one that had captured the two of them.

Every one except this one. Something had made him hang on to this one.

After his drunken rage, that terrible night when he hit rock bottom and slept in his own vomit and urine in the middle of the kitchen floor, he remembered waking up with a splitting headache and seeing that picture lying next to him. Andrew just tucked it into his wallet, and that's where it had stayed ever since.

He reached into his duffel bag, still clinging to the photograph, produced a flask of bourbon, thought about it, then tucked it back into the bag. Instead, he rummaged for his cellular phone, one of those prepaid ones, which had been a gift from his secretary last Christmas. Andrew had only used it once, when the BMW decided to lock its motor up on I-480 a couple months ago. That incident convinced him that such newfangled gadgetry wasn't all bad, and he carried it with him everywhere now. He didn't turn the thing on, though. Nothing was more annoying than hearing that stupid ring in a restaurant or a movie theater—the *Lone Ranger* theme or Beethoven's Fifth. He imagined ol' Ludwig was rolling in his grave because of that one.

On the back of the photograph, where Coralie wore a white blouse with red triangles and her brown hair was still long, Andrew had written down the phone number of his old lawyer and former best friend. This was Coralie's new home, and this was the number he could never quite finish dialing. Maybe it was the fatigue, or the fact that he spent every moment dreaming of his Coralie and how he could make up for the years of his own stupidity, but this time he finished all the digits.

"Hello," she said, sounding like he had gotten her out of bed. It was nine o'clock on a Saturday night, and that no-good boyfriend of hers wasn't out dancing with such a beautiful lady? This made Andrew furious. Saturday nights were made for showing off your wife and how well the both of you could dance. He was going to tell her all of this, but found he couldn't open his mouth to speak.

"I said, *hello*," Coralie said again. "Come on, you kids, quit wasting my time."

Still silence. So much he wanted to tell her. So much Andrew wanted to confess.

"All right, last chance before I hang up."

He opened his mouth, but could only manage a whimper. It had been two years since they'd spoken last, and even that was from behind each of their lawyers. In truth, Andrew and Coralie Falkness hadn't carried on a decent conversation in the better part of a decade.

More silence, then finally: "Cor…uh…Coralie?"

Now it was her turn to be silent for awhile. After all those years of marriage, she knew exactly who was speaking after the first word. What she didn't know was why in the world the old fool was bothering her at this hour. She wanted to give him the tongue lashing of a lifetime, and nearly began, but felt her heart soften. How could a fat, bald idiot like Andrew do that to her every time she started getting angry? He'd been doing it for years, even after their divorce.

"Andrew Falkness? Is that you?"

"Um…yeah, Cora. It's me."

Yet another awkward silence followed, before Andrew swallowed his pride and thought about his future. He was a lonely old man who ate alone, slept alone, and was scheduled to die alone. For the first time ever, he told the complete truth to someone, and it felt wonderful. Andrew told the love of his life about every affair he'd ever had, all the shady business deals and the dirty money, but he also opened the flood gates about his true feelings for her, how he had fallen in love with those green eyes the first time he'd seen them in the St. John's University Newspaper office.

He told her how sorry he was for everything, for each event that had built up to the final nail in the coffin of their marriage.

And, without any regard to what Bryn said or the work he'd already put in, or even for the money he stood to lose if she decided to call the local authorities, he spent a good half hour telling her exactly what he was currently involved in and how the money he made would finance a great future—for the both of them.

All that time she just listened to him, sitting there on the antique footstool and crying her eyes out one more time because of a man who had made her cry more than any man ever should. The sleepless nights waiting up for him, the drunken fights and fists through the walls, the other women—they all seemed to fade away as he spoke. Her husband (oops, *ex*-husband) was baring his soul to his soulmate, something her new beau had never done. He wanted her to retire and move away with him, to rekindle what little romance they had shared long ago, and build it into something wonderful.

He was a changed man now; even though he was doing something bad at present this was the last time, he swore to God. After this he would come to get her, they would ride off into the sunset like they had the night of their wedding, en route to Niagra Falls before heading south for the rest of their days.

"I guess all this doesn't amount to anything now, Coralie," he said. "But no matter what you decide to do, I can die a happy man knowing I've told you everything, and confessed how much I still love you."

The tissues were piling up on the floor of Coralie's new home now, but she paid no mind to that. Would she bite on his hook and let him try reeling her in one more time? Andrew had asked her. Had she taken the bait?

"Yes," she said, sobbing over a pile of used Kleenex. Coralie, in fact, was also unhappy with her situation, and not a day went by that she didn't think of Andrew and another chance at changing the only man she'd ever loved.

"Yes, you old fool. I'll take the bait one last time, just as soon as you can get back here to me. I'll take it hook, line, and sinker."

-3-

Paul figured he was asleep even before he hit the sleeping bag, and didn't bother taking the time to undress.

Inside his head, he was walking Shelby into her first day of kindergarten at the Martinson School, the same building he had learned to finger paint in twenty-plus years before. For the longest time, he just stood there in the doorway, watching her.

Never before had he felt so much love for anyone or anything, including his wife. Shelby Morris, who had greeted him for the first time on a cloudy December morning, was seven pounds and eight ounces of pure gold.

Even something as simple as playing "Who's got your nose?" would fascinate both father and daughter.

Paul would protect her with his own life if that's what was called for; in reality she was the only thing he had in the world which he truly, deeply loved.

He knew very little about life and how complex it really was. But what he did know was that nothing could keep him from his goals now. And when the time came, nothing would keep Shelby's neurotic, bullemic, clinically insane mother from coming near her ever again.

He knew he would spend every penny of his newfound wealth seeing to that.

But what Paul did not know was that by the time the flap closed on the sale tent the next night, the little girl he knew as Shelby Morris would no longer exist.

Chapter Twelve

The constant rumbling all night long, shouts of partying campers, and even the occasional gun shot did nothing to wake Paul and Andrew. The entire city could have gone up in one big explosion and each man would have just slept right through it. All that sweating, stale air, and hours of hard work had kept them both in a deep, dreamless sleep.

It was now 2 p.m., a time that neither man had slept until in as long as they could remember. Even when Andrew had a particularly long night at the bar and there was nothing to get up for the next morning, he would still be up by at least noon. As for Paul, growing up on a farm never really worked its way out of a person, and his latest in the past few years had been ten o'clock, after the family returned from vacation exhausted and sunburned.

"Wow," Andrew said, peeking his head into Paul's tent while checking his watch. "Somebody who didn't know us any better might think we're lazy."

Paul stretched, checked his own watch, and added, "Yeah, but I don't think anyone here can say they worked as hard as we did in the last couple days."

Before going to meet Bryn, the pair hiked into town from the campground and headed to Main Street. Motorcycles of all ages, brands, and colors lined the street in a town that was just a dot on the map the remaining 50 weeks of the year. At one end, people climbed onto a tower with their video cameras, recording the activity along the street. Women of all sizes strolled in and out of the shops, clad in leather chaps and sometimes little else. Each man bought a bottle of water from a sidewalk vendor, but found it turned instantly into sweat. The temperature had already hit 97 degrees.

Back at the sale tent, Bryn lounged behind the counter in a purple bikini top and shorts, reminding Paul instantly that it had been a good two weeks since he'd had sex of any kind, including self-induced. Maybe when this was through, he would ask her to ride off on his Harley with him, and they would raise Shelby together. Bryn had experienced a tough life from what Paul had managed to get out of her, but in the long run she actually had a good head on her shoulders. When she set her mind to something, like their current predicament, for example, she was nothing but business and seemed to know a way out of any pitfall. Paul could have used a woman like that back in his younger days.

Sunday had come, and the rally was nearing its end. On their way into town, they met more 'cycles loaded up with tents and bed rolls leaving the city than were coming in. Normally white, pasty people from around the country who stayed out of the sun now looked like lobsters, red and blistered with dark eyes that just screamed "hangover." This rally was a chance for people all over the world to get away from life for a few days, dress like a biker even if they weren't one, and just blend in with the crowd. Paul thought there were likely a handful of famous people, millionaires and the like, walking right down the street, and no one recognized them, which is exactly what they wanted sometimes.

"How's business?" Andrew asked Bryn. "Making us any more cash?"

"Nope. Every guy here does the same thing—they walk in, talk like a big shot about how their bike is better than this one or about how they'll have a chopper like that one some day, then they just leave. It's like they think we're just here for their entertainment or something. I had a guy late last night put down ten grand on a V-Rod, but that money went right to my friends."

Paul had been thinking a lot about Jorge, and how it was a terrible thing to pin the whole job on someone he hardly knew. In this business, though, that was what you did—you let someone else take the rap when you could, and did whatever was necessary so you could walk away clean. It seemed he had developed the beginning of a conscience since he had settled down, though. But when all that money crossed his hand he would soon forget about it.

"All right, boss lady," Andrew said. "What's next?"

"Well, I paid off my girlfriends and told them the new story about Jorge. They'll be here right on time later tonight just so they can be seen by some people and place themselves at the scene. Junior called this morning and said they can't release Jorge until this afternoon, so those two should be back here pretty soon. I have another favor to ask of you guys, though."

Bryn told them that she knew Junior pretty well since he was a fixture at all the Devane family functions she was taken to. Usually he was drunk, high, or both, but on the rare occasions when he was sober, Junior Devane was one smart cookie. This whole time, she imagined Junior was thinking of ways around Bryn's threats to tell the world about the real black sheep in his family.

"The plain and simple fact is, I don't trust him," she said. "If he can find a way to call up Malcolm and screw us all, you'd better believe he's going to do it. I need you guys to get us a little insurance tonight before I close down the tent. Jorge can help, and that'll keep Jorge from thinking we've turned on him, too."

The insurance was two friends of Bryn's old girlfriends who had tagged along. Both were old college buddies of the ones Bryn knew, both were tall and beautiful, but most importantly, both were black. At the bar tonight, those two were to meet Paul and Andrew after they slipped a little something in Junior's beer, for a little photo session. Besides liquor, Bryn liked a little blue pill called Tharzax, a little-known tranquilizer that had no taste or odor, and basically made you forget what you'd done for the past day or so. Shortly after she had spoken on the phone to Malcolm's little girlfriend in the kitchen that night she'd discovered the pills, and was now up to three a day. In small doses it worked a lot like asprin, but she found out that a few too many meant a trip to Blackoutville.

"I've got six of those little fellas crushed up in this pill bottle," she said, handing Paul the tiny plastic object. "Pour the whole works in Junior's second or third beer, and he won't remember a thing. Make sure you tell Jorge what you're doing too. We don't want him getting suspicious that we've turned on him."

Bryn had selected a 1999 Wideglide for Jorge's vehicle, and he would leave once 47 of the 50 remaining bikes were ready to roll. She had the VIN number written down, just like all the others, but in this case she would immediately call the police once Jorge was on the road, confirming what her friends had seen. The little foreign guy in a polo shirt would be seen handing a wad of cash to the driver of a truck with Midwest Custom Cycles on the side before he played around with the wires on his own bike and rode off. What Jorge didn't know, and a fact she almost didn't even tell Paul and Andrew, was that a listing of all 150 stolen motorcycles and their destinations would be tucked into Jorges saddlebag for the police to find.

"I know there will be a lot of cycles on the road, but the cops can't miss a bright neon green Harley with a little foreign guy riding it, especially when I tell them right where to find him."

Bryn had changed her mind that the Gearheads would head out individually as soon as their particular bike was running and had a key made. Through a couple days of phone calls, she finally established the destinations for all the bikes. While most would head to Two Harbors where the trucks had gone, some would be delivered throughout the U.S. One of Bryn's couriers had dropped by the night before as planned with a half million dollars of the money he'd collected. All the Gearheads would be given their money and directions in random order and sent out on their way. The last four cycles would be ridden by Jorge, Bryn, and Andrew, with Paul leaving last. All four were scheduled to meet in Two Harbors Tuesday morning to collect the rest of the money and divide it up, though only three would make it.

"So, with Jorge out of the picture, how much more are we getting?" Andrew asked, sounding greedy but not caring in the least.

"With the unexpected expenses we've had, and Junior wanting to start a little savings account of his own just in case he does get cut off, I figure we'll each still come away with the better part of a million, pre-laundered and ready to be spent. Junior gets his cut before we leave; he insisted on having it that way, so I need that insurance, guys."

Hopefully, the threat of even more dirt hitting the media to embarrass the Devanes would keep Junior's mouth shut long enough for them to all go their separate ways. He knew their names and had looked at Bryn's handbag full of documents about Paul and Andrew, but those few precious photographs would keep him far away from the police.

"Get him drugged up, get those pictures, and get your asses back here right after ten o'clock," she said. "And Paul, make sure your little biker buddies don't screw up again. It'll look a little conspicuous if they all come in one big heap, so have the Gearheads show up at the tent two or three at a time, maybe a group every hour or so. As you and Andrew get the keys made, and I can help too, the guys get their cash and their destinations and they're gone."

Through the crowd, the three thieves recognized two familiar faces coming toward them. One was Junior, who today had purchased another Sturgis 2003 shirt and was doing a good job of blending in. The other, who waddled along on what looked like a twisted ankle, wearing a ripped polo shirt and a black eye, was Jorge Zapate.

"Talk about *deja vu*," Paul said. "You look like you did the day we met, Jorge."

He limped over to a stool near the cash register and sat down with the effort it would have taken a man twice his age. A lump protruded from the back of his skull, likely where he had hit the table on the way down. Dried blood was frozen in a line down the back of his neck, and there were cuts on his bare forearms from the broken glass.

At first, Jorge wanted to jump up and take Paul by the throat, then bang his head against a tent pole for awhile until he felt just as bad. It was Paul's friends, Jorge had figured out last night while he tried to sleep on the paper-thin jail mattress, who had done this to him. It was a rare occasion for Jorge to take a drink of alcohol, but by no means would the two beers he'd consumed have sent him into such a rampage. Junior had also tricked him, by making him look like he was supposed to be the target. Then the rich little fool had mysteriously shown up to pay his bail. In some way or another, Jorge was angry with every member of their group, and if he had the money, he would just head for home right now and turn them all in. But the Devanes had done an excellent job of making sure he didn't save a dime.

For now, Jorge thought as he reconsidered breaking Paul's nose, *he must continue his work.*

"Well, as touching of a family reunion as this is, I really need a shower," Junior said, leaving the tent. "Come on over in awhile and get yourself cleaned up, Jorge. You look like you need a bit more than a shower."

Jorge sneered at Junior as he walked away. Junior had told him that he felt terrible for what had happened, since it should have been him on that table throwing beer bottles at strangers. He had sensed that something was up and protected himself in the only way he knew how. Just as Junior had rehearsed with Bryn, he told Jorge that everyone was friends now, and they were all working together to get Malcolm Devane's money. Jorge didn't quite believe the whole story, but once again in his life, he had no choice except to follow along.

"I do not trust him," Jorge told Bryn as Junior strolled out of sight. "He is a Devane, and that is all it takes for me not to trust him."

"Neither do I, Jorge," Bryn said. "That's why you three guys have some work to do later on tonight. Paul and Andrew will tell you about it later, but for now, just stay clear of the Gearheads and don't lose your cool."

This was too much for him. "Don't lose my cool! They think I am a child molester, Bryn! I could go to jail!"

"You won't be going to jail, Jorge. By the time they realize you're gone, you'll be on some tropical island somewhere, probably in the next hut up the beach from mine." Bryn smiled at him and placed a hand on his shoulder. She squeezed lightly and felt him flinch. There wasn't much of his body that wasn't bruised at this point, both from the bar and from a minor scuffle in the jail cell. Jorge had not told a soul about his plans to return to the place of his birth once the job was through, and right now he was very relieved about that.

Before the three men left her again, Bryn went over the night's plan so that all three could hear it in unison. Go get Junior, slip him the drug, take some photos at the Full Throttle Saloon with her two black friends, then carry him back to his motor home so he could sleep for at least a day and a half. Bryn figured that six of the pills for someone who didn't have any tolerance for them would keep Junior in dreamland at least long enough for them to make Two Harbors. Then she would call him up, say not to worry because he already had his money, and by then Jorge would likely have been arrested. Junior could call his brother, but what good would it do at that point? He would still be the hero, and he would still have to keep his mouth shut about the other participants in the crime, or else WUSF, the local NBC affiliate in The City, would get a few photos in the mail.

So would the *City Times* and *Newsworld* magazine.

"He'll be a little pissed that we slipped him the drugs," Bryn said, "but there's really nothing Junior can do about it. It just buys us some time to get where we're going just in case he gets any wild ideas."

This seemed to be good enough for Jorge. In fact, he needed to clean up and get some sleep so badly that he would have went along with anything Bryn told him. All he knew was that within the next 48 hours, there would be a lot of bad things happening to a lot of bad people. Malcolm Devane would not only be bankrupt, but he would lose the respect of his family. Malcolm's father, Jorge's too, would likely die of a heart attack when he found out that his son had been so stupid, and that his other, darker-skinned son was no longer around to take orders. And as for Junior, Jorge wanted to make sure that those photos got sent out to as many places as possible.

His mother had told him once that vengeance for the sake of profit was immoral, but vengeance for the sake of one's family was the most honorable deed of all. He only wished she could be around to be proud of her son when all this was through. At least Jorge would be able to save his sister from a terrible life…the kind of life he himself had lived.

Jorge insisted he was all right to walk himself to Junior's motor home for a shower. He would then take a much-deserved nap before Paul and Andrew were to pick him up at 7 p.m.

"It kind of sucks picking on the little guy who's already had more trouble than all of us put together," Paul said, watching the small man limp away down the sidewalk. "Just think about it—we've all had our troubles, whether it's from our wives, kids, or husband, but that guy there lost the only family he'd ever known after being shipped up here to be a slave for a father who didn't even recognize the fact that he existed. All those years…"

"That's enough, Paul," Bryn said, trying to sound stern but visibly shaken by all this. "There…there's just no other way, that's all. It has to be someone taking the fall, and it's sure not gonna be me."

She turned away from them both, not wanting them to see her cry again.

"She's right, it's the only way we can pull this off," Andrew said. "We're all elbow deep in this shit now, and someone's got to pay for it."

Andrew stared at the back of Bryn's head. This whole time, the jail when they'd first met, the diner, all those nights in her aunt's garage—there had always been something about this young woman that he remembered from before. Even her voice seemed familiar somehow.

"Well, I've got the drugs, and we'll see you back here a little after ten," he said. "How in the world did you think of that, anyway? I mean, all of this stuff, Bryn. I just gotta say that you've really surprised me."

"What can I say?" Bryn said. "This dog knows all the cool tricks."

Andrew stopped. He had that feeling about her again. Something was right in front of him but wouldn't quite click together. Maybe it was senility creeping up on him early, or did he really know something more about this girl that he couldn't quite recall?

Where had he seen Bryn Scott before?

-2-

The Full Throttle Saloon was more of a little town than a bar. It was just across the road from Paul and Andrew's new campsite, so they made their way through the traffic without need of a ride. At 6 p.m., just as planned, Bryn's friends were waiting outside. She had called them both shortly before Paul and Andrew left the sale tent, confirming what the girls would be wearing so they could be easily identified.

Both of them being black in a city with about 99 percent white people helped too.

"You our guys?" one asked as Paul approached her. She was a bit younger than Bryn, but looked as though she had lived a pretty rough life so far. Her black leather skirt revealed the bruises on her legs, and the gap-toothed smile did little for her beauty. Paul instantly thought of the photograph blown up on the wall of some swanky country club, where Junior Devane, son of one of the country's wealthiest bigots, would be pictured with his tongue inside this black woman's disgusting mouth. It was because of this vision that he smiled at her, not just out of politeness.

"Sasha Wilkins," she said, extending her hand. Paul took it, surprised at the firmness in such a small woman's grip.

The other woman, a bit heavier than Sasha but not too big, wore a white tank top that clearly showed her lack of a bra. By now, both men had gotten used to seeing such a sight, since many of the women in Sturgis were a bit larger than *Cosmopolitan* said they were supposed to be, but they happily showed off anyhow. And why not? Paul had always thought that beautiful women came in all shapes and sizes, though Andrew disagreed.

"Hi, I'm Anna Morgan," the second woman said. "Bryn says we got another little piece to our job out here, so where's our man?"

Andrew explained to the ladies, though he detested speaking to folks of color, that Junior would be along shortly. He went over the plan once more—the drugs, the brand new disposable camera he had inside his jacket (with a flash just in case the lights were too low), and how Junior's family had KKK written all over them.

"Wonderful," Sasha said, smiling at him through her chipped teeth. "I'm gonna enjoy this."

The four walked into the bar, which consisted of several little shops surrounding an open-air parking lot. All along one side people were buying saddle bags, T-shirts, and boots, and in one corner, men took turns in the burn-out pit smoking away the tires on their bikes while the crowd cheered. On stage was some local band who would make way for a bigger act later that evening. Andrew felt a bit nervous as they walked through the lot, with leather-clad bikers giving the colored women dirty looks from the catwalk strung above them. Fortunately, no one had the nerve to say anything to them. They only stared in amazement at the young man, the old man, and the two black women, all walking together.

This is a great way for us to be inconspicuous, Andrew was thinking.

Paul selected a table near the door where it would be easy to get Junior out once the little pills started working. From what Bryn had said, Junior would get a bit amorous for only a few minutes before he would be down for the count. All five of them would take a nice stroll back across the highway to the men's ten since there were no back rooms in this particular bar (a detail Bryn had overlooked), they would have their little photo session, and then just leave Junior in Paul's tent. By the time he woke up the job would likely be over already, but putting him in a stranger's tent in a campground a few miles away from his motor home and cell phone might buy them a little extra time.

They had some time before Junior and Jorge were supposed to arrive, so all four felt comfortable sitting together to have at least one beer. It turned out that Sasha was married, still living in the same trailer park she had grown up in. There were no children yet, but not for lack of trying. She waited tables at a little bar in the city of Gulch, Nevada, population 46. Her husband flew a small tour plane out of Vegas, but had recently lost his job due to a failed license renewal. It might have been his bad eyes, Sasha said, but it was more likely the fact that he polished off a fifth of Jack Daniels every few days and was caught flying drunk. Now, he just stayed at home all day and drank whiskey, driving her crazy whenever she wasn't at work.

"I'm gonna use my money from Bryn to move the hell out of that trailer," she said confidently, nursing her Budweiser. "I got an aunt in North Dakota, says I can come up and see her any time. I might just get me an apartment up there for awhile, just for a change of scenery."

The other woman's life was less like an episode of *Hee Haw*. Anna Morgan, born Anna Bigsby, was both pregnant and married by the time she was 16. This was very *Hee Haw*-like, but the rest of the story was more like a movie of the week. The father was a rich little white boy not unlike Junior Devane, who had made her life a living hell. This was part of the reason why she would enjoy their photo session with Junior so much. Alan Morgan, her "baby-daddy" as she called him, took Anna out after losing a bet with his football buddies. It was all supposed to be a joke, until poor Alan forgot to use a condom and got himself in a spot of trouble. Now she lived in the trailer park two houses down from Sasha, and didn't have to work if she didn't want to. Every week like clockwork, a big, fat check came in the mail from the Morgan family in exchange for her silence. They didn't want to see their grandchild, nor did they want their son to go near her anymore. If he did, the money stopped. Anna had decided that putting her daughter through college was more important than little Rachel Morgan knowing who her father was, so she obeyed the rules. She didn't smoke, barely ever drank, and was just enjoying getting to spend all that time with her child. Paul thought she was too good for where she was living, but that was likely the case with most of the people there.

At 7 p.m. sharp, Andrew caught sight of Junior and Jorge strolling through the parking lot. Another conspicuous combo, the little Brazilian guy and the silver-spoon-up-the-ass rich kid trying hard to look like a biker but failing miserably. Paul sent the ladies off to another table while he worked his magic with Junior.

"Now this is my kind of place," Junior said, taking a seat next to Paul. "This is my sort of crowd."

Doubtful, Paul thought, *since the man has never even been on a motorcycle in his life. His idea of being a badass is probably going without a seatbelt when he cruises in his Mercedes.*

"The women here certainly are beautiful," Jorge said. "They certainly do not like to wear much clothing."

It was interesting to see the little man away from Bryn. Whenever she was in the room, he kept his mouth shut and waited for her to give the next order. Jorge had been sort of a gift from Malcolm, who didn't have enough time anymore to boss Jorge around himself. Instead, he made sure Jorge kept an eye on his wife and was right there at her beck and call. She might have been just trailer trash, but she was his wife, after all. Why shouldn't she get some use out of the family servant?

When she was gone, though, Jorge had a sort of confidence about him that was interesting. Andrew had seen it firsthand when he got choked through the bars of his jail cell, and since then he vowed not to underestimate the little secret of the Devane family. Deep down, it pained him just as much as it did Paul to let Jorge take the fall for the heist, though even deeper down he was a little relieved that a foreigner would pay for his crime.

Paul offered to buy the first round of beers so that the four men could celebrate a job nearly completed. Junior wasn't quite sure why they had invited him here, but he wanted to believe that since he'd figured out their plan, they had come to respect him as part of their group. There weren't many groups that he fit into, and his only friends were usually strangers at a bar somewhere who would never remember him the next day when they were sober. Junior was blissfully unaware of what was happening now, though, and he was content with the concept that these men were slowly turning into his friends.

Making sure no one was looking, Junior's new "friend" Paul poured the contents of the pill bottle into Junior's beer. It fizzed a little, but the powder instantly dissolved like Bryn had said it would. With all the care of a man handling nitroglycerin, he carefully handed the booze to Junior, completely sure it was the right beer bottle.

"We need a toast, gentlemen," Junior said, raising his bottle. "To good friends, beautiful women, and a job nearly well done."

Junior looked at Jorge, the half-breed brother who was an embarrassment to the Devane family name. Soon all that would change, though. The little man would be too busy fighting off rapists in prison to tell anyone who had sired him. And for the first time ever, his father would trust Junior, his son who had saved the Devane family name and a good portion of their money, too.

He lifted the bottle and let the familiar liquid fill his throat. Though it tasted a bit funny, the beer was wonderfully refreshing after sweating all day long without a single drink. He wanted to keep his edge just in case one of his fellow gang members tried something funny with him. Yes, Junior Devane was on top of things here, and he thought it was actually he who was running the show. After all, he had been smart enough to figure out their little plan, and now he would come away with the most benefit. Hell, he didn't even have to do any work. This, he thought, made him the smartest one in the group.

As he finished the bottle in a single gulp, his head still tilted back gathering every drop from the bottle, he glanced around the table. Yes, he thought of himself as the most intelligent one in the room. And why not? He had the breeding for it, that's for sure. These other three idiots couldn't have pulled off such a complex plan without his help, anyhow. He was actually doing them a favor by helping out.

But why were they all smiling at him like that?

-3-

"You didn't say there would be three of you," the registrar said through the back door of the Kingston County Courthouse. The product of twenty years behind a desk, he was fifty pounds overweight and would have been sweating regardless, but now the man who had offered him all that money to stay a little late tonight had sprung the unexpected surprise of a child on him.

Outside the door, Shelby and Samantha Morris, with Uncle Stinky as Shelby had now gotten used to calling him, looked every bit like the weary travelers they were. Preston, Florida, was a private community just east of Miami where the young and wealthy came to escape the rest of the world. All the while, the Morris girls had been assured by their new friend that nothing but the best was ahead of them, but those pretty thoughts did little to take away the fact they'd been basically living in a car for the past couple days.

"All right, let's just get this over with," the man said finally, after exchanging smiles with Shelby. She had felt little need to smile in the past few hours, and now clung tightly to the new Teletubbie doll her mother had purchased for her shortly after their encounter in the bathroom. All Shelby knew was that she had done something wrong, horribly wrong, and she'd best keep her mouth shut and try hard not to cry. Mommy was very angry with her for some reason, but she didn't know why. Under the circumstances, she didn't feel like asking.

The registrar had been an old college friend of Stinky's, and prepared the necessary forms in exchange for twenty thousand cash. While the three sat in the waiting room, he made sure no one was left in the office and finished typing the forms. With his years of experience, he knew exactly how to push something like this through the system and not arouse suspicion, but doing so for a child still made him a bit nervous. If she was missing, her photo would be plastered all over the news stations across the county, and once found the cops would wonder who had changed her name.

"Here, I need the adults' signatures on these lines and that should be it. You are now Samantha Vanis, and this little girl here is now Shelby Vanis. All the birth dates are the same, as are the social security numbers. I rigged it up so all the new identification will be coming in the mail in a few days. Until then, you need to destroy all your old ones and just stay put. Don't drive and don't go anywhere they might ask to see I.D. If you get caught, it's my ass too, remember?"

"We get it, Artie," Chad Vanis, the artist formerly known as Stinky, said. "You just enjoy spending your money and don't worry about us."

She had been deathly afraid to mention it, but could wait no longer. Shelby wasn't sure about what was happening in the office, but she was dead sure of what was happening in her bladder. After weighing her options, she decided that asking mommy to take her to the bathroom would make her less angry than if she just wet herself. Thankfully, Samantha seemed much more calm now, and just took her daughter by the hand and led her to the potty as though nothing had happened.

"She's some find," Artie Graybald said, watching the ladies exit the room. "Where'd you find them?"

"The City, living with some prick who didn't appreciate his family," Chad said. "The mother had to come along for the ride, of course, and it pisses me off that we had to put on this whole dog and pony show just so she wouldn't get suspicious. At least she has a nice little body on her, though; that makes the nights a little easier to get through."

Both men laughed as Artie lit a cigar. It was terribly illegal to smoke in government buildings, a law that had come to pass during his administration and one he detested. He was an elected official, for goodness sake, and it was his God-given right to smoke if he wanted to.

"You gonna tell the whole story, then?" he asked, puffing away.

"Of course not," Chad said. "I never tell my wife the whole story. For all she knows, I found her the daughter she could never have, one who looks just like she did when she was that age. What the wife doesn't know won't hurt her. She'll just be happy that after all those doctors and all that money, she finally gets the kid she wants."

"And what about Samantha?"

"I send her back on my private plane to collect the rest of her things, while I tell her I want to spend some quality time with our new child. I show her the house, get her settled in for awhile so she doesn't think anything's up, and she'll trust me like they all do in no time. By the time Samantha gets back, the wife and I are well on our way to Bermuda with our new daughter. The pilot just drops her off, takes off again, and leaves her standing there. No husband, no kid, just a bunch of boxes full of toys and no one to play with them."

Artie really took off now, leaning his head back to get the full effect of his belly laugh. While Samantha Morris, now Vanis, was washing her daughter's hands, thinking about how Shelby was only the ticket for her to live the rich woman's life she'd dreamed about, the two men were planning differently.

"You truly are a heartless bastard," Artie said with admiration. "God bless you."

"Thanks, pal. After all this is through, I'll be back with the girl to get our names changed one last time. She's young enough now that in a couple years she won't even remember any of this."

Shortly after their arrival at the new house, the one where Samantha was thinking she would spend her days lounging by the pool or shopping downtown, Chad's plan would begin. Samantha would fall in love with the home, and for six million who could blame her? It was, unfortunately, just one of the many homes for sale in that neighborhood that Chad's buddies in the real estate business let him borrow on occasion. It was a display model, one of those homes where the elite came to be pampered by the real estate agent, taken out for drinks and hookers and hopefully conned into buying a similar one up the street. And as a display it was fully furnished, to give potential buyers the impression of what it would look like when they lived there.

For all Samantha knew, it was a palace that had been in her boyfriend's family for generations. He told her everything would be all right there—Shelby would go to the best school in town and Sam would never have to worry about money again. He had told her a lot of things in their time together, and she had all but forgotten who Paul Morris was. He was just one of the many obstacles in her life which had kept her from the good life. Shelby was another. As soon as possible, she planned on sending her daughter off to boarding school or something equally as ritzy, and then it would be just the two of them together in that huge house. Samantha wanted it all, and not even her own daughter would stand in her way.

"It's beautiful!" Samantha said, fighting back a tear. Through the main entrance was a fountain, right there in the middle of the room, in front of dual staircases that reminded her of one of the old musicals her mother had made her watch when she was young.

Shelby just stood there, amazed that anything under one roof could be so big, and so clean. Everything was white and gleaming, and it looked kind of cold; not like her room back home where she had posters all over the walls and her little doll stage, an old coffee table, in the corner. It was little, but she missed it just the same.

They would spend the night in the house, then Chad Vanis (God, he hated that name) would ask his little delivery girl to fly back home while he got to know his new daughter.

After a dinner of Kentucky Fried Chicken, laid out picnic style on the home's $5,000 dining room table, all three of the travelers grew even more tired. Shelby laid her head down in her arms after finishing her chicken, and promptly drifted off to sleep. Until Samantha woke her up, she and daddy were ridding a motorcycle together over countless hills, with green grass and flowers everywhere. The helmet was too big and kept slipping over her eyes, but she clung tight to Paul, knowing somehow that he would never be angry at her the way mommy was. Shelby didn't hate her mother, mostly because she didn't know what hate was yet. She was just frightened and confused, and knew that all of this was somehow her fault. If her daddy never came back, it would be because of her, but she couldn't figure out why. For now, it was best to keep her fear inside, however strong, and keep mommy happy.

"Good night, doodlebug," Samantha said, after tucking Shelby into one of the house's twelve beds. Shelby just grumbled a bit, and didn't open her eyes. She was awake, and could have kissed her mother good night, but something inside her didn't want to. That was a very mean thing to think, and Shelby was suddenly even more angry at herself for whatever she'd done to bring this on.

As her daughter lay there in the moonlight pretending to sleep, Samantha looked down at the little girl. She had no idea this would be the last time she would ever see her daughter, but even if she had known, she probably would have cared little. All her life, she could never connect herself to anyone—could never love anyone—the way it happened in the storybooks. She'd nearly run the other way on her wedding day, even though there was a man waiting for her who had stuck with her through her sicknesses, and loved her unconditionally. They said all little girls love their fathers, but Samantha never felt more for him than she did for her friends. Her mother, constantly taunting and terrorizing her, had showed her what hate was, though. Maybe that relationship had soured all the rest. She hated her mother, but respected her and wanted to please her more than anything. Samantha was amazed at how easy this had all been. She had just locked the apartment door behind her, leaving Paul to wonder forever where she'd gone. Shipping Shelby off somewhere where she only was allowed home once a year wouldn't bother her either. Something inside her, perhaps her mother's voice, kept saying it was all right. The only thing that mattered was a life of luxury, mingling with the rich and powerful and establishing herself as a pillar of the society.

Husbands with no money and children who were too cute for their own good weren't necessary.

Samantha walked to her bedroom, eyeing the expensive paintings in the hallway. She was amazed at how quickly everything had come together, but she would be even more amazed at how soon it would fall apart.

Chapter Thirteen

"So then, the guy says, '*Dude*, that's not your pie!'"

Junior looked around the table and laughed at all his new friends. Some, like little Jorge, would split into two people if you looked close enough. Being drunk was not unfamiliar to him, but getting this sort of feeling after just two beers was strange. Was he losing his edge? Could it have been too much sun? Whatever the case, his only job right now was to tell his buddies about his many escapades while wasting his father's money in college.

"And I tell him, shut your ass ya' beeotch. Just wait and see what happens. So I dump the little bag out, lift up the top of this pie, and sprinkle a little magic smokey leafy into his appley goodness."

Junior was now explaining the process of producing **kife**, a nearly-tasteless substance made from chopping up the leaves of marijuana plants. When placed in the proper baked goods, it produced a high time for the whole family. In his fourth, and final, year at college, he and some friends made a late night run to the grocery store and Junior decided to share some of the green sticky icky with a total stranger. He said his friends spent the rest of the evening waiting around in the store for someone to buy that pie, and when they did, they all watched the action from outside the man's window.

"He was probably, like, ninety or so," Junior said, motioning for the barmaid to fetch him another beer. Paul could tell it wouldn't be long before he was out like a light. "This old man was having a card party and the other couple there was getting the munchies, so he slices up this pie for 'em. Pretty soon all these old people are, like, giggling and shit, and we all start giggling outside. Then the old man hears us all by his window and he gets all paranoid, right? Finally, he sneaks over to the window, opens it up, and he yells..."

At this, Junior lost all control. The ladies at the bar who would soon be part of a Polaroid moment with the little weasel saw their opportunity and strolled over to the table. As though they had rehearsed it a thousand times, Paul and Andrew each took one of Junior's arms and they led him toward the door, with Jorge following. The people sitting around thought nothing of it, since drunks had gotten carried out of there all night. The two black women following right behind looked a bit odd, but everyone was too busy enjoying their last night at Sturgis to notice.

Just outside the bar, Junior began to gurgle, and his escorts were forced to stop while he vomited in the parking lot. His face had turned a sort of orange color, making Andrew wonder if anyone had ever taken that many of those little pills at once. Junior's long hair, now soaked with puke, flopped back against his jacket as he stood back up, pointing at the sky.

"Shmagoo! You little shits, all of ya! Shmagoo for supper!"

He looked at Paul now, like he had made some sort of interesting point which Paul was supposed to understand. Paul just chuckled, resumed the escort, and helped Junior across the highway.

"Right? That's what the old man said. Stoned out of his gourd, he was. What the fuck is a shmagoo, man?"

"You've had a few too many drinks," Andrew told Junior. "We're going to take you someplace where you can rest for awhile, all right?"

It was nearly dark now, with almost all of the cycles traveling down the highway heading away from town. The rally was over, and although Paul and Andrew hadn't seen as much of it as they would have liked to, they thought that their experience would be far more memorable than just about anyone else's. In a couple days, after cleaning up the campgrounds and sweeping the streets, the little town would be back to normal again for another 50 weeks, with just a trickle of tourists blowing through town during the off season.

They decided on Paul's tent, though both of them would be left behind when all this was over. By the time Junior woke up, he would stumble out of there into a huge parking lot, covered with empty bottles and food wrappers but with no other campers around. Everyone would be long gone by the time he was conscious again. With any luck, the motor home he'd rented would have gotten towed away too.

"All right, sweetheart," Sasha said, helping Junior to the unrolled sleeping bag. "We're gonna have us a good time for awhile."

Junior eyed the women carefully, which was quite difficult given his present state. Inside his head, he was in a wonderful place that reminded him of a long-forgotten acid trip, where everything was beautiful and the colors could sometimes change. Right now, the faces of these beautiful ladies, who were slowly stripping away his clothes, were black, but he knew enough to assume that meant nothing. Once, the girl he'd been with had turned purple, her breasts glowing with an intense white light. He had spent hours just touching them, trying to gather the brightness for himself.

"Are you…I mean…is it…black?" was all he could manage, but he wasn't concerned about getting an answer. Right now, Little Junior was calling the shots, and he was more ready for action than he had been in a long time.

Sasha looked over his equipment. "Nope, sweetie. It sure ain't black. It'd be a whole lot bigger if it was."

Paul and Andrew stood aside in the two-room tent while Jorge ran the camera. He had insisted upon being the one who got to shame his brother, and the two felt that considering the hell Jorge was about to go through, it was the least they could do. Jorge ran the show with all the flair of a Playboy photographer…or maybe a porn director.

"All right, kneel down there," he said to Anna, who was now completely naked except for her leather boots. Her dark skin and even darker nipples reminded Jorge of the woman he had first made love to back in Brazil. She was the daughter of a neighboring farmer, whose marriage to another man was already pre-arranged. He would have been run out of the country had the family found out about them.

Anna knelt in front of Junior, who obediently buried his head between her legs. Sasha, who had only her panties on at this point, licked up the length of Junior's back with her long tongue.

The camera flashed once, then twice.

This is what vengeance feels like, Jorge thought.

Junior, the obedient, drugged puppet that he was, now got himself turned around and laid on his back. Anna knelt over his face, just close enough to give the impression that Junior's tongue was inside her, and Sasha slipped Little Junior into her mouth. It tasted terrible, but all that money was what kept her from gagging.

Another camera flash.

Finally, Anna knelt on her hands and knees while Paul and Andrew helped pick Junior off the ground. Sasha slid him inside Anna, then wrapped her arms around him and licked his neck. Jorge especially liked this pose, and used all the remaining shots. It occurred to all three men simultaneously that they hadn't been with a woman in a long time, and they all envied Junior, even though he would never remember any of this. They all just stared for a minute or so as Junior pumped away furiously. Finally, Paul broke the silence.

"Too bad we couldn't find a goat, too."

That was enough for the ladies, and apparently Junior had gotten his fill, too. He toppled over suddenly, convulsed a few times, then lay still. Anna, who was currently working on finishing a CPR class, checked his pulse. It was very slow, just like Bryn had said it would be. Now there was nothing left for Junior to do but have a nice long siesta.

The women took his wallet and cell phone as well as all his clothes and the sleeping bag. Just a little bonus for their dirty work. There was nothing they hated worse than self-indulgent little white boys who thought they could have any woman in the world, and they figured Junior was a prime example of the type. Once he woke up, he would have to wear the tent wherever he was going, and would need to get there with no I.D., cash, or credit cards.

"This is almost cruel," Andrew said. As the last one out of the tent, he gave a final glance at the sleeping naked man and zipped up the flap.

"Yeah," Paul said. "Almost."

All around the campground, people had either gotten on the road already or were getting ready to do so right away in the morning. At least there were still some tents left, so Paul and Andrew's wouldn't look so suspicious. Hopefully, the campground owner would just think someone forgot their tent and wouldn't come knocking until the job was finished.

"Well, gentlemen," Anna said, winking at Paul. "You got more of a show tonight than you thought you would, am I right? Oh well, can't come to Sturgis without seeing a few tits."

"Ain't nothing we haven't done before," Sasha added. "We'll drive you guys uptown to the one- hour photo place if you'd like. I think there's a Walgreens around here someplace."

Paul and Andrew agreed, but Jorge asked to stay behind. There were many thoughts going through his mind now—the unrelenting desire to have a woman, the feeling of satisfaction from striking a blow for the Zapate family, and an unquenched thirst from sweating all day. He told his friends he would meet them back at the bar when they'd finished with the film, where he planned on drinking beer and enjoying the remainder of his time in America.

Sasha drove her Honda, packed with Anna, Paul, and Andrew, to the nearest drugstore, where they waited in the parking lot for their film to be developed. An extra hundred to the teenager working the counter insured that he wouldn't call in the police for such dirty pictures.

Anna even told him he could make some copies for himself if he wanted to. It made her proud to think of herself as the subject of a young man's jerk-off fantasies.

They took their time returning to the bar, since it was only 9:30. All five could have one celebratory drink together before Paul and Andrew returned to the sale tent and the women waited to tell their story to the police.

Paul got out of the car and barely noticed the ratty old bus in the parking lot. Nothing connected in his mind until he saw Charger running up to him.

"Hey, Paulie!" he said, out of breath from the extra thirty pounds around his middle. "You'll never guess who's here!"

Genuinely confused, Paul asked who that might be.

"Junior Devane, man! That preppy bastard you told us to take care of." Charger stood, arms folded across his chest, sounding genuinely proud of his gang. "Yeah, the boys are in there kicking his ass right now."

For a moment, the whole situation didn't make sense. Paul actually thought for a brief moment that the drugs had worn off, Junior had somehow found some clothing laying around, then he'd come back to the bar looking for the ones who had drugged him. All of this within an hour and a half was absurd, but it was the only explanation Paul could think of right then.

Andrew was thinking the same thing, until it finally clicked.

"Wait a second," he said to Charger. "What does this Junior guy look like?"

Still proud as a peacock, Charger said, "Same guy as last night. Short, brown skin, looks like a rich boy. He was the same one wearing the Midwest Custom Cycles jacket last night who got hauled off to jail, but apparently he didn't learn his lesson very good. He's right back here again, looking all cocky and rich in that polo shirt…"

And that was right. Paul remembered telling the Gearheads to pick out the rich looking man. They had never met Jorge, so they didn't know the difference. Since Jorge got tricked into wearing Junior's coat last night, and no one had bothered to tell the Gearheads they had gotten the wrong guy, they'd gotten the wrong guy again.

"Oh, *Jesus*!" Paul said, breaking into a sprint.

"No!" Andrew yelled, right behind him. "Christ, *no*!"

Jorge Zapate, the little Brazilian man who just happened to walk back into the bar at the right time, was in a world of trouble. One of the Gearheads was holding his arms while two more worked over his stomach and face with their fists. They would throw him into the booth head first, sending bottles crashing to the ground, then pick him back up and do it all over again. Before Paul and Andrew could make their way through the crowd, they heard a woman yell, "Hey, that's the child molester from T.V.!"

And that was all it took. The crowd began fighting the Gearheads for the opportunity to beat up on the suspected pedophile they'd seen on the KKER evening news last night. One woman broke a beer bottle over someone's head just to get him out of the way, then grabbed a second one to break over Jorge's head. Now it was the woman who held Jorge up, while two other strangers kicked away at him. Blood ran from one of Jorge's eyes, and the other was wide with fear. He had given up trying to struggle now; there were just too many of them. His feeling of triumph had been short-lived.

"Watch out, old man," a leather-clad woman no older than 20 said to Andrew, shoving him into a nearby food booth. She tripped over his feet as she rushed past, falling right on her face, then stood up and backhanded Andrew with all she had.

Paul tried to help him up, but not before the young woman's boyfriend landed a punch right square in his nose.

"Stay the fuck out of this, buddy," he said, sending both Paul and Andrew back into the same booth. All around them, popcorn and beer bottles were flying. Women pulled other women's hair, and some went right for the heavy stuff and punched each other. Burly bikers, unsure of why there was a fight going on but not caring either way, saw this as an opportunity to really live it up their last night here.

Friends knocked out friends just for the sake of joining in the action. All around them, people screamed and bolted for the exit, knocking others behind the bar or into the middle of the fight. Right before he was hit in the eye, Paul caught sight of Jorge getting thrown behind the bar, crashing through the lineup of liquor bottles into a large Budweiser mirror.

"Andrew!" he yelled, but Andrew was currently getting kneed in the groin by a woman just trying to get out of the place. "Andrew, we gotta get him outta here!"

Paul, after seeing what the woman was capable of, didn't feel so bad about shattering a mirror from the wall over a woman's head. She had Andrew pinned down on the table, slapping him with both hands. He pulled his partner up from the table, shook him a bit, and pointed to where Jorge had landed. They pushed their way through the crowd, stepping on people along the way, and crawled over the bar.

"Jorge!" Paul said, lightly slapping him. He had landed directly on the bottles, and large shards of glass poked through his arms and neck. It would be a miracle if he wasn't already dead, impaled by a booze bottle.

"Jorge," Andrew echoed, slapping the man's cheeks lightly. "Can you walk?"

No, in fact he could not walk. If they were able to see Jorge's ankle, which was presently covered with about twenty pounds of shattered glass, they would be able to see the bone sticking out of it. Walking was pretty much out of the question.

Paul felt the adrenaline rushing through him and picked Jorge up off the bar. He groaned in agony at being moved, but would likely have been killed had he stayed where he was. They made their way behind the bar, trying to keep away from the flying fists and bottles, and most importantly trying not to be seen. For all these people knew, the child molester was still in the middle of that big pile somewhere, and they were fighting tooth and nail to get to him.

Andrew thought of it like the old cartoons, where the dogs tackle the cat and get into a rolling, dust-flying battle, and then the cat just steps right out of the middle while the dust continues to fly and the dogs beat themselves silly. His own ankle hurt terribly, as did his groin and his right eye where he'd taken the corner of a dinner plate. Paul could walk but was limping after getting thrown into that booth, and blood that was trickling down from the gash in his forehead made everything take on a reddish tint. They had nearly made it to the exit and away from the madness when they heard "Hey, there he is!"

That kicked their adrenaline in full throttle. The men ran across the parking lot, Paul still carrying Jorge, and down to the road. They weren't sure where they were headed, just that it was as far away from here as possible.

"Jesus Christ, Paul," Andrew said, limping along as well as he could. "Don't look behind us!"

But that was exactly what Paul did. It was like when your mother told you not to touch the hot stove. What was the first thing you did? Behind them, nearly a hundred angry people were running along, and gaining on them fast. Some yelled, some threw what was left of their beer bottles. Harley engines cranked up in the background. Soon they would run them down and three men against a hundred wouldn't stand a chance. Paul and Andrew hadn't been on the news, but they were helping out the pedophile, so they would get beat just as badly.

Finally, Paul's sides felt like they were caving in and his rush ended. He fell onto the gravel shoulder, watching the headlights fly past his head as the rocks scraped into his skin. Andrew fell to his knees beside him, panting more than a man half his age should. His heart felt like it would explode, and all Andrew could think was that he would die there on some strange highway without his Coralie to hold him in her arms. All three men just laid there, deathly afraid of the mob that would soon converge on them, but too exhausted and beaten to move another inch. Fortunately for Jorge he had been knocked unconscious from the fall, and he watched the lights slowly fade into darkness. Andrew leaned on Jorge's limp body, clutching his chest and staring into the ditch. The last thing Paul remembered seeing was all those eyes looking down at him, and all the stars in the pretty South Dakota sky. He would die now for sure, leaving a wife and daughter with no money and no future. He was sure of it.

But for once, his vision was wrong.

Paul awoke first, staring up at the plain white ceiling. His first thought was that he was in a morgue, not yet covered with the sheet and perhaps not yet dead. It was like that story he'd seen on television once, where the man's heartbeat slowed down so much that they all thought he was dead, then started cutting him open while he could still feel the pain.

But this was not a morgue, and the mob had not beaten him to death. In fact, his good fortune was due to the perfect timing for two members of Sturgis' finest, who saw the crowd chasing the suspected child molester down the highway and gave chase themselves. While Officer Brett Olkin would just as soon have helped those folks beat Jorge Zapate to death, maybe with a few kicks to the balls from his twelve-year-old daughter, it was nonetheless his job to protect these people until they were proven guilty. He swooped in, found three men nearly beaten to death lying in the gravel, and pulled them into his car before the mob could dish out their own justice.

It had been Officer Olkin's experience that offenders like those who like little kids get their worst punishment from their fellow prison inmates anyhow.

"All right, sleepy head," he called through the bars at Paul, the only one whose pain killer had worn off. "Take your one call if you want it."

Paul didn't think about the other two men. He knew they would survive, since both appeared to be breathing. Right now, time was his one and only concern. He checked his watch, which read 11 p.m., exactly one hour late for their arrival at the tent. He had just one thing on his mind, and that was the subject of his single phone call. From the greasy pay phone down the hall, where countless criminals had spread their germs and pleaded their cases to mothers and wives, he carefully dialed the number he'd now committed to memory.

"Hi Bryn," he said, hearing her sigh of relief that they hadn't abandoned her. Soon, she wouldn't be so relieved, however.

"Um...Bryn...you'll never guess where we are."

-2-

To say the least, Bryn Scott was annoyed. To be more accurate, Bryn Scott was all sorts of pissed off. Not only had she been waiting there in the tent, which had closed an hour ago, but she now had to put them even further behind by making a trip downtown to post bail. And not just for her three main men, either.

What Paul told her, before she hung up the phone and slammed it down onto the counter in frustration, was that there were also seventeen members of the Gearheads incarcerated. Bail for the group this time would seriously cut into their profit, especially for Jorge Zapate, the suspected child molester. Getting him out this time would mean a hundred thousand dollars cash, since no bondsman in his right mind would post bond for such a connoisseur of kiddy porn. Jorge could easily run back home to Brazil, whatever little village he lived in, and the man would be left there holding a bond for a man he'd never find.

Of course, posting bail for Jorge wouldn't be a problem this time. Bryn decided that right away.

She checked the clock in her rental car before leaving the tent. 11:14 p.m., and time was ticking away. The traffic had thinned considerably now, since only a handful of people were hanging around until Monday morning, taking in the last of the rally before returning to their real lives. Under other circumstances, Bryn thought she might like to return to Sturgis. All those big men in leather, the rumble of the engines; the whole motorcycle girl life really appealed to her, despite what had happened to her father all those years before. All of that was in the past, and she needed to get on with her life.

Inside the front door of the police station, she was met by a gray-haired old woman who had shrunk down to about four feet tall. She was far from being a cute old lady like you'd see on television, though. Behind the counter, she climbed onto a stool and sneered down at Bryn. It was easy to see she had been working overtime with the rally going on, and had probably been called away from sleeping tonight to babysit the jailhouse full of Bryn's accomplices. From behind the old woman, Bryn could hear laughing and singing, and she couldn't help but crack a smile herself. Here was this little grandma who probably spent her time in the station house the other 50 weeks of the year dozing off or reading *Good Housekeeping*, and now she had to watch over some of the rowdiest bikers around.

"I'm here to post bail," Bryn said, trying not to giggle. The woman's thick glasses made her look like a female version of Mister Magoo.

"For whom, young lady?"

"Well, uh, for all of them, I guess."

Bryn got flashed a brief evil look as the woman considered whether or not she was joking around, but when she set the cash on the counter, the stare vanished. Grandma Magoo had probably never seen this much cash at one time in her entire life.

The Gearheads were easy. All seventeen were charged with drunk and disorderly conduct for their role in the bar fight. Paul had given Bryn their names, and she had lightened each man's pay envelope accordingly. A second visit from one of her couriers meant Bryn was lugging around a handbag with nearly three hundred thousand dollars in it, enough to pay off the Gearheads and everyone helping her out in Sturgis. She'd paid her girlfriends, wired some cash to the man at the title office, and made out the destinations for the Gearheads. Forty-six envelopes at five grand apiece meant most of her cash was gone. There was just enough to bail out Paul and Andrew and keep the three of them eating for a couple days.

"Nothing like cutting it close," Bryn said as she counted out the money. After bail, she had four hundred and ninety dollars left until Tuesday.

The woman led her into the back room, where makeshift cells had been set up to accommodate the larger-than-average prisoner load. Toward the front, Gearheads were either handcuffed or tied with plastic straps to chairs and tables, or the bars of the real cells. Inside the genuine iron bars were Paul and Andrew, two more Gearheads, and, of course, Public Enemy Number One Jorge Zapate.

She looked at Andrew first, who had a large cut across his forehead and a black and purple bruise on the other side. He sat on the wooden bench holding a towel over his cut, which probably would have needed stitches if they'd had more time to work with. Paul had a black eye, but other than that he wasn't cut up too badly. There was a pretty good bump on the back of his head from where he'd finally hit the gravel and a bit of dried blood in his hair, but he wasn't looking too bad. Most of the Gearheads looked to be in about this same shape, with cuts here and there and ripped clothing. They were used to fighting and a few scratches, and Bryn wasn't sure which bruises and bandages were from tonight and which ones they'd been carrying around all along.

Jorge was by far the worst looking of the bunch. Once again, his head was covered in white bandages that had long before needed changing. They were soaked completely through, and two trickles of fresh blood dripped down his cheek. The old lady had made up a makeshift splint for his leg, and Bryn noticed the crutches propped against the wall next to the bed he was lying on. Jorges lip was split lengthwise, and dried blood was pooling around his mouth. There was a damp cloth laid across his forehead, which was also soaked in blood.

"You're welcome to all of them but that one," the woman said, pointing at Jorge. "We've got Doc Harris coming down to take a look at him. But he's the one you're leaving anyway, right?"

Jorge lifted his head as far as he could. Something in his neck was surely broken, and all he could hear were muffled voices all around him. His ears were ringing from the kicks to his head, and the bandage blocked out most of the other sounds in the room. He could tell Bryn was speaking, but not what she was saying.

Andrew spotted her first, and stood up and walked to the end of the cell. He limped considerably, but seemed all right to ride out in the morning.

"Hey, boss lady," he said, exposing a mouth full of blood-stained teeth. Only one was missing, where Andrew had caught the edge of the liquor rack.

Paul stood up now, throwing his bloody towel into the sink. He wobbled his way over to her too, and took his place next to Andrew. It was like deja vu all over again, only this time they were a little more beat up than when Bryn had first met the boys in the Kindage County Jail a few months before.

They stood there silently for a moment, not sure whether to panic or laugh. Finally, Andrew turned to Paul and said, "Well, Stanley, this is another fine mess you've gotten us into."

"Who's Stanley?" asked Paul, knowing all about the characters from the old movies he and his grandfather used to watch, but wanting to make Andrew feel old.

Bryn looked in both men's eyes, then over to Jorge. They all turned at the same time, and suddenly realized what they had to do.

"All right, gentlemen," Grandma Magoo said, unlocking the iron door. "You're all free to go except the foreign man over there, and he shouldn't be going anywhere tonight anyhow."

This time, Jorge heard everything loud and clear. With what little strength he had left, he propped himself up against the wall, and tried to clear his eyes of the blood and sweat. Through the haze, he saw his partners all leaving the cell and the Gearheads being uncuffed.

Everyone was leaving but him.

Just as the door swung shut, he picked himself off the bed and the pain shot from his toes all the way up to his brain. His leg was surely broken, but he used it anyhow, hobbling toward Bryn. All three of them watched him limping across the cell for a second, then couldn't bear to look anymore. They had gotten him into this, and now none of them could look him in the eye.

"Bryn…" Jorge mumbled, his hand stretched out toward her. "Bryn, are we leaving now?"

Inside Paul, his heart broke in half. The consequences of what they were doing suddenly crashed down on his shoulders. All this hassle for a bit of money, and look at the innocent people who were getting hurt in the process. This wasn't just about a rich man getting hassled for his fortune; Jorge would likely spend the rest of his life in jail, and some of them would surely be caught. The gang he'd helped to start would probably be divided in half, their families ripped apart when daddy went to jail for felony theft. And for what? A couple thousand dollars? Sure, they probably needed that money pretty badly, but was it worth the sacrifice?

Andrew was a cold-hearted man, and had been his whole life. Lately, though, he'd started coming around a little. Stealing from the rich to help him retire more comfortably didn't make him lose a wink of sleep, that's for sure, but there was something about watching this poor little man hobbling across his cell that really got to him. Jorge had a father he never asked for who kept him essentially like that Harry Potter kid, in a closet under the stairs. All the guy wanted was a few dollars to get himself home, and now he would pay the ultimate price for all of them.

"Jorge, I…" was all Bryn could manage. Her vow not to cry in front of her partners had gone out the window now. She turned away from him too, until he had made his way to the end of the cell. They could all hear the confusion in his voice from the painkillers he'd been given to keep him going until the doctor arrived, and from seeing his partners—his friends— leaving him behind.

"Bryn, please…uh, why are you leaving?"

"I'm sorry, Jorge," she said to the wall, since she couldn't face him ever again. "I'm sorry, but you have to stay here. The doctor says you can't leave yet."

Jorge cared little for doctors. Where he came from, you fixed yourself up or died trying. Unless a limb had been cut off, no money would ever be wasted on a doctor. They were vultures who cared only about lining their pockets.

"We have to leave you here, Jorge," Paul said. "The doctor is coming."

And then they all started walking away. He couldn't believe his eyes. Maybe it was the drugs he'd been given, or those still in his system, but they were really walking away and leaving him here. There was no doctor coming. These greedy Americans, like all the other greedy Americans, wanted to keep all the money for themselves. They would leave him here to rot and he would never see his family—what little he had left—again.

"Do not leave me here!" he screamed with the last breath of wind and the last bit of energy he had left. The room was getting black now, and he could feel his eyes closing. With any luck, he thought, they would never open again. Perhaps that was the only way he would ever be with his family again, reunited through death.

He slid down the bars to the floor, trying to grasp at the bars but his hands would no longer obey his commands. Through the darkness, he managed one more scream.

"You did this to me! *All of you*!"

Paul made the mistake of looking over his shoulder. That was Rule One in his business of stealing—never look back. You might see who's chasing you and lose your edge, or even worse, you might see who you're really hurting. Paul had hurt a lot of people in his life, but he'd never once looked back. On one Friday night a few years back, he'd been chased down by a pickup full of men with shotguns, who fired at his tires trying to bring him down. If he'd looked back, he would have seen how close they really were, and that they weren't really shooting at the tires. He cried now too, hiding his eyes and vowing that he'd never look back again.

"Seems like we've been in this situation before," Bryn said, trying to lighten up the situation a bit.

"Yeah, but there were more of us the first time," Andrew said.

Bryn turned around, tired from a long day of making deals, a day that was ending badly. The backside of her hand connected with Andrew's cut cheek, sending blood flying. He yelped in pain and buried his face in his hands as blood dripped through his fingers. She didn't know why she had hit him, but with all the frustration inside her she had to hit something.

"Fuck you, old man!" she said, bending down to yell in his ear as he stood there doubled over in pain. "Fuck you, Andrew. What would you have me do, huh? It has to be this way, don't you understand? Get in the fucking car and finish this job, or I'll have you both right back in that jail for good."

Both men had been beaten, physically and otherwise, and gave no argument. Andrew just pulled the handkerchief from his back pocket and mopped up the blood. He had probably deserved a good slap, and figured all three of them could benefit from one right about now.

They climbed into the car and just sat there for a moment, silent.

"How long?" Paul asked finally.

"It doesn't matter, Paul. Let's just…"

"I asked you how long, you bitch!" he yelled, still unable to look at her because of his tears. "Just tell me how long and I promise I won't say another word."

Bryn couldn't look at him either.

"Thirty years, Paul. Okay? The lady said with all the charges he'll get sent away for a minimum of thirty years."

The entire trip back, with Jorge screaming simultaneously in all three of their heads, no one said another word.

Chapter Fourteen

It was clear that the streets were being rolled up for another year of normalcy, and only a few sidewalk spectators watched the mismatched group enter the dark sale tent. Four of the Gearheads accompanied Paul, Andrew, and Bryn for the first group of bikes. Those who had gotten beaten up and arrested had a few hours to sleep before their big ride, and Bryn did some switching of destinations so that the bikers who had pissed her off the most would have the longest ride ahead of them. It served them right for screwing up her plans.

It was now midnight, two hours later than they had expected to begin. Tension was already high enough without worrying about Jorge too, so the whole tent just watched silently while Paul fired up the keymaking machine. He steadied himself after breaking two blanks and miscutting another, and finally the fourth try worked.

"Eric Malone?" Bryn asked, and one of the Gearheads, a skinny man not much older than Paul, raised his hand.

"All right Eric, this is a 1999 Springer Soft Tail. It is titled to a mister Phillip Lane of Franklin, Ohio, who you will say is your uncle if you run into any trouble. You're playing mediator in a family quarrel and returning his prized bike. Don't go into too much detail, just offer to pay any tickets you get in cash, with a little extra for the policeman if he wants it. Understand?"

"What's a 'meterator'?" Eric asked, scratching his head.

"Only the best and the brightest work here," Bryn said, sending an evil glance Paul's way. "Thanks, Paul. Anyway, Eric, don't worry about it, just stick with your story. Your destination is St. Louis, Missouri. You meet the buyer at the McDonald's on Fifth and Monroe at 8 a.m. Wednesday. Got it?"

Eric nodded that he understood. He took his envelope from Bryn, which contained the full five thousand. Thanks to an incessant nosebleed, Eric had not joined his buddies at the bar the night before, and as a result he hadn't had any bail money removed from his envelope. His money was already spent, since the county attorney's office had been hounding him for back child support. But at least he could keep a little more of his paycheck after this.

Eric rumbled through the tent flap and Bryn closed it again. Just forty-nine more to go.

Paul had gotten used to the machine by now, and made the key for the next bike, a 1976 Sportster with more chrome on it than any Sportster should have. Eddie Giese rode away on this one, all three hundred and twenty pounds of him, and they laughed at how much his behind hung over the sides of the seat. Mr. Giese had also been a good boy, spending most of his time and money in a nearby strip club and not beating up Jorge Zapate. He had to be in Ortonville, Minnesota, by tomorrow evening.

By 1:15, the other two Gearheads were on their way, one on a customized 2003 V-Rod and the other on a neon pink 2000 Electra Glide Classic. Bryn was feeling a little better about how fast things were going, and called in eight more Gearheads to stand by for takeoff. As soon as possible after the sun came up the tent needed to be emptied and torn down, or the locals would start to get suspicious—something they surely didn't need.

Bryn caught a small cat nap while the boys struggled with a 1971 FLH, then handed the cash to what was perhaps the only normal looking member of the Gearheads. This young man was probably 19 at the oldest, with long blonde hair tied into a ponytail and a behind that Bryn took pleasure in watching as he saddled up on his bike. Michael Sundberg was, however, one of the brawlers from the previous night, so his destination was Modesto, California, and his pay was only four thousand.

Over the grinding of the key machine, she heard her cell phone ring shortly after 6 a.m., and thought nothing about answering it.

"Hey, Brinnie," Malcolm said from the other end of the line. "You about finished out there?"

She had expected his call, but it scared her just the same. Bryn just hung up the phone and switched the power off. Later, she would blame it on bad reception.

"Your hubby?" Paul asked, before triumphantly starting an older Wide Glide.

"Yeah," she said. "How we coming here, boys? Sun's almost up."

"Believe it or not, just a dozen to go," Andrew said, still not happy about her breaking his head back open but hiding that for now. Three more riders left after this, all jailbirds from the previous night. One even had the unfortunate task of crossing the border into Mexico. His downfall had been grabbing Bryn's ass when he came into the sale tent. Now he would pay for it with an extra two thousand miles to ride.

As the fortieth bike, the 1903, rolled off on a flatbed, Bryn could see the sun coming up over the hill and the sanitation crews out in full force cleaning the streets. Soon the police would be bored with small town life again, and would start checking tents in the campgrounds to see if the occupants were still alive. They would likely check this tent, too.

Sipping coffee and ready to ride, the final seven Gearheads entered the tent and strapped their gear onto their respective cycles. Six of them would be spread out around the region, and Bryn decided that Charger would take Jorge's place on his bike. All four of them needed to be in Two Harbors to meet the boat in just over twenty-four hours. This was 820 miles away, and left little time for errors, sleep, or eating.

Two bikes were going on the first try, and just when Paul thought he was on a roll, along came another V-Rod and its complicated ignition system. Bryn wanted to sleep again while he fiddled with the bike, but found that she couldn't. There was no chance of sleeping now, since it was already 9:30 and the men hadn't even started on their own bikes yet.

Bryn went out for sandwiches at 10, and returned to find only Charger, Paul, and Andrew left in the tent. They ate quickly, since Paul complained he could no longer see straight from hunger and lack of sleep, then he grinded Charger's key perfectly on the first try.

Three to go, but it was nearing noon.

The key fit fine on the bike Bryn would be riding, a 1979 Sportster, but starting the bike proved to be a challenge. It was obvious this was not one of the cycle maker's finest years as Paul kicked away at the starter over and over.

"You're flooding it," said Andrew.

"No, it needs more gas. Pull the choke halfway out," Charger said.

Finally Paul gave up for the time being. It would start when the time was right, he just had a feeling it would. His leg was sore and he had grown tired of listening to the advice of his colleagues.

The matching Heritage Soft Tails, not much different from the ones they had rode into town on, were no sweat, and with some furious kicking on the Sportster all four of the final bikes were warming up outside the tent by 2 p.m. That left eighteen hours for 820 miles, not including necessary stops for gas and the bathroom. No sleep would come for any of them, not for another day at least.

As the bikes rumbled behind them, the Sportster sputtering a little, all four members of the Bryn Scott Gang disassembled the tent, rolled it into a huge ball, and tried their best to hide it in the alley behind the adjacent grocery store. The counter, cash register, and chairs were all hidden nearby, and Bryn took care with a damp cloth to wipe away any possible fingerprints. She did the same on the key machine, which she threw in a nearby dumpster and buried under some trash. Now, the only evidence left of them in Sturgis would be the bikes in the storage locker a few miles down the road, and the perplexed Midwest Custom Cycles truckers who would return shortly with parts that were no longer needed.

Bryn wondered if they had found Junior yet, probably sweating to death in that tent out in the middle of the sun-baked field. This worried her some, because he was pretty crafty for such an idiot. Hopefully, his slumber wouldn't end until later in the day, but it was sometimes hard to tell with those drugs.

At 2:30 p.m., a good six hours later than anticipated, Charger, Paul, Andrew, and Bryn followed one another up Edmunds Street to I-90, which would treat them to hundreds of miles of 80-mile-an-hour riding. If they made it through the twin cities all right, they just might get there on time to meet the courier and their boat. Despite the careful planning, Bryn would still keep looking for police cars and listening for sirens the whole way. That little voice in her head, likely her mother's, was still telling her she'd be caught soon enough, and her imagination had her hearing sirens left and right.

Bryn's mother had blamed her for her father's death in that motorcycle accident, and never let her forget it. Anything in her teenage years dealing with motorcycles, or danger in any way, meant the old woman would treat her to a lecture on how such a life was nothing but trouble.

Hopefully her mother would be wrong just this once.

-2-

Every hundred miles, as they bucked the wind headed east on I-90, the Sportster's peanut tank needed gas. This meant a much needed butt break for the novice riders, and for Charger, it meant the chance to heed his nicotine craving. They stopped for dinner at a Denny's along the way, right next to Bernie and Sheila's Wild West Museum. Paul checked his gear, which included a couple more changes of clothes, plenty of deodorant, and Shelby's dinosaur book; everything but his tent. With any luck, the sleeping beauty inside that tent would still be sleeping, and Paul remembered leaving the flap open too, so the naked Junior Devane was probably covered from head to toe with mosquito bites.

After they could take it no longer, Bryn gave her approval for an hour-long nap at a rest area just outside of the twin cities. Andrew had been the most vocal one in arguing this point, that an old man like him simply needed at least some sleep to function, and riding through a big city would be tough enough without a cat nap. Neither Paul nor Charger argued for or against the stop, they were simply too tired to care either way. A person's body kind of got used to functioning on little sleep after awhile, and none of the three of them had gotten any shuteye since their wait in the jail cell Sunday night.

And even then, with Jorge moaning in pain, the winks they caught were few and far between.

Andrew unrolled his sleeping bag atop a picnic table under a small shelter, while Paul wadded up some T-shirts for a pillow. He had left his sleeping bag for Junior, who would likely use it to cover himself once he finally woke up and went to get help. Bryn leaned her sleeping bag against a soda machine, and soon the constant hum had her sleeping soundly. She set the alarm on the small portable clock she'd brought, but ignored it and hit the snooze button an unprecedented seven times.

Charger heard the alarm too, but didn't complain when she added a few more minutes. He dreamed about the new outboard he would buy for his boat with his newfound riches, so that he and his buddies could go to Canada to fish again this year. Andrew's head was full of stampeding lawyers once again, and Paul visualized hiking through the mountains of some far-off country with the Pope and Oprah Winfrey.

For Bryn, who was dreaming about running from the police while she carried her husband's severed penis, part of the dream would come true.

"Excuse me, miss," she heard the policeman say in her dream, so she threw the organ at him and kept right on running.

"Leave me alone, you can have it," she said.

"Miss, *excuse* me."

This time she felt her shoulder being shook, as her father had done to her when she was young. Malcolm would just let her sleep, since she could get awfully grouchy if woken before ten. For a moment, before the dream ended and the reality set in, it really was her father, getting her up for his ill-fated motorcycle ride on that Saturday morning so long ago.

"Daddy?" Bryn asked.

"Miss, excuse me, but you can't camp here."

She opened her eyes now to see an older black man with grey hair poking out from beneath his Minnesota State Trooper hat. He was covered head to toe in radios, pins, and patches from different departments, and wore dark sunglasses that Bryn could see her reflection in. What she also noticed was that the eastern sky had begun to lighten up.

"Oh, fuck," was the first thing she could say, and instantly regretted it. "Dammit, what time is it?"

The man checked his watch, quickly fixing his eyes back on her. She knew why right away, since she had wiggled around enough in her sleep that her tank top was pulled way down. Minus the bra she had taken off for a bit of comfort while she slept, Officer Ray Harkin was being treated to a free peep show.

"It's five fifteen, ma'am, and you should know that there's no camping in this rest area."

Paul got up now and was the first to notice that their party of four had gained a member. Had one of the Gearheads gotten caught and spilled his guts about the plan? It wasn't an unlikely scenario, since they had pretty much gotten caught doing everything else the past few days. One of them even admitted to being ticketed for public urination after relieving himself on a Honda.

The man was bent over Bryn and wasn't paying much attention to the other three campers nearby. Paul's first thought was that he could find something heavy and give the officer a good crack across the back of the head, but he quickly put that idea away. If they were in trouble, this guy probably had reinforcements on the way. Apprehending the perps who were stealing a couple million dollars worth of custom motorcycles probably required at least three or four cops.

"What seems to be the problem officer?" Paul asked, getting to his feet. After crouching in those trailers for nearly two days and spending a few more hours Sunday night on his knees, they were about ready to give out on him. He heard them crunch as he walked closer.

"What I was trying to tell your friend here is that there's no camping in a public rest area," he said, with Paul's reflection now in his dollar store sunglasses.

"We ain't campin', we're just sleepin'," Charger added, helping their case none.

The officer looked over the crew. Charger, now shirtless and hairy as a grizzly bear, looked every bit the animal. Only half his teeth were left in his mouth, and he had bruises and scars from the bar fight, in addition to those he'd had before their trip. The man hadn't showered since they'd left home, and looked like it too. As for the other men, they had their own bruises and scars. The young one had a black eye and the old guy looked like he'd been thrown through a plate glass window, with all the little cuts on his face. The girl looked clean enough, but she was awfully nervous for some reason.

"You with these fellas?" he asked Bryn, who considered the question for a moment then nodded emphatically.

He looked around again, spending a few seconds on each of the four. Three beat up grease balls and a pretty lady; something didn't add up here.

"Miss, if these men are bothering you, all you have to do is let me know—"

"Look, we're not bothering anybody," Andrew said, standing up and feeling his back protest adamantly. "We're on our way back from Sturgis, just like all the other bikers I'm sure you've been meeting on the road. We thought it would be safer if we caught a little nap before going through the cities, so we stopped in here. No harm done, right?"

Officer Harkin was not fond of this tone, especially coming from a man no older than he. As a minority in an authority position, he was making it his duty to stand up for the little guys, and he didn't take guff from anyone. Andrew caught the cop's anger right away, steadied himself, and continued.

"I'm sorry, sir, if we've broken the rules, but we thought it would be better to not be so tired when we went through a lot of traffic. If there's some ticket you have to give us, we'll gladly pay— "

"Well, there is a fine for camping in a rest area, but I imagine we can take care of this right here if you'd like."

Andrew's tension quickly drained away. Here, standing in front of him, was a man after his own heart. Although Andrew wasn't fond of his color, or anyone of color in an authority position, he had to admire the fact that in this day and age, things could still be settled under the table.

"Hundred apiece," Harkin said, waiting for them to gasp. Although their 'cycles were pretty fancy, they looked like they didn't have two nickels to rub together between the four of them. "A hundred apiece and I forget about you sleeping here, I forget about your indecent exposure, miss, and I forget about the fact that these are some awfully expensive bikes for such greasy looking losers as yourselves."

"I'm actually a lawyer," Andrew said, "I just like to fit in with the biker crowd."

"Don't care, *boy*."

This made Andrew furious. All the times he'd referred to a black man simply as "boy" had come back to haunt him. Had this darkie not been wearing a gun, he would have loved to show him a few of his old boxing moves.

Bryn was quickly doing the math. They had pooled all their money before leaving Sturgis. Both Paul and Andrew had lost their wallets and credit cards in the bar fight, and Charger lived an only cash life so that the government wouldn't figure out that he hadn't paid his taxes since 1995. Bryn also carried only cash, since Malcolm had forbiden her from bringing her credit cards along. Besides, she had loaded up all of the cards before she left, and they wouldn't have done her any good.

"We don't have— " she said, but got no further.

Officer Harkin pressed a little button on his shoulder, and began to speak into the small black box clipped to his shirt. He had bigger fish to fry elsewhere.

"Dispatch, this is twelve, I've got a possible loitering and indecent exposure— "

"Wait," Bryn said. "We've got enough. There's enough here."

He released the button on the microphone, which wasn't active anyway and was just a bluff. Harkin knew all about the millionaires who drove their fancy motor homes and trailered their new Harleys to Sturgis, then spent a week looking like blue collar mechanics. Everybody out there wanted to fit in, and that meant looking like a true biker with leather and beard stubble, even if you went yachting the other fifty weeks of the year.

"I figured you did," he said, strolling away to admire their 'cycles while they put together the cash.

Bryn fumbled through her handbag, which contained their combined funds. She had not had enough to pay Charger his five thousand (minus bail, of course), since everything the courier had advanced her had gone to bail out her crew and to bribe the others involved. His share would be deducted from the other three members' cash, but that cash wouldn't exist until they made

Two Harbors. If they fooled around any longer, they wouldn't be there on time and the boat would sail, along with the courier and the rest of their money.

She counted out the bills into Harkin's hand, trying to hold her shirt up with one elbow. He gave her a little smile as she reached four hundred, then simply turned and walked back to his car. This little windfall was going right with the rest, a fund he was saving for a motor home some day.

It would be twelve hours before Officer Harkin heard about the unprecedented theft of 150 custom and classic motorcycles during the 63rd Annual Sturgis Motorcycle Rally. He would always wonder if those folks he'd come across had been the ones responsible. All of a sudden, four hundred dollars didn't seem like so much anymore.

Fearing another officer stopping by for a handout, they packed up quickly and tried not to think about the time. They had to wind around a little more before hitting I-35 north, and even though the interstate would get them there fastest, there were still two hundred miles standing between them and Two Harbors.

"Time?" Paul asked, cranking the motor on his own bike before moving to Bryn's Sportster to kick for awhile.

"A little over two hours left," Bryn said.

"Money?" Andrew asked, suddenly very worried again.

"Sixteen dollars and seven cents," Bryn said. "That's one more tankful for each of us…almost."

Paul didn't do the math. He didn't want to. They had come too far to slump over and die now. He had been in jail twice, spent all those hours and all that sweat, and the lack of a couple dollars simply would not stand in his way.

"It's two hundred miles to Two Harbors, we've got half a tank of gas each, and I'm down to half a pack of cigarettes," Charger said.

All four of them laughed. They were tired, and strung out from the constant pounding of the wind and watching the lines fly by. A few more miles, though, and all their work would finally pay off. Everyone would have a better life, even Charger with his new boat motor.

"It's dark, and we're wearing sunglasses," Andrew finished the quote. *The Blues Brothers* was one of his favorite movies too.

"Hit it," they all answered in unison.

-3-

Rush hour hadn't yet begun, much to the relief of the Bryn Scott foursome. They cruised up I-35 in the early morning light at a steady 90 miles per hour, feeling the cool air beginning to get warmer. There were no more run-ins with Officer Harkin or his buddies, despite their traveling well over the speed limit.

They stopped for a final tank of gas in Cloquet, and distributed the last six gallons they could afford between the four cycles. Bryn made sure to use every penny and not a bit more, since getting stopped for stealing gas would sink them for sure. By now, Junior had likely found his way out of the tent and to the nearest phone, where he was probably talking to his big brother about what had happened. Knowing Malcolm, he would call every sheriff and deputy in the state to have them looking for Bryn. Monday morning had come now, and the amount of bikes still traveling had dropped to almost zero. Everyone who'd went to Sturgis was now safely back at home, drinking their morning cup of coffee and regretting another year of work before their next vacation. These four were beginning to stand out like a sore thumb amongst the cars and pickups. It wasn't often that four mismatched bikers rode their expensive, neon-colored Harleys together this early on a Monday morning.

"Hope no one was hungry," she said, returning from the counter. "That was the last of our money, boys."

"Yeah, but I can smell more of it a few miles to the north," Andrew said, cranking his motor.

The pressure had been relieved a bit now, and they adjusted their speed so that they would reach the docks at just the right time. There was no sense in speeding unnecessarily and risking a ticket. The weight on Paul and Andrew's shoulders was slowly lifting as they dreamed about their newfound riches and how they would spend it. Charger thought about fishing, but was admittedly a little jealous about how little he would be getting in comparison to the other three. No matter, though. He wasn't the fancy type that needed a lot of cash. He'd grown up on a peanut farm in Georgia, just like the ex-president, but his tastes were far from presidential.

Bryn was still a little nervous, but that was only because there was a lot more of this plan left for her. Paul sometimes caught her looking across at him as they rode side by side, and he could have sworn he saw tears in her eyes a couple times.

Was she just sad that her helpers and friends were leaving her soon, or was there more involved?

Andrew caught those looks too, but put them out of his mind. He was probably just jealous that the pretty girl was looking at the younger guy instead of him. Besides, he was quite busy keeping an eye out for their exit; as the front man on the right, that was his job. Charger was supposed to help, but Andrew doubted this guy had enough intelligence to even tie his shoes.

At a quarter of eight, with the traffic building up going both ways on the interstate, Andrew spotted the right exit number and motioned for his partners to follow him. He had done his share of business in Two Harbors, paying off freighter captains for boxes of pirated software. He knew his way around, and even remembered the exact location where they were supposed to unload.

All four cycles stopped in a parking lot as the crew scanned up and down the bay. The ship's name, which Bryn had finally clued the others in on at the last gas station, was Lady Mae, based out of Dublin, Ireland. They were to meet a woman who would be wearing a red collared shirt and khaki pants, carrying a leather duffel bag. Though Bryn was still unsure of the actual amount of the final payment, her rough math had indicated it would be a nice one.

"It's kind of like those spy movies," Andrew said, watching the people come and go along the sidewalk. Seagulls made their conversation almost impossible, as the birds darted everywhere in the parking lot scooping up bits of discarded food.

"Yeah, like cloak and dagger stuff," Charger said. "Meeting a pretty woman in a dark alley with a bag fulla greenbacks. You guys ain't gonna knife me in the back and run off with my share, now are you?"

Paul laughed first. All this time, none of them had thought of screwing over the others to take all the cash for themselves. It seemed so passe, as the French would say—something everybody does in all the spy movies. In truth, the four of them really weren't all that greedy. Bryn wasn't out to take all the money the Devanes had, she just wanted enough so that she didn't have to work in any more strip clubs for awhile. Paul didn't want to buy a mansion in Hollywood, he just wanted to take off with his daughter and make sure she grew up as good as possible before the cops caught up with him. And Andrew, he already had what most would consider a small fortune socked away. He just wanted enough so that he and Coralie could both be comfortable in their retirement years.

So why were they here?

Bryn was the answer. There had always been something about that woman that drew Paul and Andrew into this whole mess. She was very convincing, not to mention very beautiful, and when she was upset it actually made the men's hearts break. Pretty girls should never have to be upset, according to chivalry, and both Paul and Andrew were old fashioned knight-in-shining-armor types.

"Is that her?" Charger asked, pointing about half a mile down the harbor. From where they sat, they could just barely make out a red object standing near an open metal container. It looked to be the same size as a railroad car, minus the wheels.

"Good," Andrew said. "Let's get out of here and get our money. I'm so hungry I was getting ready to start fighting the seagulls over there for a discarded sandwich crust."

Bryn's Sportster had begun to sputter by the time they pulled onto the dock. Another couple of miles and they would have been done for. Bryn would do the talking here, so the others stood behind with the motorcycles as she walked up the dock toward the woman.

"Bryn Scott?" they overheard her say.

"Affirmative."

"Angie Kox," she said, shaking Bryn's hand. "Need your destination for confirmation, please."

Bryn looked over her shoulder but didn't know why. She could have trusted her partners all along with some of the information she was keeping secret, and for some reason she didn't want to let it out even now. However, this meant their job was done.

"Cape Town, South Africa, with one drop off in Hong Kong."

The woman pulled a slip of paper from her back pocket, looked at it carefully, and nodded.

"The count is one million three, give or take a couple," the red shirt woman said, handing Bryn the bag. "Everyone involved is very happy so far, I've been asked to tell you. We'll be keeping it that way, won't we?"

Bryn nodded, though she was too busy doing division in her head to understand. It was easy to forget sometimes that she had been doing business with 150 criminals from all over the world, who enjoyed the finer things in life and would likely kill if they were disappointed.

The woman held up her hand, and on command four men emerged from inside the metal box. They first looked all around to see that no one was looking, then made it a point to show the pistols tucked into their waistbands. Ms. Red Shirt pointed to the bikes, and the men obediently began walking toward Paul, Andrew, and Charger. Suddenly a bit frightened, the men quickly unstrapped their belongings and stepped away from the cycles. The final four bikes were obviously the most important ones, and would go to a king or a prince or something.

The gunmen each mounted a cycle, checked over the bikes to see that the keys were genuine and there was no damage, then cranked the motors. One had to kick over the Sportster a few times, but it sputtered to a start eventually.

"Maybe we should give him five bucks for gas," Andrew whispered in Paul's ear.

"We don't have five dollars."

Each henchman followed the first and rode the bikes into the trailer, checking around once more to see if anyone was watching. They didn't smile, didn't speak, and didn't look at Bryn, which would have been hard for any man not to do. The bikes were strapped in within seconds, and the doors to the cargo bay were closed up and locked by the woman in the red shirt, with the men still inside.

"We will consider this matter closed," she said, extending her hand again to Bryn. It bothered Andrew some to see women taking care of the business, but he kept quiet.

"Yes, we will," Bryn said.

The woman boarded the ship, and for a moment Paul was waiting for Bryn to take off running with their money or turn around and shoot all three of them. He had seen too many movies.

So had Charger, who was thinking this woman would jump right on that boat with the other one and he'd never get to see his new 75 horsepower Johnson.

But a happy ending seemed to be in store for the group, as Bryn calmly walked back up the dock to where her partners in crime were standing.

"I think we'll have that five dollars pretty soon," Andrew said.

To avoid the crowds as much as possible, they walked calmly with a fortune in unmarked, out-of-sequence hundred dollar bills to a small picnic shelter not unlike the one they'd nearly gotten arrested in earlier that morning. Bryn sat down calmly at the table, though she wanted to jump up and down and scream to the world that she had achieved her goals.

"You boys want some money?" she asked.

While Charger kept a lookout, Bryn began to divide the stacks of bills. She broke open one bundle of $10,000 and counted out half of that for Charger. In all the excitement, she'd forgotten that he owed her for bail, and he certainly wasn't going to remind her.

"It's all there, Charger," she told him, meeting his nearly toothless grin with her own.

"Tell your friends I never could have done this without their help. I hope they all make it home safely."

"Thanks," Charger said. It would be a shame to leave the side of such a pretty girl to go home to his wife Arlene, with her wide ass and passion for chewing tobacco.

All three of the remaining members watched him stroll up the boardwalk, keeping his hand firmly on the wad of bills in his front pocket. Bryn really did wish the Gearheads the best of luck, not just because it would keep her from getting in trouble, but because they seemed like the kind of men she'd grown up around. They were rude, dirty, and vulgar, but she wagered that most of them wouldn't hurt a fly. In fact, all but two of the Gearheads would end up making their destinations with no problems. Andrew "Elvis" Eck was getting pulled over right about then in Missouri for speeding. They would also find a tiny rock of methamphetamine in his back pocket and impound the cycle. Martin "Itchy" Kelseth was the other unfortunate victim. While leaving the strip club later that afternoon, he would accidentally knock over a row of cycles, getting him into a fistfight with a bunch of lawyers from Illinois. They would not only light his bike on fire in front of him, sending one more Knucklehead to the great hereafter, but they would also sue him for assault.

"Down to three," Andrew said, rubbing his palms together.

Bryn divided up the remaining cash, with $430,000 in each stack. No one complained that it was less than they were hoping for, and Paul and Andrew even put the last few assorted hundreds into Bryn's pile. They were both very wealthy now, and a few hundred dollars didn't mean much.

Paul took two thousand out of one bundle, stuffed hundreds into every available pocket, and packed the rest into his duffle bag. Bryn kept the leather bag from the red-shirted woman, and Andrew had to remove some dirty clothes to fit all of his into his own bag.

"You want some breakfast?" Paul asked Bryn. "I'm about ready to start gnawing on this picnic table myself. Come on, I'm buying."

They all laughed, but Bryn shook her head.

"I'm sorry, boys, but my flight leaves at noon and I've got to pick up my rental car still. I wish I had time to stick around some more, but I've really got to run."

"Where you headed?" Andrew asked. "Or are you still not telling?"

"Nope," she said, and reached into her handbag. Bryn produced two white envelopes, each one labeled with her partners' names. They could tell she was trying not to cry, and it finally set in that this would be the last time they would all see one another.

"These are for you guys," she said. "It's kind of embarrassing, so I need you to promise you won't open them until after I'm gone. It's kind of mushy, so wait until after breakfast or you might lose your appetite."

"Fat chance of that happening," Andrew said, smelling bacon frying at the little café across the street.

Bryn stood up, flopped her bags over her shoulder, and embraced Andrew.

"Thank you so much for all you've done for me," she said. "I never could have gotten rid of all those bikes without you. You are truly a great man, Andrew Falkness, and I'm going to miss having you around."

Andrew's eyes welled up with tears too. He had never known the joy of having children; not that he hadn't wanted any, but Coralie absolutely detested them. So, no young person had ever really said anything kind to him before. Usually it was just "Hey, old man" or "Use your turn signal, asshole."

She moved on to Paul now, a hug she had been dreading since the beginning. If there was a time that she would break, it would be now. Bryn kept telling herself to stay strong, and that it would all be forgotten soon enough. But that didn't keep the tears from flowing.

"Paul Morris," she said, sobbing into his shirt. "You are a wonderful man, too. Thank you and…"
She lowered her voice to a whisper, and put her mouth close to Paul's ear.
"…and I'm sorry, Paul. I am so terribly sorry."

Sorry for what? was what Paul was thinking, but he decided to just enjoy his last hug with his partner. In situations like these, women sometimes said things that he didn't understand. Hell, in any normal situation they were hard to understand. He held her close, feeling her hot breath on his neck and the wetness of her tears.

And then she ran away, her bags slapping against her sides. Bryn buried her head in her hands and just ran up the sidewalk, unable to look at either of them ever again. Paul and Andrew exchanged glances and considered going after her, but knew somehow that it was best to just let her go. Their job was over, and so was their short but meaningful friendship. Everybody had gotten what they wanted, the money was paid out, and now it was time to go back to reality again.

"How about you, old man?" Paul asked. "Can I interest you in some pancakes?"

"I'll race you to the door," Andrew said. He put his arm around Paul and they both strolled toward the café, carrying a combined total of nearly a million dollars in cash. It was best to let the woman go, and to make a clean break. Andrew thought maybe he and Paul could still get together, though, to have a Manhattan or two or to tell stories about their adventures in the last few weeks.

The café held only a few people, since it was now nearing 9 a.m. and most everyone had gone off to work. Through the doors Andrew caught a familiar sight that he just couldn't resist this time. In his younger days, for more than 30 years actually, Andrew Falkness had been a chain smoker. Just like John Wayne, who never died of lung cancer by the way, he would light the new one with the old one all day long. Tighter regulations and all those memos from the bureaucrats who ran his building about secondhand smoke in the workplace, along with his failing health, had finally gotten him to quit. Did he need a class? Special gum? Did he gain fifty pounds?

The verdict was no on all counts. Andrew quit cold turkey, and chose to kill his liver for awhile instead. But now, for some reason, the packs of Marlboro Reds in that display case on the way into the restaurant seemed to be calling out to him. And why not? One pack after all this time surely wouldn't hurt, would it? He would still buy a pack here and there, but found that rather than four packs a day he was smoking only one a month on the average. And considering the stress he'd been through in the last few days, he deserved a smoke.

"Miss," he called to the teenage waitress, who was probably finishing up her summer vacation by working in this dump. "Pack of Reds, please, and just add it onto our tab. We're fucking *hungry*."

She gave him a funny look and handed him the cigarettes. They selected a booth near the back, shoved their bags into it, and ordered enough breakfast for any four men. Andrew wanted three pancakes, sausage, eggs, and hash browns, while Paul ordered two servings of blueberry waffles.

While they waited for their food, Andrew fished his ratty old address book out of his pants pocket. Miraculously, or perhaps not so miraculously, he had managed to lose his wallet, credit cards, and other valuable things in their little bar fight, but his book of clients' addresses he never went without had stayed in his back pocket just fine. Of course he didn't keep any money in it, and as hungry as he was a few hours ago he was wishing he did. What he did keep in it, though, was his matchbook, with the ladies propping their naked bodies up doggy style on some random motel room bed. It was his Vegas souvenir from a couple years back, and since he rarely smoked, there were still five or six matches left in it. Besides smelling up the bathroom a bit too much, someone who just about never smoked had little need for matches.

"These dogs know *all* the tricks." He recited the slogan on its cover from memory, not needing to look at it. He unwrapped his cancer sticks and selected one, tapped it on the table, and slipped it into his mouth.

Paul, in the meantime, couldn't bring himself to wait until after breakfast to read what Bryn had written. Secretly, he was hoping she'd left instructions on where he could find her so that they could get together, but he knew it wasn't likely. What she'd said just kept running though his mind, though.

What was she so sorry about? Everything had gone smoothly.

Andrew struck a match, touched it to his cigarette, then threw it into the ashtray. It was nice to patronize a restaurant where one still had the freedom to smoke. He closed the matchbook, glanced at the ladies on the cover, and had them nearly back in his address book before he stopped.

His mouth stood wide open, dropping the lit cigarette onto the table.

On the cover of the matchbook, where those dogs knew all the tricks and were naked as the day they were born, second from the right, was Bryn Scott.

In an instant, he remembered it all. He knew why he kept getting the feeling that he'd seen her before. Andrew placed exactly where he knew her from, and why this was all happening to him.

He opened his mouth to speak, to tell Paul all about it, but it was already too late.

Paul, who had disobeyed orders and opened his letter before breakfast, needed only to read the first few words. He snatched up his bag and before he could think he was out the front door, running up the sidewalk in the direction he had watched Bryn leave. His legs pumped as hard as they could, anxious as he'd ever been about anything to reach his destination, though he didn't know where his destination was.

Andrew was shocked enough to finally have figured out where he knew Bryn that he barely noticed Paul running out the door. He would be going to prison for sure now. No more Coralie and bye bye to all that money. He did the only thing he could do—hang his head and stare at the table for a moment.

It all made perfect sense now. Why else would she need some random old man to help her out with this whole thing?

He watched his cigarette roll across the table and bump into the letter Paul had left. Rather than open his own letter, since he already knew what was inside it, he picked up Paul's and read the first line.

That was all it took before he was out the door and running too.

"Dear Paul, Malcolm and I have your daughter."

Chapter Fifteen

If Andrew Falkness hadn't felt old before, he certainly felt old now. He trailed Paul for at least three blocks before he saw, much to the relief of his knees, that the young man had slowed to a stop. He stood there by the lamp post, anxiously eyeing every car and every pedestrian that passed by. Andrew thought this was one of the few things he didn't miss out on by never being a father—that feeling of panic when you can't find your child. Multiply that by a hundred, throw in a trusted friend who had screwed you over, and add a sadistic rich boy for color, and that was about what Paul was feeling right now.

He approached Paul slowly, watching him twitch and constantly wipe the sweat from his forehead. Andrew kept his distance for a minute, listening to Paul mumble, "Shelby, little Shelby, they've got…" over and over again.

"Paul?" Andrew placed a hand on his shoulder and he jumped away, once again looking back and forth up the street. Andrew was no good at comforting anyone, which was probably the reason he had now been single for so long, but in Paul's case he was more than willing to try. He needed to put his own discovery about Bryn aside to help his friend right now.

"Sit down, Paul. Let's just sit down on this bench here and read this letter together."

Paul paced up and down the sidewalk, thought he recognized someone in one car, ran after it for a few feet then gave up. Bryn was long gone; that was why she had run away from him, not because she wanted to scoop him into her arms and tell him she wanted to be with him. It was his daughter she wanted. How did Bryn even know Paul had a daughter, anyway? He'd mentioned her a couple of times during their nights training in the garage, but that was all.

"Let's just read this through, then figure out what we're going to do,"

Andrew said again, taking Paul's shoulder. This time he didn't flinch; he was suddenly too tired to move.

Paul took his letter from Andrew, unfolded the notebook paper, and forced himself to read the entire thing. He was never one to get hot under the collar without a good explanation first, but this was his daughter, for Christ's sake!

He read it aloud for both of them.

> *Dear Paul,*
>
> *Malcolm and I have your daughter.*
>
> *As I am writing this, you and Andrew are banging around inside the second semi trailer here in Sturgis, making a terrible racket that I hope no one else will hear. You guys have been wonderful through this whole thing; you've really come to the aid of a damsel in distress, which makes it all that much tougher to do what I have to do to you.*
>
> *I guess I should start from the very beginning, which, the song says, is a very good place to start. I grew up in a trailer, a single-wide with four brothers and one sister. We lived right on the edge of Vegas, with the glittering lights on one horizon and a vast expanse of desert on the other. By the time I was into my teenage years, I had gotten just about enough of my siblings. I saved up some babysitting money, lied about my age to the nice folks at Fantasy Fred's, and got myself a steady income. Then I moved a mile down the road into another trailer park. Movin' on up, Weezie, right? Anyhow, one thing led to another, a lot of which your buddy Andrew could probably tell you, and I was down lower than I'd ever been. Through everything, my only dream was to have a child of my own, which would have been the absolute stupidest thing at that point. But, when you're 17 you don't really know what's involved with caring for a child yet. It's the weirdest thing, Paul, I never once missed my parents, but the younger brothers I took care of kept me up at night crying. Those kids I used to babysit back home kept me up too. I wanted one of my own, and tried with about every guy I dated. Something was wrong, though. My grandmother told me that God just hadn't meant for me to have a child of my own, but I've never been one to listen to anyone. I guess that's where you come in.*

Anyhow, the rest of the story is your typical fairy tale. Girl finally gets job in bar after nearly starving to death, boy meets girl, boy pays for girl for the night and they hit it off. Four hours and half a dozen kamikazes later, Malcolm Devane and myself were happily married. I didn't know then who he was or how much money his family had; I only knew that something seemed to be tying us together. Sure, he was drunk out of his mind and tried to leave me the next morning, but everything was nice and legal. He was smart, though. We got a quick divorce while he had some papers drawn up, then we were married again that next week. All this time, stupid, underage me had no idea what was going on. All I knew was that this good-looking man was paying for the hotel and for us to live it up, and I was having the time of my life. When I turned 18 a few days after, we had our other wedding, I signed his papers, and he finally let me in on how much money he had.

Sorry if I'm rambling on. So, we moved back to his place and he went back to work. I stayed home and found out what boredom really was—I was just a spoiled little rich girl. That old feeling was back again; I wanted a child so much I couldn't stand it. After some begging and pleading, Malcolm figured out that it might shut me up, and he could certainly afford to feed another mouth, so we started trying. No luck, though. Grandma was right after all, and the doctors confirmed it. We thought of adopting, but both of us had a few boo-boos on our criminal records, so that option was out. Things just got worse as time went by, and I started wanting to leave him. Maybe another man could prove those doctors wrong.

So, it was a Friday night, right after I'd decided to leave my husband. I had dreamed up this whole scheme to take his money away from him, not really because I was angry with Malcolm but because I would need money to be off on my own. There was no way I'd ever go back to the kind of work I'd done before. There I was, right in the middle of planning all this, when Malcolm sits me down at the kitchen table and starts telling me about this class he's been teaching, and about this woman he'd met there. She had a daughter, a perfect little angel from what he described about her pictures. This woman went on and on about her little girl and how wonderful she was, and I guess it got Malcolm thinking about children of his own. Finally, he and I were on the same page. He really understood the emptiness I felt in my heart, Paul. No one has ever done that for me.

I'm sure by now you've figured out who that woman was. She was Samantha Morris, just another unhappy wife wanting to better herself with a few lessons in real estate.

That whole night, we sat up and talked by the fire. Underneath all the money and family ties to the sleaziest people in the country, Malcolm Devane was actually a wonderful man. He felt so strongly for me because I loved him even before I knew about his money, even though I suspected it a little. All the women he'd know were only after his bank account, and I was the one exception. He told me about his feelings for Samantha, which were mostly for her daughter. I told him that I was planning to leave, and detailed my plan to do so. This was before I knew you guys, and before I'd really ironed the bugs out. Nonetheless, Malcolm was impressed with me. He may have been nice, but he was a Devane too, and had to give credit to anyone who could pull off such a scam.

Paul, we cried together and decided we couldn't split up. But the only thing that could keep us together was what we both wanted so badly—a child of our own. So there in the firelight, we figured out exactly how we could get what we wanted. Malcolm had a newfound respect for me after finding out that I was just as dirty as he was. It's an odd thing, and I don't expect you to understand. Rich people are funny like that. We started planning how to get what we wanted, and it made us so hot we had to make love right there. That's how intense this all was to us. I've always been a bad person, and I won't deny that.

Malcom would continue with his class, making every effort to learn as much as he could about little Shelby Morris. He told me our plan would involve him making love to her, which actually didn't bother me that much. It would get me what I wanted in the end. I'm sorry to tell you all this, Paul, but he made quite a few visits to local motels with your wife. He was enjoying himself a lot more than he should have, and I think there were actually two girls for awhile, but I just kept thinking about my new daughter and it made all the anger go away. Malcolm was intrigued with my little plan, and he soon started helping me with it. All those motorcycles, the business, and even his house are in his father's name. The old Mr. Devane believed in keeping people beneath him to make himself look high and mighty. He did it with all his sons, especially Jorge. Malcolm may have had money, but none of it is his. He wanted to get away from his father like I'd wanted to get away from him, but that would mean screwing his dad out of a couple million dollars.

He kept on fucking your wife, while I met up with you guys and we got ready for Sturgis. The lapse in the insurance was all true, but all those bikes were really in Malcolm's father's name. We planned to take his father's money and start a new life with our new daughter. This brings me up to why you're here right now, reading this letter. You were one hell of a thief in your younger days, Paul, and I really admire that. I recruited you for this little endeavor because of your skills, but mostly because I needed to distract you while Malcolm ran off with your wife and daughter. There were times when I felt guilty, but picturing you holding that bag of money that could have been mine helped ease the pain a little. I know it's not your child, but at least it's something to hold onto. All that crying to you was an act to make it look real.

I won't apologize to you for what I've done, because it's just my way of telling God that Bryn Scott makes the rules here. If I want a child, I get one. That's another thing—don't try looking for us, because we've covered all the bases. Bryn, after all, is not my real name, just a middle name I used in my dancing days. The only one left who knows who I really am is Malcolm, who had that stupid name tattooed on his arm once just to piss me off. Maybe we can get that removed some day. As for your wife, she knows Malcolm, but by the time you read this that name will have changed. Your daughter? She just knows Malcolm by his childhood nickname, Stinky. A few years down the road, she'll have forgotten all about you and Samantha. That's the beauty of youth—you forget easily. I suppose you're wondering where your wife is. Right about now, she is on a plane back to The City to collect the rest of her things before you're supposed to come home. Malcolm had Shelby stay with him so they could bond, but we'll be long gone by the time Samantha's plane lands.

Don't blame her for what she's done. Malcolm can be pretty charming when he needs to be. She seemed pretty unhappy with you—if she wasn't, she wouldn't have run off in the first place. He said he kept thinking of me while he was inside her, but I'm not sure if I really believe that. It doesn't matter now anyway. You can go find her and make another baby. That's the one luxury you have that Malcolm and I never will.

I leave you today with a bit of advice. First, don't waste your time going to the police and trying to find us. We've thought of every detail. A haircut for Shelby and some time with a psychologist who will convince her that Paul and Samantha Morris were only a dream, and we're set. I actually gave some thought to leaving him, and taking the cash and my savings and heading for the hills, but there was a pretty little girl waiting for me on the other side. Jorge, Malcolm's idiot little brother Junior—those two were just in the way and we're not sorry for what happened to them.

My other bit of advice is this—forget this ever happened. You are a good person, Paul, and good things will come your way again. Take your money and start a new life. Thank you for all you've done for me, and I promise we'll show Shelby the kind of life that you never could.

Bryn

Andrew folded the papers and set them on his knee. For a moment, both men just stared across the street into the harbor and the endless sea of blue water. Paul's first thought was to get up and run again, this time right into that water. He would just close his eyes and give in to the voices in his head telling him his life had no meaning anymore. Just sink to the bottom and close your eyes, so you can't see yourself dying. For some reason, he flashed back to his father holding him by his neck, slamming him against the wall of his war room. There too, he'd wanted to just close his eyes and let it end. The pain was so great inside him as well as on the outside that closing his eyes was all he could think of doing.

"They're gone," Paul said, still staring into the water.

He kept on saying that over and over again, as though repeating those words would somehow make him believe what had just happened.

-2-

He didn't care that renting a car in his own name would place them at the scene of the crime. Right now, there were other things to worry about.

Andrew drove down the boulevard in their rented Buick, watching the ships come and go. Besides Paul's rambling, neither man had spoken a word in nearly an hour.

"We're going to get some sleep," Andrew said finally, looking over at his passenger who was just staring out the side window. "We're getting some sleep because we both need it. Then, and only then, we'll figure out what we're going to do here."

Paul offered no argument. Like a zombie, he opened his room at the Lazy Inn, walked directly to the bed, and fell asleep on top of the covers with his clothes still on. One memory kept going through his head the whole time, repeating over and over like a skipping record. It was the morning he'd said goodbye to his daughter. That morning, which now seemed like an eternity ago, when he'd promised he'd return soon. He promised he would take her away from all this, back to a simpler place without traffic jams, shooting, and gangs.

"I broke a promise to my baby," he kept on repeating, face down on the pillow in a puddle of drool. All through his dreamless sleep, he spoke these words. Paul had never once broken a promise to Shelby, whether it was a big one like their yearly vacation, or something tiny like remembering her dinosaur book.

He agreed with Andrew. Sleep would clear his head. Unfortunately, it would also allow everything that had happened to finally sink in. Paul didn't move as he slept, and wouldn't move for the next few hours.

On the other side of the paper thin wall, Andrew Falkness sat on the floor next to his night stand. He knew what he was about to read, and that it would probably make him have a massive heart attack, so why not be that much closer to the floor? His friend had his own problems, and he thought he might help with them, but right now Andrew had an envelope of his own to contend with.

Andrew,

It's only money, sweetheart. Remember that line, you horrible son-of-a-bitch? Do you? I'll refresh your memory for you. Fantasy Fred's, Las Vegas, about seven years ago. I was 17 years old, with rent to pay and a boss just waiting for me to screw up so he could fire my ass. I couldn't dance worth shit, and I spilled more drinks than I served. So of course my boss thought it was a wonderful idea when some rich old fart asked if he could buy me for the night. I was a virgin then. Yes, believe it or not, a virgin from the trailer park. I believed in saving myself for my husband some day, but you went and fucked that up, didn't you, Andrew?

I had six dollars to my name and a stack of bills higher than I was. They told me you just wanted a massage, and I was anxious to try something new. You wanted a personal massage from the girl you saw on your matchbook cover, in that stupid photo they made me pose for my first night. But that wasn't all you wanted, was it? We went upstairs to that little room with the orange curtains and stains on the mattress. I had heard that some of the dancers took men there, but knew prostitution was illegal in Vegas too. I never dreamed you'd do what you did to me, Andrew.

Do you even remember, you fat, bald old bastard? Do you remember how you held me down? Those toys of yours that you put inside me? How I screamed for you to stop?

And when you left while I laid there crying and feeling like I'd been torn apart inside, you took your money off the night stand and just left me there with nothing. "It's only money, sweetheart," that was what you said. You took my money and left with that stupid smile on your face. I went back downstairs awhile later and you were gone. My boss fired me on the spot for not getting any money for what I'd done, but at least he drove me to the hospital after I finally passed out.

All that blood wasn't just my innocence, Andrew. You really did tear me apart inside, and not just in my head either. They said you'd broken some reproductive organs with those horrible things you did to me. They told me I could never have a child—the thing I wanted more than anything in the world. In just a couple minutes, a stranger had taken that away from me.

I nearly starved to death those next few weeks. No one would give me a job, and the bill collectors were knocking down my door. I even ate a sandwich out of a garbage can, Andrew! I had to turn to the only kind of work I could get, and that meant laying there while more dirty, smelly old men just like you took advantage of me. I thought of killing myself, since my only reason for living was now gone, and that was about the time Malcolm showed up at the whore house. I never told him about you until the night we sat up figuring out how to get away with his father's money. By this time he was really wanting a child too, and was questioning what was wrong with me. A few phone calls to some friends of his and he found you, Andrew. He found you and this time you were the one who was going to get screwed.

You should never have pissed off a rich man. Malcolm has lots of friends in lots of places, Andrew. We decided we would include you on our little trip to Sturgis, certainly not because of your ties overseas, but because you needed to pay for what you'd done to me. My hair was longer and a different color, but I actually thought you'd still recognize me when I first came to bail you out of jail. I guess you've been with enough whores that you don't remember them all, eh? I wrote all of this out for Jorge, who found Paul all right with his little out-of-gas routine, but he had some trouble tracking you down. Imagine his surprise when both of the players in the game ended up in the same bar at the same time, and later in the same jail cell! I wanted to just leave you there to rot, but I knew your money and your connections would let you go free. I needed to make you hurt like you made me hurt—right where it counts—in your pocketbook.

As soon as we hit the road for Sturgis, Malcolm's friends went to work. You're now bankrupt, Andrew, but that's not good enough. All those software makers you've screwed over are filing suit against you, with some help from my husband and his contribution to their legal fund. The SEC is investigating your ties overseas, and these papers in my handbag will help them out immensely. Your bank accounts have been rerouted. They're still in your name, but by the time we're finished, everything you've got will be spread out so much you'll never find it. The feds raided your apartment, where Malcolm's buddies planted about a pound of crystal meth in little baggies ready to be sold. There's also a typed list of the middle schools you planned on visiting to sell your awful drugs. You'll probably be in the same prison as Jorge, that little foreigner trying to take away Malcolm's money.

There's nothing for you to come home to now, Andrew. We've screwed it all up, just like you screwed up my life with your perverse toys. I'll never have a child of my own because of you, and for that you must pay. Take your money and run while you can, but I'll make sure you don't get far. I could never take away from you all that you've taken from me, but I'll certainly give it my best shot. Just remember when you're rotting away the rest of your life in prison that you fucked with the wrong little girl.

Hey, after all, it's only money, sweetheart.

Bryn

Andrew let the pages fall to the ground. He dug out the matchbook, the one that had been with him this whole time and could have clued him in to what was really going on. There she was, that little whore, right there on the cover for the world to see. Why hadn't he just bought a goddam pack of cigarettes sooner? He lit one of the final matches in the pack, set the whole pack on fire, and threw it into the ashtray by the bed.

All those years he'd worked for what he had. The road hadn't exactly been an honest one, but he had earned everything. And now it was gone, taken away by some prostitute he never expected to see again. Andrew Falkness had been a terrible person, cheating on his wife, gambling, drinking, smoking—you name it, he'd done it. And now it had all caught up with him, just when he finally wanted to turn things around. He wasn't angry at Bryn Scott, as odd as that sounded. He was suddenly very disappointed with himself for all he'd done and all the people he'd hurt. Most people his age had a nice, comfortable retirement with grandchildren and a motor home. They had no worries, they just got up in the morning and enjoyed life with their loved ones. But for him, there were no loved ones and no easy life. He was headed to prison for retirement, and he'd earned it all through his own evil deeds.

Andrew actually thought of taking a walk down the street to the hardware store, buying himself some rope, and coming back to his motel room to end it all. Why not? He'd never make it to Coralie now, and even if he did, there would be nothing to offer her. Just an old, worn-out man on the run from the law. She might have actually taken him back if he could prove he had changed, but certainly not now.

Instead of hanging himself, Andrew just sat there on the floor, staring at the stains on the ceiling. There had been little time in his life for God, and he was about as far from being a religious man as one could get, but he gave it a try anyhow.

"Well, we haven't talked much lately, have we?" he asked the ceiling. "We pretty much go our separate ways, do what we gotta do, and pay the consequences for it. You'll pardon me if I doubt you're up there sometimes, but a lot of things have been happening in this world that I just don't think you'd let happen if you were really there. I'm not talking about me either, because anything bad that happens to me is because I deserve it. I'm not saying I'm terribly fond of what's happening, but I think I had it coming. No, what I'm talking about is all the war, famine, terrorism, and all that going on in the world. It's things like those that keep me doubting you're up there."

Andrew wiped his cheek and found that he wasn't sweating. Tears had begun to trickle from his eyes.

"And another thing, what about this guy next door, huh? What did he ever do to deserve what he got? A nice kid trying to make a living for his family, and he ends up losing it all for no reason. I can understand why you want me to hurt, but why him? He's an all right guy, that Paul, and you should really rethink what you're doing to him."

It was starting to sink in now. Through all of this he had found a friend, and sort of a son too. Andrew truly cared about Paul, and felt almost as bad about Shelby as Paul did. There were no loved ones for Andrew, but Paul was as close as he would ever get. Something about the kid just made him smile. Maybe it was the laid back country way about him or the fact that he could pull off some really nasty stuff when he needed to. Paul reminded him of a young Andrew Falkness, back all those years ago.

And here he was thinking of someone other than himself, his first unselfish act in…well, ever.

"All I'm saying, Mister God, is that you should cut the kid a break. If there's any favors you owe me, I'd just as soon have you do something for Paul. He's never hurt anyone but you've sure hurt him a bunch. It's too late for me, but isn't there something you can do for him? Come on, do some good for once. You have to admit there hasn't been a great deal of good being done in the world lately."

Andrew wasn't sure what he was expecting from the stains on the ceiling. Maybe some divine voice telling him everything was going to be all right. But he knew better. The few times he had actually broken down and asked for something from the big man, nothing ever happened. This time, though, things were different. He was pleading the case for someone else, someone he could just as easily have left here in this shitty motel and never thought about again.

As he undressed and climbed under the covers, he actually thought it might work this time. Maybe a guy just had to be asking for the right reasons.

And then Andrew slept too, exhausted from going without sleep and from the weight that had just been placed on his shoulders. He dreamed of Coralie, looking young in her blue and white dress while he pushed her on the swings at their old house. As corny as it sounded, love and family were what life was all about, and he suddenly didn't miss his money anymore. Money wasn't the issue here. Helping out the only friend he had was what mattered.

Upstairs—not the real upstairs of the motel, where presently a 14-year-old was playing with himself and watching *Baywatch*—but in the upstairs where the clouds were, someone listened to Andrew Falkness for once. His turnaround late in the game had caught the interest of someone Andrew had dismissed as never listening, and just like that the wheels began to turn.

Next to Paul's bed, his cell phone began to ring.

Chapter Sixteen

"What about…Peanut? Can I call you Peanut?"

Shelby Morris threw her bag of nuts at Malcolm Devane and ran for the back of the airplane, though she had no idea where she was going. In the course of one day, her mother had left her alone with Stinky to return to The City and retrieve their things, and now she was on her very first airplane with a stranger. Only a few minutes after mommy had left, after she heard the man promise her they would be all right and would be waiting there for her when she returned, Shelby was hurried to a big, black car.

"Your mother needs to go away for awhile, and she's asked me to take care of you, Shelby," Malcolm had said on their ride to the airport. It started out that she kind of liked this man. He always seemed to be buying her a new toy or letting her eat whatever she wanted, but now he had gotten sort of creepy. She was too young to know it for sure, but something not right was happening here. What if her mother didn't want her anymore? What if she really had done something terrible to set her off in the restroom the other day, and now she was punishing Shelby by leaving her with this strange man?

They had waited in that big car for what seemed like an eternity, until a long white plane landed on a private airstrip at Ebhart Airfield. What Shelby didn't know was that this plane was supposed to be carrying her mother. It had, after all, taken her back to The City and the pilot had promised he would be right there waiting in two hours after Samantha collected her things. Instead, one of Malcolm's buddies was waiting at the gate for her when she returned to tell her that the plane had gotten called away on emergency business. It would return in eight hours, he promised her. The man in the leather coat then handed Samantha an envelope full of hundred dollar bills, and told her that Malcolm had called and wanted her to entertain herself well during this little inconvenience.

"Do some shopping; buy you and your daughter something nice," the man had said, and didn't feel the least bit guilty for doing so. To him, watching a mother stand there waiting for a plane that would never arrive with an armload of new presents for her little girl who was gone forever was the pinnacle of entertainment. He was a bad man himself, after all. Not as bad as his boss, but pretty bad. He watched her stand there from the elevated platform in the main terminal, using the new binoculars he had purchased with some of the $10,000 he'd been paid for this simple job. Yes, he was also a bad man. It actually gave him a chuckle to watch and see how long it would take for her to finally wise up, running from the terminal in the night air with an armload of presents.

Malcolm pointed out the plane to Shelby, who played in the seat opposite him with her new plastic dinosaurs. The stranger seemed to know a lot about the extinct creatures, and could tell her a story about every one of them. She listened intently, still not liking Stinky but beginning to warm up to his charm. Malcolm was a charming guy, after all, even with the youngest of ladies.

And on the plane they went, Shelby running ahead, unafraid of the roaring engines. All she wanted to do was see her mother, who had to be on board. Stinky needed to be proven wrong. Her mother didn't get called away, she was on that plane ready to scoop Shelby into her arms and say she was sorry for all the yelling she'd done. But the plane was empty except for the pilot, and it turned out that the stranger was right after all.

"Don't worry, sweetheart, your mother will be along soon enough," he told her now, as she huddled in the corner near the bathroom. She wanted to hug her new dinosaur friends, but they were back on the seat next to the stranger. They were the only thing that could comfort her now and stop her sobbing, but going to get them might mean the man would grab her and haul her away.

"Sweetheart, I— "

"My name is Shewby," she said. "Shewby Mowwis."

If there was one luxury Malcolm Devane didn't have, it was patience. He was trying hard to be calm, and not to call the little girl by her real name. His friends had told him that was important if he wanted her to forget her past. Get her a new name, or just call her "Honey" or "Sweetheart" until you do, then you can start to make her forget the rest. He'd tried that. He tried to buy her nice things and talk calmly to her, but she just ran and hid from him.

"Sweetheart, you have to come sit down. The plane's about to— "

"Shewby!" she cried, trying to keep the tears away but failing. "Shewby Mowwis!"

"Fine, just sit there, then. See if I care."

All at once the huge thing started to move, and Shelby was terrified. She had seen planes before on television, but had never been on one until now. The force pressed her against the back wall of the cabin as the engines began to power up. She could feel everything moving, so she closed her eyes and huddled into a ball, screaming at the top of her lungs for her father. He was the only one who could save her now. Her mother didn't care about her and had left her alone, but daddy would come through for her. She just knew he would.

Malcolm quickly tired of the screaming. Never in his life had he heard anything so shrill, so loud. Four hours of this would drive him insane for sure. He tried with all his might to just stay in his seat, but after five minutes of her screaming and crying he couldn't take it anymore. He sprung from his seat, picked up the child, and strapped her tightly into the seat across from him. Shelby kicked as hard as she could, connecting with his chest and groin, but he still managed to get her seated.

"Ow!" Malcolm cried as he felt the tiny shoe hit his testicles. "You fucking brat! Sit the fuck down and shut up or I'll throw you out the goddam window!"

Shelby had screamed and cried enough now that the motion of the plane, along with being thrown around, caused her to vomit in the aisle. That was enough for Malcolm. He unstrapped himself and ran to the cockpit, taking the seat next to the pilot and shutting the door. Behind him, he could still hear her screaming, but at least this was as far away from her as he could get right now.

"You look about like I do some days," the pilot said. Most people were afraid of the Devanes, but not him. Retirement was just around the corner and he cared very little for the pompous, too-rich-for-their-own-good family.

"What?" Malcolm asked, annoyed but glad to hear something other than screaming.

"I said, you look like me some days. I've got three little grandkids we're taking care of this week, and they're certainly a handful. My wife— "

"Let me ask you something," Malcolm said, staring coldly at the pilot. "Do these grandkids of yours crush your nuts for you?"

"Well…no."

"Well I will, if you don't shut the fuck up and fly this plane," Malcolm growled. "*Capice*?"

"You're the boss."

Shelby quickly tired of yelling, since no one was around to hear her. She was all alone and passed the time by counting the number of seats in the plane and thinking up names for her dinosaurs. For the past couple of days she had done nothing but cry, and didn't want to do it anymore, so she filled her head with the happiest thoughts she could find. Shelby hadn't been able to sleep the night before in that big, strange room all alone, so she had dozed off in one of the big, leather seats. She awoke to a jolt from the airplane, and then there was finally something to see out the windows. There was a lot of grass, a big pole with an orange sock hanging from it, and one tiny building off to the side. By the building was a woman, but her hair was a different color than her mother's.

Bryn watched the jet land in the old airstrip, then taxi toward her. It seemed odd that she had driven only fifteen miles from the site where she had divvied up the money with her partners. Shelby's father would be thinking his daughter could be anywhere in the world by now, when in reality she was right under his nose. But not for long. Soon enough it would all be through, and Paul Morris and the events of the last few days would be gone forever.

Malcolm emerged from the plane after checking on the child. She kept staring out the window at the field and the trees, and seemed harmless for the time being. He was pleased to see that his wife had shown up, which meant that everything had gone smoothly.

"Afternoon, Marjorie," he said, mocking her with her real name even more than the tattoo on his arm could. "I trust you've been well."

"Don't call me that, you moron," Bryn said, throwing the duffel bag at him.

There were bruises on his chest and stomach from being kicked, and the bag nearly knocked the wind out of him. Malcolm unzipped the bag and peeked in at the money. Not nearly as much as he'd laid claim to before, but at least these few hundred grand were free of his father's grasp. For once in his life, Malcolm could claim money as his own. All it took was some felony theft to get him there.

"How's the girl?" Bryn asked, anxious to see her new daughter.

"She's gonna grow up to be a soccer star, I think," Malcolm said, pulling up his shirt to show off his bruises. "I got sick of her screaming so I left her alone back there for awhile. God, do they always scream like that?"

Bryn ignored him and pushed her way to the cabin door. Up the stairs and inside, the little girl sat huddled in the corner again, surrounded by an army of plastic dinosaurs. Shelby had set them up in three rows to keep the bad people away. Only Paul Morris, and perhaps her mother, would be allowed past.

Bryn kneeled down in front of the child and the Fourth Dinosaur Regiment, and couldn't believe how beautiful this little girl was. Those big, shiny eyes that had no idea what was going on here, and those little lips were pouting away like Bryn's used to. She was perfect in every way, just like the child Bryn laid awake all those nights praying for. Now, God had delivered.

"Shewby Mowwis," the girl said, then turned her head away.

"No, sweetie, your name is…"

Bryn stopped and sat down on the floor next to Shelby, who started sobbing again. On top of everything, now there was another stranger coming to get her. Shelby summoned all the courage she had and looked into this young woman's eyes. She was about the same age as her mother, which started her thinking.

"Did you send my mommy away?" she asked. "Did you send my daddy away, too?"

Bryn couldn't believe those eyes. All the simple honesty of a child, a scared little child who didn't know where she was and what she was doing. She had been many things in her life, but never a kidnapper. One human life, one person who would never see the place where she used to live, or the parents she loved. Shelby would never again play with the little black boy down the hall who pulled her hair but whom she liked anyhow. Bryn would never again see her home, or even any part of this country. There would just be her, Malcolm, and a little girl who wasn't rightfully her own.

Yeah, she's an angel, Paul said inside her head. On their third night in the garage, he'd pulled out his wallet and started showing photos of Shelby like any proud father would. They had gotten this one done at K-Mart, with Shelby in a yellow sun dress and bonnet. *I tell you, Bryn, I thank God every day for this little girl. I don't know what I'd do without her.*

And what had Bryn done? While anyone with even a shred of conscience would have cried like a baby, she had just sat there and listened to him. She listened to him talk about the little girl who was his whole life, whom Bryn would soon be taking away. How could anyone in the world be that hard? That cold?

Now Bryn was crying too.

"Do you miss your daddy, sweetie?"

Shelby nodded, her tears dripping onto Bryn's leg.

Yes. Yes she did.

Paul checked the clock by his bed twice, then fished the watch out of his pocket to make sure it was correct. It was now 6 a.m. Wednesday morning, a full sixteen hours after he'd laid down for a quick nap. When the cell phone rang, he thought it was someone else's far away, like down the street, that *doot-doot-doodle-doodle-doot* ring that everyone had as their own. He fished around under the bed, found the object he was looking for, and brought it up to his ear.

"What?"

"Paul, it's Bryn. Please don't hang up."

He was certainly awake now. Paul jumped out of bed and ran to the window, thinking for some reason she would be in the parking lot waiting for him. His brain could not function with all the anger inside it, all the hate he had never thought it possible to feel for one human being.

"You cunt! Where's my— "

"Take it easy, Paul. She's with me."

"I swear in the name of all that's holy, when I get my hands on you— "

"Please, Paul. This is hard enough as it is. Just listen."

"The only thing I want to listen to is the sound of your neck snapping, you bitch! Now where's my daughter?"

Bryn was sobbing even more now, though she knew there would be no sympathy from the other end of the phone line. Just one look in that little girl's eyes, those eyes that looked identical to her father's, and she had to make this call.

"I am an evil person, Paul. I don't mean just a little bit, either. I sat there and listened to you brag about this little girl and all the while I was planning to take her away from you. I am so terribly sorry."

"Come visit me, you bitch. I'll make sure you're sorry."

"I just can't do it, though, Paul. I can't take something this valuable away from someone. Money, that's one thing. A person can always make more money or get it from someone else, but this…this is a real person. A real human being who no one could ever replace. She has your eyes, Paul. She looked at me with those little eyes— "

"I swear to God, if you hurt Shelby— "

"I won't hurt her, Paul. I can't even bring myself to look at her, let alone hurt her. What I've done has already hurt her enough. She didn't ask for this. It isn't her fault I'm dead inside."

Paul forced himself to take a deep breath and listen. There was nothing he could do now, and the ball was in her court. He just had to listen and wait.

"There has to be another way. I wanted a child more than anything in the world, but there has to be another way. I never thought there was a point where my conscience would take over, but I guess I was wrong. I mean, those eyes, Paul, I can't look into those innocent eyes."

"Bring her here, Bryn. Bring her here and we all go our separate ways. You want my money, you can have it; just bring my little girl to me."

Bryn was crying too hard to speak, and could only squeak into the receiver as Paul pleaded for his daughter. She looked over at the little girl and her wall of dinosaurs. All her life, this is what she had wanted, but now it just didn't feel right. There were certain things even she couldn't steal.

"We need time to get out of here, Paul. I know you'll call the police, and even though they have nothing on us, we need time to get out of here."

"Bryn, you have my word I won't say anything until Shelby is here with me."

And just like that, she believed him. Bryn listened closely as Paul recited the address of the motel, then gave him strict instructions to wait in that room at least two hours after his daughter arrived. Shelby climbed into another big car, this time with the assurance that she was on her way to see her father. The dinosaur army was quickly packed into her bag and something happened for the first time in quite a few days—she smiled.

Andrew had heard the yelling and quickly dressed himself, though he missed most of the conversation. By the time Paul hung up the phone, he was in the doorway of Paul's room. Paul ran across the room and threw his arms around Andrew, not really sure why, but he just knew he had to hug someone.

"They're sending her back," he said, burying his head into Andrew's shirt and soaking it with tears of joy. "She said she couldn't do it and they're sending my baby back to me."

Andrew was surprised at first, then gave in and put his arms around Paul. Maybe talking to that stain in the ceiling hadn't been such a bad idea after all.

"We're gonna get that bitch, son, don't you worry."

Andrew made his way across the motel parking lot to the coffee shop, where he sat down near the window with a donut and dumped sugar into his decaf. A few minutes later, a car pulled in with the pilot at the wheel and a little girl in the back seat. The man opened the door, handed the girl her backpack, and pointed her toward a row of rooms. She ran to the right one and pounded on the door.

"Paul promised not to call the cops, but they didn't say anything about me," Andrew said, dialing his cell phone. He had written down the license number and a pretty good description of the driver, which he gave to Officer Santoro while he explained the situation.

Paul heard the tiny knock on his door and bolted for it, finding Shelby on the other side.

"Daddy!" she yelled, crying once again but for a good reason this time.

"Hi, punkin head," he said, trying as hard as he could to stay calm. The last thing he wanted to do was scare his daughter any more than she'd been scared already. "Did you have fun with the babysitters?"

No, Shelby had not had any fun at all. As she told the story of the long car ride, the courthouse where they tried to change her name, the incident in the ladies room and the motel room where Mommy was moaning and yelling at her, Paul couldn't help himself. He buried his head in his daughter's chest and sobbed, and they both kneeled there in the doorway of the motel room, crying. Just this once, he couldn't help but show a little weakness in front of his little girl. He'd almost lost her forever.

"The lady said to give you this," Shelby said, reaching into her backpack. It was another letter, addressed to Paul.

"I'm so terribly sorry for this," he read aloud. "If it's any consolation, your wife is in the middle of an airport runway right now, waiting to be picked up. Malcolm tricked her, but she went along with it pretty easily. She probably thinks Shelby is with us right now, and she'll be far too embarrassed to ever call on you again, so you'll be safe with Shelby. I never knew I had a limit until there was such a wonderful little girl involved. You're truly a lucky man, Paul. Thank you, and I'm sorry. Bryn."

He crumpled up the paper and threw it aside, still hugging Shelby tight to him. She wondered where her mother had gone, but figured Mommy was still mad at her and needed a time out.

"Is Mommy comeen, too?" Shelby asked.

"No, sweetie," Paul said. "Mommy had to go away for awhile. It'll just be me and you for a bit, okay?"

Shelby nodded. She loved her mother dearly, but lately her mother had been very mean. She probably needed a rest and some time away from everybody, and for now, Shelby was just happy to have her father back.

He hadn't been mean to her yet.

Paul assembled his clothes and shoved them into the bag with his money. He wanted Shelby to meet Andrew, and the two walked hand-in-hand across the parking lot to the coffee shop. They were both very hungry too.

As Andrew watched them coming toward him, the young man with his perfect little girl and a huge smile on his face, he wondered if the man in the ceiling had anything in store for him.

"I know it's kind of greedy to ask," he said to the ceiling fan, making sure no one could hear him. "But I was wondering if I get anything out of all this. I know I'm no saint, but I really have been trying to mend my ways. All I want is to live out my days without worrying about the cops coming to break down my door. If you could help me out with that, I'd be much obliged."

Andrew watched them come closer, the little girl gripping her father's hand as tight as she could so he would never leave her sight again. And just like that, his cell phone started ringing. It scared Andrew to death, since no one ever called him on the thing. Truth be told, he hated it and kept it turned off most of the time, but he'd just finished reporting some things to the police and hadn't had the chance to switch it off yet.

"Hello?"

"I did it, Andrew. I'm a free woman now."

It was Coralie, he knew her pretty voice right away.

"You did what, honey?"

"I told my other beau I was leaving to be with you, come hell or high water. He threw a fuss for awhile, but in the end he said 'whatever makes you happy.' You do know this is your last chance, don't you?"

Andrew nodded, then realized she couldn't see him.

"Yes, Coralie. I won't let you down this time, I promise."

"I've heard that before, you know."

"Yes, I know. When can I pick you up?"

She was flying into The City Thursday morning, Gate 21, arriving at 10 a.m.

"If I have to wait more than a minute, I swear I'll— "

"Don't worry, Coralie." Andrew laughed. "I'll be there with bells on."

"You'd better be, you old fool."

He laughed even harder now. Among the things he missed the most about his Coralie was the way she could put him in his place. Only a real, old fashioned woman could do that to him, and she was quite good at it.

"I'll see you then, Coralie."

"All right. Oh, and one more thing, Andrew?"

"Yes?"

"I love you. I always have loved you, and I've never stopped."

With that she hung up the phone, just in time for his friend and a little girl to climb into the booth across from him. Paul introduced him to Shelby, the most beautiful, most perfect little girl he'd ever seen. Andrew could see why someone would want to take away such a wonderful little person, and he suddenly regretted never having children of his own. Too much time spent at work, he guessed.

"Well hello there, little person," Andrew said, shaking her tiny hand. "And what's your name? Penny McGee?"

Shelby giggled.

"Shewby Mowwis," she said, melting Andrew's heart even more with her little speech impediment. He couldn't even remember when he was that small, and he knew he'd never been anywhere near as cute.

"So what do we do now?" Paul asked, still too shocked to think straight.

"We eat pancakes," Andrew said. "Lots of them. Then, we get in the car and do a little driving. I spoke to somebody last night who I haven't talked to in quite awhile, and he really came through for me. We both got our rewards, and now we need to finally do something right for a change. You with me?"

As Shelby crashed her plastic dinosaurs into one another, Paul nodded across the table to his new friend, knowing exactly what he meant.

-3-

Around the time Junior Devane woke up naked in some stranger's tent and stumbled out to find two dozen people cleaning the campgrounds, Jorge Zapate was shackled and taken away from his still-frozen T.V. dinner breakfast. He was loaded into a van, dressed all in orange, and driven to the South Dakota State Penitentiary in Sioux Falls. There would be a lawyer appointed for him, the guards informed him as they drove, but it wouldn't do any good. Such a connoisseur of kiddie porn like himself would be a dead man soon, no matter which side of the bars he was on.

Jorge was frightened, not just for himself but for his little sister. She was all that remained of his family—the only person in the world who would even acknowledge his existence. And now she was in great danger and he was stuck here once again.

"Thirty years, they say," one guard said to the other. "That's a long time, but not nearly enough time for a freak of nature like you, boy."

"Yeah," said the other. "I've got three kids, pal. I hope your cellmate gives it to you in the butt ten times a day until you scream."

Jorge just sat quietly. He knew that there were times to speak, and this was not one of them.

The van pulled up to the gates, one of the guards pressed some numbers into a keypad, and they entered the yard. This was it, this would be the last time Jorge would see the outside world. He would be killed in here for sure, being accused of such a terrible thing. The other men wouldn't care about his innocence.

They walked him down a long hallway with cells on either side. The men yelled at him, calling him a dead man and a child molester, and saying they would make sure he had a pleasant stay. Jorge felt tears in his eyes by the time they made it to his cell and the door opened. Inside, a large black man sat in the darkness, just smiling at him as though he knew exactly what he was planning to do to Jorge.

"Jim, hold up a second," one guard said, trotting down the cell block. He whispered in the other guard's ear, and both of them seemed genuinely disgusted.

"You're kidding me," was all the first guard could say.

Then Jorge was turned around and marched back through the corridor, past those terrible men and their harsh words once more. They led him to a tiny room with only one chair and left him to sit there for nearly an hour. Was this his cell? Where would he sleep?

Finally, the door opened and he was led out into a larger area with a desk. Along the wall, and he couldn't believe his eyes, were Paul and Andrew. All these hours he had been waiting, he kept on plotting what he would like to do to the whole bunch of them who had put him in this terrible place.

"October nineteenth, ten a.m.," the guard told Paul, who nodded. "If he's one minute late, I swear to Christ I'll hunt down all three of you."

"That won't be necessary," Paul said. "He'll be here and he'll go free, too."

"But I don't— " Jorge said.

"Just wait awhile," Andrew told him. "The walls have ears."

Jorges handcuffs were taken off and he was allowed to retrieve his personal effects. He dressed right there in the hallway, afraid that if he left Paul and Andrew's sight they might leave him here again. He didn't understand any of this, but was looking forward to seeing the outside of this place again, even though he had only been there a couple hours.

They drove silently to a small restaurant on the edge of town, where each man ordered lunch. Shelby thought the little dark-skinned man in the polo shirt looked strange, but knew she shouldn't say anything. She just smiled at him and he smiled back. Finally, Jorge could take the suspense no longer.

"Why did you return for me? I thought you would blame all this on me and— "

"So did we, Jorge," Andrew said. "It was Bryn's idea to pin those thefts on you, but we're just as guilty for going along with it, and for that, I'm terribly sorry. You should know that Paul and I put our money together and got you the best lawyer in the state. He's got nearly half a million dollars to work with and I told him he can spend every penny as long as it means you get to walk free. He already arranged for your bail, which I couldn't believe myself."

"Bryn did all this as a distraction, Jorge," Paul said. "It was a distraction for all of us. While I was there, she and Malcolm took my daughter, but she found out she had a little conscience after all and brought her back. She was angry with Andrew, too, and while he was gone she and Malcolm did some dirty things to take away his company and his money."

"And what about me?" he asked from the other side of a cheeseburger.

"You were there to take the fall and stay in jail, so Malcolm didn't ever have to worry about you stepping up to claim your piece of the Devane fortune. The same with Junior. He figured that if all three Devane brothers were branded as traitors, his father's money would still have to go to one of them. And that one would probably be the brother who wasn't in jail at the time."

"But why did you men agree to all this?"

"Well," Andrew said, "Miss Bryn dug up some pretty nasty stuff on Paul and I, and it's probably on its way to the police station right about now. We were being blackmailed, but we were still greedy and stupid enough not to try finding a way out of it."

"I am sorry too. She wrote me a letter in the beginning telling me where to find you two and what she was up to. Miss Bryn said to destroy it once I had found you."

"And did you?" Paul asked, suddenly curious.

"Well, uh, no. I never had the chance. We got into that fight and ended up in jail, and I guess I just hung onto it after that. I have some other things, too."

And just what, Andrew wanted to know, were they?

Jorge reached into his jacket and pulled out a small tape recorder. He adjusted the volume and set it in the middle of the table so they all could hear. On the tape, which had been made during their first couple meetings in the diner, Bryn spoke privately to Jorge about how she was going to get these two men, and how she and Malcolm were going to work it all out so they got blamed for stealing Malcolm's father's money. Later on, they listened to their own words while Bryn threatened Paul and Andrew with the contents of her handbag.

"Sounds like conspiracy, blackmail, and extortion to me," Andrew said, suddenly very pleased at what he was hearing. "How did you think to record all that?"

"I knew Bryn was planning something illegal, and I figured if I had proof of it, she just might offer me some money for this tape so that I might return home finally."

"Wow, Jorge," Paul said. "You've got a little Devane in you after all."

The funny thing, Jorge said, was that the recorder had been a birthday present from Malcolm, who figured it would help Jorge with the book he was planning to write.

Andrew asked the waitress for some paper and began to write a letter. He explained the whole situation from start to finish, including how Bryn had tried to blackmail them and lured all three of them into her little game. He explained what the police would hear on the tape, and that the handwritten letter was Bryn's handiwork too.

The men (and young lady) finished their meal, sat for a moment to let the grease settle, then drove to the nearest post office, where Andrew looked up the address for the South Dakota state attorney's office. They listened closely to the news on the radio the whole drive, but there was nothing yet. Malcolm was in on the plan, so he probably had worked it out so his father wouldn't find out he was being stolen from until later in the week. The only other person who could pull the plug was Junior, who presently was trying to explain to the campground owner why he was naked with no identification. Clothes and some food were his first priority, not talking to the police.

"And there we have it, all in one neat little package," Andrew said, licking the flap on the brown envelope.

"Hold on a second," Paul told him, digging through his pocket. "We wouldn't want to forget this."

He produced a crumpled wad of paper, packed to the margins with fine print. On it, the names and addresses of 150 people purchasing the illegal motorcycles were written, along with how much they had paid. While Bryn was talking with the woman at the docks, Paul remembered she had planted this in Jorge's saddle bag. By that time, though, Jorge was in jail, and she had forgotten to take the list out.

Paul, however, remembered it was there.

They helped Jorge to the counter at the airport, just in case someone recognized him from the news, but no one did. Paul used some of his leftover money on a first class ticket to Sao Paulo, one way. Each man counted out five thousand dollars for Jorge, who happily accepted it.

"I will not forget this," he said, hugging both of them, then hugging little Shelby too. "You will hear from me again, I promise you."

"You just worry about getting back home," Andrew said. "You might get in some trouble if you ever came back here."

They watched Jorge walk through the gate and to his flight, as Shelby sipped on her soda. Jorge Zapate was finally going home, after all this time. All it took were a couple of good friends who could just as easily have forgotten about him. He waved once more over his shoulder, then disappeared forever.

"What do we do now?" Andrew asked. "I can't go home for my things, because there's nothing to get."

"Yeah, there's nothing for me at my house, either," Paul said. "Shelby and I may as well join you when you pick up Coralie. I have to admit, I'm anxious to meet any woman who put up with you as long as she did."

Andrew laughed and took Shelby's other hand. They picked her up as they walked, one on either side, and Shelby felt like she was flying. Only now, she knew she was flying safely.

"You know, old man, we could still get in some trouble for all of this," Paul said as they loaded into the car. "Blackmail or no blackmail, we did steal a couple million dollars worth of motorcycles and accept money for doing it."

Andrew flashed back to his time in jail—both times, actually, alongside Paul Morris. His head hurt just thinking about all they'd been through, all the fights and all the sweat and hard work. And what did he have to show for it? Each man still had about eighty thousand dollars in their bags, but neither one had a home to return to. Andrew had no nest egg, no business, and the feds were on his tail. Paul had a wife he could never trust and whom his daughter was terrified of, and he was already fired from his job since he hadn't showed up in nearly a week. Besides the Taurus and the payments that went with it, there was nothing at home for him either.

They headed west on the interstate, bound for Sturgis and a storage locker with their motorcycles in it. The weather was still all right, and they could ride around for a few months while things settled down and they lived off their newfound money. Coralie would get picked up in style, on a brand new

Heritage Soft Tail, complete with two other riders for their trip—one not-so-little and the other cute as a button in her dinosaur T-shirt.

"Yeah, Paul, I'm sure there might be some trouble waiting for us," Andrew said. "But whatever happens, son, I want you to know there's no one else I'd rather share my cell with."

Paul smiled back at the old man, who was like he'd wished his own father had been. As Shelby slurped up the last of her soda under the watchful eye of about a thousand plastic dinosaurs and her new dinosaur book, Paul nodded back.

He would share his cell with this old man anytime.

Chapter Seventeen

The winter came and went with no complaints from Paul Morris this time.

Since September of the previous year, he and his little girl had been collecting memories and sunburns along Historic Route 66, the Grand Canyon, and other exotic locales throughout the south where the snow didn't go. There would be no broken boiler and no gloves for them, not this time, at least.

After the crew picked up Coralie, the old woman simply fell in love with Shelby, and nearly threw a hissy fit when Paul tried to leave with the child. She flat out insisted that both fugitives travel together for awhile so they could team up to avoid the law while she got to know Little Shelby Munchkin, as she called her, a little bit better.

In October, they had spent some time riding their Harleys up and down the Pacific Coast Highway, stopping here and there for Shelby to play in the sand and run through the waves in her pink and yellow dinosaur swimsuit. Paul purchased a trailer shortly before Thanksgiving of that year, since his saddle bags could no longer contain his and his daughter's expanding treasure chest of souvenirs.

All the while they were guests at Andora's Trailer Village, a camping community with tons of friendly families and kids for Shelby to play with, Paul and Andrew held their breath every time someone knocked on the door. They watched the national news religiously, but never heard anything about their dirty deeds from the previous fall. Perhaps the Devanes had wanted to keep everything quiet. Paul imagined it would have been a bit embarrassing for one of the most wealthy men in the country to get screwed over by his oldest son. The Devanes knew how to keep the heat off themselves, and so far they had been doing a good job.

By the time they pulled out of Andora's, bound for Coralie's sister's house in New Mexico, it was February. Paul had begun to think about her starting school the next fall, and how he would manage to get her registered for all this without arousing suspicion. But that was assuming her mother had even reported her missing, which he doubted. Still, he worried about it. So far, they had been able to pay cash for everything, and hadn't gotten so much as a speeding ticket on their motorcycles. Shelby wore her helmet all the time, sometimes even after she had gotten off the bike. At a beachside shop in Malibu, Paul had paid $200 for the man to do a caricature of Shelby as a Tyrannosaurus Rex on the back of the helmet, and for the next week she refused to take it off. Coralie laughed until she nearly wet herself the morning she had gotten up to go to the bathroom and found a naked four-year-old in her bathtub eating cereal.

Naked, that was, except for the motorcycle helmet.

Now they had stayed too long in one place, and were on the move again. Every police car they met made Andrew nervous, and Paul admitted he was a little scared too. But, maybe their deeds had been forgotten by now. Maybe they could go back to the real world where they had identities and used their real names. Maybe once they made it to Coralie's sister's place, they would find homes close to one another. Paul was anxious to go back to work, as stupid as that sounded. He still had a good deal of cash, but that would be better spent saving for Shelby's college than feeding him while he was unemployed.

The bikes rumbled into Flemmings Gas and More on Interstate 91, a couple hours out of Albuquerque. Andrew was heating a little and Paul needed gas. They sat on a bench in the shade and drank real Coke, the kind that comes in a glass bottle. Shelby liked it very much, and performed her best belch to show her appreciation. All four of them laughed. For all anyone knew, they were a grandma, grandpa, son, and granddaughter all out for a family vacation.

"Time for a bathroom break," Paul announced, making his way back into the gas station. "You need one, Shel?"

And she did. Little girls always needed a bathroom break. They wandered through the store hand in hand, and Paul nearly passed by the television mounted over the cigarette stand.

"Hey, turn that up, would you?" he called to the boy behind the counter. Paul watched the picture and rubbed his eyes to make sure it was real. Behind the newsman, a dapper looking gent in his 70s, were photos of Bryn Scott and Malcolm Devane, each holding a sign with booking numbers on it.

"After months of investigation," the man said, "into the disappearance of more than four million dollars in antique and custom motorcycles from this year's Sturgis motorcycle rally, police turned up few leads, until they began to look into unexpected places. Midwest Custom Cycles, owned by Devane Incorporated, one of The City's largest employers, filed a claim in August for 150 motorcycles which had been shipped to Sturgis for display and had never returned. Devane's insurance company, however, stated that the business' policy had lapsed during the time of the theft, prompting a lengthy court battle which ended in defeat for Devane Incorporated. But where, they wondered, had all those cycles gone?"

Andrew and Coralie wandered into the store now, and joined Paul and Shelby, staring unbelievingly at the television.

"Authorities questioned Devane employees, who tipped investigators off to the disappearance of Devane heir Malcolm Devane, along with his wife Marjorie, a.k.a. Bryn Scott. Malcom and his wife left the country unexpectedly just hours after the thefts occurred. Perhaps due to family involvement, however, the disappearance had never been reported to police. This information, together with an anonymous package sent to the South Dakota State Attorney's office last September, led police to conclude that Devane and Scott were involved in the thefts, despite what Devane family spokesmen had been saying. Police deciphered taped conversations between Scott and other men regarding allegedly blackmailing them to aid her in the thefts. These tapes, along with a handwritten list of the150 stolen motorcycles and their buyers combined with a note in the same handwriting by Scott, meant enough evidence to continue the search and bring Devane and Scott in for questioning. Thanks in part to a new nationwide crime search program, authorities in Bermuda noticed the photos of Scott and Devane, and arrested them just hours ago. Both are charged with several counts, including conspiracy to commit a felony, extortion, and bribery of government officials. Sources tell Channel Six that the pair could face a combined sentence of up to three hundred years in connection with the incident. At this time, no other suspects are being sought in the disappearance of the motorcycles, though the names on the list have led to the arrest of some big names, we're told."

The anchorman turned to the woman beside him.

"I don't know about you, Kate, but I wouldn't want to be Malcolm Devane in jail with some of those big-time criminals his alleged list helped send to the slammer."

"Me either, Kent," she said, looking chipper as a newswoman should. "We've also been told that even if the pair were to avoid some of that jail time, they will be ordered to pay more than two million dollars in restitution to the Devane family."

Paul turned to Andrew and put his arm around him.

"Well, old man, looks like we're going to come out all right here."

They turned to leave the store, forgetting the bathroom for now, but one more story caught their attention.

"And be sure to stay tuned for our Amazing People segment," the newswoman said, flashing her pearly whites. "In this edition, we profile a young Brazilian boy, Jorge Zapate, whose father, Joseph Devane, was coincidentally the same man who lost all his motorcycles last year. We caught up with Jorge during his return to the United States to settle some legal matters. He claims the Devane family denied his existence for many years, kept him in poverty and away from his real home, and later tried to send him to jail for life to keep him silent about who his father really was."

For the next two minutes, they watched Jorge emerge triumphantly from court a free man, then playing with his young nieces and nephews back in Brazil. They spoke about the poverty he'd grown up in, the father who stole him away from his home, and his amazing secrets about the Devane family.

"I know many things about the Devane family, and I am tired of being kept silent," Jorge told the interviewer, who had traveled to Brazil to capture him at home. Jorge wore a brand new polo shirt, khaki shorts, and no shoes, and he seemed happier than they had ever seen him.

Just as they turned to leave the store again and Jorge began to spill his guts, Paul caught sight of the photo he held up, showing Junior Devane in a very compromising position with two colored women. They blurred out the good parts, but it was easy to see what he was doing. Paul covered Shelby's eyes and turned her away from the television.

"Is something wong, Daddy?" she asked from beneath his hand, as Andrew hugged his wife close to him. Coralie hugged back. Who needed money, when all Andrew ever wanted was right there in his arms? Better late than never, isn't that what they said?

"Dadeee!" Shelby called again, wiggling under his hand. They were interviewing the women in the photo now, who were admitting to how terrible a lay Junior Devane had been.

"Dadee! I said, is something wong?"

"No, sweetheart," Paul said, as the four of them walked out into their future together as a family. "No, Shelby, everything's just the way it should be."

And for the first time in his life, that was true.